Praise for

the novels of Kate White

Have You Seen Me?

"Arms linked, breath held, we drop alongside Ally Linden into Kate White's dagger-sharp, whip-smart new thriller *Have You Seen Me?*, the same questions burning like neon signs in our minds. . . . As nimbly plotted as *Before I Go to Sleep*, as winning as the best of Mary Higgins Clark, *Have You Seen Me?* showcases Kate White at her formidable best."

—A. J. Finn, #1 *New York Times* bestselling author of *The Woman in the Window*

"A well-honed thriller. . . . White skillfully maintains the pace. . . . Even the most jaded reader will be satisfied."

—*Publishers Weekly*

"Intense, nonstop suspense. . . . You won't want to miss the stunning conclusion."   —Bookreporter.com

Such a Perfect Wife

"What's not to love in Kate White's latest? . . . *Such a Perfect Wife* is deep and dark and twisty, and packed with a delicious array of questionable characters, each harboring their own secrets."

—*Entertainment Weekly*

"Intricately plotted. . . . [an] intense page-turner that never lets up."

—*Library Journal* (starred review and "Pick of the Month")

"Intrepid—and stylish!—crime reporter Bailey Weggins finds herself on the front line of a murder investigation. . . . Fun and

fast-paced. . . . Bailey is fearless, determined, and always fashionable. A grown-up Nancy Drew for grown-up girl detectives."
—*Kirkus Reviews*

"Highly entertaining. . . . The ethical and tenacious Bailey soon earns the respect of the local police, who come to see her as an ally rather than an intruder. Readers will cheer her every step of the way." —*Publishers Weekly*

"An always-entertaining series." —*Booklist*

Even If It Kills Her

"A titillating novel of secrecy and suspense, *Even If It Kills Her* will have you hanging on every word." —*Bustle*

"A twisty mystery full of clues and red herrings that are hard to distinguish between. This makes for a very thrilling read. The end is a surprise, and most readers will gasp at the unveiling of the real killer." —Bookreporter.com

"White builds suspense masterfully, and this seventh in the Bailey Weggins series has the makings of another hit. Bailey is a smart, sexy sleuth, and her exploits make for thoroughly entertaining reading." —*Booklist*

The Secrets You Keep

"A psychological thriller that doubles as a cautionary tale, *The Secrets You Keep* marks another success for a prolific author and casts an intelligent if grim eye on love—love that can warm, and love that can burn." —*Richmond Times-Dispatch*

"True to form, Kate White's *The Secrets You Keep* kept me up way past my bedtime, anxiously turning the pages. Taut, tense, and utterly gripping, I could not go to sleep until I found out whodunit."

—Jessica Knoll, *New York Times* bestselling author of *Luckiest Girl Alive*

"Suspenseful, twisty, and sharply observed, Kate White's clever psychological thriller lures us into the life of vulnerable narrator Bryn whose marriage is not what she thought it was. The uncertainty develops as the stakes ramp up ever higher, and I was holding my breath as I turned the last few pages."

—Gilly Macmillan, *New York Times* bestselling author of *What She Knew*

The Wrong Man

"A juicy beach book: a thriller with a smart female main character."

—*People*

"Breezy . . . an intriguing heroine who holds her own."

—*Kirkus Reviews*

Eyes on You

"[A] delicious tale."

—*New York Post*

"A smart, sexy sleuth with a growing fan base."

—*Booklist*

"This is a must-have summer read and an enjoyable who-dun-it."

—*Seattle Post-Intelligencer*

"Sharp as a stiletto! White captures the cut-throat world of entertainment TV where the latest star should trust no one if she's to build her show . . . or save her very life."

—Lisa Gardner, *New York Times* bestselling author

The Sixes

"You won't be able to put it down; just remember to reapply your sunscreen every so often."

—*Harper's Bazaar*, Labor Day Weekend "Must Reads"

"This is the perfect book to take on a transatlantic flight to Europe. Trust me I just did it. . . . A fast-paced plot that wraps itself up in time for you to race to the bathroom before the plane starts its descent."

—*Vanity Fair*

"A coed's gone missing at leafy Lyle College, and visiting prof Phoebe Hall is asking too many questions. A nifty spine-tingler."

—*People*

"A terrifying psychological thriller that takes 'mean girls' to a whole new level of creepy."

—Harlan Coben, #1 *New York Times* bestselling author of *Live Wire*

Hush

"A real page-turner."

—*Today* show

"A sharp-edged thriller . . . Sexy suspense."

—*New York Daily News*

"Kate White places her wily heroine in a real jam, then keeps her, as well as readers, asking 'Whodunit?' right up until the gripping finale."

—Sandra Brown, author of *Rainwater*

THE FIANCÉE

THE FIANCÉE

A Novel

KATE WHITE

HARPER

NEW YORK · LONDON · TORONTO · SYDNEY

HARPER

THE FIANCÉE. Copyright © 2021 by Kate White. All rights reserved. Printed in the United States of America. No part of this book may be used or reproduced in any manner whatsoever without written permission except in the case of brief quotations embodied in critical articles and reviews. For information, address HarperCollins Publishers, 195 Broadway, New York, NY 10007.

HarperCollins books may be purchased for educational, business, or sales promotional use. For information, please email the Special Markets Department at SPsales@harpercollins.com.

FIRST EDITION

Designed by Jamie Lynn Kerner

Library of Congress Cataloging-in-Publication Data has been applied for.

ISBN 978-0-06-294541-9 (pbk.)
ISBN 978-0-06-309272-3 (Library ed.)
ISBN 978-0-06-311345-9 (International ed.)

21 22 23 24 25 LSC 10 9 8 7 6 5 4 3 2 1

To my dazzling, wonderful friends, Nigel Campbell and Bernard Donoghue—and their cat, Tom, too

PROLOGUE

The first thing that seems wrong to her is the vultures.

There are five or six of them, perched in a cluster on the peaked roof of the old bird blind, which sits at the edge of the woods and to the right of the stream.

She freezes with a start about twenty yards away from them, unsettled by their presence. What are they doing so *close*? They're usually in the sky when she sees them, riding thermals.

One of them creeps along the base of the roof and drops its beak. Her eyes follow the movement downward and then keep going, drawn magnetically to the ground.

Three more of the birds ruffle about in the knee-high grass by the stream, and they're pecking at something long and tan colored. A deer must have staggered here and died after being maimed by a car. She watches in disgust as one of the vultures beaks the far end of the animal, then tears away a stringy red piece of flesh.

She starts to turn, unable to stomach a second more of the

grisly scene, but part of her brain has gone rogue and won't let her look away, urging her to revise her interpretation.

No, *not* a deer, she realizes. What she's staring at is a coat. And something denim colored near the lower end of it. Her heart lurches.

Stooping down, she grabs a rock off the ground and hurls it toward the vultures, who lift their wings slightly and hop backward.

It's clear now there's a body inside the coat, lying face-down, with one arm flung outward. And there's skin evident below the bottom of it, the backs of two bare calves. The denim, she now sees, is a pair of jeans that have been bunched around the ankles. Her stomach heaves.

A voice in her head screams at her to flee. Before she can propel herself away, she notices the hand protruding from the sleeve, its nails painted a vivid shade of pink. She's seen this hand before.

1

The day couldn't be more gorgeous. It's late July, and the sky is a spectacular shade of blue, with only a few tiny clouds scudding across. I'm in the passenger seat of our Volvo with my husband, Gabe, behind the wheel and my nine-year-old stepson, Henry, in the back. We're halfway to Gabe's parents' sixty-acre country home in Bucks County, Pennsylvania, for our annual family vacation there, a week that I know from experience will involve plenty of swimming, tennis, badminton, biking, hammocking, forest hikes, Frisbee-tossing, stargazing, board games, and epic conversations, to say nothing of fantastic meals and delicious cocktails.

And yet I've got a pit in my stomach that won't go away, no matter how deeply I breathe, release, and repeat.

"You okay?" Gabe asks, glancing over at me and raising a single eyebrow in that way of his.

"Not totally," I admit. "I'm kind of upset about the job I did this morning."

"Gosh, I'm sorry I didn't get a chance to ask how that went. Want to talk about it?"

I steal a glance into the back seat, where Henry, a precocious kid and world-class eavesdropper, appears engrossed in something on his iPad.

"The session turned into a real dumpster fire," I tell Gabe.

"I thought you were only recording a short story today," he says. "Wouldn't that be pretty straightforward?"

I'm an actress, and I've been concentrating for the past couple of years on voice-over work. Today's dumpster fire involved, yes, me reading one story for the audio edition of an upcoming collection by a hotshot writer.

I sigh. "The author convinced the publisher to let her sit in on the sessions, which is a bad idea on so many levels. Two minutes in she starts wrinkling her nose, like she's smelling a dead yak, and whispering to Shawna, my director. Then, if you can believe it, she started doing line readings for my benefit—to explain how things *should* sound."

"Did Shawna say anything?"

"Not really. She seemed totally intimidated by this woman. We got through the whole recording, but I think they could tell I was flustered."

"I'm sure you did fine, Summer, you always do. And besides, it's just one job."

I usually appreciate Gabe's typical glass-half-full attitude, but it's not as simple as that. Though audiobooks don't pay as well as some of the other voice-over work I do, like TV and radio commercials, and also IVR (interactive voice response)—you know, those prompts that route your call when you contact your insurance company or internet provider, the ones that sometimes make you want to hurl your phone against the wall—I love recording them. That's because it feels like *acting*, and I don't want Shawna to think twice about hiring me again.

But I just nod. Gabe's been worried lately that I give my inner critic way too much headspace, and I shouldn't look like I'm stressing as we kick off our vacation.

"How about you?" I ask. "Are you going to be able to chill this week?"

"Yeah, mostly. Marcus and I need to sit down with Dad about some business stuff, but we'll get that out of the way this weekend."

Gabe and his brother have a flourishing eight-year-old wine-importing firm, and my father-in-law's been an adviser to them, as well as an early investor.

"Will we have time to swim before dinner tonight?" Henry pipes up from the back.

"Probably, buddy," Gabe responds. "I talked to Gee earlier and she said we won't eat till seven."

We'd gotten a later start from Manhattan than we hoped for, in part because Gabe's ex, Amanda, was late dropping Henry off ("You could not *believe* the traffic."), but the GPS has us arriving by five.

"Do you think I'm gonna be able to swim every day?" Henry asks. "My mom said it's supposed to rain this week."

Gabe rolls his eyes for my benefit only. It's so much like Amanda to put a Debbie Downer spin on a fun vacation, but all things being equal, Gabe's coparenting experience could be worse. She's the one who initiated their split ("We were such different people in college, don't you think?"), and though she can be a pain in the butt, her guilt about ending the marriage seems to have kept her from turning toxic.

"There might be a few thunderstorms here and there," Gabe says. "But nothing to worry about. And you downloaded some books, right?"

"Yeah, a bunch."

"What are you reading now, Hen?" I ask.

"*Brief Answers to the Big Questions* by Stephen Hawking."

Jeez. Well, hopefully he won't ask me to elaborate on anything. My BFA theater degree meant that I made it through college without any math or science, but feel free to quiz me on what I soaked up in courses like "Freeing the Expressive Human Instrument" and "Unarmed Combat: Learning Slaps, Punches, and Found Objects."

"You know what could be fun to do if it *does* rain, honey?" I say, twisting around in my seat to look at him. "We could ask Gee to give us a cooking class."

"Wow, that would be awesome."

"Gee," aka my mother-in-law, Claire, has help from her longtime housekeeper, Bonnie, at the Bucks County house, but she also prepares many of the meals herself. A landscape designer by profession, she's a natural and talented chef.

I turn back to Gabe. "So you talked to your mom? Has anyone arrived yet?"

"Marcus and Keira drove out early, so did Blake and Wendy," he says, referring to two of his brothers and their wives. "Not sure when Nick arrives. But—major news flash: he's bringing a new girl with him."

"Oh my god!" I punch him lightly on the arm. "Why are you only telling me this *now*?"

"Because I heard it myself only a couple of hours ago."

I'm happy for Nick. His last girlfriend moved back to Belgium over a year ago, and though I'm sure my charming, dashing brother-in-law hasn't been lacking for female company, I've sensed lately he's eager for something serious. I just hope a stranger won't disturb the ecosystem of our family vacation this week.

"He really sprung it on them last minute, huh?"

"Yeah, but my mom seemed cool about it. As you know, Nick can do no wrong with her."

"Where's Uncle Nick going to stay?" Henry calls out from the back.

"Probably in the carriage house. Gee's had it totally renovated with a couple of new guest rooms."

"What about his date?" my stepson asks.

"Um, probably with him there," Gabe says.

"Does that mean they're shacking up?"

I stifle a laugh as I see Gabe's right brow shoot up.

"Yeah, but let's not refer to it that way in front of everyone else. Okay, buddy? And speaking of sleeping arrangements, are you sure you want to stay in the main house? You could always bunk down with me and Summer in the cottage."

"Thanks, but I wanna be in the big house with Gee and Grandpa. Gee said the dogs can sleep with me."

"Okay, but if you change your mind, it's not a problem."

Twenty minutes later we exit the main highway, and in another fifteen, we cross the Delaware River from New Jersey into Bucks County and end up on Durham Road. The sight of the Keatons' home—a rambling gray stone house with several wings, and dormer windows across the roof—always lifts my spirits, and I feel my work worries ease as soon as we head down the gravel road that leads to the circular driveway.

As we're parking, my father-in-law, Ash, strides from the house, his six-two frame bookended by two scampering dogs: Ginger, a golden retriever, and Bella, a pug-Chihuahua rescue mutt.

"It's only been three weeks since I saw you, but I swear you've grown two inches," Ash tells Henry, his voice booming, as he envelops him in a hug.

"Did you know you grow more when you're sleeping than when you're awake, Grandpa?" Henry asks.

"I didn't know that, but you're going to sit next to me at dinner and tell me all about it," Ash says, hugging me and Gabe in turn. Though I know my father-in-law has a reputation for being tough and exacting in his commercial real estate business, he always has plenty of warmth to spare for us. "Now let's go say hi to Gee."

We follow him in, and I'm newly struck by the fact that Gabe, with his slate-blue eyes and hawklike nose, looks a lot like his handsome dad, minus the silver hair.

Claire is in the large kitchen, wearing a cook's apron over stylish beige trousers and a cream-colored blouse, and julienning basil, which she pauses doing to hug us. As I set two bags of bagels on the countertop, I spot a few people hanging by the pool through the rear window of the kitchen.

"Can I get my trunks on?" Henry asks, noticing, too.

"You bet," Ash tells him. "Why don't you carry your bag upstairs first? You're in the room next to Gee's and mine."

"I think I'll swim, too," Gabe says. "What about you, Summer?"

"I'm going to stay here and catch up with your mom for a bit."

"Okay, I'll take our stuff to the cottage. Unless you need any help here, Mom?"

She shakes her head. "No, darling, enjoy yourself. There are snacks and drinks by the pool."

After they depart, I take a minute to let my eyes roam the room. If Gabe's business keeps growing like it has been, we're hoping to buy a small weekend home of our own, and this is the kind of kitchen I'd kill for. All the white keeps it fresh, but there's also a charming rustic feel thanks to the exposed ceiling beams, apron sink, and painted wood floor.

"How about an iced tea?" Claire asks, nodding toward the brown ceramic jug that she keeps filled on the counter.

"Not right now, thanks." My mother-in-law brews it herself with herbs like fennel and sage, and though I'm sure it has all sorts of antioxidant properties, I've always preferred the stuff that tastes like Snapple.

"You look lovely, by the way," she says. "The green in your dress perfectly matches your eyes, and the style suits you to a tee."

I cherish compliments like that from Claire as she always looks so pulled together. Her blond hair, a shade or so lighter than mine, is pulled back today in a flattering French twist.

"Do you think so? I wore it to work today. A lot of voice actors dress down for recording jobs, but I always feel I perform better when I make an effort."

"I think we all do. Like it or not, people notice our clothes and judge us on them, sometimes without even realizing it, and you pick up on those vibes in the studio, I'm sure."

I'm momentarily tempted to tell Claire what happened today at the recording. She's a fount of wisdom on everything from how much a wedding gift should cost to turning any kind of negotiation into a win-win. But I don't want to bother her when she's in the midst of making dinner for all of us.

"Where's Bonnie?" I ask.

"She went out to pick up a few more supplies. Turns out Nick's date for the week is a vegetarian and we'll have to add extra side dishes while she's here."

"Do you know anything else about her?"

"Not a thing. He only told us two days ago that he was bringing her."

She returns her attention to the basil on the butcher-block-topped island and scrapes it into a huge white bowl, one already filled with diced tomatoes, chunks of Brie, and olive oil. My mouth waters as I realize that it's for one of the delicious pasta dishes Claire loves to serve in summer.

"Do you think that after Marcus's wedding, Nick started to feel pressure to settle down?" Marcus is Nick's fraternal twin, and he married a lovely woman named Keira last summer.

Claire shakes her head. "Nick? I think the only pressure he allows himself to feel these days is work-related."

For the past several years, Nick has been involved in Ash's real estate business.

"Or," she adds smiling, "on the squash court. I just hope when he *is* inclined to marry, it's to someone as terrific as you."

"Oh, Claire, that's so kind of you to say." She's warm and generous to all three of her daughters-in-law, but I know we have a special rapport. "And, of course, it's entirely mutual. But I should have asked you before—can I help with anything?"

"No, Bonnie and I have it under control. Go start your vacation, dear."

I head out to the patio, near where Henry's already splashing around at one end of the kidney-shaped, black-bottom pool with Gabe and his grandfather. Blake, Gabe's oldest brother, is swimming laps, while Marcus, Keira, and Blake's wife, Wendy, are clustered by the beverage trolley. They wave me over.

"Great to see everyone," I say, hugging them all. "We had dinner with these two just last week," I tell Wendy, cocking my head at Marcus and Keira, "but it seems like ages since we've seen you and Blake."

"I know, that's the problem with moving to the burbs," Wendy says, flicking a strand of her chin-length hair off her face. "Plus, we've both been crazed at work lately."

"Everything good in the art world?"

"Definitely, but you can't make some of this stuff up," Wendy says. She's an art dealer who now runs her own gallery. "I sold two very expensive candle sculptures to a collector in Texas a month ago, and his wife accidentally lit them at a party she gave. He ended up ordering two more."

"Why would an artist bother making candles if he didn't want anyone to light them?" Marcus asks.

Wendy smiles, unruffled. She's been married to Blake for ten years, and she knows this is a typical response from Marcus. He's the quietest of the brothers, but when he does have something to say, he cuts straight to the chase.

"Blake asked me the same thing. He thinks a lot of modern art is the emperor's new clothes. But a good artist simply wants you to pause and stare and be provoked and maybe see things in a totally different way."

"I guess the wife missed the point. . . . Speaking of Blake, I may take a dip, too." Marcus glances at Keira. "You want to join me?"

"You go ahead," she tells her husband. "I'm going to wait until tomorrow." He nods and her eyes linger on him as he strides off toward the pool.

"I was just hearing about Keira's wonderful new job," Wendy says to me.

"Well, not wonderful yet," my other sister-in-law insists, shaking her head. "I'm still trying to get my bearings."

I don't consider either Wendy or Keira to be close friends, but I get along well with both of them, as different as they are. Wendy's outgoing and self-possessed, thirty-eight as of last month. Though she seems to favor mostly black designer clothes for work, on weekends she goes for more of that preppy-bohemian Tory Burch style of dressing, which fits well with her white-blond hair and blue-eyed good looks. I've seen her be snooty to waiters but never toward anyone in the family. It drives Gabe nuts that she talks with a faint British accent, even though she only lived in the UK for a year—and it was the year she was twenty-two. But if Madonna can be forgiven for doing it, so can Wendy, I suppose.

Keira is thirty-three like me, supersmart, and as of a few weeks ago, a relationship manager for an organization that guides philanthropists on where to donate. She's attractive, with long brown hair, brown eyes, and flawless light brown skin, and though she dresses nicely enough, it's a classic, fairly conservative style that suggests fashion didn't make the cut on her list of major priorities. Mostly she's friendly and thoughtful, though less self-assured than Wendy. Sometimes she can even be a little awkward in social situations, maybe due to anxiety. She'll walk into a room and for no obvious reason will be wearing this worried frown that makes you wonder if she knows something you don't about an approaching swarm of killer bees or a massive asteroid headed straight toward the earth.

"I hate to be a party pooper, but I have to excuse myself," Wendy says. "I need to check in quickly with a client."

"No problem," I tell her. "We'll have plenty of time together this week."

She sets down a half-empty glass of ice water and as she turns to go, I notice a tiny swell at the waist of her sundress. Could this mean she's finally pregnant? I know from Gabe that she and Blake have been trying on and off for ages, and we'd all be thrilled if they're expecting.

I turn back to Keira. "Were you able to get the whole week off?" I ask her.

"No, I'm going to take the bus back to the city early Tuesday morning, and then come out again on Friday."

"Oh, that's a bummer."

"I know, but I really need to get up to speed in the new position," she says, not looking all that sad about it.

I can't help but wonder if work is the true reason she'll be here only part of the time. She's an only child, whose parents—a Black father and Caucasian mother—divorced when she was three. Though Keira says they were both loving and did a good job of coparenting, neither remarried or had other children, and perhaps as a result, she sometimes seems uncomfortable in a big family group, especially one that can get as loud and rowdy as the Keatons.

"Of course, maybe I *should* be sticking around," she adds. "You heard about Nick's mystery guest, right?"

"Oh, yeah. But don't worry, I promise to text you regular updates if you want."

"It's not that." The tiny fissure between her eyes deepens. "She used to date *Marcus*."

"You're kidding," I say, taken aback. "When?"

"Around two years ago, right before he met me."

I can't imagine having one of Gabe's exes show up during our family vacation. "Ugh, I'm sorry. Will this be weird for you guys?"

"Marcus swears not, at least on his end. They apparently only went out a few times before he broke it off. Says she wasn't his type. So I guess I shouldn't be bothered, either."

"Of course not," I assure her. "How did Nick end up meeting her, anyway?"

"Through the same friend Marcus did. Someone they know in the city."

"Well, I feel confident you have nothing to worry about," I tell her, and I do. She and Marcus clearly have a strong bond.

The sun has now sunk low enough in the sky that it's cast a shadow across most of the water in the pool, and though Gabe and Henry are still happily splashing around, I take it as my cue to freshen up before dinner. I tell Keira I'll see her shortly and walk around to the western side of the house, then make my way down a long path to the stone guest cottage, which sits nestled against the edge of a wooded area.

Because Gabe and I often come out here on weekends, Claire offered us first dibs on the refurbished carriage house, but the little cottage will always be my first choice. In our early days of dating, it gave me a needed sense of privacy, as comfortable as I felt with Gabe's parents right from the start.

The cottage is actually an old springhouse, dating back at least a hundred years. It's where food used to be stored before refrigeration because the spring below cooled the building. The lower level features a cozy sitting room with a fireplace and a small kitchen; upstairs are two bedrooms and a bath.

After unpacking my duffel bag—and discovering that Gabe, in his typical thoughtful way, has already hung my dresses—I brew myself a cup of tea, then carry it out to the small patio in the rear. It's rimmed by a gorgeous border garden bursting with reds, blues, and purples. After settling at the table, I sweep my gaze over the Monet-like setting.

I wish I could really savor the scene, but my anxiety about the morning's recording session has somehow crept back in. I have to do better at not letting stuff like that eat at me. Besides, I shouldn't let a setback in this arena bug me. Though I enjoy voice-over work and appreciate how well it pays, the jobs are only a means to an end. If I had to spend my life recording prompts like "Please listen carefully because our menu options have changed" while people I knew were acting in movies and series or scoring lead roles off Broadway, I'd shoot myself.

What I ultimately want, and have wanted ever since my mother took me to see a touring company perform *The*

Fantasticks when I was twelve, is to engage fully in theater and film, both as an actor and writer. This fall, a short play I wrote is going to be staged as part of a small theater festival just north of the city, and I'm hoping that will help me make more inroads in the theater world at least. Plus, playwriting and possibly screenwriting, too, will be a way to stay involved in my career when Gabe and I have a baby—which we hope to do next year.

As I finish my tea, I discover to my shock that it's closing in on six thirty. I run upstairs and quickly wash my face, dab on fresh makeup, and grab a cotton sweater. I'm halfway up the path to the house when Henry comes tearing toward me, dressed now in khaki pants and a white polo shirt.

"I'm on a mission to find you," he calls out as he approaches.

"Mission accomplished. And my, don't *you* look smashing," I say, wrapping an arm around his shoulder.

"Gee bought the shirt for me," he says, wrinkling his nose.

"Don't you like it?"

"The little polo player looks stupid."

"Well, wear it just tonight," I say as we resume walking. "It'll make your grandmother happy."

"Yeah, okay. Guess what?" He flashes his dimpled smile, and his blue eyes twinkle.

"What?"

"The mystery date is here!"

This kid doesn't miss a thing. "Ah, so what do you think? Does she meet with your approval?"

"The jury's still out."

I laugh out loud at his choice of words. "I'm sure she's perfectly nice."

"And guess what else?"

"What?"

"She's an actress, too."

Oh *fabulous*. I have plenty of friends from my college acting program and years in the business, but meeting other actors is rarely fun—because an ugly compare-a-thon is almost always unavoidable. As Billy Dean, a pal from college, says, "Two actors at a dinner table is, at the very least, one actor too many."

"What's her name?"

"She told us it's Hannah, but do you think that's her real name?"

"Why do you ask?"

"Well, your name isn't really Summer. My mom said it's Sara."

Bless your heart, Amanda. I wonder how she'd feel if I told Henry everything I knew about *her*—like the fact that her "outgrowing the marriage" coincided with a fling with a coworker. Not that I'd ever do that, of course.

"Some actors have to change their names—because there's a more famous actor with the same name." What I don't add is that in my case I was mostly going for something more memorable than Sara.

Henry grabs my hand, urging me to speed up, and as we round the house to the back patio, I see that everyone else is there, talking and sipping cocktails against a soft, early evening sky. As Henry darts away to romp with the dogs, I spot Gabe in a circle with Blake and his aunt and uncle, who have

driven over from New Jersey for dinner along with their recently divorced daughter. Gabe cocks his chin up in greeting
and I signal to him that I'll be over in a sec.

I step toward the drinks trolley and pour a glass of sparkling water, knowing there'll be plenty of wine later. Spinning back around, I finally spot the mystery guest, dressed in
a summery red dress with a deep-V neckline and lips painted
to match. Nick's arm is locked around her waist, and they're
chatting with Ash, who's wearing a grin the size of a cruise
ship.

And I realize at that moment that I've met her before.
Three—no, two—years ago. We were both performing in
a theater showcase involving an evening of very short plays,
each one by a different aspiring playwright. She was in the
last one of the night, so I not only mingled with her back-
stage but also had the chance to watch her performance after
I was done.

It's no surprise I remember her. She's about five eight, a
little taller than me, with brown eyes and wavy, dark brown
hair worn just below the ear—so different from the long
hair that I and everyone else our age seem to favor. Probably
around twenty-seven. Not a bad actress, if I recall correctly,
but if she was in a showcase only two years ago, she's probably still struggling like I am.

As I rake my memory for her name, which I can't recall
at the moment, Nick spots me, flashes his trademark half-
cocked grin, and beckons me over to the trio, his light blue
eyes sparkling.

"Summer," he says, enveloping me in a hug when I reach
him. "It's been wayyyy too long."

"I know, I know. Is your dad working you to the bone?"

"Only twenty-four, six—he actually lets up a tiny bit on Sundays," he jokes, glancing at his father. Then, looking back at me, he says, "Summer, this is Hannah Kane. Hannah, this is my amazing sister-in-law Summer Redding."

Hannah Kane. Funny how I remembered her stunning looks but not her name.

"Lovely to meet you," she says, as a blend of patchouli and vanilla wafts from her creamy white skin. "Nick's absolutely gushed about you."

"Nice to meet you, too," I reply, realizing she has no recollection of me. Good to know I leave such a lasting impression.

"Summer," Ash says with mischief in his tone, "can you assure Hannah that she's under no pressure whatsoever, but that we desperately need her for the badminton tournament this week? Keira's had to bow out."

Before I can respond, Hannah does. "Oh, absolutely count me in."

"Fabulous," Ash exclaims. A split second later I see Claire signal for his assistance from the other end of the patio, and he excuses himself and hurries off.

Nick shakes his head good-naturedly. "I'd promised Hannah she wouldn't have to engage in a single group activity the entire time she's here, and now she's just been railroaded into a badminton tournament that will probably go on for days."

"I'd actually love to do it," she tells him.

"Seriously?" he asks.

"Absolutely." She eyes him flirtatiously. "I'm actually pretty good with a shuttlecock."

Oh please, I think. *Get a room.* But before I can duck away from this exchange, Nick redirects his attention to me.

"I've been so eager for you guys to meet. You're both in the same field and I'm sure you've got a ton to talk about."

He starts to elaborate, but then Henry pops over, begging Nick to pull a quarter out of his ear, and suddenly Hannah and I are left alone, like we're two characters in a movie scene in which everyone else is frozen.

"What a fabulous place this is," Hannah says, sweeping her gaze around the grounds. "You must love coming out here from the city."

"I do, very much. And I'm glad you could join us. How long have you and Nick been dating?"

"About two months," she says. "It would have been great to have met Nick's family sooner, but with work, this was my first chance."

"Actually, you and I have met before."

"*Really?*"

"We were both in the same playwriting showcase. Two Octobers ago."

She tips her head in confusion. "Showcase?"

"Yes. One with six or seven ten-minute plays. Down in the West Village."

"Hmm, I'm afraid you must have me mixed up with someone else," she says. "I've never done a showcase in the Village."

This is totally bizarre. I have no idea why, but I'm sure that she's just told me a big, fat lie.

2

---

kay, wait, maybe I'm wrong, I think, feeling a twinge of embarrassment.

But a beat later, I reconsider again. Hannah's too distinctive looking, especially with her mile-long lashes and lips full enough to be used as a flotation device. I know it was her.

"It's possible I'm remembering the location wrong," I tell her. "But you were a cat that a scientist turns into a woman, and then falls in love with. I played a failing country western singer in one of the other plays."

I expect her to raise her eyes briefly upward and to the left—that's where people look when they're trying to remember—but instead she holds my gaze, her expression blank.

"Nope, I'm sorry," she says. There's a base note of relish in her words, as if she likes proving me wrong. "I've worked in theater, but never a role like that. Though it sounds like an intriguing concept."

I guess I *am* hopelessly confused, because why would she

be reluctant to admit it? Tons of actors do showcases. And one of the biggest freaking musicals of all time has an entire cast of people pretending to be cats. I concede. "Well, you've got a doppelgänger then."

"Good to know," she says slyly. "In case I'm ever wrongly accused of murder. Though not so great for an actor, is it— someone going after the same roles?"

I force a chuckle. "Are you based full-time in New York?"

She nods. "I stayed in L.A. for a little while after I graduated from USC. You know, University of Southern California?"

Of *course* I know. It's one of the best drama programs in the country.

"But I really prefer New York," she continues. "There are so many movies and TV shows shooting in the city right now, and though I do love theater, I'm mostly concentrating on film work these days."

"Oh, like what?" I ask, barely getting the words out.

"I just finished a pilot for a Netflix series, and—fingers crossed—we'll be green-lighted this month."

It takes everything I've got to paste a smile on my face. Am I the only actor on the fucking planet not currently shooting a Netflix pilot?

"That's terrific," I say.

"What about you?"

Hmm, what should I tell her? That my main role in the past six months was an "under five" on *Law and Order: SVU*, where I played a secretary, and that two of my five lines were, "He's on a call right now so it might be a while," and "Wait, you can't go in there"?

"I do a mix of things—TV, theater, voice-over work," I say instead, trying to sound confident. "My main project right now is a short play I wrote. It's going to be part of a festival this fall."

"Oh, how fun," she says.

Fun? She makes it sound like I've informed her we're having s'mores for dessert tonight.

I'm saved from further conversation by Ash's announcement that dinner is served at the other end of the long patio. Nick reappears and takes Hannah's hand. At the same moment, Gabe heads in my direction, carrying a half glass of wine. People meld together and we make our way to dinner, the dogs practically glued to our sides.

"Shoot," Gabe says, "I never let Amanda know we arrived." He whips out his phone and quickly texts her.

"Do you think she ever misses any of this?" I ask when he's completed the task.

He shakes his head. "I doubt it. For some reason, she never took to it like you have, babe."

I think I know why the festive and celebratory atmosphere the Keatons create means so much to me. My own parents couldn't be nicer or kinder, but two years before I was born, they lost my brother, Leo, to meningitis, and a faint sadness always seemed to permeate our home, especially in the evenings.

We reach the end of the patio, where there's unified murmur of appreciation for the dinner setup. A long wooden farm table sits under the vine-laced pergola, and it's been strewn with twinkling votive candles and tiny vases bursting with lavender and other fresh herbs. Along the outer wall of the house is a rustic wooden sideboard laid with platters of antipasto—roasted vegetables, cheeses, olives, salami, and prosciutto.

"This looks fabulous," I say to Bonnie, the fiftysomething Energizer Bunny–like housekeeper who's standing by to help with serving. She's been with the Keatons for over two decades and is a total gem.

"Thanks, Summer," she says, cocking her head toward Claire, "but of course you know who the real maestro is."

After helping Henry pick and choose from the buffet, I return to the line and load up my own plate. I end up sitting between Gabe's uncle and Blake, whom I've yet to connect with today. His short, prematurely gray hair, which matches his trimmed beard and mustache, is still slightly damp from his swim, and he's dressed in slacks and a long-sleeve white linen shirt. A little formal for outdoor dining, but that's Blake for you.

"Dr. Keaton," I say, giving him a peck on the cheek. "At long last."

"I know, I know, sorry about that. Wendy's been crushed, traveling a lot for work, and I've been busier than I ever imagined."

Blake's a dermatologist, an anomaly in a family of entrepreneurs. He's forty-one and a bit square compared to his younger brothers—I could make him blush simply by saying the words *ass crack* or *lady parts*—but he's also genial and inquisitive, with a big heart. I always enjoy his company.

Before we can chat anymore, Bonnie and a young, pink-haired female helper, whom I vaguely recall from another event, approach with bottles of red and white Italian wines, compliments of Gabe and Marcus's company. When they've finished filling our glasses, my father-in-law rises and raises his glass in a toast.

"Claire, my dearest, you've done it again," he says, leveling his gaze at her. "Thank you. And to everyone else: Welcome, enjoy, and we're so glad you're able to share this wonderful family time with us."

After what seems like endless clinking of glasses, I turn back to Blake. "Well, I'm just glad that with all the work on your plate, you both managed to get away this week."

"My mother would *strangle* me if we ever skipped a year."

"Really?" It's hard for me to imagine Claire annoyed at any of her sons, but especially Blake. He's such a solid citizen.

"I'm kidding, of course. We wouldn't miss it for the world. We all have so much to catch up on."

I'm reminded suddenly of the swell in Wendy's belly. Maybe she *is* pregnant, and they're planning to tell us this week.

"The last time we spoke at length," he says, "you were picking my brain about fillers and Botox for a play you were writing. Are you still working on that?"

"Oh, you're sweet to remember, Blake. Yes, I'm still tweaking it. It's about five women planning to do an intervention with a friend and at first you think it's about alcohol or drugs—if I'm doing my job right—but then you realize it's about the friend having had way too many cosmetic procedures. The good news is that it was accepted into a small playwriting festival and is going to be staged in November."

"How clever, Summer. It sounds wonderful."

Well, it's not a damn *Netflix* pilot, but it's something. "Thank you, Blake."

"Is there a part for you, I hope?"

I smile. "Better be."

"The voice-over stuff sounds great, too. When we were in the pool, Gabe mentioned that you set up a recording studio right in the loft."

"True, though it's nothing fancy. I just put up some acoustical foam in a walk-in closet. But I can do a lot of voice-over jobs that way—even if it sometimes seems like I'm in a padded cell."

"Ah, but to have so much freedom in your professional life. There are days when I feel like I'm stuck on a gerbil wheel."

The comment surprises me. I always assumed Blake, the responsible oldest child, was thriving in his work or at least convinced it was worth all the spoils: a huge house in the suburbs; a condo in Aspen; weekend jaunts to the Caribbean. Is it possible he'd like a break from always having to follow the rules?

"What about a short sabbatical?"

"It's hard to do in my world, and I don't know if it would help. I've always envied Gabe. He parlayed his passions for wine and travel into a business and gets to do what he really loves every day. I like medicine, but it's hard to be passionate about removing endless moles from people who refuse to stay out of the sun."

Before I can ask him to elaborate, he switches gears back to the voice-over work. Though I appreciate his friendly questions, they have the unfortunate effect of forcing my mind on the morning's recording session, and I start to wonder if I should have attempted any kind of damage control with the director.

As Bonnie and her helper clear away the plates from the first course, I excuse myself, head to the powder room off the main hall in the house, and shoot Shawna a text.

Sorry abt all the back and forth today. Hope everyone's happy with the final results.

I give it a minute, waiting to see if she'll respond. No reply appears. I slip my phone back into my purse and step outside, but I don't return to the table yet. Instead, I pause in the corridor, leaning against the row of tan slickers that hang on wall pegs, placed there by Claire for anyone in the house to borrow in foul weather.

There's something else on my mind and I fish my phone from my purse again and send another text, this one to Billy Dean, my college friend who is now an actor-barista-tour guide in New York. It happens that he was in that West Village showcase with me.

Crazy Q 4u. I was thinking of those plays we did abt 2 years ago at the Lilac Theater on West 13th St. Do u remember the name of the girl who played the cat who turned into a woman? In the last play?

By the time I return, the pasta with tomatoes and melted Brie is being served, and the volume of the conversation has gone up a decibel or two. Dusk has begun to dissolve into darkness, and fireflies dance in the yard beyond the patio, oblivious to all of us.

During this part of the meal, I chat with Gabe's uncle,

and I also have the chance to observe Hannah in action. She's to the left of Aunt Jean, Ash's sister, with Nick on her other side, his arm draped around her shoulder like a pashmina she's brought along in case the weather cools.

While nodding and smiling during the conversation I'm pretending to be engaged in, I manage to hear Hannah entertaining Nick, Jean, and Wendy with a story about her first day on a film set. When she heard the term "honey wagon," she tells them, her voice sparkling, she assumed it was where food and beverages were served, but it turned out to be the trailer with the toilets. She's greeted with warm laughter from her listeners.

As I watch her from the corner of my eye, I'm struck by how totally unselfconscious she seems. Her hands move a little for emphasis or illustration when she's telling a story, but she never touches her face, twirls her hair, or nibbles a cuticle, which is my go-to nervous habit. During my first years in New York, when I wasn't chasing auditions or waiting tables, I took endless acting workshops and classes, and the best ones focused on training you to look natural and spontaneous when you performed—acting teachers call it being "unentangled." The legendary Stanislavski—whom I did *not* study with needless to say—stressed that actors need to learn "public solitude," meaning that even with people watching you, you're at ease. Hannah's more than nailed the technique.

Discreetly, I steal a glance toward Marcus at the far end of the table, wondering how he's handling Hannah's presence. He seems fully absorbed in conversation with Claire and his cousin. But a few seconds later, as I'm about to ask

Gabe's uncle a question, Marcus shifts slightly in his seat and reaches for the breadbasket, and as he does, his gaze shifts to Hannah. He stares hard at her, seemingly unable to look away.

Has he misled Keira, I wonder, allowing her to believe he was never serious about Hannah? Maybe he'd been as enthralled with her as Nick is. And if that's the case, I can't imagine how uncomfortable he must be, not just from Hannah's being here but also the fact that she's bedding down with his twin.

I can see how Hannah would have been attracted to both of them initially. As fraternal twins, Marcus and Nick aren't supposed to look any more alike than regular brothers, but there's an uncanny resemblance. They're both about six feet tall, a little shorter than Gabe, with light blue eyes like their mother and her blond hair, as well, though slightly darker.

That said, they lack the magical bond so many *identical* twins have. They get along well enough most of the time, but from what Gabe has told me, and what I've seen with my own eyes, there's always been a subtle, unspoken rivalry between them. By all accounts, Nick was an easygoing and fun kid, a natural athlete whom others glommed on to, whereas Marcus was a chubby, introspective child, who spent hours in his room and didn't fully come into his own—and his looks—until his midtwenties, around the time he and Gabe began their partnership. And though Marcus is now happily married and runs a successful business with Gabe, due in no small part to his excellent head for numbers, I sense he's still envious of Nick at times.

And though this is far *less* obvious, I suspect Nick has moments when he envies Marcus. For being so brainy. For not needing to charm people until their cheeks hurt from smiling.

Once the heavenly tiramisu has been served and eaten, I rise and make my way over to Henry, who's been entertaining Ash through the meal and now has his eyes at half-mast. Gabe joins us.

"Want me to tuck him in?" I ask.

"No, I better do it," Gabe says. "I want to make sure he feels really comfortable sleeping in a different house from us. I'll meet you at the cottage, okay?"

I nod. "Night, honey," I say to Henry, tousling his silky light brown hair.

"Can you do Peter and Wendy tonight?" he asks, looking up at me.

I've been reading *Peter Pan* to him when he stays at our loft in the city, acting out the characters, but it's clear he'd pass out tonight before I uttered a line. Plus, it's good to give Gabe some time alone with Henry. He's got great natural instincts as a father, but I know he's always working at being an even better one. His marriage broke up when Henry was only two, and he initially felt fairly hapless as a single dad, along with petrified that Amanda would sense his insecurity and use it to press for full custody. He stockpiled dozens of parenting books and even did sessions with a child therapist to help him gain more confidence and skill.

"Some other night this week, I promise. When you're not so sleepy."

Gabe sweeps him up in his arms and off they go. Moments later, the extended family members say their good-byes before they start back to New Jersey, and Blake and Wendy announce they're turning in. Before they head up to the carriage house, which they're sharing with Nick and Hannah, Ash announces to everyone that the badminton tournament kicks off Monday at four so we have the weekend to simply relax. *Too bad*, I think. *I'm going to have to wait two whole days to see the mistress of the shuttlecock in action.*

After wishing the remaining guests good night, I wander up to the cottage. The sky is cloudless, scattered everywhere with bright white stars, and the night air is filled with the insistent, magical calls of katydids and crickets.

Inside the cottage, I curl up on the sofa, waiting for Gabe. My tummy, I notice, is still doing a vaguely nervous jig. I check my phone, but there's still nothing from Shawna. Which makes sense, of course. Why would she bother answering a work text on a Friday night in the summer?

There is, however, a text from my mom, asking how things are going in Pennsylvania. Nice, I tell her. Good to see everybody. Will give you a call this week. I know it's not necessary, but when I talk to my mother, I often find myself underplaying how much fun I have with the Keatons. Despite their sadness, my parents tried their best to give my sister and me a happy home, and I don't ever want her to think that our family was lacking.

Fifteen minutes later, Gabe still isn't back, and I realize he's probably having a hard time getting Henry down. I mount the stairs and change for bed, telling myself I'll read until Gabe returns, but when I feel him crawl in bed beside me, I realize I've dozed off with the lights on.

"Hi," I murmur, happy to finally see him again. "Where've you been?"

"I ended up walking Nick and Hannah over to the carriage house after I put Henry to bed."

"Oh. What did you think?"

"My mom did a really great job with it. Open plan downstairs, two bedrooms on the second floor."

"No, I mean what do you think of Hannah?"

"Oh, the mystery woman," he says, reaching across me and turning off the light on my bedside table. "Yeah, she seems nice, fun. Certainly an improvement over the girl Nick brought to our apartment a few months ago."

"Did you know that she used to date Marcus?"

"Yeah, so I hear. But he says it wasn't a big deal. Apparently, she was a little too flashy for his taste."

"Did he sleep with her, do you know?"

"He admitted he did, but says it didn't mean anything."

"Your father seemed to like her."

"Yeah, but as Nick knows, Mom's the tougher critic."

"Any idea what she thinks?"

"None at all," he says, wrapping an arm around me. "But don't worry, babe. No matter who Nick ends up with, you're always gonna be her favorite daughter-in-law. Night."

I try to get back to sleep, but I can't seem to. After about thirty minutes, I slip downstairs, where I pour a glass of water, and park myself on the couch again. My phone's still on the coffee table and I notice two text alerts on the screen. The first text is a reply from Shawna:

Thanks for going with the flow. Have a nice weekend.

Not what you'd call a direct response to my comment about hoping everyone was happy, but I don't want to bug her and press for more.

And there's a message from Billy, sent only ten minutes ago.

I'll give you the name but first tell me why you're so hot to know.

That's typical of Billy. He likes to use gossip as a bargaining chip. Confident he's still up, I tap his number and call him.

"Why aren't you in bed with that hunky hubby of yours, the wine impresario?" he says.

"What makes you think I'm not?"

"Let me hear him snoring."

"No. What about *you*, the playboy of the Western world? It's Friday night."

"She just left."

"*Right.* So do you remember the girl I'm talking about?"

"Of course, but tell me, why so curious?"

"Uh, I was at a party at my in-laws' tonight and I thought a woman I was talking to might be her." That's the most I'm revealing to Mr. Blabby. "I've been racking my brain to think of her name."

"Well, the actress's name—excuse me, *actor's* name—was Hannah. Hannah Kane."

So my memory had been correct after all. It's possible Hannah's simply forgotten, but that seems unlikely. The showcase was only two years ago, and most actors can tell you every part they ever played, right down to roles like "Shepherd #1" in the fourth-grade Nativity play.

"Not her then?" Billy says into the silence.

"Actually, it *is*. But she swore she wasn't in that showcase. Why would she lie?"

"Maybe she wants to pretend that whole nasty experience with the other actress never happened."

The skin on the back of my neck begins to crawl. "What nasty experience?"

"You don't remember? The night of the dress rehearsal turned into a real shitstorm. Because Hannah stole a wad of cash from the other actress."

3

y heart skips. Nick's new girlfriend isn't only a liar, she might be a thief, too?

"How much cash are you talking about?" I ask.

"I think it was close to a hundred bucks," Billy says. "But that actually wasn't the worst part. She also took a pricey necklace, which the chick said was a gift from her parents."

"Who was this other actress, anyway?"

"Cary something. She was in the same play as me. Curly brown hair, overacted as if the fate of Western civilization depended on it."

I know exactly who he's talking about. One evening she and I had gotten to talking and realized we both loved the play *Skylight* by David Hare, how our dream would be to star in it. We'd even gone out for coffee after an early rehearsal and had promised to stay in touch, but as often happens, neither of us ever reached out.

"And she was sure Hannah did it?"

"Well, Hannah wasn't required to open her purse or consent to a strip search if that's what you mean. But Cary

Whatever-Her-Last-Name-Is said that they'd changed clothes at the same time in that pit of a dressing room, and she caught Hannah watching her during the process. If I remember correctly—and I'm trying not to tax too many brain cells doing so—Cary said she'd forgotten she'd worn the necklace that day, and stuck it into the toe of her boot because she couldn't wear it during dress rehearsal. She's clearly one of those actors who believe in total authenticity. . . . Don't tell me none of this is ringing a bell?"

I've combed through my memories as we've been speaking, pulling up a few images from the run of the showcase: the overcrowded coed dressing room that reeked of someone's BO; a director going nuclear on one actress who wasn't off book by dress rehearsal; Gabe applauding wildly as I took my bow on opening night. But I finally realize why I missed the showdown Billy's talking about.

"I needed to meet Gabe at an event that night, and I had to leave the second my own dress rehearsal was over," I tell him.

"Too bad, because the drama in the dressing room was better than anything those playwrights had written. I almost thought Cary wouldn't show for the play the next night, but someone apparently talked the poor thing off the ledge."

"And Cary's only evidence was that she'd noticed Hannah watching her undress?"

"No, there was also some maintenance guy who was dragged into the mess. He claimed he'd seen Hannah alone in the room at one point, in the corner by Cary's stuff."

A bed creaks on the floor directly above me, and I pause for a sec, wondering if I've woken Gabe, but the cottage goes quiet again.

"Do you think Hannah really stole the stuff?" I ask.

"Probably. She denied it and claimed the maintenance guy was pissed because she'd given him the deep freeze after he'd tried to flirt with her. But there was something off about her whole demeanor that night. She seemed almost bemused by the accusation, not at all embarrassed."

"Wow."

"Yeah, wow. I'd thought about asking her out for a drink but changed my mind. You know I like edgy, Summer, but I draw the line at sociopaths."

"Glad to hear you were looking out for yourself. Anyway, I appreciate the info. And I better let us both turn in now."

We sign off, and I tiptoe back upstairs, crawling into bed in the pitch-darkness. I flip onto my back and lie there with my eyes wide open and my curiosity on fire.

Did Hannah really steal the cash and the necklace? I've only got Billy's version of events, but the fact that she lied to me about being in the showcase suggests she has something to hide.

It's hard to draw a bigger conclusion from it, though. Maybe stealing's something she did once out of total financial desperation. I certainly felt a little desperate for cash myself in the years before I began landing regular voice-over work and married Gabe. True, I never *stole* anything, but when I was waiting tables for extra income, eager for the biggest tips possible, I regularly upsold my customers desserts like Anjou pear crisps and pumpkin mousses they *so* didn't need.

It's kind of a moot point, anyway, I think as I finally drift off to sleep. If Nick's recent history is anything to go on, his

relationship with Hannah is hardly likely to progress beyond
a sex-fueled fling.

When I wake the next morning, Gabe's side of the bed is
empty, and I find a note from him on the dresser explaining
he's at the tennis court hitting balls with Henry. I'm shocked
to discover that my watch says it's eight o'clock. Peering out
the window, I see that it's another drop-dead gorgeous day,
the kind of weather that reminds me I should be relishing the
week ahead, but I still feel oddly unsettled—about yesterday's recording session, and about Hannah.

After a quick shower, I start up the path to the house,
where I know Claire and Bonnie will have set the sideboard
on the patio with a continental breakfast. Fortunately for
me, late sleepers are never penalized here. Off in the distance,
I hear friendly shouts from the tennis court and the *plock,
plock* of a ball in play.

Nearing the house, I pass one of Claire's larger gardens
and a favorite of mine. It's an extraordinary mix of not only
colors but textures, too, and abuts a grove of boxwood clouds,
bushes that have been pruned into massive balls of green with
a small glade in the middle, like something from the pages of
Alice in Wonderland.

There's a wrought-iron table at the edge of the garden,
and this morning a mug is resting there along with a floral
plate hosting a half-eaten piece of dry toast. Thinking they've
been left behind, I start to grab both to take indoors, but
then notice that the mug is filled with what looks like tea.

A moment later, I hear murmuring and the snap of a

branch as Wendy steps out from behind one of the box-woods, talking quietly on her cell phone. She's dressed in a filmy, pale orange tunic and white capris, with a thick gold bangle on her wrist. I view the loose top—along with the dry toast—as an additional hint that she might be pregnant.

It takes her a second to notice me, and when I see that she's about to jump off the call, I shake my head to convey that I'll catch her later. But she quickly murmurs a farewell, disconnects, and moves toward me.

"Sorry," she says. "*Work.* Clients don't consider Saturday an off-duty day."

"Blake said you've been on the road a lot lately, too."

"Unfortunately, yes. I've got a client in Palm Beach I see several times a month. And two in Texas. One's a friend from Yale who's already made a fortune in oil and gas."

That's something else that works Gabe's last nerve—Wendy doesn't like to let a conversation go by without a re-minder that she went to Yale.

"Are you feeling more pressure now that you have the gallery?"

"A bit, but I so prefer running my own show. Of course, what I do comes down to helping very rich people sell pic-tures to other very rich people, as opposed to, say, trying to solve the climate crisis."

"Well, what would the world be without art?"

"Ah, thank you, Summer. By the way, Blake told me about your play. It sounds brilliant."

"Well, I don't think I'd use the word 'brilliant,' but I'm excited. It was great, by the way, to catch up a little with Blake last night. It'd been way too long."

"Yes, he's been crazed at work, too. Sometimes I sense that he'd like to bag it and never look at another squamous cell carcinoma again. As long as he can still get his hands on Botox, I'm fine with that," she says, grinning, and I notice the lack of lines on her high, smooth forehead.

"Ha, I'm going to need that myself before long. . . . Do you know if anyone's still at the breakfast table?"

"Keira and Hannah were both having coffee when I left. They might still be there."

Okay, that's interesting—Keira sharing a meal with her husband's ex. I wonder what that must be like for her.

"Oh, good, I'll join them. . . . It's nice, isn't it, that Nick could bring someone out for the week?"

I know I'm fishing here, but it's just a line in the water, to see what bites.

"Yes, though frankly, I've started to lose track of the names of some of his objects of affection."

I quickly glance around the area, making sure we still have it to ourselves. "I noticed you sat near Hannah. Did you have much of a chance to chat with her?"

"I did actually. And of all things, we ended up talking about *dressage* for a while. It turns out she trained, too, so it gave us a lot to discuss."

Dressage. Until I was about twenty-five, I thought it was French for putting on fancy clothes for a night on the town, but it's actually a kind of horseback riding. Apparently, Wendy studied it as a kid, part of her equestrian training. Though she didn't grow up in a family nearly as well-off as the Keatons, Gabe heard no expense was spared on her and her brother when they were young.

"That must have been fun to connect over."

"It was. I almost never meet people who've done it."

"Well, I'd better hightail it to breakfast. See you later."

"You bet. Ciao."

I return to the path and close the distance to the house. Through one of the side kitchen windows, I spy Claire at the table, glued to her iPad. She wouldn't mind me dropping in, but over time I've noticed that she likes to have this part of the day to herself, or to spend with her husband. Usually Ash is sitting next to her, but not this morning.

As I round the corner, I spot Keira at the table on the patio, and Hannah standing to the side of her, dressed in white shorts and a cropped yellow top. She's even more svelte than I realized last night, as if she hasn't consumed a bad carbohydrate in her adult life. She finishes her conversation with Keira and leaves a moment later without appearing to notice me.

"Morning, Keira," I say, approaching the table.

"Morning. Sleep well?"

"Yup; you? You're in the main house, right?"

"Yes, in the guest suite at the far end of the second floor."

"You didn't want to give the carriage house a try?"

She presses her lips together. "I don't love being away from the main house. And there's a little kitchenette in the suite, with a toaster oven and a half fridge, so we can fix stuff there if we need to."

I'm not sure why they'd need a toaster oven—there's one here on the sideboard, along with a Nespresso machine and a carafe of brewed coffee. There are also bowls of strawberries and raspberries, baskets of croissants and the bagels Gabe and I brought, a wooden cutting board topped with artisan bread, a large glass jar of granola, as well as small containers of yogurt set in a basin of ice water.

After making a cappuccino and grabbing a yogurt, I join Keira, who's wearing a white cover-up over a bathing suit that looks damp.

"So how's it going with Hannah?" I say, lowering my voice. "Any awkwardness?"

"No, it's actually fine. To be honest, the *main* reason I didn't want to be in the carriage house was because she'd be there, but Marcus is clearly a very distant memory for her."

"And Marcus—is he okay with it, too?"

I can still picture him at last night's table, his eyes glued to Hannah and his face set like stone.

"He says it's fine, too." She glances left and right, making sure we're alone. "She was nothing more than a blip on the radar. He's just glad Nick at least gave him a heads-up before they arrived."

"She clearly feels comfortable with *you*."

Her deep brown eyes register puzzlement.

"I saw you talking when I came around the corner."

"Oh, that. She's actually going to do me a big favor. This director she's working with on the Netflix show is involved with some major clean water initiatives, and Hannah said she could convince him to do a luncheon with some of our clients. That could really help move one of our initiatives along, plus it would assure I'd win a few points in my new job."

Okay, I see what Hannah's up to. Her modus operandi this week is a full-on charm offensive. I'm sure Claire and Ash have been subjected to it, too, though last night she seemed to have no interest whatsoever in wooing *me*. "How thoughtful of her," I say, using my best fake sincere voice.

After Keira excuses herself to change out of her wet swimsuit, I finish my cappuccino at a leisurely pace and decide it's an okay time to pop into the kitchen. Claire's still in the room, fussing at the counter, with the dogs hovering nearby.

"There you are, darling," she says. "How is your morning so far?"

"Lovely." I stoop down and give both dogs a pat, and they immediately roll over in anticipation of having their bellies scratched. "How do you think Henry did last night?"

"He says great. I heard his toilet flush around six, but I assume he fell right back to sleep."

"On his way to being a big boy. Now tell me how I can help you with lunch."

"We seem to be all set, so just enjoy the day."

"Okay, but let me know if you think of anything. I'm going to go grab my tennis shoes and head down to the court."

But when I open the door to the cottage a couple of minutes later, I spot Gabe's tennis racket leaning against the couch and notice the steady drum of shower water upstairs.

When it ceases, Gabe calls out, "That you?"

"Yeah," I shout back. "I was hoping to hit some balls with you."

"Sorry, we all called it quits. It's getting too hot."

Two minutes later, he bounds down the stairs, dressed in swim trunks and a T-shirt that matches his blue eyes, and smelling of mango-scented bodywash.

"How's Henry's game coming?" I ask.

"Really good. He's probably never going to be the kind of

kid who ends up starring on the school basketball team, but he's definitely good at tennis. We ended up playing against Nick and Hannah, which was fun, and then Hannah hit with him for a while."

Okay, this is starting to get ridiculous.

"So she's a tennis player, too?"

"Not a superskilled one, but she's game."

"Speaking of Hannah," I say, grabbing a spot on the couch, "there's something I wanted to tell you."

Gabe sits down next to me and sweeps a hand through his short dark brown hair. "What's up?"

"She told me a lie last night. And I can't figure out why."

"A lie? What do you mean?"

I explain: her weird deception about the showcase, plus Billy's intel about the missing money and necklace. As I speak, Gabe's brow furrows in obvious concern.

"Is that who you were talking to after I went to bed?" he asks.

"Yeah. I was texting with him but it seemed easier to speak on the phone."

His brow wrinkles even more. "Jesus."

"I know. I'm a little concerned by it."

"No, I mean Jesus, I can't believe you were calling up a friend in the middle of the night to try to dig for gossip about my brother's new girlfriend."

I was not expecting this reaction. "Gabe, it wasn't in the middle of the night—and it's not idle gossip. I found it really odd that she would lie that way, and I wanted to look into it a bit more—for Nick's sake."

"Hannah probably just forgot the show. Or she's embarrassed about her performance and didn't want to discuss it. As for the missing money, I wouldn't trust anything Billy Dean tells you."

He's never liked Billy. Not for a second.

"I know he can be a jerk, but he doesn't have any reason to make this up, Gabe."

"Maybe not," he says. "I just hate the way he flirts with you in front of me. Regardless, Hannah seems nice enough, and I don't see the point in focusing on some old rumor."

Wow, I'm getting nowhere fast.

Obviously sensing my frustration, Gabe gives me a wry smile. "Besides," he says, "you know as well as I do that in a month, Nick will be dating someone totally new."

"Fine," I say reluctantly. "I'll drop it."

"Thanks for understanding. I want everything to be as harmonious as possible this week."

"What do you mean?"

"It's just been so long since we've seen Blake and Wendy, and Nick's been hard to pin down lately, too. Plus, since Marcus and I need to talk to Dad about work stuff, I want him in a good mood. He gets on edge if he thinks there's any sibling friction."

"Okay, *okay*, I'll let it go. What are you planning to do for the rest of the morning?"

"Henry wants to swim now, so I told him I'd play lifeguard. You want to join us?"

"This afternoon, for sure. I should work on my play for a little bit now. And get a walk in before lunch."

"See you later then," he says. He plants a quick kiss on my lips and springs up from the couch.

As the door shuts behind him, I reflect that he's probably right, that just as I thought earlier, this might be the last time we ever see Hannah. She's not worth the mental energy I'm devoting to her.

I grab my laptop, wander outside, and settle at the table on the small patio. Though my play's been accepted into the festival, I still have the opportunity to fiddle with it, and I need to make sure the dialogue is as strong as possible and do some work cementing the theme.

The stakes of the festival are high for me. After I arrived in the city straight out of college, I managed through a combination of luck and hard work to land some TV commercials, a bunch of under-five parts on television shows, two small roles in limited-run off-Broadway plays, and a ton of roles in off-*off*-Broadway productions. Those were held in so-called black box theaters—where the minuscule audiences are almost entirely composed of the casts' blood relatives and friends, many of whom probably wish they were someplace else—but I was able to work pretty consistently and felt like I was on a bit of a roll.

But several years ago, it became clear, to my utter dismay, that my career was stalled. Yes, it's a brutal business and I'd seen pals from college bag it altogether, but I also knew plenty of people who were working, especially with so many opportunities opening up in streaming. Was the problem because at twenty-nine I was no longer an ingenue? In my world you can never be sure. Rather than collapse into a heap on my apartment floor, however (which I was *briefly* tempted to do), I began seriously going after the voice-over work. And I also decided to start writing plays. If I can make some headway as a playwright, it will garner me respect and possibly jump-start my career.

I know my play's amusing—the judges stressed that—but I want to guarantee it's more than a sketch. A good play, even a short one, needs an arc with a central question at the core, and I feel I still need to crystalize my question.

But as hard as I try, I can't seem to focus this morning. Because I'm having a hard time shaking my conversation with Gabe.

Maybe Hannah really didn't steal the money and the necklace. But what if she *did* and stealing is a regular habit with her? What if she were to steal something from the house here, something of real value to the Keatons? I think of all the cherished items they've brought back from their travels, as well as the miniature sterling silver animals by a British artist Claire collects. And since the rooms have an enchanting, unfussy dishabille—cashmere throws tossed on sofas rather than folded neatly, books splayed on chair arms—it might be days before anyone noticed something was missing.

But above all, there's Nick to consider. Even if this is a short-term thing for him, there's still a chance he could end up hurt.

I get that Gabe, the perennial peacekeeper, doesn't want any friction. He's always been the one, for instance, to smooth over the occasional issues that arise between Marcus and Nick, and this is our hard-earned vacation week, after all.

But something just doesn't feel right about Hannah. I know it. And I hate that I seem to be the only one who does.

4

---

nstead of trying to focus on my play any longer, I decide to head outside now and come back to it later in the day when my mind is clearer. I collect my hiking boots and lace them up, then leave the cottage, veering off the flagstone path and moving north across the expanse of sloping lawn. Eventually, it gives way to a wide grass path flanked and topped by rustic trellises and running through a lightly wooded area. Though I appreciate the manicured parts of the property, this is where the real magic happens for me. Relishing the stillness, I walk at a moderate pace, and after a couple of minutes I emerge from between the trellises into a meadow of riotously colored wildflowers. When she designed it, Claire meant for it to be a total surprise to the eye, and no matter how many times I come upon it, it always makes me smile.

I traipse through the meadow, admiring the endless mix of pink, red, blue, orange, and yellow. At the far side, a totally different meadow begins, this one consisting of various wild grasses, some of them really high. There's a distinct path through it, but one Claire designed in an enchanting, serpentine way, so that when you meander along, you almost feel as if you're in a maze.

Finally, I reach the far side and after tramping a bit farther come to the stream that gushes along the border of a heavily wooded area, a continuation of the woods behind our cottage. I hadn't planned to be gone for too long, but I lower myself onto a rock beside the gurgling stream and savor the sound of it. There's an old bird blind a few yards ahead of me and to the right of the stream. Sometimes Henry and I will brush away the cobwebs inside and sit for a while, watching and waiting. Or we'll search the nearby area for deer antlers or abandoned box turtle shells. I've made many happy memories with him here.

But mostly I love this spot because it's where Gabe proposed to me.

We'd met around six years ago in a wine bar in the city, where I'd gone with several nonactor friends to celebrate one girl's acceptance to business school. The wine bar owner was Gabe's client, I later learned, and he'd only stopped by that evening to say hello. My friends and I were clustered by the bar and Gabe was sitting on a stool behind me. At some point I turned, as if drawn by a force field, and when I met his gaze, I felt as if I'd been struck by the proverbial thunderbolt. Maybe it was those slate-blue eyes, or hawk nose, or fetching dark scruff, or the way he held his wineglass like such a pro. We chatted for a couple of minutes, exchanging first names and a little bit about our professional lives, and what was so special about the Bordeaux he was drinking—he had the bartender pour me a taste—but then my friends were dragging me off to another location, and I couldn't think of a slick way to say, "Here's my number."

I went back to the wine bar twice, hoping he'd be there, but no such luck. Two weeks later, though, I spotted him in the audience at the tiny theater where I was performing in the play I'd mentioned to him. I was so stunned by the sight, I almost dropped a line, but managed to keep it together. And when I left the theater, he was waiting outside and invited me for a late pasta dinner.

That night I discovered there was even more to like than the blue eyes and hawk nose: his wit, his thoughtfulness, his straightforward style, his passion for his work, and his evident devotion to his toddler son. To say nothing of the fact that he'd remembered the name of the play I was in, tracked down a ticket, and actually showed up.

Yes, it was clear he was still a little shell-shocked from his divorce and struggling at moments with being a single dad, but after meeting Henry and seeing how sweet Gabe was with him, I was smitten. And so when he went down on one knee with a big grin six months later, right here in this spot, I didn't hesitate to say yes.

The sudden sound of a branch cracking in the woods startles me, and I spin around. Probably just a deer or groundhog rooting around the undergrowth, I decide, but it's time for me to get back anyway. I retrace my steps to the house, concentrating on the minty smell of the ornamental grasses, the swish of my boots through the meadows, and the sight of two bluebirds darting above the flowers. When I reach the start of the trellis-covered path, I notice Nick up ahead, walking in my direction.

He spots me at the same moment and lifts his hand in a wave, which I return. Where's Hannah? I wonder, snidely. Maybe she's busy coming up with fresh, toady ways to preserve her standing as everyone's favorite houseguest.

By the time I near the middle of the path, I realize that it's actually Marcus coming toward me. I've made this mistake in the past since the twins look so much alike.

"Morning," he calls out as he closes the gap between us.

"Hi there. Just doing a walkabout?"

"Sort of. I heard something fairly noisy prowling around outside my window last night, and I figured it was a raccoon or a fox, but my father got an email from a neighbor on the road this morning saying he'd spotted a coywolf in the area. I thought I'd have a look around."

"A coywolf? Is that a real animal?"

"It's an eastern coyote. They've bred with gray wolves over time, so they're a little larger, more the size of a German shepherd."

"Yikes. Do they attack humans?"

"Not unless provoked, but we should all keep an eye out. And be extra careful with the dogs."

"Good to know. Are you really thinking you might come across one now?"

"No, fortunately coyotes aren't usually out in the daytime. I'm just on the lookout for any signs one's been around."

Ever since he was a little kid, Marcus has apparently been a nut about nature. Claire once told me that while the other three boys were devoting their summers out here to tennis, swimming, and Wiffle ball, Marcus would be memorizing the names of tree species, hunting for owl pellets, and identifying animal droppings—earning him the name Scat Man from Nick.

"Let me know what you find, will you?" I say. "How's your weekend going anyway?"

I'm trying to make the question sound casual, but I'm curious if he'd ever admit how he feels about Nick dating Hannah. Because of the wine business, I've spent more time with Marcus than my other brothers-in-law, and sometimes with me he'll lower the cards he so often plays close to the vest.

"It's okay. Yours?"

"Good. You excited to be here with the whole gang?"

"Yup."

Well, I guess he's not going to cough up much today. As I observe him, something crystallizes for me. Though he and his twin have similar features, on Marcus they come together in a less compelling way than they do on Nick, almost like a piece of fabric faded by the sun. Nick's jaw is a little stronger, his eyes more vivid, his hair more golden, or maybe you just think that because of the sheer force of his personality.

"Sorry to hear Keira can't stay for the full week," I say.

"Yeah, you know, new job stuff. And it's probably for the best. Unlike you, she always finds these vacations a bit overwhelming."

I smile. "It's a lot of people in one place, and she didn't grow up in a big family."

"No, I mean more the whole country estate thing. The

decor, the gardens, the fancy-pants lettuces for dinner, the guest suites with sheets that cost as much as a used car."

I get it. The Keatons aren't billionaires, but they've clearly got plenty of millions, and their apartment in New York and their estate here are both spectacular. They also have a winter home in Palm Beach, a small but stunning house landscaped with saw grasses, cactus, and a gorgeous selection of palms. There's an incredible easy, natural feel to all three places, and to the way the Keatons live, which is a trick in itself. Not everyone with big bucks is able to pull it off.

"Well, you guys have only been together a couple of years. The more she visits here, the more comfortable she'll be."

He shrugs. "I hope you're right. I should get moving, Summer. Lunch is in less than an hour."

"See you then."

As I head back to the house, I find myself mulling over Marcus's comment about how Keira feels being here. This spread certainly bears no resemblance to what I experienced growing up. My father has a small accounting firm and my mom's a social worker, and we were brought up in a comfortable ranch-style house with a cute backyard in West Hartford, Connecticut, but we certainly didn't have a full-time housekeeper or landscapers, bartenders, and cooks around.

And yet I've never felt ill at ease with Gabe's parents. The first time I met them was at their sprawling Park Avenue apartment, which they'd gutted in the center to make it feel like a loft, wowing you the moment you open the door. But both Ash and Claire were warm and welcoming, seemingly eager to put me at ease with wine and appetizers on their terrace. As I commented on how much I liked the artichoke dip, his mother told a funny story about how once, as a young hostess, she served whole artichokes without realizing they needed to be steamed first. Everything about their world had the potential to be intimidating, but somehow I managed to find it enchanting instead, like I'd been cast in a play that involved performing on an enthralling stage set.

I return to the cottage, where I exchange my hiking boots for sandals, and then make my way to the main house. I can hear someone splashing in the pool, but Gabe, Henry, Blake, Nick, and Hannah are all sitting under the pergola, playing cards. Sidling up to the table, I see they're still in swimsuits, though Hannah's got a flowy vermillion cover-up over hers. She's wearing makeup, too, applied in that artful way that probably makes even smart guys stupidly think she's totally barefaced, sporting that natural look they claim to love.

"Summer," Henry calls out, "come play B.S. with us, okay?"

Henry knows it's really called Bullshit, but Gabe won't let him use that word in mixed company.

"You're not in the middle of a game?" I ask.

"No, we just finished a hand," Gabe says. "Can I deal you in?"

"Sure," I respond and slip into an empty spot next to my husband.

"I hear you've been working on your play this morning," Blake says to me. "You're making the rest of us look like slackers."

"Blake, you couldn't look like a slacker if you tried," Nick says good-naturedly.

"Well, my goal for my forties is to tap into my inner lazy guy. Lots of golf and long walks."

"Just so you know, I squeezed in a walk myself this morning," I say, feeling a twinge of guilt over abandoning my play.

After an adroit shuffle, Gabe delivers everyone a hand. The goal of the game is to end up with no cards, and the action moves around the table, starting with the number two and requiring players to place a card or cards facedown in sequence while announcing what they've played—such as "four threes" and "one four." You're supposed to put down *something*, which means you have to fib at certain points if you don't have a card with the right denomination or face, and you can even lie and add more cards to the pile than you're admitting. If someone suspects you're bluffing, he can call out "B.S.," which obligates you to turn over the cards you played. If they're indeed what you claimed, the person who called B.S. must add the entire discard pile to his or her hand. If you were lying, though, *you* inherit the entire pile.

"I should warn you," Nick says to Hannah once all the cards have been dealt. "Summer could play on the B.S. pro circuit."

"There's a *pro* circuit, Uncle Nick?" Henry exclaims.

"Yeah, I'm pretty sure," Nick tells him. "Maybe the two of us could join it one day. Head out to Vegas for the winter."

"Nick, *stop*," Gabe says, smiling. "He's going to think you're serious."

I take a minute to order the cards I'm holding. It's a good hand, not a great one, but that's okay. As Nick says, I'm a wiz at this game. That's because, thanks to years of drama training, I excel at bluffing as well as spotting other people's tells.

With six players, the game takes a while, and I keep a fairly low profile throughout, mostly observing. At one point I notice that Gabe seems close to winning, but Henry correctly calls "B.S." and Gabe is forced to swoop up a fistful of cards.

"Oh, Henry, you're ruthless," Hannah says with a laugh, though she's already nailed Blake, Nick, and Gabe for bluffing.

"You gotta do what you gotta do," Henry replies.

I can't tell if Hannah's actually having fun or just pretending to. She's across the table from me and seems to be mostly focused on the massage Nick is giving the back of her neck. At one point I catch her awarding him an intense I-can't-wait-to-get-you-between-the-sheets-later stare that makes me want to gag.

But after a while, I realize the flirty stuff is a diversion. She's holding her hand discreetly, but I can tell she's down to a tiny number of cards, possibly only one, and her turn is coming up. The discard pile, at this point, happens to be enormous.

When the play reaches Hannah, she sits up a bit straighter with her hands in her lap. She pulls up a card from the hand she's holding, lowers her eyes, and tosses it quickly onto the pile. *Too* quickly.

"One jack," she says carefully. *Too* carefully. As she glances up again, her gaze meets mine and I detect a smidgen of nerves.

"B.S.," I declare, surprising myself with how loud it comes out.

Hannah purses her full lips and gives a little shrug. She reaches out with a perfectly manicured hand and slowly flips over the card.

It's a fucking jack.

"Oh, no, Summer," Henry exclaims, as I gather up the cards. "You're gonna need both hands to hold all those."

"But now I won't have to bother with any bicep curls today," I say, plastering a grin on my face.

It turns out Hannah still has a card or possibly two in her hand and the game continues. When it's her turn again, she lays down what I now realize is her final card and announces, "One two."

"B.S.," Blake says quickly.

After she proves *him* wrong, she raises two empty hands and says, "All done."

"Oh my god. Bravo!" Nick exclaims.

I smile and congratulate her on her win, but inside I'm stewing. She was playing me the entire time, trying to prove which of us is the best actress.

Mercifully, Bonnie and her pink-haired helper emerge from the house at that exact moment, carrying trays of sandwiches and wraps and setting them on the sideboard. They return a minute later with bowls of pickles, olives, and homemade coleslaw. Claire appears, too, and announces that lunch is totally casual today and we should sit anywhere we want.

Claire, Blake, Wendy, Nick, and Hannah end up in a circle of white Adirondack chairs on the lawn, with both dogs at their feet. After grabbing a chicken wrap, I head as far away as I can get, to the umbrella table on the pool deck where Ash is sitting with Gabe and Henry.

"Summer," Ash says, "I've posted the badminton teams and times on the wall in the kitchen. I've partnered you with Nick."

"Excellent," I say. "I'm looking forward to it."

Gabe suggests Henry tell his grandfather about the Hawking book he's currently reading, and as my stepson launches into a mini-dissertation, I see that Marcus and Keira have finally shown up and settled into lounge chairs by the pool. Things seem fine between them, but I can't forget the way Marcus stared at Hannah last night, as if he hadn't really let go of her.

Eventually Bonnie appears on the pool deck and passes around a platter of chocolate chip cookies the size of hubcaps, but I excuse myself to go change into my swimsuit. Ash follows me up to the patio, confessing that he's in search of another sandwich.

And suddenly there's Hannah again, filling a glass with sparkling water at the sideboard, with Ginger and Bella glued to her side, tails wagging. Aren't dogs supposed to emit a low growl in the presence of a sociopath, rather than trying to mount a leg, the way Bella appears eager to do? But these dogs seem totally won over by Hannah, like everyone else. And yet I *know* something's off with her. And she knows I know. That's why she worked so hard to show me up in the card game.

"Hannah," Ash says, still studying the offerings on the sideboard, "I just mentioned to Summer that the badminton teams and times are posted in the kitchen, so take a look. I hope you're not going to mind having me as a partner."

"Not at all," she says with a smile. "In fact, I'm honored."

"I need to warn you, though. We have several family

members, Nick being one of them, who play the game as a killer sport. Isn't that right, Summer?"

"True," I say, "but what fun would it be without a few broken bones?"

Hannah laughs, but she doesn't take her attention off Ash. "Forewarned is forearmed."

"Have you two ladies had a chance to chat yet?" Ash asks, a fresh sandwich in his hand.

"A bit, yes," Hannah replies.

"I'm sure you must know some of the same people," he says. "Though Hannah, you're mostly doing film at the moment, right? Summer's been focusing on theater lately, getting her play ready for a festival."

"Oh, Hannah does theater, too," I say, glancing in her direction and forcing her to meet my gaze. There's a flicker of surprise in her eyes, as if I've caught her off guard, and this time I don't think she's acting.

"Oh really, in New York?" Ash inquires.

"Now and then," she says. "Schedule permitting."

I let my eyes slide briefly toward the pool deck, making sure Gabe is still down there and out of earshot.

"We were actually even once in the same showcase," I tell Ash before looking back at Hannah. "By the way, I double-checked, and you were definitely involved. The Lilac Theater on West Thirteenth Street. Are you sure you don't remember? It was two years ago this October."

She hesitates, and I can almost hear the wheels of her brain spinning.

"The Lilac Theater, of course," she says after a couple of beats. "I *was* in a showcase there."

"Maybe I confused you somehow when we spoke about it last night," I say, trying to keep my tone neutral.

"Just a little," Hannah says. "But no harm done. You thought I was in a play about a woman who had amnesia. But it was actually about a scientist who turns a cat into a woman and then falls hopelessly in love with her."

That's *exactly* what I told her last night, and she knows it. Her lips curve up in the tiniest of smiles, and I realize she's not just lying now. She's trying to gaslight me.

5

take a long, slow breath as I try to drum up the right response. I can't have Ash picking up on any tension between us, but I also don't want Hannah to think I'm unnerved by her ruse.

"Well, whatever," I say, with a little wave of my hand. "We'll catch up more later. I need to grab my bathing suit."

I leave without giving her a chance to respond, but the second I start up the path, I kick myself for having gotten into that exchange in the first place. What's the point in trying to show someone like Hannah that I'm wise to her? It's hardly going to chase her off the property, and any obvious game playing could make my in-laws think less of me. What's the old expression? *Never wrestle with a pig. You both get dirty and the pig enjoys it.*

The smartest strategy is for me to cut her a wide berth and pray that Nick sees through her soon enough.

A rustling stirs me from my thoughts, and I glance up to see Claire emerging from the glade of cloud boxwoods. She's dressed today in a casual, salmon-colored tunic dress that she's belted around the waist and paired with the sneakers she always wears for gardening. A camera dangles from her neck.

"Is everything all right, darling?"

Clearly, I'm wearing my consternation on my face.

"Um, yes, fine. I was just trying to remember something."

"Have you had a nice day so far?" she asks, stepping closer. Even in bright daylight, her skin looks creamy and naturally youthful, like she's in her fifties rather than early seventies.

"Absolutely. Before lunch I took a walk down to the stream, which was heavenly—though I hear I should be keeping an eye out for coyotes."

"That's what our neighbor says. Frankly, I've been more concerned about hunters this year. Even though our property's posted, we've spotted them sneaking through our woods."

"How annoying." I nod toward her camera. "Gabe mentioned last week that you might be taking on a new landscaping job. Does that mean you're considering coming out of retirement?"

"Yes, I'm working on a small project but not for commission. Friends of ours in Palm Beach want to give a jungle garden feel to their property, and I said I would create the design as a favor because I absolutely love doing those. I had to fly down a couple of weeks ago to take a closer look at their property, but it gave me the chance to check on our house. While we're on the subject of gardens," she adds, "I promised Hannah a tour at four today. I know you've been on plenty before but please join us if you feel like it."

I flash a smile, despite how much the mention of Hannah's name irritates me. "Thank you, Claire, but I'm sure it will be more fun for her if the tour's a private one."

"That's sweet of you to say, Summer. And she does seem very eager to learn."

I wish I could tell Claire that Hannah's simply trying to ingratiate herself, but knowing how catty it would sound, I instead wish her good-bye and promise to see her later. After changing into my swimsuit at the cottage, I return to the pool area and end up playing Marco Polo with Henry, Gabe, and eventually Nick. By the last round, I'm wondering what kind of sadist invented this game.

"One more game?" Henry begs as I hoist myself out of the pool.

"Tomorrow, okay, sweetie?" I tell him. "I'm too water-logged today. Why don't you read for a while?"

"Hey, Henry," Nick calls out. "Dive for coins with me, okay?"

He eagerly agrees, and I give Nick a grateful thumbs-up. As I do, I notice that Hannah's sunbathing facedown at the far end of the pool, near Blake and Wendy. I'm glad she's at the other end. This is as close as I hope to get to her for the rest of the week.

I collapse onto a lounge chair next to Gabe, who has a slightly damp Nordic thriller splayed on his torso. He rolls over onto his side, rests a hand on my stomach, and stares at me intently.

"If we have a little boy, do you mind naming him that?" he asks.

"Nick? Won't your other brothers mind?"

"No, Marco. Marco Polo."

"Very funny," I say, grinning. I open my mouth, intend-ing to tell him that I suspect Wendy's pregnant—but realize that if it's true, Blake will want to surprise Gabe with the news himself.

"What were you going to say?"

"Just that I'm excited about us trying for a baby this winter."

"Me, too."

I appreciate the fact that Gabe hasn't pushed to start before then, as keen as he is for Henry to have a sibling. He's been really supportive of my career and knows I want to see my first short play staged and start on a second before I get pregnant.

"In fact," he adds, "how about some practice this afternoon? My dad's taking Henry to the farmers' market in a little while."

I glance at my phone on the wrought-iron table. It's two forty-five, and I'd promised myself I'd return to my play this afternoon, but Gabe and I so rarely have the chance for afternoon sex anymore.

"What a good idea. Why don't I go make myself beautiful?" I say.

"That will take all of four seconds. I'll see Dad and Henry off, then meet you there."

Back at the cottage, I shower quickly, and straighten the bedding from this morning. When Gabe arrives, I hear him bound up the stairs.

"Very beautiful indeed," he says, running his eyes over my body.

Though it's warm outside, the bedroom feels cool, inviting. We make love at a languorous pace, and afterward, as Gabe dozes, I watch the filmy white curtains flutter in the breeze and let the rest of the world recede for a while.

Eventually, I leave him sleeping, change into a sundress,

and tiptoe downstairs. Blake promised he'd play tennis with Henry after he returned from the farmers' market, so we have a bit more downtime. I slide out a bottle of rosé that Gabe stashed in the fridge, set it in a bucket of ice, and grab a can of nuts from the lightly stocked pantry. As I'm setting them out on the antique wooden trunk that serves as a coffee table, I hear him start the shower.

How nice for Gabe and me to have a little time for ourselves. Though I appreciate that our life is rich with family and friends, I always feel my marriage is at its strongest when we make time for the two of us, whether it's going to wine tastings, or seeing plays, which Gabe has embraced with gusto, or even simply watching Netflix thrillers at home.

My attention is caught by the muted sounds of two female voices coming from outside, not far from the patio. Glancing out the French doors, I spot Claire and Hannah, their backs to me, meandering alongside one of the gardens on this part of the property. I tug the cream-colored muslin drapes closed, but I don't back away from the window. Instead, I practically hug the fabric with my body as I listen.

"Absolutely dazzling," Hannah exclaims. They're moving closer, and before long their voices are so distinct I realize they're by the border garden that runs along the edge of the cottage patio. "And what are *these* called?"

"Here we have mostly foxgloves, alliums, and artemisias," Claire explains. "But I added some iris and ornamental chartreuse Japanese forest grasses to make the mix more interesting."

"Did you always have amazing instincts when it came to gardening, Claire?"

Oh my god. Could she be any more of a suck-up?

"I think I always had a sense of what worked visually, but as a professional gardener, your aesthetic interests don't matter unless you're aware of what grows where and when."

"You mean, like knowing whether a certain plant prefers sun or shade?"

"Yes, and the type of soil plants favor, and which climates, and even what they like or dislike as neighbors. I once planted a garden not far from an English walnut tree, which I didn't realize is toxic to many flowers. Everything started to die."

"Ouch."

"Yes, ouch indeed. I had to eat the cost. But I learned over time."

There's a moment of silence and then a whoosh of fabric. I sense Claire stooping down, probably touching a plant.

"Do you always wear those gloves?" Hannah asks.

"I do. There are thorns to worry about, of course, and lots of bacteria in the soil. And some plants are toxic, not just to other plants but to humans and animals. Like oleander. Monkshood. And foxgloves. That's why I don't use them in indoor arrangements. I wouldn't want the dogs sampling any petals that might have dropped to the floor."

"Why even grow them, then?"

"Because they're glorious to look at." I hear Claire chuckle lightly. "And of course, it's nice to think a passing fox has access to a pair of gloves on a stormy night if she needs them. . . . We should be getting back. I need to check on dinner."

As they move away, Hannah asks her another question,

which regrettably I can't hear. No sooner have I leaned in a little closer than I feel something behind me, and I spin around to find Gabe standing there.

"What in the world are you doing?" he asks, squinting at me.

"I was pulling the drapes closed."

He steps forward and tugs the curtain back with a finger. His mother and Hannah are in his line of sight, making their way back to the main house.

"Not spying?"

"*Spying?* Don't be ridiculous."

"Come on, fess up."

"I wasn't *spying*, Gabe. I heard voices, and I was closing the drapes for a little privacy." I conjure up my most mischievous grin. "I've got this wicked postorgasmic glow thing going, and I'm not interested in showing it off to the world."

"You *do* look pretty radiant," Gabe says, smiling.

"Ready for some rosé?" I cock my chin toward the coffee table.

"Definitely, though cut me off after one handful of cashews, will you? I'd like to avoid packing on five pounds here like I did last July."

I pour us each a glass of the ice-cold wine and then we flop side by side on the couch. The crook of Gabe's shoulder beckons and I lean into it, relishing the feel of his chest through his slightly damp T-shirt. Like Henry, Gabe doesn't have the patience to dry himself off fully after a shower.

"Oh, this wine is perfect," I say after taking a sip.

"I thought you'd like this one. It's Tuscan. . . . Are you feeling more relaxed now?"

"About work?" He nods. "I guess. I got an annoyingly vague text from Shawna saying, 'Thanks for going with the flow.' If she was really happy with my recording, she probably would have come right out and said so."

"Okay, maybe it wasn't your best day, but no one hits it out of the park every time, Summer." He props a bare foot on the trunk and I sense a comment hovering in the air.

"Is something else on your mind?" I ask.

"I was wondering, too, if you're feeling more relaxed about Hannah."

"*Hannah?* Well, in all honesty, no. But if the topic's going to annoy you, I'm not getting into it."

"Is there more to say?"

"Actually, yes."

He leans forward a little.

"What?"

I tell him about my conversation with her and his father, and how unsettled it left me.

"You thought she might have forgotten about the show-case when I first asked her," I add, "but that's clearly not what happened. It's obvious she didn't want to admit it last night because she was afraid I might know about the theft. So now that she can't deny she was in the play, she's pretending that *I* was the one who was confused about it."

Gabe presses his index finger sideways across his mouth, a gesture that always signals he's taking things seriously. "Don't you think it's possible she *did* misunderstand you?"

"No. How does 'a cat who turned into a woman' sound like 'a woman who's suffering from amnesia'? Plus, I hated the way she tried to embarrass me in front of your father."

"What do you mean?"

"Why not just say she'd misunderstood me, instead of making it look like I was an idiot?"

"I guarantee my father doesn't think you're an idiot."

"I know, I know. But the bottom line is that she lies and probably steals, too, and now she's dating your brother."

"But there was never any proof Hannah took the money and bracelet or necklace or whatever it was."

"God, Gabe, I feel like I'm trying to hold on to a wet bar of soap. Can't you see my side of things?"

"I *do* see your side of things. I just don't want you getting all agitated about something that isn't going to matter in the long run."

"It might matter to Nick. Even if he only sees her for the short term, he could be vulnerable."

"Well, if his wallet ends up missing, I promise I'll tell him what you heard."

"But won't he resent us for not having warned him?"

"Nick's a big boy. He can take care of himself."

I let out a loud sigh, realizing it's pointless to continue. "Fine. Let's move on to a different subject, okay?"

He reaches up and rests a hand on my back. "Great idea, babe. You really shouldn't let girls like her bother you."

I feel myself start to bristle. "What exactly do you mean?"

"I know it's not always easy for you to be around other actresses. But you can't let her agitate you. You're in a crazy, totally unfair business, you've always known that."

I *soooo* don't like where he's going with this.

"You think I'm 'agitated' because I'm *envious* of Hannah?"

"I'm not saying that, but it has to be a little tough to be

in close proximity to someone doing the kind of work you want to be doing," he says. Sensing this isn't going well, he starts to overexplain. "But what you're doing these days is great, I mean. And so much saner than playing the Hollywood game."

I feel my whole mood shift, as fast as an actor dropping through a trapdoor on the stage. I have to do everything in my power not to jump down his throat.

"Gabe," I say, rising from the couch, "I appreciate your support, I really do, but I don't need you making judgment calls about what I should or should not be doing professionally, or whether I should be playing the Hollywood game or not. I don't advise you on the wine business, do I?"

"Look, I'm sorry," he says. "Don't take it the wrong way. I was—Where are you going?"

I'm halfway out of the room. "I need to put on some makeup before dinner."

"Summer—"

"Please, can we finally table this? There's really nothing more to say."

I scurry up the stairs and shut myself in the bathroom, giving the door a forceful shove to close it. I pile my hair into a sloppy bun and dab on foundation and blush, stewing the whole time. Up until ten minutes ago, it had been such a lovely, perfect afternoon.

I'm not sure what's pissing me off more: Gabe's unwillingness to acknowledge that there might be something unsavory about Hannah or his hint—despite his attempt to backtrack—that he thinks I'm motivated by envy. Does he

really believe I was so undone by the notion of Hannah shooting a Netflix pilot that I've lost sight of what's important?

I nearly tear off the top of the lipstick tube and swipe
color across my lips. I wish now that I'd never confessed to
Gabe how annoyed I was by an actress who was a fellow guest
at a dinner party we attended last year. She was a college
friend of one of the couple hosting the dinner, L.A. based but
in town to shoot a movie, and she totally monopolized the
conversation, regaling us with tales about this actor and that
actor, using the nicknames they use in real life—like Jen instead of Jennifer—to let us know she was a member of their
secret club.

There's a knock at the bathroom door.

"Babe, we need to go. They want to eat early since it might
rain later."

"Fine," I mutter.

"I'm really sorry, okay?"

"Okay."

I slap on a smile because I want this week to be special,
and I'm certainly not going to let Hannah drive a wedge
between me and Gabe. And you know what? I've done my
part. If something valuable goes missing this week, it won't
be my fault.

We're halfway up the path when I detect the delicious
scent of food grilling over an open flame, and soon Henry
comes tearing around the corner of the house, announcing
he's shucked twenty pieces of corn for dinner. We all head
over to the large built-in outdoor grill, where Ash, with Nick
and Marcus at his side, is gingerly rotating kabobs, some

with chicken and vegetables, others simple vegetarian ones, obviously for Hannah.

"So tell me about the wines for tonight," Nick says to Gabe and Marcus. "What are you treating us to this time?"

"We've got a really nice French pinot noir," Gabe tells him. "I think you'll like it."

"Not white?" Nick asks.

Marcus shoots him a look. "The only people who still think you have to drink white wine with chicken are the ones who keep those tags on their pillows that say, 'Do not remove under penalty of law.'"

"Oh, you know us philistines," Nick says with a laugh and then turns to Henry. "If I use the wrong fork tonight, can you correct your old uncle Nick right away?"

It might be only good-natured ribbing—Marcus and Nick get into that at times—but I sense extra tension tonight. Ash seems to make a point of ignoring them, though, and asks Henry to let Bonnie know that the kabobs are done and it's time to eat.

At the table, I park myself as far away as possible from Hannah and motion for Henry to sit by my side. Gabe leaves his phone at the place across from me and joins Marcus in pouring the wine. They've no sooner taken their seats when everyone's attention is drawn to Blake, who's tapping his wine goblet with a knife. We all focus his way as he rises from his seat.

"First," he says, "I'd like to thank Mom and Dad for another wonderful day. They say living well is the best revenge and I suppose that's true. But living well is also a testament to following your passion, working incredibly hard, and always striving for the best. And that's what your lives have been about."

People smile and Gabe calls out, "Hear, hear."

"Second," he says with a smile, "Wendy and I have an important announcement to make."

Wow, seems like I might have been right about the pregnancy.

"I'm thrilled to tell you all," he continues, "that we're *expecting*. And needless to say, we're over the moon about it."

The whole table erupts in applause and shouts of congratulations. Gabe looks especially happy, and to my surprise, I even find myself blinking back tears.

As the others at the table barrage Blake and Wendy with questions—"When are you due?" ("December"); "Do you know the sex?" ("Not yet, but we want to and will let everyone know"); "Have you had any morning sickness?" ("A little")—Henry tugs on my arm.

"Does expecting mean a *baby*?" he whispers in my ear.

"Yes, that's right. You'll finally have a cousin, sweetie."

"Cool, though we'll be nine years apart, right? So it's not like we can go to Disney World together, or anything."

"No, but it will be so much fun to have him or her in the family."

As if on cue, Bonnie and her helper, the dogs trailing behind them, emerge from the house and set a huge blue ceramic bowl of potato salad on the table along with a platter of steaming corn on the cob, then return with two trays of kabobs.

Ash, I notice, is still beaming as we pass the food up and down the table—and though I can't see Claire from where

I'm sitting, I'm sure she's in heaven, too. She sometimes plays her cards close to the vest, like Marcus, but I sense that she's fretted about Blake and Wendy's fertility struggles.

Speaking of Marcus, as I glance down the table, I catch him stealing a look at Hannah, his expression hard like it was last night. It's so not a look that says, *You know, she was never my type, but I'm really glad my twin brother seems to like her.*

And then once again, there's a tinkle of metal on glass, but this time it's Nick who rises out of his seat.

"I want to express what I know we're all feeling right now," he says, grinning ear to ear. "Blake, we still have no idea in the world how you ended up as a dermatologist, and, man, a golfer to boot, but we love you to death and are incredibly happy for you and Wendy. And since this seems to be a good night for announcements, I have one to make myself. Or rather, Hannah and I do."

The bottom falls out of my stomach. This can't be happening. Everyone at the table seems to freeze, lips parted, utensils in midair.

"I know this may come as a surprise to everyone," he continues, "and in some ways it's even a surprise to me. But sometimes good things come at you when you least expect them."

He pauses and I hold my breath.

"I've asked Hannah to marry me, and to my delight she's said yes."

6

What follows is a nearly deafening silence, except for the sound of Bella's snorting as she noses around under the table. None of us appear to be breathing, let alone speaking. I steal a glance at Gabe, who's staring right at Nick, his expression blank, but from the infinitesimal, telltale wrinkle of his brow it's clear that the news has stunned him.

Though I manage to pick my stomach up off the ground, it quickly starts to roil. My adorable, charming brother-in-law, the kid brother I never had, is planning to marry a woman he's known for only two months. And who might be a thief, and possibly a sociopath. Which means my life with my in-laws—every future family dinner at Gabe's parents' apartment, every group weekend out here, every family vacation—is about to be irrevocably altered by her presence.

Nick has remained on his feet, and he's looking uncharacteristically flustered now, as if he has no idea why he's left a patio full of people dumbfounded. Hannah appears flustered, too. Her triumphant smile has begun to contract, like ice before it starts to crack.

"Gosh," he says. "I think this might be the only time in my life that the Keatons have been at a loss for words. I'm sure it's in part because Hannah and I only met two months ago. But in that short period, we've spent every possible moment together, and we know what we've got is very special."

Someone clears his throat. I watch as Ash reaches for his wineglass and slowly raises it.

"It *is* a bit of a shock, Nick, but we love you, and of course we're very pleased for both of you," he says. "We wish you great happiness and look forward to getting to know Hannah better over the coming months—*and* years."

"Hear, hear," Gabe says once more tonight, though this time there's a catch in his voice. He awkwardly raises his own glass in salute, and I notice Blake and Wendy do the same, both of them smiling politely. Obviously, they're still in the afterglow of their baby announcement.

"Thank you so much everyone," Hannah says. "I couldn't love Nick more, and I'm thrilled to be joining this amazing family."

There are a few more "Hear hears," and I notice Keira raise her own glass. I'm unable to see either Marcus or Claire, though as far as I know, they're following suit. But I can't bring myself to fake it. Instead I lean down toward Henry, as if I'm answering another question of his.

"So you know what this means, right?" I whisper to him.

"Uncle Nick's getting married?"

"Yup."

"Oh. Wow."

"Yeah, wow."

To keep from having to look up, I go out of my way to help Henry, using a fork to slide chicken and veggies off the second kabob stick on his plate. I hear Blake ask Nick and Hannah if they've set a date yet.

"Not yet," Nick replies. Thank god for small favors. "We need to determine what Hannah's shooting schedule will be once the show is picked up. And we still need to go ring shopping."

"Are you from this part of the country, Hannah?" Ash asks.

"No, Miami, actually," she replies. "Sadly, my parents both passed away, but I have a wonderful sister, and I'm looking forward to introducing Nick to her."

"Well, we look forward to meeting her, as well," Ash says.

"You all set with food?" I murmur to Henry, still awarding him my full attention.

"Yeah." He wrinkles his little brow, looking like Gabe as he does it, and stares down the length of the table. Then he presses his mouth so tightly against my ear that it tickles. "Can I ask you another question?"

"Of course." *Please*, I think, *give me something else to do. Tell me you're tired and you want me to take you up to bed and read you a story.* I don't want to be here for one more second.

"Does Gee wish Uncle Nick wasn't doing it?"

"Why—?" But instead of finishing, I lift my head and follow his gaze to the other end of the table, where my mother-in-law is now in my line of sight, standing and holding up the bowl of potato salad.

"Who'd like more?" she asks. "Anyone?"

She's smiling, but I can tell, just as Henry obviously can, that she's pasted it on, using only the muscles around her mouth and not her eyes. She's not happy about this turn in events, not in the least, despite whatever bonding she did with Hannah during their ladies' garden tour.

I look toward Gabe next, and finally we lock eyes. Part of me expects an expression that says, *You were right, we've got major trouble here.* But all he does is smile wanly.

The potato salad bowl ends up being passed down the table, with no one taking seconds, and the conversation shifts awkwardly to how delicious the meal is.

Then, miraculously, from off in the distance, there's a muted rumble of thunder, and seconds later a couple of fat drops of rain plop onto the table. A mad scramble ensues as we all grab plates, bowls, and utensils, and Bonnie and her helper rush out to assist us. In theater it's called *deus ex machina,* or "god from the machine," a plot device once frequently used by ancient Greek and Roman playwrights whereby a seemingly unsolvable problem in a story is suddenly and abruptly resolved by an unexpected and seemingly unlikely occurrence. No respectable modern play relies on one, but right now all I can do is be grateful.

At first everyone ends up in the kitchen, setting plates and platters onto countertops, but then Claire and Bonnie herd us all out of the room, promising that coffee and dessert will be served shortly.

We cluster in the large living room, a space decorated invitingly in cream, mint, and lavender and featuring vases of Claire's flowers on several surfaces. After realizing that Gabe is missing in action, I check the long corridor that runs perpendicular to the main hall, poking my head into the den but not seeing him there. I finally locate him on the screened porch at the east end of the house, staring out at the rain.

"Hey," I say, coming up next to him. "You okay?"

"Yeah, I guess." He rakes a hand through his hair. "It's just a lot to digest."

There's almost a pulse to his unease, I realize, one I can practically feel. Good, maybe he's finally catching on to how big of an issue the Nick-Hannah romance is.

"Did you have any sense this was coming?" I ask.

"Of course not. I would have told you."

"Gabe, it wasn't an accusation. I was just wondering whether in hindsight you realize there were hints he was this serious."

"No, there weren't. I mean, he's clearly besotted—you couldn't miss *that* from the International Space Station—but I've seen him that way before."

"How do you think your parents feel? Your mom seems to be putting on a brave face, but something tells me she's pretty dismayed."

He shrugs. "They know Nick's a smart guy—my dad wouldn't have brought him into the business otherwise. But they're also aware that in his personal life, he doesn't always think things through."

"Is there some way to convince him to take his time?"

"I'm not sure of the best tack." He's continued to face the lawn as we've been speaking, but he turns now in my direction. "But I'll tell you what's *not* going to help? Stuff like looking totally bummed and refusing to join a toast in their honor."

He's right, I know. "I'm sorry. I'm just not any good at pretending I'm happy about this."

"I thought you were an actress."

"That's a cheap shot, Gabe," I say as anger flares in me.

"Agreed. Sorry. But we're all going to have to fake it for now. And who knows? Maybe it will turn out better than we imagine. My parents only knew each other six months before they were married, and look how well that's worked—"

"Wait, you really think the issue is that Nick and Hannah haven't had enough time to get to know each other? And not that she's untrustworthy?"

Even in the dusky light, I see the muscles of his face tense.

"Summer, let's not get into that again, okay? Like I told you before, I'm not giving any credence to something based on hearsay. . . . I think we'd better show our faces in there or else we're going to seem totally rude."

I'm still bristling, but I don't want to make things any worse tonight than they already are, so I nod and start for the interior of the house. Gabe suddenly pulls me close and kisses the top of my head.

"Babe, I know you care about Nick, and you don't want anything bad to happen to him. But let's give them a chance, okay?"

"Sure."

I follow him back down the corridor toward the sound of voices, ending up in the dining room this time. Everyone's milling around the table, where there are two large stoneware baking dishes with blueberry crumble and a huge bowl of vanilla ice cream for topping. Claire still seems to be in the kitchen, though, and I don't see Marcus, either.

By now I've lost my appetite, and fruit crumble sounds about as appealing as a plateful of hair, but I join Gabe at the table, where a short line has formed. Henry's at the front and has already managed to secure himself a piece of the crumble and top it with a giant mound of ice cream.

"Buddy, let me help you carry that into the living room," Gabe tells him.

As they depart the room, I drift toward the coffee carafes on the sideboard. Hannah, I notice, is already serving herself a tiny sliver of crumble. As she rounds the far end of the table, dessert plate in one hand and coffee mug in the other, she glances backward and for the first time since the announcement, we make eye contact. She stares, as if daring me to look away—which I finally do—before she goes to sit with her *fiancé.*

Soon, Keira and I are the only ones left in the dining room, both serving ourselves coffee. She looks even more pensive than normal.

"Where's Marcus?" I ask.

"Already in bed. He felt a cold coming on, and he wants to see if he can nip it in the bud."

"Good idea," I say, though I can't help but wonder if what's really bothering him is the idea of his twin marrying a woman he might still have the hots for.

"Of course," Keira says, lowering her voice, "if there are any more big announcements, I'll have to run up and get him."

"I think two is all I can handle in one evening."

"I'm thrilled for Wendy, of course. But I don't know what to make about the other . . . thing. Do you?"

"No," I tell her. "But they seem really happy so hopefully it will all work out."

See, I can behave. And when I want to be, I'm a damn good actress.

"What worries me, though, is that it's a distraction," Keira says. The thin fissure above the bridge of her nose deepens. "And Marcus and Gabe need to have Ash in full focus mode."

"You think it will get in the way of them talking business?"

"I'm sure Ash will sit down with them—he promised he would—but if he's preoccupied with all this family stuff, he may not want to discuss the loan."

The *loan*? This is total news to me. Gabe's assured me that the business is nicely in the black these days, so I don't know why there'd be any need for a loan. Maybe they're just trying to secure a promise of investment money down the road. Either way, I haven't heard a word about it and I don't know why.

"Right, the loan," I say. "Well, I'm sure Ash will be able to focus. That's his middle name."

She nods and glances into the living room, where Henry is now demonstrating one of his dozen or so card tricks. "I guess we should join them."

"I'll be right in," I tell her, but after she leaves, I linger, slowly stirring my coffee and hoping Claire might emerge shortly. Is she as upset as she looked?

She doesn't appear, but the clanging sounds coming from the kitchen have subsided, meaning the cleanup must be nearly complete. I push open the swinging door and step in to find my mother-in-law by herself, sitting at the island and scribbling on a pad. The rain's stopped by now, and through the screened windows I hear the thud of a garbage bag being dropped into the big trash bin, followed by the murmur of voices. Bonnie and her helper must be headed out for the night.

"Hello, darling," Claire says, glancing up. "Do you need something?"

"No, I was just wondering where you were. Are you going to join us?"

"In a minute, yes. I need to make a few notes for tomorrow."

There's nothing about her tone or demeanor to suggest that she's particularly distressed, though I spot the same tension in her face I noticed earlier, and the rims of her eyes seem pinker than usual, not quite as if she's been crying but like she's on high alert. And of course, there's the fact that she's in here, and not with the rest of the family.

"Notes?"

"Just some reminders for Bonnie tomorrow. Everything going smoothly in the other room?"

"It seems so. Henry's entertaining the troops with sleights of hand."

She sets down the pen and smiles again, this time with her eyes, too, like she's finally registering that I'm in the room.

"Nick introduced Henry to magic, of course," she says, "but I know you're the one who bought him those books and really encouraged his interest. That was so great of you to do."

"It was my pleasure—and Gabe and I get such a kick out of watching him."

"It's exactly what we need tonight, isn't it? A bit of misdirection."

Is she hinting that she wants to be distracted from the surprise engagement? Sounds like it.

"*I* certainly need it," I say, despite my promise to Gabe to cease and desist about Hannah. "I . . . I feel worried about Nick. Making such a, you know, hasty decision."

She sighs, without losing her smile. "I so appreciate your concern, Summer dear. That's one of the many things I love about you. But no need to worry. I think this will—how shall I put it?—run its course."

"You don't think they'll get married?" I say, surprised by her comment.

"I don't. Just between us, I have Hannah's number. I've had it almost since the moment our little *USC* graduate arrived."

I stare at her, shocked by the revelation. I also note the emphasis she put on USC. What could she mean by that?

"So . . . ?"

"Let's just bide our time for the moment, shall we?" She scoots her stool back so that it makes a scraping sound on the wooden floor. "*Now*, why don't we go see some magic?"

Claire and I watch with the others. Thank god for the show. Because other than Henry's instructions and the "oohs" and "aahs" from the crowd when he completes each trick, no one is saying a word.

"Okay, Hen, let's save a few for the rest of the week," Gabe tells him eventually.

The performer takes his leave, accepting a final round of applause, before Gabe ushers him upstairs, with me tagging along.

After tucking Henry into bed, we return downstairs, bid the others good night, and set off on the path to the cottage. It's wet and shiny from the rain and glows here and there where the toadstool-shaped fixtures along the way reflect light onto the flagstone.

"You going to bed?" Gabe asks once we're inside the cottage.

"Yeah, guess so," I say and start to head up the stairs. "I'm pretty tired."

I'm still rattled, too, not only from the engagement drama, but also from what Keira revealed about the loan. I want to ask Gabe about it, but that's a discussion best tabled until the morning.

"Me, too," he says, following me up.

After quickly stripping off his clothes, he slides into bed and looks up at me. "You ended up speaking to my mom, I noticed. Did she say anything of note?"

Because of my promise to butt out, I'm hardly going to tell him we talked about Hannah, and besides, Claire said it was "between us."

"No, nothing in particular," I say, slipping into bed next to him. "But like I said earlier, she didn't look thrilled."

"Well, you know my mom. There's nothing she can't handle."

Based on how annoyed Gabe seemed earlier, I'm surprised when he moves closer and snuggles up to me. Within a couple of minutes, I hear his breathing deepen.

I try to will myself to sleep, but my mind refuses to quiet. It would have been wrong to betray his mother's confidence, and yet I'm uncomfortable hiding something from Gabe. But given how unwilling he is to accept the truth about Hannah and consider the impact she's going to have on Nick, I'm not sure I'd get through to him anyway.

I keep circling back to my conversation with Claire. She claimed to have Hannah's number, but what does that mean exactly? Has she discovered more about Hannah than I already know myself? *Our little* USC *graduate*, she'd said. Could she mean that Hannah lied about going there?

Finally, too exhausted to ruminate any further, I drift off to sleep. But then I'm awake again, stirring as I feel Gabe slipping back into bed.

"Everything okay?" I mumble.

"Yeah, I was just getting some water."

I'm thirsty, too, I realize, and head down to the kitchen a minute later, where the clock tells me it's 1:30 A.M. As I'm filling a glass with ice water, I jerk in surprise at a movement I hear on the other side of the front door.

I tiptoe into the sitting room and stare at the wooden door. Someone or something is clearly out there, scuffing the ground. It could be deer, or a raccoon. Or the darn *coywolf.*

And then a different sound, a light but frantic rapping on the door.

Holding my breath, I inch toward it.

"Who's there?" I call out.

Silence.

"Who's *there*?" I repeat, but this time louder.

"Daddy," a voice calls, almost a wail. "Daddy, please let me in. Pleeeease."

I fling open the door, and there, standing in the dark,

is Henry in his Spider-Man pajamas, his face streaked with tears.

"Oh my god, honey, what's the matter?" I exclaim.

"Something," he says. His chest heaves as he speaks.

"Something what?"

"Something bad happened."

7

Gasping, I yank Henry inside, kick the door closed with my bare foot, and wrap an arm around him.

"Can you tell me what happened?" I ask, trying to keep my voice calm as my shock morphs into dread.

"Gee," he says. "It . . . it's about Gee."

My heart nearly stops.

"Is she okay? Is she sick?"

"Not sick. She's really mad."

"At *you*, honey?" I can't imagine that.

"No . . . at someone else." He starts to cry again, softly, and swipes his tears away with the back of his hand. "I heard her when I was in my room—and I got really scared."

Okay, none of this is making any sense, but at least the house isn't burning to the ground like Manderley.

"Come sit. I'll get you a glass of water and we can talk about it some more."

I lead him to the couch, flicking on a light as we go. The back of his pajama top, I realize, is damp with perspiration.

"Is Daddy here?" he asks mournfully as I turn toward the kitchen.

"Yes, of course. Want me to wake him up?"

But I don't have to. Suddenly there's the sound of feet barreling down the enclosed staircase, and Gabe emerges dressed only in his boxer briefs. His gaze immediately falls on Henry and he rushes toward him.

"Hen, what's happened?"

Henry glances at me, like he's wondering if he should start at the beginning again.

"He thought he heard your mother yelling at someone in the house, and it frightened him," I say.

"Not *yelling*," Henry corrects me. "She was scolding the person. And it wasn't in the house. It was outside my window."

Outside? Had Claire encountered a would-be intruder prowling around the house?

"What was Gee saying?" Gabe asks, dropping onto the couch next to Henry.

"She was telling them she knew what they were up to. And that they better do the right thing."

No, not a stranger then. Someone in the family—or the person's partner. Could she have been talking to Hannah? Based on what Claire told me, I'd assumed she'd be biding her time, but maybe she decided to bring the situation to a head tonight.

"But you don't know who Gee was talking to?" I ask.

Henry shakes his head.

"And when did this happen, buddy?" Gabe prods. "Just now?"

"Uh, I don't know. I think I went back to sleep for a while. But I can't sleep now. Please, I don't want to be in the big house anymore."

Gabe pulls Henry toward him in an embrace. "You don't have to be there. You can stay right here in the cottage with me and Summer. The bed's already made up in the spare room."

Henry whimpers in relief and then asks if he can have a glass of water now.

"Summer will get it for you and take you upstairs while I run to the house for a second, okay? I want to make sure everything's all right over there."

Henry nods, and Gabe jumps up and follows me to the kitchen.

"What the hell do you think is going on?" he whispers. "It's the middle of the night. Who could my mother have been talking to outside?"

"I think it might be just what he said—that he heard it earlier and then fell back to sleep."

I've managed to avoid answering my husband's second question. *Who?*

"And maybe," I add, "he only *thought* he heard it out his window. It could have taken place in the living room or the screened porch."

"Yeah, well, whatever and wherever, I don't like the sound of it and I want to check things out. I have my house key."

"Okay, but take the flashlight, too. And honey, be careful. We have no idea what's really going on."

Gabe nods and hurries upstairs for his pants and shoes, then grabs the flashlight from the kitchen drawer. He tells

Henry not to worry, swings open the cottage door, and disappears into the darkness outside.

I've never felt jittery on the Keatons' property at night, but I do now. After Henry's nursed his water for as long as possible, I lead him upstairs to the second bedroom. Because the space hasn't been used in a while, it smells musty, and I wiggle open the windows, allowing fresh air to seep in through the screens. I also plug in the night-light so he won't get scared when I switch off the bedside lamp.

"I can stay here the rest of the week, right?" Henry asks.

"Of course. Daddy will bring your bag over tomorrow. And why don't we have you wear one of his T-shirts to bed? Your PJ top is a little sweaty."

I grab one from Gabe's drawer, and as I'm slipping it onto Henry's small frame, I realize that it was probably a mistake to ever let him stay in the main house. He seemed so excited initially—especially about the chance to sleep with the dogs—and of course, I'd been all for the idea of Gabe and me having the cottage as our private love nest, but Henry's a bit young to be on his own that way.

This switch is for the best, then, though there probably won't be dreamy afternoon sex from this point forward.

"You feeling any better?" I ask, pulling the cotton blanket over him. I take a seat on the edge of the bed.

"Yeah, I guess. Is Daddy going to be okay?"

"For sure, and he won't be long. . . . Is there anything more you can remember about what you heard?"

"No, just what I told you. . . . Oh, wait. Gee said if the person didn't do the right thing, *she* would."

"I wouldn't worry about it," I tell Henry, even though the

hair on the back of my neck is standing up now. "Maybe she only sounded mad because she was tired." I kiss his forehead and rise. "Night, night. I'll leave your door open and ours, too."

From the glow of the night-light, I can see the outline of his hand giving me a thumbs-up.

Descending again to the sitting room, I pace, fretting. Was it Hannah whom Claire had been speaking to? Or could it have been *Ash* she was addressing? No, that seems unlikely. That's not the way their relationship operates—at least as far as I've witnessed.

Another thought flickers in my head, one I probably should have considered initially: Could Henry have simply *dreamed* the exchange?

After ten minutes have passed and Gabe hasn't materialized, my stomach feels like a big hard ball of rubber bands. Five minutes more go by, and I wish I'd told him to take his phone.

Finally, as I'm nearly out of my mind, I spot the beam of a flashlight bouncing between the branches of the shrub in front of the sitting room window. Gabe pushes the door open before I have the time to cross the room, and his expression reads perplexed rather than alarmed.

"*So?*" I ask quietly.

"The house is dark, and no one's up—or seems to be. I looked all around and climbed to the top of the stairs, and I could hear my dad snoring. And the dogs are now sitting outside my parents' room."

"No sign of anything unusual?"

"None. The door at this side of the house was partly open—that's obviously how Henry got out—but I closed and locked it as I left."

I nod. "What are you going to do next?"

"I'll have to talk to my mom in the morning, explain why Henry's not there anymore. But I feel a little weird bringing it up—it sounds like it was a sensitive conversation."

"Marcus and Keira are staying in the main house. Maybe they overheard it, too, and can fill you in so you don't have to ask your mom."

"But they're in the big guest room, all the way at the other end of the house, so I doubt they heard anything. I'll just have to suck it up and be frank with my mother, I guess. Did Henry go to bed okay?"

"Yeah, he seemed pretty relieved to be here. Do you think it's possible he dreamed the whole thing?"

Gabe scrunches his mouth in thought. "Or . . ." he says, lowering his voice, "what if it's all the product of a nine-year-old's overactive imagination—and he made it up as a way to get out of staying in the house without having to ask directly?"

"Possible. And he might not have fabricated *everything*. Maybe he heard something, and it got twisted in his mind."

Gabe shrugs. "Right. Hopefully we'll know more in the morning."

We trudge up to our room and crawl back under the sheet. The room feels slightly more humid than earlier, but I don't have the psychic energy to activate the air conditioning. From sheer fatigue, I drift off into a restless sleep.

I wake the next day to the sound of laughter coming from below. Gabe and Henry. I roll over on my side. It's 7:04. Sleepily, I pull on shorts and a T-shirt.

Downstairs I find the two of them drinking orange juice at the kitchen table. Henry's playing a game on Gabe's phone and grinning so widely that I almost wonder if last night was something *I* must have dreamed.

"Hi, guys," I say, my voice froggy still from sleep. "Everything good?"

"Yup, all good," Gabe announces.

"Dad said I could play *Subway Surfers* for fifteen minutes," Henry tells me without looking up. "Then I have to stop."

Sitting in front of Henry, I notice, is a plate scattered with toast crumbs, and there are strawberries and plums in a bowl, neither of which were in our kitchen here yesterday. I shoot Gabe a questioning look.

"Hey, Hen," he says, "why don't you take the phone upstairs while you get dressed? I left your duffel bag on the luggage rack in your room. And then when you're ready, we'll take the dogs for a long walk."

"Gee says the dogs can't go in the woods this week because of hunters," Henry says.

"We'll walk them on the road with their leashes, then," Gabe assures him.

As soon as Henry's scampered upstairs, Gabe eases the kitchen door shut with his foot.

"So you've been over to the house already?" I say.

"Yeah, I realized I'd better be there when my mom woke up so she wouldn't go into Henry's room and find him missing."

"Did you learn anything?"

Using his foot again, Gabe shoves a chair away from the table for me to sit on.

"Turns out Henry was right," he says. "He *did* hear my mom reading the riot act to someone outside his window."

"Who *was* it?"

"You know the girl who's been working with Bonnie? The one with the pink hair? My mother caught her helping herself to a couple of bottles of wine on the way out last night and confronted her out on the patio."

It takes a second for the answer to register since it's not what I was expecting.

"You mean after we took Henry up to bed?"

"Yeah, though there were still people around in the house. My mom didn't want to spoil the mood, so she kept it to herself. Henry obviously *did* fall asleep after hearing the conversation and only came over here after he woke up in the middle of the night."

I feel a weird, diluted kind of relief. On one hand I'm glad there's no major family conflict, but part of me was hoping that Claire *had* put Hannah on notice.

"Does your mom know Henry's staying here now?"

Gabe takes a couple of moments to chug his coffee. "Yeah, and she gets it—that he's not quite ready to bunk down at the main house on his own. Though she was upset to hear he was out in the dark like that."

I pour a mugful of coffee for myself and feel a frown form on my face, as if the muscles around my mouth have a mind of their own.

"What is it?" Gabe asks, his eyes curious.

"After you went over to the house last night, Henry remembered one more thing about the conversation. He said your mom told the person that if they didn't do the right thing, *she* would. How does that jibe with your mom catching a girl stealing bottles of wine?"

"Hmm. Well, I doubt Henry's memory of the exchange is a hundred percent accurate—especially if he fell asleep right after. And my mother could have meant she wanted the girl to tell Bonnie what had happened—or she would."

"That makes sense, I guess," I say, even though it seems like a stretch.

"By the way, my mom wants to keep this low-profile, so don't mention it to anyone, okay?"

"Got it."

Gabe grabs a plum and leans over to kiss me on the lips. "I figured we'd get out of your hair for a while today so you can work on your play," he adds.

"Thanks, I appreciate that." Gabe, I'm happy to see, seems to be doing his best to bring us back on an even keel. "Shall we meet up before lunch?"

"Maybe *at* lunch. Marcus and I are going to talk shop with Dad before then."

"Wait," I say, remembering something else as he starts to rise from the table. "Are you planning to ask your dad for a loan?"

His brow wrinkles. "Who told you *that*?"

"Keira mentioned it last night. I felt stupid not knowing."

"She's clearly misunderstood what Marcus told her," Gabe says, obviously frustrated by Keira getting it wrong. "No, we don't need money at the moment, but Dad's been promising some investment funds and we have to nail down the details if we want to expand going forward."

"Okay, that's what I figured it might be." I'm relieved not only that Gabe's business is okay but also that he hasn't hidden any problems from me.

After they take off, I serve myself a bowl of yogurt from the fridge and open my laptop on the kitchen table, thinking there'll be fewer distractions in here than out on the patio. But before long I'm groaning in frustration. I just can't concentrate.

My mind keeps replaying the events of last night. Not only Henry bursting in from the dark like a scene out of a Harry Potter movie, but all the tension that preceded it: the engagement announcement, Gabe complaining about my behavior, Claire sharing her concern.

And as I sit there, a spoon dangling in my hand, a memory rushes into my brain like an animal suddenly darting across the road at night: Claire and me in the kitchen, speaking quietly, the rhythmic calls of katydids and crickets coming through the windows. Voices, too. Bonnie and her helper chatting as they dropped a trash bag into the bin outside, and then the firing of their car engines as they departed for the night. All before we went in to admire Henry's magic tricks.

Which means the pink-haired helper was long gone by the time he went up to bed. Which means she wasn't the person Claire confronted.

Who was she talking to then? And why would she concoct a story for Gabe?

I replay the fragments of conversation that Henry claimed to have overheard: *I know what you're up to. . . . You'd better do the right thing. . . . And if you don't, I will.*

So what "right thing" could she be referring to? For Hannah to confess to Nick? And possibly back out of her engagement?

I'm too antsy now to look at my computer, so I decide simply to make some notes about how to clarify the arc of my story and the question it involves. I grab my notebook and start up the path to the house, in search of an espresso and a spot where I can sit and scribble, maybe the boxwood glade.

To my surprise, I seem to have the entire grounds to myself. Granted, it's early still, but I'd expect on a Sunday to hear sounds of people playing tennis or someone splashing in the pool, but there aren't any. And the table under the pergola is abandoned. It feels as if I've showed up at an event on the wrong day or at the wrong time.

But clearly people have been here earlier—the croissant basket on the sideboard, I notice, is only half full.

"Morning," I call out, stepping into the kitchen. But no one's in there.

I enter the dining room next, as the swinging door yawns behind me. The space has been tidied up from last night, and the living room is pristine, too. You'd hardly know we'd been gathered there.

Curious, I begin to wander, from room to room, corridor to corridor, practically the length of the house, and the quiet is almost eerie.

Finally, back in the living room, I glance into the adjoining study, a room I think of as mostly Ash's turf. Though the fireplace probably hasn't been used in months, I can pick up the lingering hint of woodsmoke even from the doorway. I don't see anyone in here, either, but as I turn to leave, I sense a motion on the other end of the room and spin quickly to the right. Wendy's standing by the wall of floor-to-ceiling bookshelves, and I've clearly surprised her, too.

"Oh sorry, I didn't mean to intrude," I say.

"No problem. I was just looking for something to read. My iPad seems to have died."

"You've got your choice of classics here, I guess, but there are a couple of thrillers in the cottage bookshelf if you want more options. . . . Where is everyone, do you know? It's like a ghost town this morning."

"Blake went for a drive along the river, and Nick and Hannah haven't emerged from their room yet."

She says the last part with a faint smirk on her face.

"What about Claire and Ash? And Bonnie?"

"Bonnie's at church apparently and not due until later. I saw Ash leave with his bike about ten minutes ago. He said Claire had gone to the farmers' market."

"Sounds like there might be more corn on the cob in our future." I step a little closer to her. "Wendy, I have to say again how thrilled I am for you and Blake. You must be in seventh heaven."

"We are, thank you."

A rogue lock of blond hair has fallen in her eyes, and as she sweeps it back, I notice something vexed about her expression. Maybe more perturbed than vexed, actually.

"Is everything all right?"

"What do you mean?"

"Are you feeling okay? You look . . ."

"Oh, sorry. . . . It's just, you know, sometimes things don't turn out exactly as you hope they will."

My heart skips. "Is there something wrong with the baby?"

"God, no—sorry. I didn't mean it that way. I was talking about the announcement. We were so looking forward to telling everyone. I mean, it's taken us so many years to get to this place. And to be honest, it felt kind of lousy to have Nick share his big news right after."

Of course. I wasn't the only one struck by the poor timing of the second announcement.

"I have to admit, it surprised me. They could have waited until another night this week."

Wendy shrugs. "I don't think Nick was given much of a choice."

"How so?"

"He apologized to Blake later, saying he got caught up in the happy family moment, but I think he was actually pushed into doing it." She leans toward me as if to share a secret. "When we were answering questions about the due date and sex, I felt Hannah give Nick a kick under the table. Like she was urging him to speak up."

What a brat, I think. But since I'm still trying to be a good girl, I don't utter it aloud.

"That's a shame. But we're all so excited for you and Blake, Wendy, and nothing could overshadow that."

"Thanks, that means a lot," she tells me. "Actually, instead of reading, I think I'll hit some tennis balls against the backboard."

Wow, I think, as she hurries off. What a difference a day makes. Twenty-four hours ago, I figured I was the only one with a distaste for Hannah, but now there are three of us.

After exiting the house and fixing an espresso to go on the sideboard, I make my way across the yard toward the boxwoods, planning to finally park myself on the bench inside the glade. But someone's already inside, I realize. At least two someones actually. I hear a male voice—and though it's too low for me to make out the words, his tone seems very hostile.

Instinctively, I freeze and take a step backward. As I shift positions, I'm suddenly able to see into the glade through a small, open space in one of the boxwoods. It's Nick in there—and he's with Hannah. They're standing only a few inches apart from each other, and though he's in profile, I can see enough of his mouth to know it's twisted in anger.

Are things between them beginning to unravel? Maybe Hannah's responded to Claire's ultimatum and revealed a truth about herself that Nick can't accept. In that case, she may be in our rearview mirror before the day's over.

I watch as she reaches up and lays a hand gently on Nick's cheek. He attempts to shrug it off with a flick of his head, but she places it there again, and this time he doesn't resist.

Move, I command myself. However intense my curiosity, I know it's inappropriate for me to be watching this. Before I can inch backward, though, Nick shifts slightly so I can see more of his face. And I realize that it's not *Nick* standing there with Hannah's hand resting on his cheek.

It's Marcus.

8

Oh boy. I turn away immediately, being careful not to slosh my espresso onto the grass, and start toward the path, still holding my breath. I'm in such a discombobulated state that I soon realize I'm heading back to the house even though that wasn't my intention.

What the hell did I just witness? I've wondered since Friday night whether Marcus has a lingering romantic interest in Hannah, and their heated conversation and body language suggest my instinct was right.

And it doesn't appear to be a one-way street. The way Hannah laid her hand on Marcus's cheek looked very intimate.

When I reach the patio, I set my notebook and cup on the table, so lost in thought it takes a minute to notice that Keira's appeared, dressed in a bathing suit and cover-up.

"Morning," she says.

"Oh, hi, good morning." I swallow hard, thinking about the scene playing out not all that far from us. "Going for a swim?"

"In a minute, yes. It's so warm today. Have you seen Marcus, by the way? He came downstairs earlier, saying he was headed to the pool."

My heart sinks. Should I tell her what her husband is up to? I'd certainly want her to clue *me* in if she spotted Gabe in a tête-à-tête with a woman he used to have sex with.

Before I can respond, she moves her gaze over my shoulder toward the cottage path, as if her attention's being drawn there by an unseen force.

"Um, I thought I saw him a minute or two ago," I blurt out. "Near the boxwood grove."

"Over *there*?" she says. "Okay, I'll track him down. See you in a bit."

She crosses the patio and steps off onto the path in that direction, and I stay glued to the spot, stunned by what I've done. Yes, it's only fair that my sister-in-law know the truth, but it's really not my business to orchestrate the revelation, especially in a way that could humiliate her. I have to catch her before she walks into the glade.

I rush across the patio and hurry up the path, trying to come up with a little white lie to tell her, maybe that I think I just heard Marcus's voice coming from the pool area.

But I'm too late.

When I spot Keira, she's many yards ahead of me and walking purposely toward the grove, her ponytail bouncing. Before I can call to her, she disappears into the center of the boxwoods. I feel like I've pulled the pin from a hand grenade and it's about to explode.

But a second later, she emerges, her expression intent rather than crushed or livid. Marcus and Hannah must have moved on. I exhale with relief. Maybe I won't burn in hell after all.

"No luck?" I call out from the path.

She shakes her head as she strides in my direction. "How long ago did you see him?" she asks.

"A minute or two before you and I spoke. He might have gone back to your room since then—or he's down by the pool now."

I realize as I'm standing there that I'm barely thinking straight and left my notebook on the patio. "Are you going that way?" I add. "I need to get something."

She nods, but now she looks puzzled. Has she grown suspicious of Marcus this weekend?

"Or maybe he went to look for Gabe?" I volunteer as we start up the path. "To connect before the meeting with Ash?"

She doesn't answer but abruptly stops and cocks her head.

"Marcus wasn't in the glade, but *Hannah* was."

"Huh," is all I manage.

"Do you think they'd been in there together?" she asks.

"*Together?*" I decide I need to quit while I'm ahead and not admit to what I saw. "Why would they be together?"

"I don't know." She scrunches her mouth. "But it's kind of a weird coincidence, don't you think? That they were both there in the last few minutes? It's not like the boxwoods are a spot people tend to congregate in."

"Keira, are you worried about Marcus and Hannah?"

She shrugs halfheartedly. "No. I mean, he hasn't done anything to make me worry. But you always feel vulnerable when you're married, don't you? There are so many distrac-

tions for guys, and so many women who operate like preda-
tors."

"Even though Marcus dated Hannah for only a short
time, it might be weird for him to have his brother engaged
to her," I say carefully. "Why don't you talk to him and see
what's on his mind?"

"When Nick first called and said he was dating Hannah,
Marcus told me that he didn't exactly end things well with
her. He ghosted her, just stopped calling, and she later sent
him a kind of pissy text. Do you think being with Nick is her
way of getting back at Marcus?"

"Marrying someone's brother seems like a pretty drastic
way to get even, but who knows. Either way, Keira, the person you really need to talk to is Marcus."

She nods. "You're right."

We reach the patio, where I grab my notebook and say
good-bye. Abandoning the idea of trying to work outside—
too many land mines at the moment—I return to the cottage. After making a cup of tea, I settle at the table in the
sitting room, which is cooler than outside thanks to the stone
walls and closed drapes.

I manage to scribble down only a couple of notes because
by now my mind is a jumble of thoughts and emotions. I'm
ashamed of myself for almost sending Keira into an ambush.
I'm also angry at both Marcus and Hannah for whatever that
conversation was about. But most of all, I can't stand the
idea of Hannah invading this family. She's already messing
with our dynamic and throwing the whole ecosystem out of
whack.

As I attempt to force my attention back to my play, I

hear the faint buzz of bees permeating the glass of the French doors, and then a few moments later the *snip, snip* of flowers being cut. Claire must be back from her trip to the farmers' market and collecting stems from the garden. Briefly, life here feels back to normal.

And then, as if confirming that thought, Henry bounds into the cottage with a grin on his face.

"How was the dog walk?" I ask.

"Good. Dad had to hold Bella's leash because she kept wanting to run off the road and into the woods."

"Where is Dad, anyway?"

"He's in the house talking to Grandpa and Uncle Marcus. Can I go to the pool? Uncle Blake's gonna swim with me."

"Okay, but you can only go in the water if he's in there with you or watching, okay?"

He shoots me a look that says, *I hate being treated like a baby*, but then dashes upstairs to change into his trunks.

I deliberate following him to the pool myself, but as soon as Henry's out the door, I'm nailed by a wave of fatigue, the result of how few hours of sleep I clocked last night. I shift to the couch and stretch out, closing my eyes.

The slam of the front door wakes me. I blink a couple of times and sit up slowly to see Gabe standing in the entranceway.

"So how'd it go? Did—?"

And then I take him in more fully. He looks stricken.

"Gabe, what's the matter?"

"It's a fucking mess."

My heart jumps. "*What* is?"

Rather than join me, he strides into the kitchen, where I hear him yank open the refrigerator. "Is it too early for a beer?" he calls out. He obviously decides it is because by the time I join him in the kitchen, he's chugging seltzer water from a liter bottle.

"Gabe, please," I urge. "Tell me what's going on."

"That vineyard in Spain that Marcus and I invested so much in? It's going bankrupt."

"No," I say, trying to keep panic out of my voice. "And you just found this out today?"

"*I* did, but Marcus has known for over a week."

That explains why Keira seemed so concerned about the meeting.

"Here, sit," I say, motioning to a chair at the kitchen table and taking a seat across from it. "How much will this set you back?" What I'm not asking but, of course, also wondering is how much will this set *us* back.

"We're not in danger of going under, but we lose all our investment in the vineyard, plus anything we expected to draw from it. And now there won't be money for the initiatives we planned for next year. Marcus and I will both probably have to take a pay cut."

"But what about the money your dad was going to invest?"

He sighs in frustration. "That's not happening apparently."

"What?"

"Despite his hints otherwise, he's decided not to give us any more money, at least for a while."

I'm flabbergasted. Ash has seemed so eager to help with Gabe's business.

"Maybe he needs time to think about it?" I ask.

"He's *had* time. Turns out, Marcus called him last week and gave him a heads-up so he'd have the chance to look over the paperwork before we met. Again, all unbeknownst to me."

"I can't believe Marcus would keep this from you. What was he thinking?"

"Oh, he's got this whole justification—I'm the front person for the company, doing sales and marketing, and he's the numbers guy. He says he didn't want to burden me until he had proof things were really coming undone."

"You think that's true?"

As smart as Marcus is, he apparently floundered a bit professionally in his early twenties, and it wasn't until Gabe asked him to join the fledgling wine business that he seemed to find himself. He's been a great partner, but Gabe is the face of the company and thus gets most of the attention. Maybe by attempting to solve the problem on his own, Marcus was trying to prove his own importance.

"Not sure why it wouldn't be. He's seemed a little moody over the past couple of weeks, but I guess it was probably from trying to handle this solo."

I set my elbows on the table and sink my face into my hands, and another thought pushes into the front of my mind. "Do you think your dad could be having money troubles?"

Gabe shakes his head. "No, and he assured me this doesn't affect anything for us personally. He and my mother are still going to be paying for Henry's school and contributing to his college fund. And they're still taking us skiing at Christmastime."

"Then what's the reason? I don't get it."

"It seems to be about spreading the wealth around when it comes to his investment dollars. Dad feels he's been more than generous to Marcus and me for the time being, and of course, he helped Wendy start her gallery. And now he feels he should do something for Nick, who's got some side real estate project he's trying to launch. Dad has every right to turn us down, but I just didn't see this coming."

My stomach feels like a fist by now. I hate seeing Gabe unhappy for any reason, but this one's especially troubling. It will surely cast a pall over the vacation, and it'll ultimately have ramifications on the personal front. Should we really plan to try for a baby next year if his salary could be reduced? I'd been hoping to step back from any voice-over work while my play's in the festival, but I realize I won't be able to do that now. We have bills to pay and a mortgage on our loft, and that means we'll have to continue to count on income from me every week.

"Gabe, I'm so sorry," I say. "Are you going to be able to handle the week ahead out here?"

He shrugs with both shoulders, his expression defeated.

"I don't have a choice. I'll just have to suck it up."

He takes another long swig of water from the bottle, and after wiping his mouth, says he's going to take a short hike before lunch to burn off his agitation. Do I mind, he asks, keeping an eye on Henry for the next hour or so? Not at all, I say, and half jokingly urge him to steer clear of coywolves.

After he leaves, I flop back on the sofa, my whole body thrumming with dread. It's hard to believe that two days ago I was nearly giddy over the idea of our vacation here. In our six years together, I've never seen Gabe face any issue this size with his family, and I have no idea how this might play out over the next days.

Desperate for a distraction myself, I set out in search of Henry and find him on the lawn finishing a game of horseshoes with Blake, his cherry red trunks still damp from the pool. I usher him back to the cottage, and an hour later, as we're playing our thousandth hand of Uno, Gabe returns, lugging a wicker basket filled with sandwiches, chips, pickles, and soft drinks.

"Bonnie helped me put it together," he says, with Henry out of range. "I just couldn't face sitting around that table. I blamed it on Henry being up last night and us all being wiped."

"That's fine," I say. "It'll be nice to have one meal with only the three of us."

I help Gabe set out the food and drinks on the kitchen table and we eat there, a light breeze mercifully finding its way in through the window. By the time Henry's finished his sandwich, he looks almost comatose with fatigue, so Gabe urges him upstairs, promising to read to him up there.

While they rest, I decide to make an appearance at the house. Though I'm unsettled by Ash's decision, it won't help anything if we seem to be sulking. Plus, I might have an opportunity to connect with Claire, and if she's still in a sharing mood, maybe she'll tell me who she was *really* confronting last night.

I grab the basket and go. The day's really muggy now, and I'm sweating by the time I reach the patio, which turns out to be empty. No one down by the pool, either. I peer through a kitchen window, but the gauze curtain is drawn, so I tug open the door to find that the lights are off and the only sound is the faint hum of the dishwasher.

But there's Claire sitting on a stool at the butcher-block-topped island. All by herself, in the dimness.

"Hello, darling," she says softly.

"Claire, hi. Where is everyone?"

"I believe most people have opted for a short siesta this afternoon."

"That makes sense in this heat. . . . Want me to turn a light on?"

"No, that's all right, dear. It was feeling a little too bright. . . . Can I get you anything?"

"Thank you, I'm fine," I say. "I just wanted to say hello."

After setting down the basket, I step closer so I can see her better. Her hair's pulled back today, with a few silvery-blond tendrils curled by her ears, and her face looks unusually shiny, probably from the humidity. In front of her on the island is an empty drinking glass, the jug she uses to make her special iced tea, and a plate with an untouched sandwich. She taps her index finger to her lips a few times, as if she's sensing the start of a fever blister.

"You know what?" she says. "We should set aside a time this week to take a walk together. I feel like I haven't had much chance to catch up with you yet."

"Great thought. What about right now?" I ask.

"Would you mind waiting until later? I might take a siesta myself since I'm feeling slightly drained from the heat."

"Of course. Whenever works for you."

Sensing that she'd like to be alone, I say good-bye and turn to leave.

"Summer," she says quietly as I near the door. I pivot. "Have you colored your hair lately, darling?"

"My *hair*?"

"It looks lighter to me this weekend."

"Uh, no, just the usual highlights I indulge in every few months."

A minute later, while I'm pouring myself an ice water on the patio, I feel a hot swell of anger. This week has already gone to hell, and it's only Sunday. Gabe's not only upset with his Dad, he's pissed at Marcus as well. Claire's distressed about Nick's engagement, and I'm pretty sure Marcus is, too. Keira's feeling worried about her marriage. And I'm too agitated to concentrate on my play. I know Hannah's not responsible for *all* of it—but life would be so much better if she weren't here.

How fitting that at this exact moment, I catch a glimpse of her in the distance, all by herself and heading down the path that connects the pool area with the carriage house. She's dressed in a cutoff jean skirt and T-shirt, and there's total confidence in her stride. If she was actually the one Claire confronted last night, the experience certainly hasn't undone her. And neither has the encounter with Marcus. Or perhaps she's an even better actress than I realize.

When I reenter the cottage, Gabe's still reading to Henry—I hear the murmur of their voices from above. I read myself for an hour or so, though my eyes keep sliding off the screen of my iPad. I feel restless, unable to relax. A hike helped Gabe clear his head, and maybe I need some exercise, too. By now I'm picking up the sound of Gabe's light snoring from the spare bedroom, meaning they're *both* asleep—so I write a note explaining my intended whereabouts before changing into running shoes and slathering on a glob of sunscreen. Then I head to the front of the property and onto Durham Road.

Granted, it's a lousy day to jog, not only hot but humid. As I accelerate my speed, pounding the road hard, I feel the heat radiating from the blacktop through my shoes. Gnats swarm around my face, trying to shoot up my nostrils. But it's nice to move my legs and good to have a change of scenery.

I don't pass a single car on the road as I go, and the only person I spot is a farmer riding a tractor in a distant field. The solitude feels good, even essential, right now. After about fifteen minutes, my tension begins to subside, and after another ten, I do a U-turn and start back at a slower pace.

And then, just as I'm jogging the last stretch, not even minding that my top is clinging to my torso, I have a revelation. Things will work out with the wine business. They *will*. Gabe is incredibly clever, and he'll sort out the problem with the vineyard. He'll insist that Marcus be more forthcoming in the future and he'll smooth things over with his dad. Because the Keatons don't do family drama.

I'm almost back at the house when my attention is diverted by the wail of a siren, from a fire truck or maybe an ambulance. It's about half a mile ahead, I guess, barreling in this direction. Instinctively, I step even closer to the edge of the road.

Abruptly, the siren ceases—but the vehicle never passes

me. My heart skips and I hasten my pace. Could it have stopped at *our* house? I move even faster, breaking into a run, and tearing up the gravel drive.

And there it is, an ambulance smack in front of the house.

Panic surges through me. My first thought is Henry. Has something happened to him?

"What's going on?" I shout to the two paramedics who have jumped out the back of the vehicle.

"We need to get inside," one of them yells as they grab equipment and charge into the house.

I race behind them through the foyer and into the center hall.

The first thing I notice is the sound of the dogs yelping from the kitchen and frantically scratching on the closed door. From the corner of my eye, I catch a movement in the living room and turn to see a cluster of people there. Blake is at the far end, kneeling, his back to me and his arms moving like pistons. *Chest compressions.*

As soon as I see the shoes, I know that it's Claire sprawled out on the floor. And that Blake is trying to save her life.

9

"We need you to please step away now," one of the paramedics tells Blake.

He rises and lurches backward. In the second before the ambulance crew take over, I catch a glimpse of my mother-in-law. She's deadly pale, her eyes are closed, and her mouth is twisted into a terrible grimace.

Did she have a heart attack? I wonder, my breath trapped in my chest.

I quickly absorb the rest of the scene. Ash, his face nearly as white as Claire's, is standing nearby and Blake has placed an arm around him protectively. Marcus, Nick, Wendy, and Bonnie are here, too, in a ragged semicircle, looking on in horror.

"What happened?" I whisper to Marcus, stepping closer and grasping his arm.

"Not sure," he mutters. "We were all out by the pool, and Bonnie came running out to get us. God—"

"What about Gabe? Does he know?"

"No, it all happened so fast. I'm not sure where he is."

He must still be in the cottage.

My whole body feels weighted down by dread, but I force myself to run there. *Please, please,* I pray as I propel myself along the flagstone path, *please let her be okay.* It seems to take forever to reach the cottage, like I'm trying to run through water, but I finally shove open the front door to find Gabe and Henry on the couch, watching a video on Gabe's laptop. The volume's so high, neither one hears me arrive, and clearly they didn't hear the siren, either.

"Gabe," I shout from the doorway. When he glances up with a start, I flick my hand in a beckoning motion for him to come to me.

"Keep watching," he tells Henry as he jumps up and hurries toward me, barefoot.

"You need to get over to the house," I whisper. "Your mom collapsed for some reason and paramedics are here, working on her."

"Jesus." There's panic in his eyes. He takes five frantic seconds to shove his feet into a pair of espadrilles by the coffee table, and then he's off, charging up the path toward the house.

"Is something the matter?" Henry asks, finally tearing his eyes off the screen.

"Gee's not feeling well, and Dad needs to check on her."

"Should I pause the movie?"

"Uh, no, why don't you keep watching, sweetie. And do you mind staying here for a little while by yourself? I want to check on Gee, too."

"Okay. Is she throwing up?"

"No, not throwing up," I tell him. If only it were that simple.

Though I'm only a minute or so behind Gabe, he must have run like crazy because I don't spot him ahead on the path. By the time I burst through the side door of the house and reach the living room, no one's there. I find them all in the circular driveway, joined now by Keira and Hannah, watching in anguish as Claire is hoisted on a gurney into the back of the ambulance. Blake and Ash are talking to the driver through the window about which hospital she's being taken to. The paramedics jump into the back of the ambulance and pull the doors shut with a double clang.

"Okay, Dad and I are going to follow them to the hospital in Doylestown," Blake announces as the ambulance pulls out of the driveway. It's a town I know is about twenty-five minutes away. "Who's coming with us?"

Marcus and Nick shout in unison that they are.

"Wh-why don't I drive my own car," Gabe says. "The keys are in it. And it'll be better to have two there."

"I'm coming, too," Wendy announces and grabs Blake's hand.

"I want to go," I tell Gabe, "but someone needs to stay with Henry."

He nods distractedly, like he's clicking onto automatic pilot. "I'll call you as soon as we know anything."

Keira and Hannah quickly ask if they can accompany the group, but Blake nixes that idea.

"We need people to hold down the fort here," he calls out as he hurries toward his Mercedes with Wendy and Ash alongside him.

Seconds later the cars are roaring out of the driveway: Blake, Ash, Wendy, and Marcus in one, Gabe and Nick in the other. I stare helplessly, feeling like I'm watching a movie about another person's life.

Behind me I hear someone choke back a sob, and I turn to find Bonnie with her hands pressed to her face.

"I can't believe this," she murmurs.

"Why don't we go to the kitchen," I say, touching her shoulder. "I'll fix us each up a cup of tea."

Before we retreat, I turn back to Hannah and Keira, making eye contact with only my sister-in-law.

"Are you coming in the house?" I ask.

"Yes—I think I'll wait in the living room with my phone. I don't know what else there is to do beyond that."

"I'll come check in on you in a little while, okay?"

Keira nods while Hannah simply stands there, looking surprisingly unsure of how to play the scene. Could she be secretly happy that she's been granted a momentary reprieve? If she was the one Claire was chewing out, there's certainly nothing to be done about it at the moment.

I lead Bonnie by the arm to the kitchen, where Ginger and Bella are waiting on the other side of the door, all stressed out.

"It's okay," I say, giving each dog a couple of pats on the head. "Go lie down now."

After encouraging Bonnie to sit at the table, I fill the electric teakettle with water and flick it on. I seem to be functioning on autopilot now, too, trying my best to hold my anxiety at bay.

"Do you think it's a heart attack?" Bonnie asks bleakly, her sun-weathered cheeks wet from tears.

"Maybe. Do you know if she had any heart issues?"

I doubt that Claire would have told Bonnie if she had— she's too private for that—but as housekeeper, Bonnie might have noticed certain medications tucked in a cabinet or drawer.

She shakes her head. "Not that I'm aware of."

But certainly it's a possibility, a problem Claire might not have even been cognizant of. Claire, after all, is seventy-two. Or is it seventy-three? On the other hand, she's superfit for her age. When I spoke with her after lunch, she'd seemed uncharacteristically subdued, but hardly unwell, and if she'd been experiencing any chest pain, she'd done a good job of disguising it.

Of course, maybe she's collapsed for some other reason altogether—a brain aneurysm or a seizure of some kind. Just thinking those words makes my stomach clench.

"You were the one who found her?" I ask Bonnie.

"Yes, it was me," she says. "I'd come back from my break at four and started getting stuff ready for dinner. Claire's usually in the kitchen around that time, but she never showed up, so I finally went looking for her and saw her at the end of the living room."

"Was she conscious?"

"I'm not sure, to be honest. Her eyes were closed. And she was writhing on the floor, like she was in a lot of pain. I ran outside and yelled down at the pool for Ash and Blake, and they came running. Blake started CPR right away."

I shudder. It's horrible to think of Claire suffering like that. "I'm so glad you found her when you did."

"I just pray she's okay," Bonnie says.

"She *will* be," I insist. "You know how strong Claire is."

The kettle clicks off and I fill two mugs with hot water. As I'm grabbing tea bags, my eyes fall on a row of empty ceramic vases on the counter, still waiting for Claire to fill them with her glorious arrangements. What if she never has the chance? No, I can't allow myself to think that way. I carry the mugs to the table and join Bonnie there.

"I know it seems awful to worry about this now," Bonnie says, cupping her mug, "but what about dinner tonight? I was planning on grilling flank steaks. People will need to eat—though we have no idea when."

"You could always serve it at room temperature, right? And put out some sliced tomatoes and maybe one of those great pasta salads you do."

"That would work."

I think suddenly of my mother's macaroni salad, to which she added hard-boiled eggs, peas, onions, celery, and gobs of mayo. She used to make it for friends if they lost a loved one or had a family member in the hospital. It was a dish that could keep in the fridge for a few days and people could help themselves to when they had a chance to eat. Not the kind of thing that would ever get whipped up in this kitchen, but it's exactly the type of comfort food I could use right now.

"I'm going to check on Henry," I announce, rising from my chair and abandoning my tea, "but I'll be back—and I'll let you know if I hear anything." I pause for a moment. "Um, do you have any help coming later?"

My motive for asking is partly practical, but I still want to get to the bottom of what happened last night. What if the stress of the conversation triggered some sort of medical issue in Claire?

"Yes, but someone new," Bonnie tells me. "Not the girl who was here this weekend."

Wait, does this mean the pink-haired helper really had been the person Claire confronted?

"How come?" I ask.

"She'd only been able to give me a couple of days since she's getting ready to attend her college orientation program. I have a young guy coming who's done a few dinner parties with me here."

So then it clearly *wasn't* the helper whom Claire gave the ultimatum to, especially when you add in the fact that I heard Bonnie and the girl leave the premises while Claire and I were in the kitchen.

I jog back to the cottage, desperate not only to check on Henry but also to grab my phone. Though the ambulance probably won't reach the hospital for another ten minutes, Gabe will surely call after that with any news.

With a start I discover that the ground floor of the cottage is empty, and Gabe's laptop is resting on the coffee table, its screen dark.

"Henry," I call out. "Where are you?"

No reply.

"Henry," I yell, this time frantically.

"I'm up here," he shouts back from the second floor.

"What are you doing up there?"

"Changing out of my trunks."

"Well, come down."

"Okay, okay."

"Sorry about yelling," I say as he emerges from the stairwell, dressed in a T-shirt and shorts. "I was just worried when I didn't see you."

"I'm not a little kid anymore, you know."

Yes, you are I want to say, but this isn't the moment.

"Look, why don't you start another movie on Dad's computer? I have to use my computer for a minute."

"Yeah, all right. Are we gonna eat dinner soon?"

"It might be a little later than usual. Sweetie, Gee ended up having to go to the hospital and Dad went with her."

His face wrinkles in confusion and concern.

"Is she going to be okay?"

"Yes, I'm sure. They took her to a really good hospital, with really good doctors."

I give myself a D for my performance. Even *I* hear the uncertainty in my voice.

"I guess I can watch *Rise of Skywalker*," Henry says hesitantly, sensing perhaps there's more going on than I'm admitting to. He trudges over to the couch, plops down, and cues up the movie.

After changing out of my running clothes, I grab my own laptop and sit beside him, but I angle my screen so that he can't see what I'm doing, which is searching medical sites for "signs of a heart attack in a woman."

It turns out that in women, there's not always chest pain in the minutes or hours before a cardiac arrest. They often experience vague or even "silent" symptoms, like fatigue, nausea or indigestion, light-headedness, and a cold sweat. I flash back to my encounter with Claire in the kitchen: her vaguely listless manner, which could have been a sign of fatigue; the uneaten sandwich, which might have laid there untouched because she was feeling nauseated. And her face slightly shiny from perspiration.

If it *was* a heart attack, that doesn't mean it's a death sentence. People have bypass surgery or get stents put in all the time. Like I told Bonnie, Claire's incredibly strong, and she also has a ferocious zest for life.

Please, I think, *let her be okay. She* has *to be.*

I check the time on my laptop. It's now close to seven o'clock, and Claire should be at the hospital by now, hopefully being seen right away by a great team. I wish Gabe would find a way to call.

I snap my laptop closed and glance over at Henry, who's transfixed by the movie. A thought about Claire skirts around the edges of my mind, toying with my attention. But as hard as I try, I can't manage to catch a hold of it.

"You hungry for a snack?" I ask.

"I thought you said to watch another movie."

"I did, but if you're hungry we can go up to the house and grab something for you."

"Okay, yeah. Is Dad coming back?"

"Not for a while probably," I tell him, hating to be so vague.

We end up entering the kitchen at the same time Bonnie is carrying in several finished flank steaks from the outdoor grill. She introduces us to a twentysomething-year-old guy named Jake, who is slicing tomatoes at the counter and then she helps me cobble together a plateful of items for Henry. I set him up at the kitchen table.

"You want a Coke with that?" I ask.

"My mom says I'm not supposed to drink soda with dinner."

"Why don't we make an exception tonight, since things are kind of crazy?"

"*Really?*"

The violation of house rules seems to brighten his mood, and while he digs into his dinner, I leave the kitchen in search of Keira. She's alone in the living room, perched on the edge of a chair.

"I haven't heard anything, have you?" I say.

"No, nothing."

I sense she's about to say more, but doesn't. Maybe she's annoyed we're stuck holding down the fort while Wendy is at ground zero.

I find myself exhaling, a long, raggedy breath that's been caught in my chest.

And then, nearly in unison, both our phones ring. Without thinking, I back a few steps into the front hall to answer mine. Gabe's name is on the screen, and my heart skips as I answer. All I hear from the other end is a low, guttural sound, like an animal in pain.

"Honey, what's happening?" I say. "Tell me."

"Oh god," he exclaims. "Mom didn't make it. She's dead, Summer."

10

M y knees buckle. *No*, I think. This can't be true. But
I hear my husband choke back tears and know it
must be.

"Oh, Gabe," I tell him. "I'm so sorry. Where are you—in
the ER?"

"Yeah. She had a whole team working on her, but they
couldn't save her. They said it was a massive heart attack."

I start to cry, the kind of hard cry that makes my shoulders shake, but I take a couple of fast breaths and force myself
to pull it together. My sobbing won't help Gabe a bit.

"What can I do?" I ask. "Want me to come down there?
I could take one of the cars that's still here."

"No, don't. I mean, it would be good to have you with
me, but there's no point. Blake and my dad are going to stay
for a while to handle the paperwork, but the rest of us are
heading home in a few minutes."

"Okay. How's your dad holding up?"

"He's still in a state of shock. I guess we all are."

"God, I, I—"

"I know," he says, his voice cracking. "It's so hard to grasp."

"What about Henry? You want to tell him yourself, right?"

"Yeah, I will as soon as I'm there."

"Okay, I'll see you in a little while. And call me if there's anything I can do between now and when you get home."

"Yup."

He hangs up, and as I stuff the phone into my pocket, I notice that my hand is trembling.

My poor husband. He may be in a state of shock now, but when reality sinks in, it will be shattering for him.

And for me, too. Claire's been such a key presence and positive force in our lives. We've spent so many hours in her company, not only here but back home in Manhattan, too.

I'm jostled from my thoughts by the sight of Keira moving toward me, holding her own phone in her hand, with a heightened watchfulness in her eyes. Maybe she's got the right approach to life. If you're always on alert, then you're better prepared for moments like this.

"Was that Gabe?" she asks.

"Yeah. You heard, too?"

She nods grimly.

"I can't believe it," I say. "I feel like I'm going to wake up in a little while and none of it will be true. . . . How did Marcus sound?"

"He's devastated, but he knows he has to stay strong for his dad."

"I'm sure Gabe is feeling that way, too."

"Are we supposed to *do* anything, call anyone?"

"Not for the time being, I'd say—What happened to Hannah, anyway?"

"I have no clue. I'm sure Nick will call her."

There's a trace of dismissiveness in her tone, suggesting she hasn't abandoned her concerns about Hannah and Marcus.

"I should tell Bonnie. She's putting together a cold buffet."

"It's hard to imagine anyone having an appetite tonight."

"True, but they'll still need to eat. By the way, Henry doesn't know yet. Gabe wants to be the one to tell him."

"Understood."

I make a move to return to the kitchen but catch myself. "How about you, Keira? Are you okay?"

Though I sense she's feeling a mix of shock and grief, I couldn't guess the ratio. From what I've gathered, she wasn't particularly close to Claire, but they seemed to like and respect each other.

"Yes, thanks for asking. I just feel so sad for Marcus— and for everyone, of course."

"Me, too. . . . I guess I'd better break the news to Bonnie. See you in a little while."

I return to the kitchen, but don't go past the doorway. Henry's still at the table, his little head bent over as he noisily drains his Coke with a straw. Bonnie looks up from a conversation with Jake, and I motion silently that I need to talk to her. She quickly steps into the dining room, closing the door behind us.

She breaks down when I tell her. "Poor Ash," she says, using the bottom of her apron to dab at her eyes. "Poor all of us. I can't imagine life without Claire."

"I know. Me, either."

"Does this mean she *did* have heart problems? She never said a word."

"Maybe she didn't know."

"Well, this week certainly didn't help." My face must have fallen, because she adds, "Oh, please don't take that the wrong way, honey. But you know how she was. She tried so hard to make everything perfect, and sometimes I think it stressed her out."

"I'm sure," I say, but I doubt being a gracious hostess this weekend stressed Claire out any more than normal. If there's any culprit, it's *Hannah*.

Bonnie dabs more tears away.

"Should I lay out the food in here?" she asks, indicating the sideboard. "I doubt anyone will want to eat on the patio."

I think she's referencing the mugginess, but how could any of us bear to eat under the pergola tonight, no matter how glorious the weather was? It's the place where Claire made so much joy happen—and it would be a harsh reminder of what's been wrenched away.

"Yes, in here is good."

My phone pings with a text and I glance down to see it's from Gabe.

Headed home now. Meet you at the cottage.

"You ready to head back?" I ask Henry once Bonnie and I are back in the kitchen. He's on the floor now with Bella and Ginger, and quizzing Jake about his canine knowledge.

"*Now?* We just got here. And Bonnie said I could have ice cream."

He's rarely whiny like this, and I know it's probably a sign he's picked up on the tension in the air. The dogs seem to sense it, too, looking up at me imploringly.

"You can bring it with you, okay?"

Henry shrugs in resignation, clearly confused, and I scoop the chocolate ice cream myself so that Bonnie can return to her dinner prep. As I do so, my gaze falls once again onto the row of empty vases on the side counter. Suddenly my mind catches on a memory from this morning, the faint sound of Claire in the garden behind the cottage, the snip-snip of flowers being clipped.

"What happened to the flowers Claire picked today?" I ask Bonnie.

She turns toward me, her face pinched. "Flowers? I don't think she got a chance to do any cutting today."

It must not have been Claire who I heard, then. Maybe it was a deer rooting through the garden and helping itself to the flowers. Claire always used to say they were the bane of her existence.

No more, I think woefully.

With the bowl of ice cream in one hand, and Henry's soft palm in the other, I lead him back to the cottage. He kicks stones absentmindedly along the path and watches them skip across the flagstone. My heart aches. In a matter of minutes, his small world will be turned upside down.

As I wait for Gabe on the couch in the sitting room, with Henry beside me, I realize how this is one of those pivotal moments in a marriage—when you have the opportunity to provide your spouse with the comfort he craves. I want to do the best job possible at that.

Before long I spot Gabe through the window, hurrying along the path. His shoulders are sagging, his expression heartsick. Leaving Henry to his movie, I pop out of the cottage, hurry toward my husband, and hug him tightly.

"Oh Gabe."

"It's totally surreal," he says, his lips against my hair. After a minute he pulls back. Every muscle in his face is taut, as if he's doing his damnedest not to sob. "Last night she's passing potato salad around the table and cutting a blueberry crumble, and now she's just gone. *Gone.*"

"Sit for a moment, will you?"

"Yeah, good idea," he says and collapses onto the wooden bench outside the cottage. "I need to pull myself together a little before I talk to Henry."

"Do you want to speak to him alone?"

"I think it might be best. Would you mind?"

"Not at all. But if there's anything I can do, just let me know."

"Thanks. I'm sure he'll need comforting over the next few days."

"We'll go back to the city for the service, right?"

"Uh, doesn't look that way. According to Dad, my mom made it clear over the years that she wanted a very private memorial service out here—for family, mostly." He snorts, sadly. "Oh, and get this. She told him she wanted one of those natural burials, where they put you in some kind of shroud and drop you in a hole in the ground."

"Well, it's not what we're used to, but it's fitting for someone who loved nature as much as she did. . . . So they think it was definitely a heart attack?"

"Yeah, looks like it."

"Had she ever had any heart issues?"

"Not that I knew of, but Blake told them in the ER that

she'd been on medication for high blood pressure—a diuretic and something called a calcium channel blocker. A couple of years ago, my mom had asked for his professional opinion about taking them."

"But those drugs didn't do their job?"

"It's not clear exactly what happened. Maybe she didn't take her meds religiously. The ER doctor said that she might have actually developed a pulmonary embolism that caused her heart to stop—or even had a stroke."

Gabe drops his head into his hands.

"Oh honey," I say, rubbing the back of his neck.

"It just doesn't make any sense. She looked so great over the weekend. Like she was in perfect health."

I don't want to upset Gabe any more than necessary but I decide it's best to mention what I'd noticed earlier. I bring up his mother's lack of interest in eating, the indication of fatigue, ordinary details that only with hindsight appear to be warning signs.

"And she told you she was going up to take a nap? What time was that?"

"Around two thirty."

"My mother *never* takes naps, so yeah, that clearly meant something." He shakes his head in despair. "If only she told one of us she wasn't feeling right."

"Maybe it didn't seem that significant at first."

Gabe releases a gust of breath.

"What?" I ask. I sense words on the tip of his tongue, perhaps a thought or emotion he wishes he could convey.

"I . . . I guess I'd better get to Henry."

"Just so you know, I didn't let on to him how serious the situation was, only that Gee was feeling unwell. But he seems to have picked up on the sadness in the air."

Gabe nods solemnly. "Why don't we meet you over at the house," he suggests as he rises from the bench. "My dad and Blake ended up leaving right after us."

When I enter the main house through the side door, it's Ash whom I spot first, standing at the end of the corridor that leads to the main hall. I care a lot for my father-in-law, but I've never been as close to him as Claire, and our typical friendly banter hasn't exactly prepared me for this moment. I gird myself, though, and rush forward.

"Ash, I'm so sorry," I say, tears springing into my eyes as I embrace him.

"Oh, sweetheart, I know you are." He holds me tightly. "Claire was crazy about you, you realize that, of course."

"Yes, I know. And the feeling was so mutual."

He nods. "Will you excuse me for a minute? I need to call my sister, Jean, and break the news, and I want to get it out of the way while I'm still standing."

"Of course."

I follow him down the corridor and as he veers right, probably pointed toward his study, I head to the dining room, where Gabe's brothers are milling around with Wendy, Keira, and Hannah, who's surfaced again, now wearing a somber look. A few people have helped themselves to food, others just to wine. I embrace each of my brothers-in-law, without bothering to stifle my tears. Marcus and Blake seem to be trying hard to hold themselves together, while Nick's eyes are rimmed with red. As soon as I release him from a hug, Hannah snakes an arm possessively around his waist again. Maybe I should remind her I already have a Keaton and I'm not in the market for a second one.

Still, I have to applaud her acting skills. The corners of her deep brown eyes are turned down, and so are the ends of her mouth, as if she's devastated on Nick's behalf—and her own, too. And her straight-backed posture suggests she feels she has every right to be standing smack in the middle of our group, grieving, even though most of us have known her for only two days.

Does she have any idea, I wonder, *that the stress she subjected Claire to might have played a role in her death?* Doubtful. Hannah's got too big of an ego for a thought like that. She might even be secretly gloating over the fact that she's been handed a get-out-of-jail-free card after her stern talking-to by Claire last night. There must be just one niggling worry: that Ash is wise to whatever Claire threatened her about.

"Here you go, love," Blake says to Wendy, handing her a large glass of sparkling water. "You need to stay hydrated."

"Thanks," she says. She looks not only sad but tense, making me wonder if she's second-guessed her decision to have accompanied people to the hospital. That kind of stress can't be good when you're newly pregnant.

"How's Henry doing?" Blake asks, directing his attention to me.

"Gabe's telling him now. I'm sure he'll be really upset."

"She was an incredible grandmother. It's terrible to realize that our own child will never meet her," he says, looking at Wendy.

And neither, I think, *will the ones I hope to have with Gabe.*

"I'm glad she learned about the baby, Blake," I say. "It must have made her so happy."

"I only wish I'd gotten to her sooner today," he says, taking the conversation in a different direction. "God knows how long she lay there while we were all outside the house, including my dad and the dogs."

"I saw her around two thirty in the kitchen, and she said she was going up for a nap. So maybe she'd come downstairs right before you found her."

He nods soberly.

"I should probably force myself to eat a little something," Wendy interjects. "And then go to bed."

"Yes, sweetheart, I think that's best," Blake tells her. "Make sure you get some protein, and let me know when you're ready to head to the carriage house."

Wendy starts off toward the sideboard, and my phone pings again. When I see it's a text from Gabe, I excuse myself and step aside to read it.

H is pretty upset. Gonna stay for a while, help him fall asleep. Can you relieve me in a bit so that I can head back over to the house?

Of course. I'll be back soon.

I say good night to everyone, and after smearing a wedge of blue cheese onto a piece of bread to go, exit the way I came. It will take Gabe a while to get Henry to sleep, so I linger in the dusk along the path, admiring Claire's large garden near the boxwoods. The landscape people who work the property will continue to maintain everything, but as certain plants die, they'll be replaced with less imaginative choices, and these gardens are bound to lose their uniqueness before too long. Over the next day or two, I decide, I'll take pictures of them with my phone so I can capture them as they are right now.

When I reach the cottage, I round the building to the little patio in the back. The border garden here is much smaller than others on the property, but no less enchanting. I pause in the fading light, admiring the ingenious mix of bold and subtle colors, soft and thorny textures.

There are definitely some flowers missing from it, though. I stare at a small, ragged gap in the garden, one, I realize, that a hungry deer couldn't actually be to blame for. As Claire always told me, deer usually gobble blossoms, not the stalks, too. The missing flowers appear to have been clipped off at the very base.

I step closer. The flowers surrounding the gap are foxgloves, tall stems lined with purple, trumpet-shaped blossoms. Which means the missing ones must be foxgloves, too.

How weird, though. Because as I heard Claire tell Hannah, foxgloves shouldn't be used in bouquets. They're deadly to animals. And to humans, as well.

11

I n the fading light, it's hard for me to see. Slipping my phone from my pocket, I activate the flashlight and direct it toward the stumps of the missing flowers, then run the beam over the surrounding clusters of foxgloves to get a closer look at their stalks. It's pretty clear that they match up.

Since Claire would never have picked the foxgloves herself, someone else must have. But why? They're *poisonous*. Unless . . . My skin crawls. Unless someone picked them *because* they're poisonous.

That's crazy, I tell myself. No one here at the house would choose to hurt someone else. Unless they secretly despised that person, or felt threatened by them.

Well, Hannah has surely felt threatened lately, right? *You do the right thing—or I will.*

No, it's not possible, I chide myself again. There's got to be another explanation for the missing flowers. Maybe someone who didn't know better clipped them for a bedroom arrangement.

A soft neighing sound startles me, and I nearly drop

the phone. Tightening my grip, I spin around and point the beam outward. All I can see are yards and yards of lawn, and farther away, shrubbery bleeding into the edge of the woods. The neighing comes again, plaintive this time, and I realize it's from high up in one of the trees. It must be a screech owl, a sound Marcus identified for me once.

I quickly snap a photo of the gap in the flowers and scurry around to the front of the cottage. As I swing open the front door, Gabe's emerging from the stairwell.

"Was that you in the back of the cottage just now?" he asks. "I thought I heard someone."

"Yeah, it was only me."

"What were you doing?"

"I was taking a look at the gardens and thinking of your mom. And all the magic she created."

Gabe nods, walks over to the butler's table in the sitting room, and grabs a bottle of red wine. "The gardens, the house, the ambience, *everything*," he says, uncorking the bottle. "I can't imagine how it's all going to exist without her."

"Oh, Gabe, I know. Your mother was so remarkable."

He looks off, and though I sense he's about to elaborate, he doesn't.

"What?" I ask.

"Nothing. Frankly, I'm at a loss for words tonight. It all still seems so surreal to me." He pours us each a goblet of wine.

Should I mention the missing foxgloves? I wonder, then decide against it. Suggesting, without any evidence, that his mother might have been poisoned would be on par with telling him I suspect she died from the bite of a vampire bat. Besides, I'm clearly wrung out from everything that's happened, and tomorrow there's bound to be a totally rational explanation staring me in the face.

Gabe plops down on the couch to drink his wine, where I join him.

"So tell me about Henry," I say. "It must have been so hard to break the news."

"I wish I'd had time to google the right things to say, but I guess I did okay. At least I avoided stupid euphemisms, like 'She's in a better place' and shit like that."

"I'm sure you did a great job. Did he seem to get it?"

"I *think* so. Nine is probably a tricky age for fully processing this stuff. You're old enough to know that death is permanent, but you still don't quite understand it all."

"You're planning on having him stay for the memorial service, right?"

"Definitely. I called Amanda right before you came back and filled her in. I could tell she wasn't thrilled about the idea of Henry being here for the service, but I'm not going to let her pressure me out of it."

"I'm sure he'll be able to handle it," I say, thinking of how I attended my grandfather's funeral when I was ten and have always been glad that I did.

We sit in silence for a while, sipping our wine. Gabe appears misleadingly at ease—one leg stretched out across the coffee table and his hand dangling the wineglass—but with our bodies touching lightly, I can almost feel the emotions churn inside him. Grief, anguish, possibly anger at how unfair life can be.

"I know you need to get back over to the house," I say

after he's drained his glass. "I'll stay here with Henry. And please eat something, honey. Even if you don't feel hungry."

"Will do."

As soon as he leaves, I find myself with a sudden urge to phone my mom, to tell her about Claire and to hear the words of comfort I know she'll offer. But she and my dad go to bed early these days, and it wouldn't be fair to wake her. The call will have to wait until tomorrow.

I should probably try to read, but I'm too distraught about Claire to focus on a book. I'm also still unsettled by that gaping hole in the garden. I grab my laptop from the table and take it back to the couch with me. I know that it would be foolish to jump to any conclusions, and even worse to spout off to Gabe about it, but I can at least google *foxglove poisoning*, right?

I open the first link that pops up, a site devoted to dangerous plants, and there's no mincing of words. Foxgloves contain something called digoxin and can be extremely toxic—not only the flowers, but also the stems, leaves, and seeds. Over a century ago, small amounts of the plant were used for medicinal purposes, and later foxglove extract actually became the basis for the heart medication digitalis—though too high a dose can dangerously interfere with the electrical signals that keep the heart beating.

I quickly scroll down to the symptoms of foxglove toxicity: irregular or slowed heart rate; low blood pressure; rashes or hives; weakness or drowsiness; loss of appetite; stomach pain; vomiting, nausea, or diarrhea; blurred vision; headache; confusion; fainting.

Could this be what I observed in Claire today? She was

clearly tired, acting a little confused, and she didn't appear to have much appetite.

But I remind myself, these symptoms overlap with those of a woman having a heart attack. I snap my laptop shut. Going down this internet rabbit hole is not how I should be spending my time tonight.

I fill the next hour tidying up the cottage, checking twice on Henry, trying to read the news on my phone, and wishing I could dash over to the house. But what if Henry woke up, came downstairs, and found himself alone? I don't want to add any stress onto what he's already dealing with tonight.

Finally, the door creaks open and Gabe trudges in looking wearier than I've ever seen him. He has an update on the memorial service. It's going to be held on Tuesday morning at eleven here at the house, attended only by immediate family and Claire's closest friends, and followed by a simple outdoor luncheon that Bonnie will put together. Ash is also thinking of asking a meditation instructor friend of Claire's to offer a spiritual reading. As for the burial, that will most likely be Thursday, down by the lower woods where the stream is.

"There are probably a few other things I'm forgetting," Gabe says, "but my brain has stalled."

"No problem, honey. Let's go to bed."

We collapse onto the mattress, though not before I've mustered enough energy to switch on the AC.

Gabe sleeps fitfully through the night, moaning incoherently at times, and at six, after his constant thrashing's woken me for the third time, I slip out of bed and steal downstairs.

I feel more ragged than I did last night, and my heart's even heavier. So many hurdles loom ahead this week—

helping Gabe and Henry cope with their grief as well as dealing with my own, weathering the memorial service and burial. And there's still *Hannah* to contend with.

As if caught in an undertow, my thoughts are dragged back to the missing foxgloves. I realize I won't be able to clear my mind until I've discovered where they went. Maybe someone who didn't know better really did clip them for a bedroom bouquet. Unlikely, but in order to eliminate that as a possibility, I'll have to figure out an excuse to snoop around, especially in the carriage house. After a couple of seconds, I come up with one.

I'm setting out breakfast when the stairwell door creaks open, and Henry pads into the kitchen, wearing his Incredible Hulk pajama top with the matching green shorts.

"Hey, Hen."

"Morning. Is it still true? Is Gee dead?"

"Yes, honey." I wrap my arms gently around him. He smells that lovely rumpled way kids do in the morning. "I'm so sorry."

"I don't want her to be gone," he says, sinking into my embrace.

"I know. We're all going to miss her so much."

"Does this mean we won't have a vacation?"

"No, we can still stay here. And though you'll feel sad, you can do the things you planned on—like swim and play with the dogs. In fact, the dogs look really sad themselves, so the more you hang with them, the better."

I fix him a slice of peanut butter toast and let him play *Subway Surfers* on my phone until Gabe materializes, bleary-eyed and barefoot.

"Morning," he murmurs.

"Morning," I say and give his arm a squeeze. "Did you get much sleep?"

"A few hours." He turns toward Henry, who's immersed in the game. "Buddy, give me a hug, okay?"

Henry obliges with an extra-long one, and when he finally pulls away, Gabe settles at the table, too. I pour him a cup of coffee.

"You need anything else?" I ask. "I thought I'd go over to the house now and check what's happening in the kitchen."

"Nah, I'll probably just have coffee anyway."

I come up behind his seat, wrap my arms around his chest, and kiss the top of his head. "I love you, honey."

"Me, too. I'm so glad you're here."

When I reach the main house a few minutes later, I enter through the side door rather than the kitchen and immediately do a lap through the downstairs, hunting to see if foxgloves have somehow ended up in a bouquet on a table or shelf. Other than a mason jar filled charmingly with rosemary, sage, and mint in the powder room off the main hall, there's not a vase in sight.

The one first-floor room I don't inspect is the study because the door is closed, meaning Ash is most likely ensconced in there. As I start to back away, I pick up the deep timbre of his voice, and I assume he's on a phone call. But then, after a pause, I hear another voice, which I think belongs to Blake. It makes sense that he'd be the one Ash is relying on—he's the oldest child and plays that role—but I hope Gabe isn't going to be excluded from chunks of the memorial planning, or the twins, either.

As I'm returning to the front hall, I spot Keira descending the staircase from the second floor, dressed in crisp pants and with her hair pulled back in a low ponytail. *Good*, I think, *this saves me from having to find an excuse to knock on her bedroom door.*

"Morning," we say in unison, each offering a wan smile.

"How's Marcus doing today?" I ask.

"He's really suffering. I'm sure Gabe is, too."

"Definitely. It's all so out of the blue. By the way, I was thinking of putting some flowers out, like Claire did. Do you want any in your bedroom? Unless you already picked some for it."

She looks befuddled. "I didn't think we were supposed to pick them. But I hate the smell of flowers in a bedroom anyway."

"Okay, sure, just asking."

"Speaking of Marcus, did you see him down here by any chance? He left the room a while ago and hasn't come back."

Oh, great, don't tell me he's off canoodling with Hannah again.

"No, sorry. But if I run into him, I'll let him know you were looking for him."

My next stop is the kitchen. I find Bonnie working on her usual eight cylinders, though she looks frayed around the edges and her short blond hair is frizzed from the heat. Jake's there, too, and politely asks if I'd like an omelet.

"No, Jake, breakfast here is always a continental buffet, okay?" Bonnie tells him over her shoulder. "There's no omelet stand." She returns her attention to me, wiping her brow with the back of her hand. "How you doin' today, hon?"

"Surviving, I guess." I wander over to the dog beds and give the glum-looking Ginger and Bella each a pat. "How about you?"

"Still in a state of shock, but I'm trying to stay strong for Ash's sake."

I nod. "We really appreciate that, Bonnie. Do you have all the help you need?"

"I think I'm covered. I've got Jake on board for the rest of the week, and as far as the meals go, I'm going to follow the menus Claire and I planned out."

"What about food for the luncheon tomorrow?"

"Ash told me to use my own judgment. I figured I'd serve sliced roasted turkey breast and some salads, including a pasta one Claire especially liked. And I rented extra tables and chairs from the place we always use for big parties."

"That all sounds perfect. Can I do anything?"

"When you get the chance, can you eyeball the lawn and decide on the best spot for the tables?"

"Of course. You know what else I think I'll do today? Deal with the vases Claire never got around to filling yesterday and then distribute them around."

"That's a nice idea," she says.

"I know my arrangements will pale utterly to what Claire would have done," I add, pouring it on a little thick, "but at least there'll be flowers in the house."

"Yes, good point. You know, don't you, only to take them from the cutting gardens?"

"Yup. Just one last thing. Are these all the vases there are?"

Bonnie looks over and silently counts each one off with a nod of her head.

"I think that's it," she says.

With three vases in my arms, I make my way next to the potting shed near the eastern end of the house, not far from the garage and the carriage house. It's a simple wood structure, used as a work space and storage area for gardening supplies, though it also seemed to be a kind of sanctuary for Claire, and one she was nice enough to welcome me to. As soon as I step inside, the familiar smell—a sweet, ripe mix from clay pots and bags of soil—comes at me like a punch, triggering another spasm of sadness.

I set down the vases on one of the unfinished wood counters lining the walls, and my eyes quickly fall on the gardening gloves lying nearby. They're still puckered a little from the last time Claire wore them, as if anticipating her return. The sight of them is almost unbearable.

Since I've promised Bonnie I'm going to fill all the vases, I have no choice but to follow through, but my priority right now is to inspect the carriage house, and I only need a single vase for that purpose. After snatching a pair of cutting shears from a hook on the wall, I hurry outside to one of the nearby cutting gardens, quickly clip a mixed assortment of flowers, and return with them to the shed. With little attention to design, I stuff all the flowers into a vase. Henry could have probably done a better job, but I don't have the time to fuss.

I'm halfway down the path to the carriage house when I notice Wendy emerge from the doorway.

"How you doing this morning?" I ask when we meet up. She looks as if she slept as poorly as I did.

"It's a nightmare, isn't it?" she says. "I'm just trying to go easy, not stress out too much."

"That sounds wise. Listen, I was planning to drop off this arrangement in the carriage house. Are there any already there, do you know?"

"How nice of you. I don't think we have any—oh, wait, there's a jar of fresh herbs in our bathroom."

"Okay, I'll find a spot for these then. Is anyone still inside?"

"Blake is up at the big house with his dad, and Nick and his lady must have gone to breakfast. I heard their door shut a little while ago."

Good, I think, *I can get into her room*, and then I notice Wendy's mouth morph into a faint grimace.

"What?" I ask.

"It's just a shame that in the middle of this, we have to deal with that . . . that interloper."

Oh wow, however bad the timing, this is an opportunity I didn't see coming. "Did something happen with Hannah—besides her hijacking your announcement?"

"Between us girls? I'm not so sure that I like her. For one thing, I think she made up her experience with dressage. I asked her a question about it yesterday at the pool, and she clearly had no idea what I was talking about. Totally clueless."

"Why would she have done that? To ingratiate herself with you?"

"That's my guess. I bet that Nick told her about my interest and she researched it before she came out here."

"How strange," I say, keeping my tone casual. "I wonder what that says about her."

"Me, too. Hopefully Nick will catch his breath and take some time to figure her out before they set a date. Sorry, I should stop. I don't want to sound like a total bitch."

I hardly fault her for it. In fact, I'm relieved she's gone from simply being offended by Hannah's action the other night to spotting the cracks in her facade.

"No, I hear your concerns," I say, before we wish each other good-bye and continue in opposite directions.

Though I saw the renovation of the carriage house in process, this is my first glimpse of the final results, and they're impressive. It's double-heighted downstairs, a great room with an open living and dining area and a small separate kitchen at the far end. The couch and chairs are comfy looking, and there are a few antiques scattered about, echoing the style of the main house, but the overall design is modern. I scan the space, confirming that there are no flowers anywhere, unless I count the framed botanical prints on the wall.

After taking a quick peek out the window to make sure no one is coming along the path, I carry the vase up the stairs to the open landing that runs the width of the house. There are two doors, which, if I remember the plans correctly, each lead to an en suite bedroom. I twist open the handle of the first one and slowly push it open until I notice Wendy's Louis Vuitton duffel bag on the whitewashed bench at the end of the bed. I close the door and inch down the landing until I've reached the next room. The only sound besides my shallow breathing is from a bird outside one of the windows chirping "Peter, peter, peter." I slowly twist the handle and ease the door open.

The room is nearly identical to Blake and Wendy's, though one side of it is strewn with shoes, shorts, and T-shirts that obviously belong to Nick. The cloying scent of Hannah's patchouli-vanilla mix still clings to the air.

I scan the room. There aren't any flowers in here, either, which means neither Hannah nor Nick stupidly picked the foxgloves and stuffed a vase with them. As I start to back out into the hallway, ready to beat a retreat, I hear the soft tread of footsteps. I swivel in place, and my heart skips as I see Hannah standing at the top of the stairs.

"Looking for me?" she asks, raising a thick, perfectly groomed eyebrow.

"Yes. I mean, sort of. I've been dropping off flowers this morning."

For a moment she says nothing, simply takes me in with her eyes, which in the dimness of the landing seem coal black, not brown.

Her lips swell briefly into a pout and then she opens her mouth. "Don't you know it's not nice to go into someone's room without their permission?"

I feel my chest flush, followed by my cheeks, like there's a red tide surging up through my body. "I wasn't going *into* the room. I was planning to set the flowers inside the door." I shrug, a pathetic attempt at nonchalance. "But I can hand them to you instead."

"If you don't mind, actually, I'll pick my own."

"Fine." Get out of here, I command myself. *Shut up and leave.* But I can't resist. "Be careful, though. Some of the flowers around here are poisonous and shouldn't be brought into the house. Like foxgloves."

"Thanks, I didn't know that," she says, her expression even. "I'll keep it in mind."

That's one more lie she's told me.

12

Hannah stares straight at me, unblinking, committed to this falsehood. I think of Billy's comment—that Hannah Kane has ice in her veins.

"If you'll excuse me," I say, "I'm going to do some more deliveries."

She doesn't hug the wall to let me pass, just swivels her torso an inch or so to the left. As I edge past her, I'm unable to avoid contact, and the bare skin of my arm brushes unpleasantly against hers. I also detect a whiff of cigarette smoke. Hannah clearly has a bad habit that she's hiding from the rest of us.

As soon as I descend the stairs, I hear a soft click, her bedroom door closing behind her. I wonder if she's smiling. Because it must absolutely delight her that she's unnerved me—and I'm not a good enough actress to disguise the fact.

"Couldn't find any place to put them?"

Again, I'm caught by surprise. This time it's Wendy, standing a foot or so inside the front door, holding an orange. I must look like an idiot, still lugging the fucking vase around.

"Sorry, I'm operating in a daze today," I say. I set the vase down on a side table with a soft thud. "I guess this spot is as good as any."

"Did I hear you talking to someone?"

"Yes, Hannah's back."

"Ahh. Well, thanks for the flowers."

I end up taking the long way back to the cottage, doing a sweep down beyond the pool and across the bright green lawn, and gnawing at one of my cuticles. It's clear to me now that the missing foxgloves aren't anywhere on the property, that no one clipped them for a bouquet, unaware that they're toxic. So perhaps someone—and Hannah's name is at the top of my list—*did* do something horrible with them. Like kill Claire.

No, that's *insane,* I admonish myself. Claire had high blood pressure and there's no proof she died of anything but a heart attack. And maybe Hannah was so busy kissing up during the garden tour that she didn't pay attention to what Claire was actually saying about various plants. Besides, even if Hannah *is* some kind of sociopath, as Billy insinuated, how could she have pulled off poisoning Claire? She could hardly have tucked a few blossoms into Claire's sandwich on Sunday because she would have noticed them. And, in fact, Claire didn't even eat her sandwich that day.

I have to calm down and step away from the vehicle. There must be an explanation for the missing foxgloves that I'm too wired to see.

And more than anything right now, I need my mom. I fish my phone from my pocket and call her cell.

"Oh, Sara, hi," she says. "What a nice way for me to start a Monday."

After I launched my acting career and started referring to

myself as Summer, my dad came on board, but my mother has never switched over, and I've tried not to mind it too much.

"Hey, Mom, nice for me to hear your voice, too. You and Dad good?"

"Yes, and I was actually about to call *you* today. We were driving to some friends' house last evening and heard a commercial for sunscreen on the radio. We're positive it was your voice."

"A sport cream, paraben-free?"

"I believe so, though I have no clue what paraben is."

"Yup, that was me."

"Oh, what a kick for us. I may have to even go out and buy some now."

"That's so sweet of you, Mom. But actually, there's a specific reason for my call today."

I blurt it out then, trying not to blubber as I do. Because the Keatons live in Manhattan, I've spent more time with them in recent years than with my own parents, and I don't want my mom to think that I was closer to Claire than to her—because I wasn't.

"Goodness, no," she exclaims. "Oh, Sara, this must be so hard for Gabe. And for you, too."

"Yes, everybody's very shaken."

She peppers me gently with questions, and once I've told her what I know, she says how sorry she is. "Dad and I will come down to New York for the funeral, of course."

I explain that the service is being held here in Bucks County and for only immediate family. A brief silence follows, and I sense she's hurt.

"I would love to have you and Dad here," I add. "But I

want to respect Ash's wishes. Wendy's and Keira's parents won't be here, either."

"I understand," she says. "For some families, a small service works best."

"I'd better go," I tell her. "But I'll call in a day or so and fill you in."

"Let us know if there's any way we can help, honey."

"Will do." I'm about to say good-bye when I catch myself. "Mom, just one more thing. Do you have any words of wisdom on the right way for me to support Gabe right now?"

"That's such a good question, Sara. I . . . I would say that the best thing you can do is follow his lead, and sense what he needs from you rather than simply deciding. And don't tell him how he feels or *should* feel."

My heart aches a little. I know she's basing her advice not only on her experience as a social worker, but also on how people treated her when my brother, Leo, died.

"Thanks, Mom, that's very helpful."

After signing off, I mull over her advice, still making my way to the cottage. My mother's words remind me of a lesson they pound into your head in drama classes: the best acting is *reacting*, really listening to the other actors and responding to them instead of constantly focusing on the line you're supposed to say next.

Have I been doing that with Gabe? *Mostly*, I think.

Stepping inside a minute later, I discover a note from him saying that he and Henry have taken the dogs for a walk again, which sounds like a perfect way to normalize things. I serve myself the remaining coffee from the carafe and wander with the mug into the sitting room, where my laptop is still on the table. It seems to shoot me a withering look that says, *Your play's not going to get any better if all you do is sit on your ass*, so I plop down and hover the cursor over the document. But I don't open it. Instead, I google two words for the second time: *foxglove poisoning*.

Since the missing flowers aren't in a vase somewhere on the property, it suggests someone had a plan for them that wasn't decorative. But just because foxgloves are toxic doesn't mean it's easy to poison someone with them. If the process is really complicated, and unlikely for someone here to have pulled off, then I can quit obsessing. Needless to say, there's no post titled "How to Poison Someone with Pretty Purple Plants from Your Garden," so I start reading some of the additional posts on dangerous plants to see what turns up.

It doesn't take long for me to learn that over the years foxgloves have definitely been linked to homicides. Plus, there were instances of accidental poisoning back in the day when the plant was used medicinally because it was hard for medical practitioners to get the dosage right.

Accidents have also occurred more recently, and not from an incorrect dosage. It says in one of the posts that the leaves of the foxglove plant have been mistaken for comfrey, a plant from the borage family that's sometimes used to make tea.

To make *tea*. I sit up stick straight as an image flashes in my mind. The pitcher of herbal iced tea that Claire drank from nearly every day during the summer. The one that was sitting on the kitchen island the last time I spoke to her.

Could Claire have accidentally poisoned *herself*? Would she have mistaken foxglove leaves for borage—whatever the hell that is? It seems impossible, given her expertise with plants.

But someone could have brewed poisonous tea *for* her.

My pulse racing, I keep scrolling, and deep into another post, one from a medical journal, I find this: "An unusual side effect of digoxin is a disturbance of color vision (mostly yellow and green) called xanthopsia. Van Gogh's 'Yellow Period' may have somehow been influenced by concurrent digitalis therapy. . . . Evidence of his use is supported by multiple self-portraits that include the foxglove plant."

Again, I picture the main kitchen as it was during my very last conversation with Claire: the curtains oddly closed on a sunny day, the lights off. And then there was her final question: "Have you colored your hair lately, darling? It looks lighter to me this weekend."

I choke back a sob.

Frantically, I google heart attack symptoms again to refresh my memory. A few *are* similar to the ones associated with digitalis poisoning, like nausea and tiredness, but there's no mention of distorted vision—the green or yellow halo effect. Was Claire's vision yellowed because she'd been poisoned with digoxin?

Finally, I search for *digitalis*. Though the drug is still prescribed in certain instances for heart problems, there are newer meds now. In one of the posts is yet another detail that makes my breath quicken: An overdose of digitalis is more likely to be fatal if a person's potassium levels are low. And one cause of lowered potassium levels is the use of a diuretic.

Which Claire was taking for her high blood pressure.

If someone intent on murdering her knew what drugs she'd been prescribed, they were probably aware that the diuretic improved their chances of success.

I snap the laptop closed and stand up. There's something I need to do in the main house before Gabe and Henry return: Get my hands on the iced-tea jug Claire always used. If Claire *was* poisoned, maybe there are still traces of the toxic tea.

I swing open the front door, and to my surprise, Nick is on the other side, dressed in a weathered Bucknell T-shirt and shorts, his arm raised as if ready to knock.

"Oh, Summer, gosh," he says. "You look distraught. Give me a hug."

"Thanks, Nick," I tell him as we quickly embrace. "I *am* distraught."

"Totally understood. You and my mom had such a great connection."

As we pull apart, I notice that his eyes are bloodshot, suggesting he's had his share of crying jags since yesterday.

"Your mom was so generous. I bet a lot of people feel that way."

"No, the two of you had a special bond." He flashes one of his trademarked half-cocked grins. "In fact, you're part of the reason I felt so comfortable bringing Hannah out here and sharing the news about our engagement. I knew my mom clearly had a soft spot for actresses."

Nothing in his words or demeanor suggests that he had any clue about Claire's reservations regarding Hannah or that he's aware of their confrontation. I work at keeping the smile on my face as he goes on. "Of course," he adds, "she also loved how bighearted you are."

"That means a lot, Nick. Though for a bighearted person, I haven't even asked how *you're* doing."

"Miserable. I still can't believe it's true. It hit me this

morning that my mom won't be there for my wedding. But Hannah and I will get through it. We have to."

I can barely meet his eyes, but I nod. "I'm sure you will."

"Hey, is Gabe around? I was hoping to grab a few minutes with him."

"He and Henry are walking the dogs, but they should be back before long. Is there anything I can help you with?"

"Uh, no, I can drop by later, I guess." He scrunches his handsome face, clearly deliberating. "There *is* one thing that maybe I could ask you, though."

"Shoot. Anything, Nick."

"Is Gabe pissed at me?"

"*Pissed* at you?" I say, caught off guard. "Of course not. What reason could he possibly have?"

"You heard about how my father turned him and Marcus down for money?"

It clicks. Ash had justified his choice by saying that he'd already been generous to Gabe and Marcus and now it was Nick's turn, and Nick clearly feels guilty.

"I'm sure Gabe doesn't fault you for that. It was your dad's decision, after all."

He drops his eyes to the ground, kicks at a stone with his Top-Sider. "Yeah, Dad's decision—partly," he says looking back at me. "But apparently mostly my mom's. She was the one who told Dad that it wasn't fair to me, and I needed a turn."

I stare at him, hiding my confusion. Gabe hadn't mentioned that his mother had been part of the decision-making process related to the wine business. To my knowledge, in fact, she'd never been involved before. "How do you know this?"

"Marcus told me that Dad admitted it at their meeting, after Gabe and Marcus prodded. You hadn't heard?"

I shake my head.

"Gabe probably didn't want to throw my mom under the bus. Can you act surprised when he brings it up? I'm sure he will at some point."

"Okay," I say, still reeling a bit. I can't believe Claire would have stopped Ash from helping Gabe and Marcus, simply because it violated some previously unknown protocol she'd established about how much they should support each son financially.

"And I'll talk to him when we get a chance," he says. "I just feel so bad that this happened right before she died."

"I'm sure Gabe put it all into perspective," I say.

Nick looks stricken. "No, he was upset with her, Marcus told me. Really upset. He didn't know why she'd do something like that."

For a moment, I can't even think how to respond. Is this what Gabe was about to tell me as we sat on the bench outside the cottage? It must be eating at him, the idea that his mother died while he was so angry with her.

"Um, well, yes, do talk to him about it, Nick. He'll be around later."

He hugs me again then takes off down the path at a sprint. I give him a minute to put a little distance between us and then start off for the house myself, noticing how warm the day's gotten. It must be in the mideighties by now.

I enter the house through the kitchen. Jake's alone in there, scooping tuna salad onto slices of bread.

"Hi again," I say. "Is Bonnie around?"

"She ran upstairs to make the beds."

"Okay, I'll futz around here until she gets back."

He returns to his task and I begin the one I came for. Though the kitchen has always been Bonnie and Claire's domain, I've never felt it was off-limits to me. I swing the fridge door open, but there's no iced tea on any of the shelves. I proceed to a cabinet at the far end of the kitchen and scan the inside. No jug there, either. Okay, it's got to be someplace else in the room. I'm pivoting on my heels when Bonnie enters the room, clearly a little winded.

"You need something, hon?" she asks.

"Actually, yes." I wish I didn't have to burden her with another task, but it's important. "I was looking for the jug Claire always used for her iced tea."

"There's iced tea out on the patio already."

"Okay, thanks, but as silly as this sounds, I was hoping to use Claire's jug and make some herbal tea. For, you know, sentimental reasons."

"Sure," she says agreeably enough. "We actually keep it in here."

I trail behind her into the pantry, where she tugs open a long cupboard I've never looked inside before. One of the interior shelves is lined with nine or ten pitchers and jugs, some glass but also ceramic ones in the shape of things like peaches, oranges, rabbits, and monkeys.

I watch her sweep the collection with her eyes, absentmindedly fingering the small gold cross she wears around her neck.

"That's odd," she says. "It's not here anymore."

13

Shaking her head, Bonnie lingers before the shelf, obviously perplexed. This is her turf, and the mystery has snagged her attention. With her brow furrowed, she closes the door of the cupboard and pulls open another one. And another.

"For Pete's sake, where'd it go?" she says. "I'm sorry, Summer. Someone's clearly using it."

"When was the last time you saw it?" My heart's thrumming from what all this might mean.

"It was upside down on the drainboard when I came back from my break yesterday. Claire must have washed it before she left the room."

Her face clouds as she speaks. A short time later, of course, she would find Claire writhing on the living room floor.

"But what would someone be using it for?" I say.

She shrugs. "Maybe they wanted water in their bedroom. I'm sure it will turn up at some point."

Will it? I mean, the pantry is nearly bursting with a brigade of fruit- and animal-shaped alternatives, so why would anyone take the container Claire used, unless they wanted to be sure it couldn't be found?

"Okay, I'll have regular iced tea for now. . . . Bonnie, can I ask you one more question?" I lower my voice, and she observes me quizzically. "When you found Claire yesterday—do you think she'd just come downstairs from a nap? Or do you suppose she'd never gone up?"

I've been wondering that ever since last night.

"Gosh, Summer, I don't have any idea."

"Why, if she wasn't feeling well, do you think she would have gone into the living room instead of coming out here and trying to find help?"

Her face contorts in anguish. "Maybe she was looking for Ash in his study. To tell you the truth, it's too tough for me to even think about."

I feel guilty making Bonnie relive the tragedy, but I need to in order to figure things out. "I understand. And I'm sorry to bring it up. I only hope she wasn't suffering for too long."

"I know; me, too."

I start to exit the house by the kitchen door, but a glance out the window reveals Keira and Marcus standing on the patio, their faces grim. He shakes his head, not angrily but with a firmness that says she's wrong about something or that he's not going to change his mind. There's no way I'm going to intrude on the moment.

But I need a quiet place to think. I slip into the dining room and follow the long corridor to the eastern end of the house. Once I reach the screened-in porch, I settle on one of the wicker couches and exhale.

Okay, let's say that the terrifying theory I've been toying

with is really true and Claire was poisoned to death by a drink made from foxgloves. How would the tea have been brewed? I wonder. The killer must have dried out the leaves from the plant after they'd been picked. But where? An oven seems like the only possibility given the tight time frame, though using the oven in this kitchen would have been too risky with everyone around. And *yet* . . . it would have been easy enough to do during a quiet moment in the carriage house kitchen. The carriage house where Hannah is staying.

Once the leaves were dried and crumbled, the poisonous tea could have been made and substituted for Claire's daily iced tea, or possibly added to it. Thinking it through, the latter makes more sense to me, because the taste of the foxglove leaves would have been better disguised that way.

The trickiest part of the plan would have been adding the poison tea to Claire's jug without being observed because the kitchen here often resembles Grand Central Station at rush hour. Yet the room *wasn't* bustling on Sunday morning, was it? Claire was at the farmers' market, Ash was on a bike ride, and Bonnie was at church.

There would have been one more matter to deal with: the jug. Someone washed it and placed it in the drainer after Claire drank the tea, and it probably wasn't her, since she was beginning to feel unwell. But then the jug was removed later. Did the killer decide it was smarter to get rid of it altogether?

I lean back against the couch pillows, bewildered. Though it's easy to imagine how someone might have orchestrated the poisoning, when I take a few steps backward, the whole idea seems preposterous, including the notion of Hannah as a poisoner. She might be a liar and thief but that doesn't make her a cold-blooded murderer. Right?

I glance at my watch. It's after noon. I want to check in on Gabe and Henry and I also need to find Ash, to see if he needs any help.

Shaking away thoughts of dried leaves and toxic tea, I wind my way back through the house into the front hall, where standing in a circle are Ash, all four sons . . . and also, with her back to me, Hannah. Exactly the person I'm trying to avoid.

She turns at the sound of my footsteps and to my surprise I discover it's not Hannah, after all, but Ash's executive assistant, who must have driven out here from the city this morning. Her hair is similarly dark and chin-length, and she's Hannah's height. Though her looks are striking, as well, she doesn't dazzle quite the same way Hannah does. Even I have to admit that.

"Sorry to interrupt," I say, beginning to retreat from the impromptu family conference that seems to be happening.

"No problem, dear," Ash says. "We're talking over plans for the service tomorrow."

"I've already discussed a menu with Bonnie," I say. "Is there anything else I can do?"

"That's kind of you, Summer. We seem to have things under control otherwise. You remember Jillian Herrera, of course."

"Yes, hi," I say, and she smiles in greeting. I've only met her a handful of times and know little about her beyond the fact she's in her early forties, recently divorced, and is supposedly very, very good at her job.

"Keira just took Henry down to the tennis court to hit a few balls," Gabe says.

"I'll relieve her in a bit," I tell him. "I want to head out to the patio and take care of one thing for the luncheon I promised Bonnie I'd do."

"Why don't I go with you, Summer?" Jillian says. "I can review a few details with you about the service."

She follows me out to the patio, where we have the space to ourselves. I motion for her to have a seat at the table.

"I'm so sorry for your loss, Summer," she says. She touches my arm, a warmer gesture than I'm used to with her. "I know everyone must be devastated."

"Yes, it's been brutal."

"I'm helping Ash coordinate as much as possible— writing the obit, alerting colleagues, inviting people to the service—but if there's anything you can think of, please let me know."

Though Jillian's title is executive assistant, her job is apparently broader than that. She not only ensures that Ash's work life runs smoothly, but I've been told she has her eye on the business, too, making certain that none of the spinning plates is about to drop and shatter. During the times I've been in her presence, she's been polite but no-nonsense, the kind of woman who seems to like everything just-so. I'm sure she keeps her panties rolled like little sausages in a paper-lined underwear drawer, but they're probably sexy, empowering panties from brands like Agent Provocateur.

"Nothing off the top of my head. How many people do you expect?"

"It will be only family and several friends of Claire's who

Ash felt we needed to include. And she has a cousin who apparently wants to fly in from Pittsburgh. I'd tell Bonnie to plan on about twenty-five people, not including the musical quartet we've hired."

Thirty. I understand the desire to keep the service intimate, and yet it seems like such a paltry gathering to celebrate the kind of life Claire led.

"And it's set for eleven A.M.?"

"That's right. After a short welcome from Blake, Claire's meditation teacher is going to do a reading, and then any friends or family members who wish to speak may do so."

"Um, okay." I hadn't even considered that there would be such an opportunity. *I'm sure Gabe will want to say a few words. Should I do the same?*

Before I can really think about it, Jillian asks what Bonnie plans to serve at the luncheon.

"Cold roast turkey?" she says with a wrinkle of her nose after I run through the menu.

"Bonnie does a great aioli sauce on the side. It's a really delicious combo."

Her expression is unchanged. "You know what might be lovely to add?" She taps her perfectly manicured nails on the wood table twice for emphasis. "Cold-poached salmon."

That seems like a pain for Bonnie, but Jillian works for Ash so I have to act reasonably receptive.

"I'll see if there's time for Bonnie to order or prepare one."

"Good. As for the event tomorrow afternoon, there's no need to make a fuss. But it might be nice to have coffee in the room."

"What's tomorrow afternoon?"

"When the lawyer reads the will. It needs to happen this week, and Ash prefers to have the reading done here at the house rather than making people troop into Manhattan and convene at the law office."

"Sure, we'll put coffee out," I say casually, though she's actually thrown me for a loop. This is the first I've heard about a will being read. Doesn't Claire's half of the estate simply go to Ash?

"Well, I think that's it then," Jillian says, all efficient again, and we rise in unison. "I should see what else Ash needs."

"Thanks for filling me in."

After she leaves, I survey the lawn per Bonnie's request, and as I'm deciding on the best spot to put the tables tomorrow, Keira and Henry come trudging toward me along the patio, Henry dragging his tennis racket so that it scrapes loudly on the flagstone. His cheeks are red, suggesting Gabe's forgotten to apply sunscreen. He looks a little sullen, too, as does Keira, making me wonder if he's not been his usual winning self with her on the court. She confided in me once that she and Marcus aren't planning to have kids, and she might not have had the patience to deal with Henry today.

"Hi guys," I call out. "Henry, please don't let your racket drag like that. It's not good for it."

"Where's Dad?" he asks.

"He's talking to your uncles and grandfather. Why don't you take a seat? Lunch should be out before long." I turn to Keira. "Thanks so much for lending a hand."

"Happy to," she says, staring over my shoulder. She's got that worried look again, though it suddenly dissolves. I follow her gaze to see Marcus rounding the house from the side, followed by Gabe and Nick. I try to catch my husband's eye, but he focuses all his attention on Henry.

"You okay, buddy?" Gabe asks him.

"I'm thirsty," he whines, sounding ready to bawl. "And hungry."

"Well, let's get you something to drink for starters."

People glumly begin serving themselves drinks from the sideboard, and moments later Bonnie and Jake emerge from the kitchen with a platter of sandwiches and wraps as well as bowls of pickles, olives, and fancy potato chips. When Bonnie's hands are free, I take her aside and suggest setting the tables under the maple trees tomorrow, since they'll provide shade while people are eating. I also mention Jillian's salmon idea. She nods, but looks understandably annoyed.

We take turns grabbing food and are soon joined by Blake and Wendy. Bonnie lingers to make plates for Ash and Jillian, who plan to eat while working in the study, she reports. And Nick mentions that Hannah won't be joining us. Apparently she's on a long call with her agent that couldn't be rescheduled.

I feel relieved to have a meal without her, and yet I can't help but wonder if the agent call is real. Maybe she's actually in hiding, agitated with worry. Could my comment about foxgloves have alerted her to my suspicions?

Stop, I chide myself once again. I have no proof whatsoever that Hannah's done anything wrong.

The group is smaller than usual and we make a stab at conversation—about how hot it is, about an article in the *New York Times*, about Claire's cousin from Pittsburgh whom only Blake remembers. But beneath the desultory chatter, I sense tension, a tautness that practically hums. Nick, I realize, barely glances in my direction. Is he sorry he shared his concerns with me earlier? And there's a chill coming off Gabe, as well. He could still be upset with Marcus about the vineyard news—and with Nick, too, as Nick himself suggested.

But halfway through the meal, I begin to suspect that some of the chill is directed *my* way. Each time I attempt to make eye contact with Gabe, his gaze pings off a split second later. Is he annoyed that I disappeared earlier, feeling that I'm not helping him enough?

Wendy excuses herself to call a client and for the first time it registers that this is *Monday*, a workday to the rest of the world. I haven't checked texts or emails today, and I need to do that. I can't afford to respond late if my agent has tried to book me for a voice-over job.

"Excuse me, too," I announce. "I'll be back in a couple of minutes."

I'm halfway to the cottage when I hear footsteps from behind, and I turn to discover Gabe trying to catch up with me.

"Where are you off to?" he asks, slightly out of breath and not very friendly. Maybe it's grief that's making him act sullen toward me.

"I'm just grabbing my phone to check messages. I won't be more than a minute."

He studies me, his brow wrinkled.

"And then I'll be glad to watch Henry as much as you need," I add. "Tomorrow morning, too, during the service. And later, when the meeting happens."

"Meeting?"

"Jillian said a lawyer is coming. To talk about the will."

"Oh, that. Right."

"There's not some issue, is there? I was kind of surprised when she brought it up."

"There's no issue," he says, brusquely. "My parents have a will in which the person who dies first leaves his or her half of the estate in trust to the surviving spouse. It's always been that way."

"Gabe, what's the matter? You seem, I don't know, slightly perturbed."

He folds his arms against his chest, briefly looks off, and then returns his gaze to me. This time he doesn't let go.

"Tell me honestly," he says. "Did you really sneak into Nick and Hannah's room this morning?"

14

Oh my god, Hannah tattled on me. What a bitch.

"Yes, I did go into their room," I tell him. "Well, not *into* it. I opened the door in order to set a vase of flowers on the floor. . . . Did she say something to you about it?"

"Nick did. Hannah found it really disturbing, and so did he. I don't get it, Summer."

"I was only trying to be *nice*, Gabe. No one answered my knock, and I decided to leave the vase in the room rather than lug it back downstairs." I hate being untruthful with Gabe, but I don't want to tell him why I was on a quest to find the missing foxgloves.

"Why not leave them outside the room?"

"I guess I didn't see any harm in opening the door for two seconds. It wasn't as if I expected to see bondage equipment in there, or bags of heroin."

I can tell from his expression that he doesn't appreciate my attempt at humor. And this isn't the time for it anyway.

"Look, I see your point," I say, switching gears. "I've

never viewed your parents' home as a place where we need to stand on ceremony, but Nick has someone new in his life, and I should have respected their privacy."

He studies me, obviously trying to assess how sincere I am.

"Okay," he says finally. "I'm glad you get it. You'd hardly want Hannah coming into *our* room uninvited, would you?"

"Of course not. Please tell Nick I'm sorry."

He nods. "See you back at the table then."

Frustrated, I hurry the rest of the way to the cottage. In the bathroom mirror I discover that I look as agitated as I feel. My face has turned lumpy and red, like I have a bout of diaper rash on my cheeks and chin, and my T-shirt is streaked with dirt from lugging around the vases earlier. I change into a new one, and press a cold wet washcloth to my face for a minute, then dab on a concealer and foundation.

Back downstairs I take a minute to peruse the small bookcase, loaded with volumes for weekend guests, and dig out a book of poetry by Mary Oliver. Thumbing through it quickly, I come upon "Why I Wake Early," the poem the collection takes its title from. I've decided that if Gabe feels comfortable with me speaking tomorrow at the service, I'll read this because Claire once told me it was a favorite of hers. It begins with the line, "Hello sun in my face," and goes on to talk about tulips and morning glories and how the sun holds us in its hands of light. It perfectly reflects Claire's love of nature.

Before I return to the patio, I bookmark the page with a scrap of paper and grab my phone from the charger in the kitchen. There are a bunch of emails and text alerts, but I don't start reading until I'm on the path. And that's when things get even shittier. The first text is from Shawna.

Hey, just a heads-up. They decided to re-record that story with another actor. Pls don't take this personally. They wanted the voice to sound a little older. Talk soon.

Oh, lovely. I couldn't manage to nail a job reading a story about two women taking the world's most boring road trip together—they don't even meet a hot drifter who steals their money, let alone drive their car into the Grand Canyon. Is Shawna being honest when she says we'll talk soon— meaning she'll book me for another recording? It's impossible to tell.

To my dismay, there are no requests for voice-over auditions from my agent, and the only other professional message in my in-box is from a Columbia University grad student who'd had me read twice for a student film he's directing. "Thank you for your time," he writes. "Unfortunately, we've decided to go in another direction." I've learned that "other direction" generally means they want someone younger, prettier, thinner, hotter, bigger boobed, shorter chinned (yup, I was told that once), or in their view, more talented. Or all the above.

I shouldn't let this stuff get to me, but it's impossible not to. And right now, it's piling on top of everything else—my sorrow over losing Claire, the mystery of the missing foxgloves and jug, to say nothing of the tension between me and Gabe.

By the time I return to the table, most of the diners have left, but Gabe and Henry are listlessly working on a bowl of cherries, and Blake's lost in thought. I imagine he might be struggling to make sense of his mother's death, wondering if there could have been a way to save her. I pick at what remains from the inside of my wrap.

When he comes out of his reverie, Blake looks at Gabe. "You up for smacking a tennis ball around?" I sense he's looking for distraction more than exercise.

"Man, I'd love that," Gabe says.

"But, Dad, I thought we were going to swim now," Henry says despondently.

"Um, you're right, buddy. Blake, how 'bout later?"

I flash back to the advice my mother offered earlier, about how important it is to sense what a loved one needs when they're grieving. And I know Gabe's been missing his regular get-togethers with Blake this past year.

"Honey, play tennis," I insist. "I'll hang by the pool with Henry, and you can come by when you're done."

"That would be great." He sounds appreciative, and I hope he's no longer miffed.

I send Henry off to change into his trunks, and by the time he's back, I've set up two lounge chairs with beach towels and grabbed us a couple of cans of sugar-free lemonade. For the next half hour, I watch him splash around in the pool and rate his handstands Olympic-style from one to ten. It's about as exciting as waiting in line at the DMV, but it seems to lift Henry's spirits.

I only wish there was something that could lift *mine*. Everything seems off without Claire here, and I've experienced a sense of mounting dread since I woke up. Right now, it's as hard to ignore as a toothache, and it's coupled with the embarrassment I feel about being caught going into Nick and Hannah's room. And the hot sun isn't helping.

As Henry performs what must be his fiftieth handstand, Wendy wanders onto the deck in a black one-piece bathing suit and flip-flops with the double Gucci G and settles into a lounge chair on the other side of the pool, iPad in hand. We wave at each other across the water. Watching her triggers a memory of the conversation we had earlier today about her dislike of Hannah. Maybe we can commiserate.

I convince Henry to take a break so I can apply more sunscreen on him and he can jiggle the water out of his ears. He's brought his own iPad from the cottage, and soon falls asleep on the lounge chair before he's read more than a page or two.

I round the pool to where Wendy's sitting.

"I'm not interrupting, am I?" I ask.

"No, no, please sit," she says, stuffing the iPad into her squishy leather tote. "And while you're at it maybe you can tell me how to develop the endless patience you have as a mom. You're brilliant at it."

"I appreciate the compliment," I say, lowering myself onto the chaise lounge next to her. She's gotten a light tan, which looks fetching with her pale blond hair. "And I wish I could say it came naturally to me, but it really has to do with Henry. He's always been such an easy, undemanding kid. Not sure how I'd handle a spoiled brat. Regardless, you shouldn't worry, Wendy. I know you and Blake will be fabulous parents."

"I hope so. I've wanted this baby for so long."

"Are you feeling any less stressed this afternoon?"

"Honestly? No. I'd kill for a glass of rosé right now, but that's not a possibility."

"I know how you feel." I break into a grin. "Tell you what—I'll drink a rosé for both of us later."

"Go for it."

"Hey, I wanted to ask you about something you mentioned earlier—the so-called interloper."

Wendy raises her pale blond eyebrows above the rims of her tortoise-framed Ray-Bans. "Have you had your own concerns?"

"Actually, yes. I recognized Hannah as soon as I saw her Friday night—we were in the same playwrights' showcase a couple of years ago. But she lied and said I was mistaking her for someone else."

"How strange. Why would she do that, I wonder?"

"I didn't know this at the time, but she supposedly stole money and jewelry from another actress in the showcase and I guess she didn't want me to connect the dots. I'm worried about what this means for Nick. For all of us, frankly."

"You've mentioned this to Gabe, I assume?"

"Yes, but he's got so much else on his mind, even before Claire died, and he hasn't taken it seriously."

She shifts a little in the chair, crossing her long, slim arms over her chest. "I'm not sure what recourse either of us has. Let's say you or I took Nick aside and confided in him. He's hardly going to send Hannah packing because she told a little white lie about dressage, or that you heard a rumor she stole something. And he'd probably resent us for interfering."

"What if it were more serious than that?"

"Serious how?"

On and off since Saturday night, I've replayed my conversation with Claire, and one phrase keeps echoing in my head: *Our little* USC *graduate.*

"It's possible Hannah lied about where she went to college."

"That's pretty shady."

"I know. It's not the kind of lie that could cause any real damage, but it says something about her character. . . . You spend a fair amount of time in Florida, don't you?"

She looks surprised. "What do you mean?"

"I just mean you do business there, right? Do you think there's a way to find out anything about Hannah's background—if her parents are both really dead, if she's even *from* there?"

Wendy looks off, seeming to mull over my request. "I can do a little digging. My gallery runs a background check on anyone we're considering doing a major transaction with— it's called KYC for 'Know Your Client.' I can ask my guy about Hannah and see what turns up."

"That would be great. I know it might seem like an extreme step, but I don't want Nick to find himself in a terrible situation one day."

"I don't, either."

"And would you mind not saying anything to Blake for the moment, since I haven't totally looped Gabe in?"

She nods. "Of course, understood. And speaking of Blake, I promised I'd watch him and Gabe play." She rolls her eyes. "He barely lets me out of his sight these days."

"I don't blame him. And thanks again, Wendy."

She propels herself off the lounge chair and no sooner is

she gone, descending the small hill to the tennis court, than I'm gripped by second thoughts. Did I make a mistake by involving Wendy? What if she talks to Blake and it gets back to Gabe, or worse, Nick?

No, it was the right thing to do, I tell myself. If Wendy finds out that Hannah's who she says she is, fair enough. And if she turns up incriminating information, it will help me make my case to Gabe.

Plus, Wendy is incredibly discreet. I know from the family grapevine that she's had her share of famous clients over the years and hasn't breathed a word about them. She's always struck me as someone for whom the pleasure is in having the secret all to herself and savoring it.

I drift back to my original lounge chair, and it's not long before Henry stirs. When a freshly showered Gabe joins us, we spend the next half hour or so playing gin. Blake appears at one point, dressed in swim trunks, and dives into the deep end of the pool and begins slicing through the water with perfectly synchronized stokes. From where I'm sitting, I have a view of the patio and I can see Keira, sunglasses perched on top of her head, perusing folders that are probably work-related.

In so many ways, everything appears absolutely normal. If Claire hadn't died, this might be exactly what we'd all be doing anyway—swimming, lounging, playing cards, reading at the table. But there's a pall over everything, like a smog thick enough to make it hard to breathe.

Eventually needing to pee, I decide to use the powder room in the main house, rather than walk all the way to the cottage. The door's locked, so I hang for a minute in the side corridor, leaning into the folds of slickers hanging from pegs. When the door opens, Keira emerges, having changed from her earlier shorts and top outfit into navy cotton pants and a crisp button-down. Her hair's a little wavier than usual, probably from the heat, and she's pulled it into a low ponytail.

"You headed someplace?" I ask.

"Marcus and I are driving into Doylestown in a few minutes," she replies, and I shudder inwardly hearing the name of the town where Claire died. "We're just going to walk around a little, get an ice cream cone."

Of course, there's a freezer in the house with about twenty-seven tubs of ice cream, all in different flavors, but my guess is that she needs a break from all of us.

"Sounds like a good diversion. Will you be able to stick around past Tuesday?"

"Yes, I'm staying all week now. Work was totally understanding about the situation, of course."

"I'm glad. It'll be good to have you here."

"Thanks, Summer, I appreciate that." She glances one way down the hall and then the other, as if making sure we won't be overheard. "You and I haven't actually gotten a chance to talk in the last day, and I was worried you might be upset with me."

That came out of left field. "Upset? Why?"

"Because of Marcus not telling Gabe right away about the mess at work. I know he was only trying to spare him unnecessary worry."

"Keira, I don't fault you for any of that. It's between the two of them, and they'll sort it out. I just hope they can find a way to get it under control in the midst of everything else they're coping with."

She bites her lip, as if there's more she wants to say but doesn't know how to broach it.

"What?" I ask.

"Maybe there'll be less to sort out now."

"I'm not following."

Before she can respond, our attention's diverted by the crunch of car tires on gravel coming from outside.

"Is Ash expecting someone else?"

"I think that's Jillian leaving. I saw her a few minutes ago and she said she was staying at that B&B along the river so she won't have to drive all the way back from the city to-morrow for the service. You know what, I should get going myself. I told Marcus I'd be right back."

She smiles wanly and pivots, hurrying down the corridor. Her remark lingers in the air. *Maybe there'll be less to sort out.*

Is she suggesting that with Claire dead, Marcus and Gabe can convince Ash to give them the money they need? It seems like a crude point for her to make now, though, and really unlike her to think that way.

By the time I return to the pool, Blake's gone, but Ash has taken over one of the lounge chairs. He's not in a swim-suit today, instead wearing a business casual green polo shirt and khakis—and a face taut from distress. He's staring down at his phone and appears to be writing an email, practically stabbing at the screen. Without a word to any of us, he strug-gles up out of his chair, strides across the deck, and heads over to the house.

Seeing Ash this way, when he's usually so comfortable in

his own skin, is jarring, but I'm sure he's handling his grief as best as he can.

I've had a question I've been wanting to ask Gabe and I slide back onto the lounge chair next to his. "Would you mind—or would your dad mind—if I spoke at the service tomorrow?" I say. "I thought I could read a poem."

"That would be really nice, Summer. Please, yes."

"There's one by Mary Oliver that I know your mom loved. I could show it to you if you'd like."

"No, I don't need to see it. I trust you totally."

"Okay, good. You're planning to say something, right?"

"Yeah, of course. I'm still working it out in my head."

I'm grateful for Gabe's support of my decision to do a reading, but I sense that things are still a little off between us—and I'm not sure how to remedy that without making me the focus when what he needs to do is grieve.

As the afternoon slips away, Henry and Gabe opt for one more dip, but I decide to return to the cottage, saying I'll see them there later.

It's really dim inside when I arrive, and I fumble for the wall switch to the right of the door. Once the light comes on, I discover that Gabe has pulled the muslin drapes closed for some reason.

I pick up the book of poems on the coffee table and turn again to the one I bookmarked earlier with a scrap of paper: I read it several times aloud, familiarizing myself more deeply with the words.

I calculate that I have enough time for a quick shower, and while toweling off afterward, I consider my outfit options for dinner. There's a dress I haven't worn yet on this trip, but I decide to save it for the service tomorrow. Instead, I yank a cotton skirt off a hanger in the closet and open the dresser drawer to find an appropriate top.

My eyes light on a sleeveless jersey tank, and as I lift it from its spot, something falls into the drawer—a small piece of purple cloth that must have been caught in its folds.

But no, that's not it. As I stare into the drawer, I finally realize that what's fluttered down isn't a piece of cloth.

It's a trumpet-shaped bloom from a foxglove.

gulp air, trying to catch a breath.

Someone snuck into the bedroom and tucked the blossom among my things. I rifle through the drawer, and the one below it, chucking items of clothing onto the bed. Nothing else is out of place. I scan the room next, but there are no other nasty leave-behinds that I can see.

After stuffing my clothes back into the drawers, I sink onto the mattress and press both hands to my mouth.

There's only one possible explanation: Hannah left the blossom. It has to be her because she's the only one I've mentioned foxgloves to. Which means she might very well have killed Claire. I've dismissed the idea each time it's wiggled into my mind, but why would Hannah hide a blossom in my drawer if something wasn't going on?

It's like she's issuing a warning: *Back off or you'll be next.*

So what the hell do I do now? I need to talk to Wendy as soon as possible—to see if she's managed to dig up anything, even though it's only been a couple of hours. And as Laertes says to Ophelia, "Best safety lies in fear." I have to let

Hannah scare the living daylights out of me, meaning my guard must be up at all times.

"You okay?" Gabe asks.

I've been so immersed in my thoughts, I didn't hear him come up the stairs. I twist around to face him, and see an unusual wariness in his eyes.

"Uh, just tired," I say. The sound of my heartbeat seems so loud I bet he can hear it. "How about you? You must be exhausted."

"Yeah, I'm probably gonna crash right after dinner tonight. I'll need all the energy I can summon for tomorrow."

"Henry's with you?"

"In his room changing."

Gabe unwinds the white beach towel around his waist, yanks off his suit, and digs a pair of boxer briefs out of his duffel bag. Ordinarily I'd feel a swell of desire at a moment like this, simply from catching a glimpse of his tanned, toned body, but I'm too scared and unsettled to experience even a twinge of lust.

As the three of us prepare to leave the cottage a few minutes later, I glance toward the French doors leading out to the patio.

"Did you close the drapes in here?" I ask Gabe.

"No, I thought you did. It must have been Bonnie. I noticed she emptied the wastebaskets earlier."

Bonnie might have dealt with the wastebaskets, but my money's on Hannah having closed the drapes so that no one would spot her moving around in here.

When we arrive on the patio for dinner, everyone's already gathered, slowly taking their seats, and I make a point of picking one as far away from Hannah as possible.

Most of us seem less shell-shocked at this meal than we were at lunch, and even Ash appears more himself. There's a bit of friendly chatter as the wine is poured, and Blake, his voice cracking, offers a toast to his mother's memory. Over crab cakes and salad, Nick, with tears in his eyes, tells us several laugh-out-loud stories about Claire, one involving her teaching him the names of the constellations as they wandered around the pool deck one night. She became so caught up in the lesson that she accidentally stepped off into the water, dressed in pants, a button-down sweater, and her favorite pair of Tod's suede loafers—but resumed the lesson as soon as she emerged, as if nothing had happened.

The chatter continues, but my focus shifts to the right, as if pulled by a magnetic force, and suddenly I'm staring right into Hannah's eyes. The edges of her mouth turn upward into a tiny, mischievous smile. She knows I found the blossom—and that I'm rattled. *Stay scared*, I warn myself, as I quickly glance away.

Toward the end of the meal, I manage to snag Wendy's attention. I cock my head as if to ask, *Find anything?*, and she gives me a tiny nod. Thank god.

By the time Bonnie and Jake are clearing the plates, Ash looks distracted and restless again, and he excuses himself before dessert is served. Blake and Wendy soon make motions to leave, too, and I realize I need to act fast. As Gabe helps Henry select a brownie from the platter on the table, I rise and edge over to her.

"Do you have a sec?" I say casually, careful not to pique anyone's interest. "I'd love your advice on something for tomorrow."

She turns to Blake. "You go back to the carriage house," she tells him. "I'll walk over in a minute once I've spoken to Summer."

He cups the side of her head with his hand, lacing his fingers through some of the silky strands.

"No, no, I'll wait."

"Blake, I'll be fine, I swear. I'm not the first woman on the planet to have a baby."

"I don't mind hanging here. I'll grab a brandy and sit with the others for a while."

She shrugs, rises, and takes my arm, and as the two of us walk onto the lawn in the direction of the Adirondack chairs, I can almost feel Hannah's eyes on my back.

"Blake mentioned you're planning to read a Mary Oliver poem tomorrow," Wendy says. "That's such a thoughtful idea."

I realize with a stab of guilt that I should have given Wendy and Keira a heads-up that I intended to speak. At least Gabe has spread the word.

"It's just a short one, but Claire mentioned once she loved it. Are you going to say anything?"

"I considered it—and I know Blake would be pleased if I did—but I get really teary at funerals, and I don't want to distract from the service by blubbering all over the place."

It's hard to imagine Wendy blubbering, but I know funerals can bring out extreme emotions.

"I'm also trying to keep my stress level down," she adds. "I generally don't mind public speaking, but tomorrow will be intense."

"Sounds like a smart decision."

We reach the chairs and sink into them. Fireflies have

begun to blink their lights all around us, and the delicious scent of honeysuckle clings to the air. It could almost seem like just another summer evening here, but, of course, it isn't.

"So, tell me," I say, my voice barely above a whisper. "You found something?"

"Keep in mind I only had time to make a superficial request, but yes, I had a bit of luck. And you're not going to believe it."

I hold my breath for a couple of seconds. "*What?*" I finally ask.

"Things checked out. She definitely went to USC. And she's from Miami, exactly as she told us. Her parents died a short time apart several years ago, in their fifties and both from illnesses. She's never been arrested and doesn't have any debt to speak of. Of course, as I said, this is only the top-line stuff."

I can almost feel myself deflating, like a beach ball that's been popped with a fork.

"Okay, then it must be something else," I say.

"What must be something else?"

"What Claire discovered. I thought it had to do with USC, but I guess not. We're going to have to dig deeper to figure it out."

Wendy swats at her arm, trying to kill a buzzing mosquito.

"I'm not sure what it could be. Hannah certainly doesn't look like a meth head. And she's not lying about the Netflix pilot—she showed Blake and me a clip from it, and it seems like she's landed a big role."

"But it's there, somewhere. I know Claire found something."

"She told you?"

"More or less. She said she had Hannah's number, and I could tell she didn't think Nick should marry her."

"Hmm. Is it possible Claire was simply being super-protective? I know Nick's, what, a minute younger than Marcus? But Claire considered him her baby and has always held on to him tightly."

Should I tell her about the foxgloves? I wonder. *Or the fight that Henry overheard?* No, I can't. Not now.

"Please, don't take this the wrong way," she continues. "I was very fond of Claire, we all were, but let's face it, you were her favorite, and I think it was hard for you to see how judgmental she could be at times. And, well, how *premeditated* she was when it came to her sons."

Maybe Claire and I had a strong connection, but that hardly means I was oblivious to who she was. Yes, she apparently had certain expectations of the boys when they were younger, but as they grew older, she let them become their own men. Regardless, this isn't about Claire being Claire. It's about how dangerous Hannah is.

"Okay, maybe Claire didn't love the idea of Nick getting married," I say, "but I think there was something else at play. And we have to keep looking."

Wendy's face is hard to read in the twilight, but I can hear the sigh that escapes her lips and the swish of her dress as she shifts position in the chair.

"Summer, I know you've got the best intentions," she says, "but I think we need to leave this alone now. If Hannah's not right for Nick, he'll find out soon enough."

"But—"

"And to be perfectly honest, I'm uncomfortable with the

idea of doing any more snooping. By the time I got off the phone today, I felt like I'd been dumpster diving."

Since I'm the one who promoted the so-called dumpster diving, her comment triggers a ripple of resentment through me. I open my mouth in protest, but quickly bite my tongue. It's pretty obvious she just doesn't get it—and if I keep desperately trying to make the case, Wendy might think I'm suffering from a bad case of Hannah envy, the way Gabe does.

"Sure, I understand," I say steadily. "And I appreciate your looking into it. It's reassuring to know the basic facts line up."

"I should go back," she says, smacking another mosquito. "Blake's waiting, and I know he's as knackered as I am. You must be, too."

Yeah, but I say tired, not knackered, I'm tempted to tell her, *because I didn't live in the UK for fifteen minutes a million years ago.*

I know I shouldn't be annoyed with Wendy. Since I haven't told her about the fight, or the foxgloves, I can hardly fault her lack of urgency. And yet I was counting on her, and I hate this sudden goody-two-shoes moralizing from someone who sells multimillion-dollar paintings of nothing but polka dots. Plus, it means I'm totally on my own again.

Blake's waiting on the patio as promised, brandy snifter in hand, and Gabe and Henry are there, too, brownie crumbs scattered on the table in front of them. As Blake and Wendy head off to the carriage house, Gabe hoists a sleepy Henry in his arms, and we trudge to the cottage. The night air is filled now with the insistent, rhythmic mating calls of countless katydids and crickets, a sound I usually find soothing, but tonight it grates against my nerves, making me even edgier.

While Gabe puts Henry to bed, I not only turn the lock on the front door but fasten the brass chain we never use. By the time he returns downstairs, I've turned on all the lights in the sitting room and poured us each a glass of rioja from a bottle I found on the butler's table.

"I thought you might like this," I say, offering him the goblet.

"Yeah, thanks. I had my share at dinner but one more won't kill me."

"He asleep?"

"Out like a light. He seems pretty exhausted from everything."

"I know. He even took a nap at the pool. I'm sure the memorial service will be sad for him, but I'm glad he's staying for it."

He takes a long sip of wine, and as he lowers the glass, his eyes meet mine.

"What were you and Wendy talking about out in the yard?"

"The memorial," I say. Which is *partly* true. "She'd heard I'm reading a poem, but she's decided not to speak. She's afraid of getting too emotional."

I settle on the sofa, wineglass in hand, and Gabe follows suit, but just far enough away from me that our bodies don't touch. Is that by chance, or by choice on his part?

"Have you worked out what you're going to say tomorrow?" I ask.

"Yeah, I decided to read a letter my mother wrote me at summer camp when I was Henry's age, one with a few good life lessons that have stuck with me. I made a digital copy of it once, and so I've got access."

"What a wonderful idea," I say. "I can't wait to hear what she wrote."

From there we drift into what feels like an awkward silence. Or maybe Gabe is simply grief-stricken and I'm reading it wrong. Finally, he drains his wineglass in a single gulp and announces he's going to bed.

"I'll be up in a minute," I say. I cock my chin to the poetry book on the coffee table. "I want to read over the poem a few more times tonight."

When I slip into bed ten minutes later, Gabe's already asleep, and snoring heavily. It sounds like there's a woodland animal rooting around in his chest, snorting, snuffling, emitting a low, troubled growl. I drag the pillow over my head, but it doesn't help.

That's not the only thing that's keeping me from a good night's sleep. There's also a huge ugly knot in my stomach. I'm nervous, I realize, over the idea of reading the poem at the service tomorrow. Sure, I've performed onstage countless times, but it's never an anxiety-free experience, and these are especially difficult circumstances. I'm also worried about Gabe and me. There's been this odd clunkiness between us since he found out about my snooping. Or really, ever since I first told him about Hannah's lie.

But mostly it's a knot of fear. I keep thinking of Hannah's wicked little smile tonight, when she'd clearly realized I'd found the foxglove blossom. She seems completely unafraid of tipping her hand to me. She must have concluded by now that if I accuse her of murder in front of the Keatons, everyone will think I'm crazy.

But she's the one who's crazy—and dangerous. The blossom was a threat, but would she go so far as to hurt me? She snuck into the cottage once before, and she could do it again.

The patio door, I suddenly think, bolting up in bed. I never checked whether it was locked. I nearly fly down the stairs and, holding my breath, tug back the muslin curtains. The lock is in place. And there's nothing beyond the window but a wall of darkness.

Before returning to our bedroom, I check in on Henry. The bedding is twisted crazily around his torso, and I take a minute to untangle the top sheet before laying it over him again and returning to the other bedroom.

Though I eventually drift off to sleep, I'm awake again at around one thirty, once more after three, and again near six, this time without even the hint of grogginess that promises a possible return to slumber. I struggle out of bed, dress as quietly as possible, and tiptoe downstairs.

Pale morning light greets me on the ground floor, seeping in from around the edges of the curtains, and when I peek through the window, I see the sky is smeared with pink. For a brief moment, my fears from the night before seem overwrought, even ridiculous. But they're not, I tell myself. *Red sky in morning, sailor's warning.*

Though it's only six o'clock now, there's a slight chance Bonnie's already in the kitchen, prepping for the luncheon. I decide to head over there and see if she needs any help. Coming down the path, I can see the side door of the house is closed, and probably still locked, but when I round the corner, I find the interior kitchen door open and the scent of fresh coffee wafting from inside. I ease open the screen door, and there's Marcus sitting at the table with a mug in front of him, staring off into the middle distance.

"Hi," he says when he notices me.

"Good morning. You couldn't sleep, either?"

"Not really. I kept hearing some animal prowling around again last night. I'm not sure if it was only a raccoon or that damn coywolf. You want coffee? Bonnie apparently isn't coming until seven, so I went ahead and made a pot."

"Coffee sounds great, thanks."

I fill a mug and join Marcus at the table. The two of us, I realize, have had practically no one-on-one time this week.

"Are you and I the only ones up?" I ask.

"Looks that way, though the study door's shut, meaning my father might be in there." He lets his gaze sweep the room. "I thought it would be nice to sit in the kitchen for a while. I don't think I've done that since I was a kid."

"You must have been, what, three or four, when your parents bought this place, right?"

"Yup. Though of course it wasn't scaled up then like it is now. In those days you could have a Fudgsicle in the kitchen on a summer afternoon, and not worry if it dripped all over everything."

"Are you ready for this morning?" I ask.

"I guess as ready as I'll ever be. Gabe says you're speaking. That's nice, Summer."

"I'm just reading a short poem I know your mom liked."

"Keira decided not to say anything. Talking in public kind of terrifies her."

"Understood. I guess I'm the only in-law speaking then."

"Unless you count Hannah," he says, with a hard edge to his voice.

I almost spit out my coffee. "*Hannah?* What could she possibly have to say? She knew your mother for two days."

And probably murdered her, I think.

"You'll have to ask her. Or Nick."

It's clearly a ploy on Hannah's part to cement the image of herself as the grieving future daughter-in-law.

"What's your take on her, anyway?" I ask, feeling like he's given me an opening.

He shrugs, his expression blank. "I don't really have one. I guess you know I dated her briefly, but I haven't said more than two words to her the entire time she's been here."

Should I tell him his pants are about to explode into flames?

Before I can craft the right response in my head, I hear the far-off sound of tires on gravel.

"Who could that be?" Marcus says, pushing back his chair. "Maybe it's the truck with the rental tables and chairs."

I trail him through the house to the living room and join him at one of the windows that faces the drive.

A cobalt blue BMW has pulled in, and Ash is already striding toward it, both dogs bounding along beside him. He must have been in the study, after all. I squint, curious about who's here so early, and see Jillian unfold herself from the driver's side, dressed in a sleeveless black dress and strappy sandals.

Ash closes the distance to the car, and as Marcus and I stand there watching silently, he takes Jillian into his arms and embraces her.

16

"Tell me I'm not seeing what I'm seeing," Marcus says under his breath.

"I—"

But I'm at a loss for words. It's like I'm watching a play in which all the actors have strayed disastrously away from the script.

When Ash and Jillian break apart and turn in the direction of the house, Marcus grabs my wrist.

"Let's go," he hisses. "We can't let them see us."

We hurry back through the house to the kitchen, making sure the swinging door closes behind us. Marcus's cheeks have reddened from shock, and probably anger, too.

"Marcus," I say, my voice low. "It might not be what it seems."

"Oh yeah? You mean my father and his assistant weren't really clinging to each other in the fucking driveway?"

"No. But maybe it was nothing more than a comforting hug."

Do I actually mean that? I don't have any idea. All I know is that I feel sick to my stomach.

"Bosses and employees hugging to comfort each other?" he says, his tone still brimming with sarcasm. "I didn't think that was supposed to happen even before the Me Too era."

"I'm not saying it's common, but a director I once worked with bear-hugged everybody, and I doubt it was ever sexual. Your dad's a paternal kind of guy and Jillian's been with him for at least five or six years, right?"

From far off comes the dull thud of the front door closing, and we both straighten, but no audible footsteps follow. Chances are Ash and Jillian have retreated to the study, where they spent so much of yesterday, something that didn't raise a red flag then but perhaps should have.

Marcus expels a long, rough sigh and sinks into a chair at the table. "Maybe. But . . ." His voice trails off and he kneads his temples with his fingertips.

"But what?"

"Lately, I had this weird sense that . . . there was a distance between my parents. They didn't seem to talk a lot to each other, or even make eye contact as much as usual."

"But your dad made that beautiful toast at dinner the night we arrived. He—" As I flash back to that moment, however, other memories nudge it out of place. Claire eating breakfast alone in the kitchen. Claire eating lunch alone. Ash going on a bike ride alone when in the past they generally went out together on Sundays. The fact that I rarely saw them interact over the weekend. I'd been so preoccupied, I hadn't let those details snag my attention.

"Maybe it had to do with them being superbusy. They

had *nine* houseguests, after all. Or they were just going through a little rough patch."

He shrugs, unconvinced, and drops his gaze to the table. "Yeah, maybe."

"What are you going to do?"

"Not sure." His eyes cut quickly to mine. "But listen, don't say anything to Gabe, okay?"

I throw up a hand. "Whoa, Marcus, you can't make me promise that. I think Gabe would feel he has a right to know."

What I don't add is that my husband's probably still smarting from the Spanish vineyard kerfuffle, and Marcus keeping another secret from him would go over really poorly.

"Okay, okay. But can you hold off a little while? I . . . I'll talk to my father, ask him about Jillian. Maybe it's what you said—a comforting hug."

"All right," I respond, without enthusiasm. He's suggesting that he leave Gabe in the dark again until he supposedly gathers more information—but this time I'm in on the deception. As I hurry toward the cottage a few minutes later, I realize that I wouldn't tell Gabe right now anyway. I don't want to knock the wind out of his sails before the memorial service.

Gabe's not on the first floor of the cottage when I arrive, but I can hear him clomping around upstairs. I quickly start the coffee machine and grab bread, and butter and yogurt from the fridge.

By the time he enters the kitchen, the coffee's already dripping into the carafe.

"Hey, morning," he says.

"Morning, honey. Henry still sleeping?"

"Yeah, he's so wiped, I'm going to wait to wake him. You been out already?"

"Yeah, I was going to check if Bonnie needed anything, but she's not coming till seven. I'll have a cup of coffee with you and then go back over there."

He doesn't ask if anyone else was up already, which thankfully means I don't have to dance around the truth with him.

I pour us each a cup, and Gabe slices off a piece of bread from the loaf. As I watch him drop it into the toaster, with his shoulders uncharacteristically slumped, I realize how much I want to be there for him right now, and yet I'm not sure exactly how. Does he want to talk about his grief, try to shape it into words, or would he prefer to seek comfort in silence? I once again conjure up the advice my mom offered me on the phone: Follow his lead.

Rather than talk, Gabe sits at the table and scans his phone, pressing his index finger against his lip. In the awkward quiet, I end up fixing a piece of toast for myself, something I haven't done in ages, not since I made a full-bore commitment to trying to be cast as the female lead and not her carb-loving, wiseass best friend. It tastes incredible, making me realize how much I'm in need of comfort food.

But the dread that hounded me last night soon rears its head again. I feel disconnected from my husband, when I should be helping him. Ash might be having an affair with his assistant. And there's probably a murderer on the property, one who knows I'm wise to her.

"It's almost seven," I tell Gabe. "I think I'll scoot over to the house again and check in with Bonnie. I'll be back to help get Henry dressed."

"Thanks," he says distractedly, eyes still glued to his phone.

"Let me know if there's anything else, will you?" I kiss the top of his head good-bye.

"By the way," he calls out as I approach the door. "Dad worked out the order for the service. Blake will welcome everyone. Then there'll be some kind of spiritual reading. Two of Mom's friends will speak next, followed by Hannah, you, and us four guys at the end."

"Got it. Are you sure you don't want to see the poem I picked? It's called 'Why I Wake Early.'"

"No, like I said, I trust your judgment. And I want to be surprised."

I'm touched by this. Maybe once the service is over, things will feel less stiff between us.

Bonnie's in the kitchen when I arrive, along with Jake and two additional helpers, both twentysomething women. They're all in black pants and white collared shirts beneath their aprons, though Jake's shirt looks like it might have been recently balled up in a hamper.

"You guys look nice," I say.

Bonnie blows a strand of hair out of her eyes. "Yeah, well, Jake is going to tend bar so he needs to iron his shirt, but there are a few items ahead of it on the list," she says.

"You want any help?" I ask.

"I think we have everything under control. Oh, actually, there *is* something you can do." She steps closer, dropping her voice. "You can do your best to keep Jillian off my case."

"Has she been a problem?" I ask, my heart skipping. That worrisome scene from the driveway keeps replaying in my mind.

"She's been up in my business since yesterday. Making sure I'd bought the salmon, telling me what we should wear today as if I didn't know, even asking me what's in the damn salads."

And then as if on cue, the door from the dining room swings open, and Jillian steps into the room. I quickly set my facial expression to neutral, but Bonnie's is frozen in annoyance.

"Morning, Summer," Jillian says and then shifts her attention to Bonnie without uttering her name. "Everything for lunch on schedule?"

"Yup. Though we have to get breakfast out of the way first."

"Understood. But wouldn't it make sense to at least start setting up the dining room?"

Bonnie looks startled by the suggestion. "But we're not using the dining room. We're serving lunch outside."

"*Outside?*" Jillian says. "I don't think we want the reception to feel like a Fourth of July picnic, do we?"

Bonnie's shoulders sag, as if she's decided she's no match for Jillian, and angry indignation stirs inside me. Regardless of what may or may not be going on with Ash, Jillian is his assistant, not the lady of the house. At least not yet. I shift my body to square my shoulders with hers.

"Actually, Jillian, I think outdoors is exactly what Claire would have wanted," I say. "She loved entertaining guests al fresco."

"If that's what you'd like," she says crisply. "I'm simply trying to make sure things go smoothly for Ash's sake."

"Of course. But Bonnie has this covered. She was Claire's right hand in the kitchen for years."

I may be out of line here, but I don't care.

Jillian doesn't slink off. That's not her style. Instead, she gives us a tight smile and turns on her heel.

"Thank you," Bonnie says as soon as she's gone. "That's one less thing to worry about now."

It seems like the right moment to take my leave, too, and I head outside through the back door. Clacking sounds fill the air, and as I round the corner of the house, I see that Blake is supervising as two groundskeepers set up the rented white folding chairs in rows on the lawn. If I didn't know better, I'd think someone was getting married here today.

And what a beautiful day the lucky couple would have. For the first time I take note of the bright blue sky. So much for red sky in the morning, sailor's warning.

The next several hours go by in a blur. Back at the cottage I find Henry awake and Gabe urging him into the shower. I rummage through Henry's duffel and dig out khaki pants and the one collared shirt he's brought, then press them on the kitchen table with an iron from under the sink. When Gabe and Henry depart in search of another round of breakfast, I shower quickly, blow-dry my hair, and apply foundation, blush, eye shadow, mascara, and lipstick. Once downstairs again, I reach for the Mary Oliver book, which is still lying on the coffee table, and open it to "Why I Wake Early."

By now I have the poem memorized, but I plan to hold

the book when I'm speaking and glance down a few times so that it looks as if I'm reading, not reciting, which I've decided will seem more natural and appropriate for the occasion. I say it aloud a few more times, to make certain I have the beats and emphases right, and I practice making eye contact, using the sitting room furniture as stand-ins for people. I've only been in one or two plays where the actors "broke the fourth wall," that is, acknowledged the presence of the audience, and I need to be comfortable doing it today. Done practicing, I tuck the book into my purse.

By ten fifteen, Henry and Gabe have returned, and the three of us are ready, as spruced up as we can be, considering we obviously hadn't packed anything for a funeral. I'm wearing a flowy black dress dotted with small pink flowers, and Gabe's in navy slacks and a blue-and-white-striped dress shirt. The deep circles under my husband's eyes betray how tough this morning is for him.

Though there's still forty-five minutes to go until the service, a few people are already mingling on the lawn when we show up there. Some of them turn out to be the members of the string quartet, and I also spot Denton Healy, Claire's friend and former business partner, who retired a year or two before she did. He's with his husband, who's helping him set up several gorgeous floral arrangements he's designed and brought for the occasion. Blake's here, too, I notice, now sporting a navy blazer. As far as I know, he's never left home without one.

Wendy arrives a few minutes later, followed by Keira and Marcus, and my stomach churns as I wait for Hannah's grand entrance. And then suddenly she's there, holding hands with Nick and dressed in dark pants and a bright pink blouse. Her choice of outfit surprises me, since she's worn a dress for dinner every night so far. But I realize that her sundresses tend to reveal a fair amount of cleavage, so perhaps she's decided that this is not the moment to be treating us all to the sight of her breasts.

As Henry scampers through the grass with Bella and Ginger—and the quartet begins to play a soft classical music piece—Gabe and his brothers merge into a loose conversational group, along with us, their partners. There's no effort from Hannah to make any eye contact with me this time, which I take as a small blessing. Maybe she's busy mentally prepping for a reading she's hoping to wow the crowd with. What could she possibly say about Claire that could be meaningful to anyone here?

Soon, Claire's long-lost cousin arrives, and shortly after that I spot her college friend, Ellen, emerging from the side of the house. She's tall, probably six feet, with superstraight posture, which enhances how stunning she looks in the black summer suit she's chosen for today. While Blake and Gabe greet their mother's cousin, I make my way toward Ellen and pull her into a hug.

After we separate, she pushes her sunglasses up into her silver hair, to reveal eyes that are bloodshot and puffy.

"Oh, Ellen," I say, "I'm so sorry. You knew Claire longer than any of us."

She manages a smile. "Goodness, this is so dreadful. I've been on a crying jag for two days."

I nod. "It's completely understandable. We're all so unbearably sad."

"This isn't the moment, but can I call you later this week

to hear more about what happened to Claire? Ash told me a little, but this seemed to come out of nowhere."

"I'd be glad to fill you in, though I don't know much." Would I ever dare share my theory with her? Ellen seems like a shrewd judge of character. Not at this juncture, I decide.

"Good, I'd appreciate that." She scans the small crowd and absentmindedly touches the Hermès scarf tied loosely around her neck. "Who's the beauty in hot pink with Nick? Is that his latest squeeze? I've been up in Maine since late June, with miserable Wi-Fi, so Claire and I weren't emailing as much as usual."

Sounds like she hasn't heard about the engagement. And since she's been out of the loop, it also means she might not have heard if any trouble had been brewing in Claire's marriage.

"Yep, his latest." I can't bring myself to spit out the word *fiancée.*

"Well, well. . . . I should speak to Ash and the boys. But before I do, let me offer my condolences to *you*, Summer. You know of course that Claire adored you."

"Thank you. I don't know if adore is the right word, but I always felt such affection from her. We all did. Claire was such a giving person."

She lifts her eyebrows. "You must know, Summer, that the connection you had with Claire was unique. Claire was not only a tiger mom, but she could also be very judgmental, a tough critic. But never about you."

Judgmental. That's the same word Wendy used last night.

"But if she was judgmental, why would she think well of me?" I ask. "When I met her, I didn't exactly have it together. I was waiting tables and performing in tiny black box theaters."

"But look at what you did for Gabe. Amanda had pulled the rug out from under him, and at first he struggled not only with being betrayed, but with coparenting a toddler. Once you entered his life, you opened your heart to Henry as much as Gabe and made a wonderful home for both of them. That meant so much to Claire. You could have been a pole dancer and she probably wouldn't have cared."

I can't help but laugh. "I'm not so sure about that, but I appreciate it, Ellen."

After she hurries off, I glance around and see that there are about fifteen or so outside guests here, meaning that everyone has probably arrived. Ash is saying hello to people now, looking tired but stoic, summoning charm the way politicians do when they have to concede defeat at a podium. And Jillian is here, of course, though she seems to be keeping her distance from Ash. Is she purposely doing that to throw off suspicion?

And then suddenly the music stops, signaling it's time for people to take their seats. I find Gabe and the two of us head to the front row with Henry, positioning him in a chair between us. As I give Henry's hand an affectionate squeeze, he leans his head against my arm, almost breaking my heart. *Dear Claire*, I think, *you didn't have to be grateful to me. Henry's been so easy to love.*

A hush falls over the crowd as Blake walks to the front of the seating area. Behind him, lush cumulous clouds chase one another across the sky. He welcomes everyone, his voice breaking once or twice as he speaks, and introduces Claire's friend and meditation instructor, who will start things off with a spiritual reading. The reading is nice, a little woo-woo probably for Claire's taste, but overall it sets the right tone. Next, Denton speaks about his long, wonderful partnership with Claire and quotes from emails former clients have sent, gushing about her talent. Another friend of Claire's, one I don't know, shares a story of Claire nursing her through a serious illness.

And then finally it's time for Hannah, who's sitting with Nick across the aisle from us. As she rises, I see that she's holding an index card in one of her perfectly manicured hands, with nails painted to match her top. She strides the short distance to the front, her butt swaying a little as she walks but her expression sober. The sight of her forces the taste of bile into my throat. How does she have the fucking *nerve*?

"Good morning, I'm Hannah Kane, Nick's fiancée, and I so appreciate the chance to speak today," she says with a restrained but confident smile. "Sadly, I knew Claire for only a very short while, but the hours we spent together were some of the most wonderful ones in my life. I felt an instant connection to her, especially on our tour of her magnificent gardens."

I have to fight off the urge to dry heave.

"I realize," Hannah continues, "that it would be silly of me to share impressions of Claire with people who knew her so much better than me, so I decided instead to read a poem that I know was one of her favorites.

"It's called 'Why I Wake Early' by Mary Oliver."

17

You've GOT to be kidding me. I sit there, stunned, as the words spill from her lips, the poem *I* was going to read. It can't be a fluke. No, no, she's very clearly done this on purpose.

My fury is quickly overtaken by panic. What the hell am I supposed to do? We hardly covered this kind of situation in the year's worth of improv workshops I did.

Think, *think*. The poem's short and she's almost finished. I sense Gabe eyeing me, and when I turn to him, I see surprise on his face. But it's not indignant surprise. He flips over both hands, palms up, as if to say, *Yikes, what a lousy coincidence. What are you going to do?*

My hands are trembling in my lap, and I raise a finger as discreetly as I can to indicate *I've got this*. I sure as hell *don't* have it, but somehow I'm going to have to. I'm a damn actress, right?

Hannah has finished and bows her head slightly in thanks. She lingers at the front for a moment, as if expecting a round of applause, before striding back to her seat.

As I rise from my own, my mind grasps desperately for memories. Claire and Gabe. Claire and me. Claire and her gardens. *Impromptu can work*, I tell myself, *as long as it's sincere.*

Reaching the front, I turn, face forward, and pause. Though there are fewer than thirty or so people, it feels like an ocean of faces. I take a breath from as deep in my diaphragm as I can manage and slowly exhale.

"Thank you so much for giving me the opportunity to speak today," I say, still rooting around for words. "I was so lucky to have Claire as my mother-in-law for the past four years, and knowing her was one of the most meaningful experiences of my life. She not only was a terrific mother to my husband, Gabe, and a fantastic grandmother to my stepson, Henry . . . but she also brought such joy into my own life. She taught me how to grow basil all winter long on my kitchen counter, and to set the kind of table people love to linger at . . . and, um, how to make a divine pasta sauce when all you have are lemons and cream."

The faces in the group are kind and receptive, but I have no freaking idea where I'm going next, and the back of my dress is all sweaty now, as if Henry's doused me with his Super Soaker. Suddenly, though, a memory snags in my mind.

"And most of all," I continue, "Claire taught me the importance of cherishing every day, rather than always fantasizing about the future. She came to see me once in a short Chekhov play off-off-Broadway, one called *The Bear*. She took me to dinner after, and as we were discussing that incredible playwright who knew so much about human nature, I mentioned a quote from him I'd read: 'The life of a man is like a flower, blooming so gaily in a field. Then, along comes a goat, he eats it and the flower is gone.'

"'That line—it always crushes me,' I told Claire. 'To think it's all over in an instant.' And . . . and do you know what she said? She said, 'But oh, to be that gaily blooming flower, if only for a little while.'

"Oh, Claire, what a flower you were. Thank you with all my heart for letting me—letting all of us—be witness to it."

My god, I think as soon as I stop, *I've made it sound as if Claire's been devoured by a* goat. But people are nodding, their expressions approving. Some are sniffling, and Ellen is dabbing at her eyes with a tissue.

Then there's Hannah. She's staring straight ahead, her gaze fastened to some distant point on the horizon. I wish I could gloat, because she didn't derail me as she'd planned, but I'm too shaken to do anything other than smile weakly and return to my chair. As soon as I'm seated, Gabe reaches across Henry, grasps my arm, and smiles appreciatively.

As the service continues, I try to focus on the remarks from Nick and Marcus, but the blood's pounding in my head, and all I can think of is Hannah, and what she's done. How had she figured out what poem I was planning to read? Had Gabe told Nick, who then told her? But I didn't even mention the exact name of the poem to Gabe until a couple of hours ago.

Wait, I know how she figured it out. When she snuck into the cottage yesterday to leave her ominous calling card, she probably snooped around and spotted the book of poems on the coffee table with "Why I Wake Early" bookmarked. By then she'd heard I was reading a poem, and now she knew which one.

When Gabe rises from his seat, I finally manage to focus again on the service. He briefly gives the context for the letter he's chosen, then proceeds to read his mother's wonderful advice: "Study the night sky and spot at least one shooting star; ask three kids to tell you the thing they like best about their hometowns; run so fast you break a flip-flop and have to use your backup pair," and so on. It's a list, Gabe says, that not only kept him happy at camp, but has served as a guide for life in general. It's a simple but lovely tribute, beautifully delivered, and I feel a swell of pride.

Blake finishes up the service with a short eulogy of his own and then Ash makes his way to the front, thanking everyone for coming to celebrate the life of his amazing Claire, whose death has broken his heart.

"Is it over?" Henry whispers to me as Ash retreats from the front.

"Yes, except for the lunch."

"But do they bury Gee now? Right here in the yard?"

"No, not here, sweetie. Down by the woods. Later this week."

"Can I have the list Gee wrote for Dad? And do all the stuff on it?"

"Of course. That's a great idea."

People are on their feet now, starting to mingle again. Henry spots the dogs and galumphs dispiritedly in their direction, but once they raise their heads in anticipation, he breaks into a run.

"Summer, how on earth did you pull that off?" Gabe says, closing the gap between us. He's radiating concern, and for a moment I feel in sync with him again.

"I have no clue," I say. "It was like I was having an out-of-body experience, and . . . and I just started racing through my memories of your mom." I don't add that the exchange I quoted might not have been word-for-word correct. But it was true in essence and essence was as good as I could come up with today.

"I can't believe Hannah picked the same poem to read as you did," he says. "Though I guess it makes sense when you consider—"

"Gabe," I interrupt, scanning the crowd to see if Hannah's looking at me. "Let's talk about it a little later, okay?"

"Sure," he replies, his expression wary. He senses trouble. And though he may not like it, I'm going to have to tell him everything. Because who knows what Hannah will try next?

We merge with the crowd, and the first person I see is Ash, who hugs me and thanks me for my words about Claire. Soon, like a school of fish, we all move in unison toward the patio, where we load up our plates and then retreat back to the white, round wooden tables the groundskeepers have set up in the shade of the maple trees.

Gabe, Henry, and I end up at a table with Keira and Marcus, as well as Gabe's aunt, uncle, and cousin. Keira looks even more watchful than usual, and beyond complimenting my tribute, she says very little. I wonder if she's regretting not speaking. Is she grieving in her own way? Or is she still deliberating whether a marriage can survive if one of the partners is still hung up on his former lover?

While the others make polite but strained small talk, my eyes roam the yard in search of Hannah, who's seated with Wendy and Blake, among others. Because she's got her back to me, there's no way for me to see her expression, but I'm dying to know if she's pissed because I wasn't undone by her nasty little ploy.

Wendy's to her left, her profile to me, and I watch as she touches Hannah's arm and smiles. Seeing her make nice to the woman she yesterday tagged as an interloper tells me I should never have confided in Wendy about my concerns.

When people start to wander back to the patio for slices of carrot cake, I use the moment to pop into the kitchen and check on Bonnie.

"Wow, what a fantastic lunch," I say, though I barely ate a bite.

"Thanks, Summer. And what a perfect day to eat outside."

I lower my voice. "Did Jillian give you any more trouble?"

"Thanks to you, no. The only time I saw her was a few minutes ago when she came in to thank me."

"Good. Did you have the sense she's planning to hang around today?"

"Don't think so. She and Blake went into the dining room for a minute, and when he came back into the kitchen, he said she was leaving, going back to the city."

That's a relief. And it might be a sign that there's really nothing going on, but I think Marcus still needs to talk to Ash about what we saw.

I check my watch as I head back outside. The meeting with the lawyer is only a couple of hours away, and I could use a break. Gabe and I decide that I'll take Henry back to the cottage and he'll meet us there as soon as the last guests have left. Once Henry and I are ensconced in the sitting room, and he's scribbled down everything he remembers from Gabe's summer camp list, I somehow manage to convince him to take a reading break in his room with a glass of Coke. If Amanda finds out, she'll report me to the national dental authorities, but she's the least of my concerns right now. When Gabe returns, I have to tell him everything I know about Hannah, and I need to convince him that this isn't a matter of me being envious or snoopy. Hannah could be a murderer. And she's a potential threat to all of us.

In my college acting program, I learned that to come across as authentic and credible as a character, one of the keys is to not sound fanatical. Most great theatrical characters are plagued by doubts at times—well, maybe not Antigone—and I need to indicate that I've weighed all sides of the situation. I'm still thinking this through when Gabe pushes open the door.

"Everybody get off okay?" I ask.

"Just about," he says. "Where's Hen?"

"Upstairs reading, though he may have conked out by now. I loved what you had to say today, Gabe, and so did Henry. He's been busy writing down all the items on the list."

"Thanks—but I didn't have to miraculously make it up on the spot. You have to tell me how you did it."

"Let me ask you something first," I say, closing the door to the stairwell so Henry won't overhear. "Did Nick know exactly what I was planning to read today?"

"Nick? No. He just asked if you were speaking and I told him you were reading a poem. I didn't tell him the name because I didn't know it myself at the time. I'm sure it was all just a rotten coincidence."

I take a deep breath. "I wish. But there was no coincidence, Gabe. Hannah figured out the poem I'd chosen, and she decided to read it herself, knowing that I'd be left high and dry."

"*What?*" he says, looking incredulous. "How can you think that?"

"I don't think it, I'm sure of it."

"Summer, she's not a mind reader. How could she have known? And why would she do something like that anyway? You two might not have hit it off, but that would be a pretty aggressive move on her part."

"Well, she *is* aggressive." I point to the volume of poetry on the coffee table. "She figured out which one it was because she snuck into the cottage and saw the bookmark on the page."

Gabe's gawking at me but he doesn't say a word.

"Look, I know it seems hard to believe," I say, "but I need to share something difficult with you, okay? It's something that at first I thought couldn't possibly be true, *prayed* wasn't true, but despite my initial doubts, I've come to see it probably *is* true. . . . I think Hannah might have murdered your mother."

He straightens in shock, then steps a few feet backward, finally collapsing on the sofa, his eyes on the ground. But he still doesn't say a word.

It all spills out of me then: how his mother lied to him about who she'd confronted on the patio that night; my strange conversation with her the day she died; the missing foxgloves; my fruitless search for the flowers; the disappearing jug; Hannah pretending she didn't know about the dangers of foxgloves; the blossom tucked diabolically in my drawer. Finally, I present a minute-and-a-half course on digitalis, how it's especially dangerous for anyone on a diuretic and why it can lead to cardiac arrest.

I give Gabe a chance to respond, but he remains silent, staring now at something in the middle distance. After what feels like an hour, he looks in my direction and pushes himself up off the couch. *Okay*, I think, *he's going to take me in his arms and say that it all makes sense, and that he's horrified I've had to deal with this solo.*

But he doesn't. He simply says, "Show me the place in the garden where the flowers are missing."

"Of course," I respond, feeling an iota of relief. I hurry across the room, part the drapes, and tug open the doors to the patio, beckoning him to follow. A cloud has passed across the sun, dulling the garden colors, but the air is ripe with the sweet scent of the artemisias.

"There," I say, pointing to the spot but training my eyes on Gabe. Instantly I see the surprise on his face. He gets it. He finally does.

But when I drop my eyes to the garden a second later, I see there's no gap anymore. It's now filled entirely with stalks of purple foxgloves.

18

For a second I freeze, my feet bolted to the ground. But then I bend my knees for a closer inspection and I discover right away what's happened. The soil around a handful of the foxgloves is rough and knobby, making it clear that someone has dug there in the last day or two, and the flowers themselves are a little limp.

"Okay, there's no gap now, but it's pretty obvious why not," I say, hearing the desperate edge to my voice. "She clearly found these foxgloves in another one of the gardens, dug them up, and planted them to replace the ones she clipped."

But *when*? Probably after I'd stupidly mentioned foxgloves to Hannah, telegraphing my suspicions.

Gabe doesn't move. He's next to me, his eyes on the border garden.

"Summer," he says, finally pivoting to me. His tone is plaintive, the way guys get when they're about to tell you they slept with a girl they met on a business trip to Dayton or have come to realize they never really loved you after all.

"Wait," I say, squinting as the sun sneaks from behind a cloud. "I took a picture. I can show you."

He trails me back into the sitting room where I grab my phone, click on the photo I took Sunday night, and thrust it toward him. "Here, see," I say.

He sighs and lowers his gaze. A second later, using his thumb, he swipes a few frames forward and then backward, obviously searching for additional photos.

"Is this the only one you have? Because there's really nothing here."

I snatch the phone back and as I glance at the photo, my heart sinks. It was even darker out than I realized when I took it, and the flash never went off. Though I know exactly where the gaping hole is, to anyone else looking at the photo, it might appear to be simply a mush of dark plants and shadows.

"Gabe," I plead. "You have to believe me. There was a hole there. Someone dug up the foxgloves the day your mother died."

"I believe you, Summer."

I tear up. Maybe I *am* getting somewhere. "So what do you think we should do?"

Gabe shakes his head forlornly. "Nothing."

"But why not?" I feel my stomach twisting. "If you believe me."

"I *do* believe you saw a gap. I understand that the jug isn't in the cupboard anymore. I'm sure there was one of those foxglove buds or blossoms or whatever you call it in your drawer. But I also think you're looking at everything from the wrong angle. Or maybe it's been refracted somehow, like when Henry makes a pencil look bent in a glass of water."

"*Refracted?* Gabe, I saw the hole. It was there."

"Let's sit, okay?" he says, gesturing toward the couch, and I oblige because I only have a chance of convincing him if I seem as level-headed as possible.

"What I mean," Gabe says when we've settled onto opposite ends of the couch, "is that it might have seemed like a gap when you saw it, but the wind or the heat had probably parted the flowers a certain way at the time. Plus, it was clearly dark then—so maybe it looked like a bigger gap than it was."

I grit my teeth. "What about the jug then?" I say. "And the flower in my drawer?"

"The jug—I'm sure it's in the house *somewhere*, or maybe that new guy Bonnie's using broke it, swept up the pieces, and threw it away. . . . As for the flower in your drawer, you said you were carrying vases around yesterday. The blossom part probably snagged onto whatever you were wearing and then ended up in the drawer."

"And your mom saying that thing about my hair being lighter?"

"It *is* lighter. You've been in the sun a lot this summer."

Frustration nearly overwhelms me, but I force calm into my voice. "So what you're saying is that after your mother basically threatened to expose Hannah, Hannah simply let it roll off her back. And all these other things are pure coincidence?"

"There's no evidence whatsoever that my mother was talking to Hannah that night."

"But then who was she fighting with?"

"I don't know," he says, throwing up his hands. "One of my brothers? My father?"

"Your *father*?" Does Gabe suspect an issue in his parents' marriage?

"That was only a suggestion. My point is that we don't know. She might not have even been all that upset. We have only a sleepy little boy's transcript of what she said."

"And the poem today?"

"I'm sure my mother also told Hannah she loved it. She probably told every woman who's come out here that it was her favorite."

Somewhere in there is a dig, but I ignore it. I clasp my arms against my chest, wondering how things have gone so horribly wrong. Gabe doesn't get it at all.

"Summer," he says with eerie calm, like a cop trying to talk a potential jumper off a ledge, "what I'm asking is that you take a long deep breath and try to see this all from another perspective."

Obviously, he hasn't noticed that I've been breathing so deeply I've nearly sucked all the air from the room.

"Gabe, please. . . ." I look at him, imploring. "Can't *you* try to see it from another perspective? You seem so . . . so quick to come to Hannah's defense."

"I'm not," he snaps. "There's simply no evidence she's done anything wrong."

As I search desperately for a response, I notice that his eyes are now glistening with tears. In the moment, I've lost sight of the fact that Gabe is distraught and grief-stricken, and this conversation is only making him feel worse.

"Gabe, I'm sorry. I didn't mean to upset you today. But I had to tell you all this. How could I forgive myself if I didn't?"

"Fine, and thank you. You've told me. But now you have to let it go, okay? My mother's dead, dead from a massive heart attack, and supporting my dad and Henry is what I need to focus on."

"Of course," I say, chastened. "And I want to be there for you, and your dad, and Henry."

"Great, so let's move on. Seriously, Summer, I can't have another crazy conversation like this. You have to figure out a way to stop obsessing about Hannah."

So that's it, isn't it? That's what he thinks this is all about. Me crazily fixated on Hannah and her success. Jealous and unable to stop trash-talking. I feel an urge to hurl something at the wall, but instead I smother my anger. More talk or flying objects won't open his eyes, and I need to stop exacerbating his distress over his mother's death.

"I hear you," I say, probably a little too brightly. "I do. And you're right, let's move on."

He eyes me quizzically, his tan brow wrinkled, as if he's not sure if I'm sincere or giving a Drama-Desk-Award-caliber performance. But I sense a resignation beneath the surface, that he's going to take me at my word.

"I should check on Henry," he says, rising and raking both hands through his hair.

"I'll watch him during the meeting with the lawyer, of course," I volunteer. "Maybe fix him an early dinner."

"But you're supposed to be at the meeting, too."

"I am? I thought only you and your brothers were invited."

"Well, wives, too. Dad's expecting you."

"Sure, I'm happy to be included. It's just a formality, right?"

"That's what I hear." He's moving toward the stairwell, his face still tense.

"Okay, why don't I go over to the house and see if Henry can hang in the kitchen with Bonnie during the meeting, then?"

Gabe's lips part, as if he's about to suggest *Hannah could always watch him*, but in the end he just nods.

I don't head directly to the house, though. Instead I wander halfway down the path, veer off toward the cloud boxwood grove, and slip into the glade. This was another one of Claire's sanctuaries, and it's not hard to understand why. The space is so serene and Zen-like, a spot where the rest of the world can feel completely removed.

But it doesn't today. As I lower myself onto one of the two weathered benches, my problems seem to bulldoze their way through the boxwoods. Hannah's out there someplace, a potential danger to me and to others. And my conversation with Gabe has only intensified the big, fat wedge between us.

Something else is churning in me, too, something besides frustration and anguish. I feel . . . *pissed*, I realize. I didn't expect Gabe to leap from his seat like Dr. Watson and shout, *My god, you're right, why didn't I see it?* But I expected him to at least listen carefully, consider my points, and accept that though all I had was circumstantial evidence, it warranted investigation.

Instead, he completely dismissed my theory. And chalked it all up to a personal issue. But I'm *not* obsessed with Hannah's career. Yes, I want what she has, have *always* wanted it, but I'm opening other doors for myself. No, this is simply about the truth and trying to convince Gabe to see it, too.

What I need is an ally, I decide. Not Wendy, obviously, since she now seems to be cozying up to Hannah. No, it has to be someone else, someone receptive.

Marcus. There's a chance he's still lusting for Hannah, of course, but based on how he looked at her right here in this spot, I think that he's feeling anger, too. And perhaps, as I once considered, he might be privy to details about her that make him want to prevent a marriage between her and Nick. I can also probably count on Marcus to be discreet, since the two of us are sharing another secret.

With my mind made up, I leave the grove and hurry to the house. The tables and chairs have been carted off, and the sole reminders of the service that took place are the indentations in the grass. As I round the house toward the pool, I can hear a Rihanna song playing faintly from the kitchen. Claire's not even buried yet and her "only classical music in the kitchen" policy has already bitten the dust.

Marcus isn't at the pool, nor is anyone else, hardly a surprise. Chances are he's in the guest suite, resting or steeling himself for the next gathering. I make my way to the eastern end of the house, knowing that the door to the screened-in porch is always unlocked. There's a back stairway in this section of the house that will take me right to the guest suite.

Several large fir trees shade the porch, keeping the light in there dim, and it isn't until I'm a few feet into the space that I notice someone lying faceup on the wicker couch. Wendy. Like me, she's still in the clothes she wore to the service, and her hand is pressed against her forehead. I'm shocked to see a goblet of what might be chardonnay parked on the coffee table beside her.

"Oh, hi," she mutters, scooting up a little. Her face is as white as candle wax.

"Is everything okay?"

"Yes, I—Oh, you're looking at my drink. Don't worry, it's water. I grabbed the closest glass I could find."

"Wendy, are you sure you're feeling okay?" I perch on the rocker across from her so I can see her better in the dimness. "Want me to find Blake?"

"I'm fine, really." She scooches up even more so she's almost in a seated position, but her legs are still stretched out in front of her. "Well, maybe not so fine. To be perfectly honest—and you can't breathe a word of this to anyone—I was feeling crampy a little while ago, and it freaked me out. I thought I might be miscarrying."

My breath quickens. "You have to let me get Blake. He'll know what to do."

"No, please. I don't want to scare him if nothing's wrong. And besides, if I *am* having a miscarriage, there's no way he can help."

"Are you sure?" I ask, though I know practically nothing on the subject.

"Trust me, after years of trying, I'm practically an expert on everything related to pregnancy," she says, a shadow passing over her face.

"It's good you're resting, at least."

She snickers. "You know, doctors used to advise bed rest for a possible miscarriage, but it's apparently useless. I'm just lying down for my own sanity. I can't bear the idea of possibly losing this baby."

"Oh, Wendy, I can only imagine. The cramps—they're gone now?"

"Yes, they subsided a little while ago. And I'm not bleeding, so hopefully it's a false alarm."

"Thank god. . . . I'm sure the situation here isn't helping matters."

"You can say that again." There's more than a hint of exasperation in her voice. "Are we supposed to simply continue here, pretending we're all on vacation?"

"I'm sure people would understand if you left in the next day or two."

"Maybe. I'll have to see what Blake thinks."

She lowers herself back on the cushion and brings a hand to her brow again.

"Why don't I let you rest," I say, rising. "Do you have your phone? In case of an emergency?"

"Yes, it's in my pocket." She slowly closes her eyes. "Thanks, Summer. I appreciate it."

"Take care." I wish I had better words of comfort to offer.

I head from the porch into the house and toward the back stairs. Though I've always been comfortable in every part of the Keatons' property, I can't help but feel a little sheepish about going up to the guest suite now, particularly after Hannah found me outside her room. Once I'm at the top of the stairs, I hurry to the far end of the hall and rap lightly on the bedroom door.

I hear footsteps drawing close, and soon Marcus swings open the door, wearing only a pair of dark slacks. "Hey," he says, frowning. "Everything okay?"

"Yup. I was just hoping to talk for a second."

The sitting area behind him, I notice, looks like a tornado hit it. There are papers spread about, shirts tossed over chairs, and through the open door to the galley kitchen, I can see a plate piled with orange rinds on the counter along with a couple of stained wineglasses.

"Ignore the mess," Marcus says. "I told Bonnie not to bother tidying up while we're here. What did you want to talk about?"

I've only been able to come up with one bad excuse for instigating a conversation. "The thing this morning."

"Now? We've got the meeting with the lawyer coming up."

"I know, but this won't take long."

"Okay, let's do it someplace else, though. Keira's napping in the bedroom."

He retreats back into the sitting area, grabs his shirt from a chair arm, and throws it on as we descend the stairs. When I mention that Wendy is resting on the screened porch, Marcus points to the door on the side of the house, and we exit there, ending up not far from the garage and the potting shed. There isn't a soul in sight.

"Is there some new development since this morning? I heard Jillian took off a while ago."

"No, nothing new. But I was wondering if you'd had a chance to speak to your father yet?"

He straightens, his expression darkening. "Summer, you're

kidding. Was I supposed to have raised the topic before my mother's *memorial* service?"

I can hardly blame him for being irritated. It was a stupid excuse for asking to see him, I know. Time to switch gears.

"No, of course not. I'm sorry. I just hate keeping secrets from Gabe. And . . . there's other crap going on here, too."

"Like what?"

"That poem Hannah read? That was the one *I* was planning on reading. I had to come up with my remarks as I walked to the front."

"Christ, Summer, that's crazy. You pulled it off, though."

"Thanks, but I'm still reeling a little. . . . What do you *really* think of her, Marcus?"

"Who?"

"*Who?* Hannah."

He gives a shrug that smacks of studied nonchalance. "As I told you before, I hardly know the woman."

"But you dated her. Do you think she could be dangerous for Nick?"

"You mean is she a massive bitch? A gold digger? I have no idea. Nick will have to figure that one out for himself."

Had I really thought that he'd suddenly share his honest feelings with me?

"Okay, sorry to bother you. See you at the meeting."

"Sure." He touches my arm as I turn to go. "Summer, sorry, I didn't mean to sound so abrupt. But I've been going over the same ground again and again with Keira. Hannah and I dated for a couple forgettable weeks, ages ago, and there was nothing to it."

"Got it," I say, feeling deflated from the complete waste

of time and energy—and the fact that there's no one in the world I can count on for support right now.

By the time I detour to the kitchen to speak with Bonnie and then return to the cottage, it's way later than I'd realized, but Gabe doesn't seem to notice. As we're walking over to the house together, with Henry trudging behind us, I'm tempted to slip my hand into my husband's and give it a squeeze, but I don't. Though I want to be in sync with him again, want to comfort him, it's hard to forget how dismissive he was an hour ago.

After dropping Henry in the kitchen, we make our way to the living room, right on time but the last to arrive. Like Gabe, his brothers are still in their clothes from the service, as if preferring not to look too casual. I take a seat on the sofa next to Wendy, who's gotten the color back in her cheeks, and Gabe settles next to me on the other side.

"How are you doing?" I whisper to Wendy. I'm a little surprised she felt up to attending the meeting.

"Still no bleeding, so I think I'm okay," she whispers back.

Before I can respond, Ash crosses to the doorway of the study, pokes his head in, and announces, "We're ready."

Based on my sense of estate lawyers, I'm expecting some avuncular-type male with white hair and a barrel chest, but the person who emerges is female, Black, and probably in her midforties.

"Everyone, meet Letena Smith," Ash says. "Letena's been helping with our estate planning for a number of years now."

After setting a folder down on the card table, Letena moves around the room, graciously introducing herself to us one by one. Her hair is short and wavy, and she's wearing a killer navy pantsuit that I assume is Armani, but I hardly have the firsthand experience to know for sure.

"Let me begin by saying how sorry I am for your loss," Letena says, returning to where Ash is standing. "Claire was an amazing, accomplished woman as well as a devoted wife and mother, and I know it's tough for you to be doing this so soon after her passing. But Ash felt we should get the proceedings out of the way so life could go on.

"This will be brief," she continues. "And it's all very straightforward." She takes a moment to step back toward the table and withdraw a sheet of paper from the folder, then scans it quickly. "The bulk of your mother's half of your parents' financial assets will be held in trust for your father. As you've been informed in the past, upon your father's death, the assets in that trust will go to you—Blake, Gabriel, Marcus, and Nicolas—along with your father's share of assets. But a few months ago, your mother decided to update the will with a new provision in case she predeceased your father. She wanted to leave each of you an immediate financial gift to be used however you wish."

She pauses. People straighten in surprise. I have no clue where this is going.

"Claire," she says, "bequeathed each of you the sum of one million dollars."

19

I t takes a few extra seconds for my brain cells to process the words, and when they finally do, my jaw nearly hits the floor. I feel as if I'm on some kind of game show and we're about to watch a dozen women in low-cut dresses and stilettos emerge from the study with numbered silver suitcases. Or maybe the host—the Armani-clad lawyer—is going to ask if we'd like to try to double our money.

But it's not a game show. It's really happening. Though we'd all assumed that Claire's half of the estate would be going to Ash, Gabe and his brothers are getting a chunk of it. Even with estate taxes and legal fees, my husband and I are about to receive a *lot* of money.

I steal a glance at Gabe, but his face is a total blank. I know this is as big a shock to him as it is to me, and it must also be horribly bittersweet. The only reason we're receiving this windfall is a tragic one. But still, this means funds to put aside for the baby we hope to have, to help Gabe deal with the mess at work, to finally redo the grungy second bathroom in our loft.

Trying not to seem obvious, I inch my gaze over toward Ash. His arms are folded over his chest, in a tight, almost protective way, but nothing about his demeanor suggests this news has caught him off guard.

Letena shares a few quick details about how and when the money will be distributed and asks if there are any questions. At first no one says a word or even moves a muscle, but then Blake rises, his hands on the waist of his perfectly pressed black pants. Clearing his throat, he looks directly at Ash.

"Dad, are you really okay with this?" he asks.

"Of course," Ash says. "Your mother and I worked it out together."

"But when you and Mom had the estate discussion with us a few years ago, this wasn't the plan."

"I know, Blake, but we decided to shift things around a little." Ash's arms still guard his torso. "Your mother certainly wasn't expecting to die at seventy-two, but she decided that if she passed away relatively young, there ought to be money for you each to use right now. Toward a new home, artwork, investments. It's your call. And I have all the money I need."

A few heads nod, Gabe's included. Still, there's a weird, almost palpable tension in the room. Keira's hand is resting on Marcus's arm, but his eyes are glued to the rug. This has to be so emotionally charged for all Claire's sons.

"No more questions?" the lawyer asks, glancing from one brother to the next.

Before anyone can speak, Ash steps forward. "Letena, I'm sure there'll be questions once everyone has a chance to digest this. Why don't you give each of the boys a card, and they'll contact you next week? Can I have our housekeeper fix you a plate of food before you head back to the city?"

"I appreciate that, Ash, but it's not necessary," she says, obviously knowing how to follow a cue. She slides a small silver case from her purse, withdraws several cards, and passes them around the room.

Ash tells us he'll see everyone outside for dinner shortly since he's asked Bonnie to serve the meal early tonight. As we file out of the room, he lingers behind to speak to Letena, who's slipping the folder into a soft leather briefcase.

"Honey, this must be such a shock," I say to Gabe. We're alone in the dining room now, the others having scattered in different directions.

"That's for sure."

"Your dad didn't warn you this was happening today?"

"No, not a word."

"That was wonderful of your mother. I'm happy for you."

"Yeah, well, we've got plenty of ways to spend it now. . . . Look, I'm going to see how Henry's doing. He doesn't seem like himself today."

I nod, feeling a pinch of guilt. I've been going through the motions a little with Henry over the last two days. "Why don't the three of us watch a movie together tonight? We can probably commandeer the TV in the den, right?"

"Sure. There are a million old DVDs in there, and I'm sure we can find something he'll like."

"I'll meet you outside in two minutes. I'm going to run to the bathroom."

As Gabe enters the kitchen, I retrace my steps through

the dining room, and right before I enter the front hall, I catch a glimpse of Keira and Marcus through the window. They're standing in the side yard, at this end of the boxwood grove, and from Keira's pinched expression I can tell their conversation isn't a pleasant one. Marcus has his back to me, the sleeves of his pale blue shirt rolled to his elbows, and as he gestures in what looks like frustration, I think of what he said earlier, about covering the same ground with Keira again and again. Based on the moment I witnessed between him and Hannah, his reassurances are bullshit, though. Feeling like I shouldn't be watching them any longer, I move on.

I'm about to turn the handle on the powder room door when Wendy emerges from inside. I glance up and down the corridor, making sure we have the area to ourselves.

"How are you doing?" I ask.

"I think I'm okay," she says, though I can almost see the worry pulsing from inside her. "I left a message for my OB, and I'll see what she says."

"So, for now, you and Blake will be staying out here?"

"Yes, at least for the burial, though I'd love to be any-where else on the planet. This is all just too much to take. And what a slap in the face that announcement was to Ash."

Her comment takes me aback.

"But Ash said he knew about it," I say, lowering my voice further.

Wendy rolls her pale blue eyes. "He knew about it, sure, but that doesn't mean he *liked* it. We see this in my business, too. A spouse suddenly changing the will to leave some of the artwork to the kids."

"Is that such a bad thing?"

"Not the gesture itself, but sometimes the motives behind it are. The person who makes the change is often worried that when he or she dies, the spouse will marry someone who has designs on the money and then when *he* dies, he'll leave everything to the new squeeze and the kids won't get a bloody dime."

"But it's hard to believe—" An image of Jillian and Ash's embrace pops in my mind. "Wait, do you think Claire had reason to be concerned about something like that?"

Wendy shrugs. "I don't know. But it seems like she was trying to make a point—and take Ash down a notch. Look, if you don't mind, I should find Blake. I want to fill him in on the cramping now that things don't look so dire."

"Of course," I say, still a bit stunned by her comments. "I'll catch up with you later."

Once I'm in the powder room, I lower the toilet seat and settle on it, my eyes closed and my hands over my face. Like Wendy said, the events of the past few days now seem overwhelming. That Claire is dead. That a million dollars has weirdly been dropped into our laps. That Ash might have been cheating on Claire. That Gabe and I have had a real breakdown in communication. That Claire was likely poisoned by Hannah. And that if I don't figure out a way to expose her, she could get away with it.

Hannah. She's on the patio mingling with all the others when I emerge from the house. Right away, I sense her attempting to catch my gaze, but I'm not going to give her the satisfaction. Instead, I glue myself to Henry's side, telling him we're thinking of watching a movie later and he'll have a ton of choices to pick from.

The dinner's already been laid on the sideboard, some leftovers Bonnie's doctored from the luncheon along with a fresh green salad, and the various Keatons begin to load up their plates. I linger by the sideboard, waiting for Hannah to take her seat, and once she does, I choose one at the opposite end of the table and urge Henry to park himself next to me. Before any of us can take a bite, Ash rises from his seat and clears his throat.

"It's hard to believe we're sitting at this table without our dearest Claire here," he says. "She was so proud of you boys, and I only wish she could have heard your terrific tributes to her today. We'll go on, because we *must*, because what would make her happiest is knowing we'll embrace our lives as fully as she did her own. What was it you said, Summer? Relish being the flower. And Henry, a special thank you for being here. Gee loved you with all her heart."

Ash is a polished speaker, in the way supremely confident men are even if it's not part of their day-to-day jobs, and he could probably offer a loving and seemingly authentic tribute to the yard crew if he had to. So is his grief genuine? Or is he eager to rush into another woman's arms?

"Beautifully put, Dad," Blake says, and the rest of us murmur in assent, except for Marcus who stares ahead, looking particularly glum. As I study him, a thought stirs in me, but before I can grab hold of it, it flutters away.

Nearly in unison, we all tuck into our food, and people make a decent attempt at conversation. Next to me Henry indifferently stabs at a piece of lettuce with his fork.

"I know today's been hard," I say quietly to him. "But see how good it's made Grandpa feel to have you here?"

"Where's Gee *now*? Is anyone watching her?"

"For the time being, she's in what's called a funeral home. After she's buried near the woods, we can pay our respects to her whenever we're walking there."

"But it gets so dark down there at night."

I have to fight the urge to wince, my heart aching over his concern. I, too, hate to think of her being in those dark, dark woods. "Don't worry, honey. When you die, you don't feel pain or fear anymore, so Gee won't be scared."

A listless nod. Henry's floundering, and what we need is to burrow into the den tonight and watch something outrageously funny. I'm relieved when Jake finally passes around slices from the remains of the carrot cake, and I reach across Henry to touch Gabe's arm. "Movie now?" I ask.

After making our excuses and grabbing fresh drinks for ourselves, Gabe, Henry, and I head down the back corridor to the small, comfy den, with Ginger and Bella choosing to join us. For the first time all day, the dogs seem to perk up and they leap onto the couch, perhaps in anticipation of Claire, who used to snuggle in here with them after dinner. Henry and Gabe drop to the floor and begin fishing through the rows of DVDs lining the lower shelves on each side of the fireplace. I'm hoping the next couple of hours will not only help boost Henry's spirits, but also ease the tension between Gabe and me.

"Hey, you know what we could use?" I announce. "Popcorn. Why don't I nuke some while you guys decide on a movie?"

"With butter, pretty please," Henry calls out as I leave.

I follow the hallway toward the kitchen, where I can hear

the sounds of chatter and splashing water from Bonnie and Jake, but most of the house is still. The rest of the family must have retired for the night.

Bonnie looks fairly bushed, but happily helps me locate popcorn. Once I've made it, I thank her and Jake again for their efforts today, wish them good night, and, bowl in hand, retrace my steps to the den. Someone, maybe Ash, has flicked off the corridor light since I was here a few minutes ago, but I can see well enough. As I'm about to open the door, I sense someone behind me, and spin around to see who it is.

I nearly jump back in shock. Hannah is standing three feet away from me.

"What's up?" I say, trying to keep my tone casual over the drumbeat of my heart.

"I wanted to speak to you for a minute."

"What about?"

Even in the dimness of the corridor, I see her lips turn up in a tiny smile. "I think I owe you an apology."

Ha. For putting a foxglove in my drawer? For killing my mother-in-law? I wait to see what she'll say next.

"I found out a little while ago that you'd planned to read the same poem today."

I inhale deeply, wondering where she's going with this. It's surely a booby trap of some kind. "Who told you that?" I ask.

At that moment the den door opens with a creak and Gabe steps over the threshold.

"Hannah," he says, clearly surprised to see her next to me.

"Hello, Gabe. I was looking for Summer so I could apologize. I found out that I recited the same poem she'd intended to share at the service. I'm so sorry."

"Who told you that?" I repeat, hoping that Gabe will see me catch her in a lie.

"Nick. He heard from Marcus, I believe."

"And Claire just happened to mention that poem to you during the brief one-on-one time you had with her before she died?"

"*Summer*," Gabe says, as if I'm five years old and just called my kindergarten teacher a "caca head."

"She did—on a tour she gave me of the gardens."

I feel a sudden urge to throttle her, to squeeze the truth out of her as she gasps for air, but I sense the tension in Gabe, and his words from earlier echo in my head: *You have to stop obsessing about Hannah.*

"Apology accepted," I say. "I appreciate it."

I've caught her off guard with my response. Somehow, as unnerved as I feel, I've managed to find the perfect tone, the kind that sounds unchallengingly authentic, but the person you're talking to knows it's fake as fuck.

"See you tomorrow then," she says. She pivots and retreats down the corridor.

Gabe doesn't seem exactly pleased as I follow him back into the den and settle in with him, Henry, and the dogs, but he doesn't say anything.

While I was making popcorn, the two of them selected *Home Alone*, a movie Henry has never seen. It ends up being just what the doctor ordered. Henry, wedged between Bella and Ginger on the sofa, is riveted from the very first scene, and he howls with laughter through much of the film. Though Gabe and I each saw it years ago, we laugh out loud in our respective leather armchairs.

But despite how diverting the movie is, worry gnaws away at me. I'm not sure how Hannah's apology works into her overall plan, but it *must*, because from what I've seen so far, she *always* has an agenda.

When the movie ends, Henry insists on watching the credits, but before they're over, he's slumped against Ginger, fast asleep.

"I hate to wake him," Gabe says. "Why don't I carry him back to the cottage?"

"Okay." I glance at the floor, which is strewn with rejected DVDs and popcorn kernels. "I'll tidy up in here and be over in a minute."

After their footsteps fade, along with the sounds of Gabe shooing the dogs upstairs, I realize how absolutely quiet the house is. I stack up the DVDs quickly, stick them back in the shelves, and scoop up the kernels with my hands.

When I start down the corridor a minute later, I spot light seeping from beneath the kitchen door, and pick up the sound of rustling from inside. *It can't be Bonnie*, I think. I'd heard a couple of cars pulling out of the driveway while we were watching the movie.

I'm just about to investigate when the door swings open and Keira emerges into the corridor, wearing a terry cloth bathrobe over her pajamas.

"Gosh, you scared me," she says. "I didn't realize anyone else was still down here."

"Sorry. Everything okay?"

In the light flooding from the kitchen, I have my first recent glimpse of her without makeup this week, and I notice that her light brown skin, always so flawless, is dotted with blemishes, and the area beneath each eye is a puffy crescent. It seems like the past couple of days have taken a toll on her, as well.

"Yeah." She looks down and I see that she has a man's dress shirt draped over one arm. "Marcus spilled some red wine on his shirt, and I volunteered to put vinegar on it. It always gets that kind of stain out."

"Wow, as a wife, I have zero tricks like that up my sleeve."

"Trust me, this is my only one. Is Gabe still around? Marcus was looking for him a while ago."

"He's gone back to the cottage, but I'll tell him."

"Thanks . . . I should get back upstairs."

We say good night, and as I turn to leave, my eye catches on the shirt. And the fluttering thought I couldn't quite snag at the dinner is finally in my grasp. The shirt Marcus was wearing tonight is white, not blue. It was *Nick* who was wearing a pale blue shirt. And that means it was Nick whom Keira was confronting in the side yard before we all sat down for dinner.

What would they have had to discuss in such a heated way? Was she sharing her suspicions about Marcus and Hannah? I'm losing the ability to make sense of things.

Outside, the beautiful day has turned into an overcast evening, and despite the walkway lights on, the area along the path is mostly shrouded in darkness.

I'm halfway to the cottage when I see it—a large form, low to the ground and darting behind a shrub on the side of the path where the main lawn is. My heart jumps. Is it one of the dogs?

"Ginger," I call out weakly, and then stronger a second time. How did she get out of the house?

But it can't be her. I heard Gabe urging the dogs up to Ash's room fifteen minutes ago.

And then it's there again, shooting out from behind the shrub and across the lawn. It's almost as big as Ginger but more lithe, with an extra-long snout. In a flash it disappears into the darkness.

It must be the coyote. I gulp for air and tear up the rest of the path. By the time I reach the cottage, my lungs are on fire. Before grasping the doorknob, I spin around and stare into the night, checking all around me. There's no sign of any animal now, and all I can hear are the usual insect sounds from the treetops: *katydid; she didn't; she did; she didn't.*

Maybe it wasn't a coywolf. Maybe only a possum or raccoon. Or it was nothing at all, simply all my fears metamorphosing into a darting shadow. But I can't shake it from my mind—the fast dash across the grass, the ominous shape of the snout.

It feels like an omen. Telling me that in this serene, lovely place, a place I've always loved, more terrible things are in store for us.

20

Once I thrust open the door to the cottage, I find Gabe sitting in the middle of the couch, lost in his thoughts.

"What's the matter?" he asks, reading the distress on my face.

"I think I saw the coyote near one of the shrubs. Or the coywolf—or whatever it's called."

"You're kidding." He makes a move for the door.

"Please, Gabe, don't go out there. And besides, it's gone now. It ran across the lawn toward the woods after it spotted me."

"Damn, that must be what Marcus has been hearing. I'll let my father know first thing in the morning."

"Henry's in bed, I take it?"

"Yeah, he barely stirred when I laid him down."

"The movie seemed to cheer him up a little."

"For now. Amanda called me this afternoon and said he's been sounding morose when they talk, and she's lobbying to drive out and pick him up before the week is out."

"What do you think?"

"I'm partly tempted to say yes and that we'll make up the vacation time with him later in the summer. It might actually be a good idea for him to skip the burial."

"I think you're right. He asked me earlier if Gee would be scared in the woods, so it's clearly causing a lot of anxiety."

"I'll call her in the morning, then, and suggest she pick him up early Thursday."

We're communicating at least. Navigating regular parenting stuff. But there's still a wall between us that's hard to ignore.

"You going up now?" I ask.

"I might sit here for a minute, try to decompress from the day."

What I want is for him to decompress with *me*. Spoon me in bed, stroke my hair, let me sleep in his arms.

"Okay, see you up there," I say.

Swiveling back toward the door, I turn the lock.

"When you left the house, did you think to lock that door behind you?" Gabe asks.

"Yup. And that reminds me. I ran into Keira, who said Marcus was looking for you earlier."

"Thanks."

Upstairs, I dress for bed and dig out my phone from my purse, looking for news about the rest of my life. There's a missed call from my mom, and a voice mail asking how the memorial service went. I wish I'd had time to check in with her today. But how do I even begin to explain—about the poem, about Hannah, about the poisoning?

As for work, my agent's booked me for a voice-over job at the end of next week, which I appreciate, but I can't help but note there's nothing from Shawna, no *Hey, sorry that other job turned into a shitshow, but we'd love you to record the next Liane Moriarty novel.*

There are also a couple of texts from friends, who want to know how my vacation is going, and I'm reminded that I haven't had a chance to tell any of them yet about Claire. Finally, I see a text from Billy Dean asking if I've bumped into Hannah again. It doesn't surprise me—the guy never met a piece of gossip he didn't love. But maybe there's a chance he could be of help.

Yeah, unfortunately she turned up AGAIN, I text back. You have friends from USC, right? Anyone know her when she was there?

I'm thinking again of Claire's comment—*Our little* USC *graduate.* Wendy learned Hannah had actually attended the school, but maybe Claire meant something else by her remark, that perhaps Hannah did something at college that wasn't on the up-and-up.

On it, he replies.

Of course, I'll end up having to pay Billy back somehow, probably in Moscow Mules. And that's regardless of whether or not he manages to produce information. But at least I'm not sitting here doing nothing.

Before crawling between the sheets, I make a final run to the bathroom and as I cross the hall, I hear Gabe on his phone downstairs. I pick up the word *vineyard*, which makes me think it's Marcus on the other end.

"Right, right," Gabe says, his voice low.

There's a long pause, Marcus clearly elaborating on a point. Twice Gabe attempts to interrupt him to no avail.

"Look," he says finally. "Let's not get ahead of ourselves. The bottom line is that we now have the cushion we need."

As relieved as I am that the sudden influx of cash will enable Gabe to deal with his work crisis, the idea leaves me slightly queasy. The newfound safety net exists only because Claire is dead.

Once I'm back in bed, sleep overtakes me quickly. But at around four, I'm woken by a nightmare in which a huge dog chews through not only my suitcase but also all the clothes packed inside, so I'm left naked, and then finally the animal bares its vicious teeth at me. And that's when I bolt awake.

With my pulse racing, I yank the covers up to my chin and force my breaths to slow. Gabe's snoring lightly beside me. After a moment I start to make out the shapes in the room: the dresser with the carved mirror above it, the slipper chair, the filmy white curtains fluttering a little in the breeze. There's no Hound of the Baskervilles after me or my luggage.

I finally manage to fall back to sleep and wake again at close to seven. Leaving Gabe in bed, I dress quietly and creep down the stairs. Before heading into the kitchen, I tug back a curtain on one of the sitting room windows to see that it's utterly gloomy out, the early morning sky gray and distended.

In the kitchen, I make coffee and slip outside with my mug. The temperature is probably in the seasonal range, but the dampness in the air makes it feel a little raw and unpleasant, such a far cry from the past couple of days.

Leaving the path, I cross the lawn toward the row of

shrubs I saw that animal shoot behind last night. I know it's unlikely I'll find a tuft of fur snagged on a branch, or, ha, a pile of scat I can ask Marcus to analyze, but I'm hoping there might be some paw prints in the dirt around the bushes. But there's nothing. I might as well be looking for signs of Bigfoot.

Still, the lack of evidence doesn't leave me any less rattled—not only about what I saw, but the idea that it felt like a harbinger of something bad.

Gabe and Henry are both stirring when I return, and we eat breakfast together. Afterward, determined to give Henry more of my undivided attention, I act out part of a chapter of *Peter Pan* for him. Once that's run its course, we all settle in the sitting room—Gabe with his dog-eared thriller, Henry with his iPad, and me with my laptop.

From time to time I sense Gabe studying me from the corner of his eye. Is he wondering if I've done what he asked—taken a long deep breath and let the Hannah business go? I'm certainly using all my acting chops to look like I have. There's no way he can tell from my I'm-just-perusing-scented-candles-on-Amazon expression that I'm actually doing a deep dive on digitalis. From what I've read so far, it stays in the system for days, which means that if an autopsy is done on Claire before she's buried, the authorities will be able to tell if she had ingested it prior to her death. But first, of course, someone would have to *alert* the authorities.

Shortly before ten Gabe asks if I'd mind if he went for a run on the road while the weather's still decent, and I tell him of course, offering a smile.

"Are we gonna be in the cottage all day?" Henry asks

after he leaves. Curious rather than whiny, with a sliver of hope that I'm going to answer in the negative.

"Well, it's not really swimming weather. How 'bout a game of horseshoes?"

He shrugs, unenthused. "Can we go play with Bella and Ginger in the big house?"

"Great idea," I tell him. I feel desperate to escape the cottage, too. Maybe if I clear my head, my next steps will become evident to me.

In the kitchen, we greet Bonnie, and Henry drops to the floor with the dogs.

"Anything going on?" I ask her.

"It's been real quiet so far this morning," she reports, setting down the whisk she's been using on an aluminum bowl filled with raw eggs. Next to it are a half dozen empty tart crusts. "Ash has been in the study with the door closed, and Wendy had her dry toast and tea in the dining room, but I think she's since gone back to the carriage house."

"No one else is stirring?"

"Not that I've seen. Oh, Hannah was here a little while ago, getting coffee." She lowers her voice. "I feel sorry for that girl."

Beneath my sleeves, goose bumps roll up my arms. "What do you mean?"

Bonnie lowers her voice so Henry can't overhear, though he's probably doing his best to do so. "This can't be easy for her. Coming out here for the first time, getting engaged, and then having her future mother-in-law die. I think it's putting a strain on things."

"On her, you mean . . . or the relationship?"

"Both. I shouldn't be talking out of turn, but you're so bighearted, Summer, maybe you could reach out to her, see if you could help."

"Of course, of course. But why do you suspect there's a problem?" I ask lightly, then hold my breath.

"They were in a tiff last night after dinner," she says, whispering now. "I heard them right before I left."

"Do you know what they were arguing about?"

"No idea. But Nick seemed pissed. And you know Nick. He never gets pissed."

In a split second, some of the tension coiled in my body unwinds. Maybe Nick is finally coming to his senses. It could have something to do with whatever Keira told him right before dinner. Maybe she discovered that Marcus, despite his protestations to the contrary, had been meeting privately with Hannah, and she conveyed as much to Nick.

"Summer?"

I've been so lost in my thoughts, it takes me a couple of seconds to realize Bonnie's still talking to me.

"Yes, I know what you mean," I say. "Let me see what I can do."

"You're a doll."

If she only knew.

Henry and I end up taking Bella and Ginger outside and romping with them in the yard at the far side of the pool. I doubt anyone's played with them since Sunday and they seem in heaven.

Once we've tired out the dogs, we drop them off in the kitchen and return to the cottage, and Gabe shows up a while later, carrying one of the freshly baked goat cheese and asparagus tarts that Bonnie made. "I figured we'd eat lunch here," he says.

I appreciate the thought, but his tone and body language toward me still feel really distant.

While Henry and I set the table, Gabe slices the tart and uses a spatula to wiggle three slices onto plates. "Don't let me forget," he says. "I promised Bonnie I'd return the tart pan so she doesn't lose track of it."

"Does Bonnie always wash her hands when she makes our food?" Henry asks. It's the kind of question I've never heard him utter.

"Of course. What brings that up, Hen?" Gabe says, clearly surprised, too.

"My mom says you always have to wash your hands before food preparation, or people can get sick."

"That's true, and Bonnie always does it."

"And what about the people who help her? Do they wash their hands, too?"

"You bet. Bonnie would kick some serious butt if they didn't."

Gabe and I make brief and puzzled eye contact, and I can't help but wonder if Henry's preoccupied by sickness because of his grandmother's death.

After lunch, Gabe and Henry retreat to the couch again, but I feel even antsier than I did this morning. With each hour that ticks by, I'm further away from proving what I know. I need to stretch my legs and think.

"Hey," I call out to Gabe and Henry, who barely look up. "I'm going to take the tart pan back to Bonnie."

Only Jake is in the kitchen when I arrive, loading glasses

into the dishwasher and bobbing his head to a song on his iPod I can't hear. Wondering if anyone else is still around postlunch, I open the dining room door an inch to see Keira at the table, drinking an espresso and studying the contents of a folder, probably for work. Instead of disturbing her, I quietly ease the door closed.

"Bonnie nearby?" I ask Jake.

He plucks out his wireless earbuds. "Hmm, I think she's at the carriage house. She said she wanted to tidy up over there."

"Okay."

"No, wait," he adds. "I saw her out the window so she's already back. She must be in the woods now."

"The *woods*?"

"Yeah, she said that after she was finished, she was going to walk down to the spot where they're going to do the burial. For, you know, for Mrs. Keaton. Bonnie wanted to check it out before it rained."

That would be just like Bonnie, wanting to see where Claire will be laid to rest and make sure everything is in order.

I feel a slight pinch of worry, though. There's a coyote roaming around. Would it ever come out in daytime? Gabe was supposed to mention my sighting to his father, but the news might not have made its way to Bonnie.

I press a finger to my lips, wondering if I should head to the stream myself and alert her. As I stand staring into space, something Jake said works its way back through my mind. Bonnie tidied up at the carriage house this morning. Though Marcus told her to skip the guest suite, she's been taking care of the rest of us—swapping in fresh towels, emptying waste-baskets, stocking the fridges.

If Hannah used the kitchen in the carriage house to dry foxglove leaves for a tea, Bonnie might have noticed something without being aware of its significance. Maybe this is my opportunity to ask her without others around.

"If anyone's looking for me, tell them I'll be back shortly," I call to Jake as I'm halfway out the back door. Once I'm off the patio, I break into a jog across the lawn. The sky's even darker now, like it's been smeared with soot, and the air feels damp. Rain's coming at some point.

I reach the trellis-lined pathway, and cover it, still moving at a clip. Vines have threaded through the rustic slats at the top, shrouding the path in near darkness today, and I'm relieved when I finally emerge into the wildflower meadow. There's only one easy route to the stream from here—through the two meadows—so surely I'll run into Bonnie on her way back. I don't spot her in this meadow, however, or the next one, either. A stitch has started in my side, and I slow my pace, grabbing a few extra breaths.

And then finally I hear footsteps. And someone panting, even gasping for air. I burst from the grass meadow to find Bonnie standing off to the left near the start of the woods, her eyes wide with what looks like fear.

"What's wrong?" I call out as I race to her side. "Is it the coywolf?"

"No, no," she says, shaking her head. She jabs her free arm in the direction of the stream. "There . . . near the water . . . omigod . . ."

"Show me what you mean," I urge.

Grasping her arm, I pull her cautiously along the edge of the woods in the direction of the stream, less than a minute away.

Before long I see what's scared her. Vultures. There's a cluster of them parked on the peaked roof of the old, weathered bird blind. They're huge, the size of toddlers, though they look primordial—brownish black-feathered bodies with wrinkly, blood-red heads.

"There must be a dead animal around—"

But then my gaze is drawn to the ground about fifteen or so yards ahead of me. There are three more vultures in the weeds along the stream—and a body lying stretched out beside them, facedown. The vultures are pecking at the base of the skull with their beaks, one with a claw clasped around the skull.

Bile surges up into my throat.

It's a woman wearing one of the tan slickers that hang in the side corridor of the house. And jeans. Jeans that have been yanked down to her ankles, revealing the flesh of her calves.

My gaze flies back to the woman's head. Her hair's dark brown, and though the face isn't visible, I can see a hand, poking out from the sleeve of the slicker. The fingernails are painted a glossy pink.

It's Hannah, I realize. Lying dead by the stream.

21

gasp, rooted in place.

Is she really dead? Maybe she's only injured, but it looks like a devastating injury. And why else would the vultures have come? I drop Bonnie's arm and force myself forward a few steps. The vultures stop pecking, but barely deterred, they hop back less than a foot.

It's enough for me to have a better view, though, and the sight makes me recoil. Hannah's hair is matted and wet with blood, especially near the base of her skull. There's a hole there, and pieces of flesh stuck in the ooze surrounding it.

"We have to go," I say to Bonnie in a hoarse whisper.

"Is it——?"

"Hannah? Yeah, it must be."

"I tried to throw a rock——to make the birds go away, but . . ."

"Bonnie, I don't think there's anything you could have done. She must be dead."

As Bonnie lets out a moan, I grab her arm again and haul her away from the stream. I try to run, the two of us entwined, but the best I manage is a slow jog, hampered by my panic. Someone brutally attacked Hannah, right here on my in-laws' property. Every few steps I twist my neck and check behind us, making sure no one is following.

We reach the first meadow, where the higher grasses block our view, and each time we approach another curve in the serpentine path, my fear balloons further, as I wonder what's on the other side. But we don't see anyone, and finally burst into the flower meadow. At the end of it I check behind me yet again, almost tripping as I swing back around.

We're halfway through the trellised path when Bonnie begs me to stop.

"I've got to rest for a sec," she says.

"Of course," I tell her. We halt and both lean forward at the waist, gasping for air. At least from here, we can see the house, up the slope and far across the lawn.

"I can't believe this," Bonnie says, a sob caught in her throat. She's practically dripping with sweat, and in the contained space of the path, I pick up its sour smell. "Was she raped, do you think?"

"Maybe. Or someone intended that and when she tried to fight him off, he killed her."

"Oh god, the poor girl. But who could have done it?"

So far, I've been too terrified to wonder, but now a thought takes shape. "Claire said something the other day about hunters coming onto the property."

"Yes, more than once," Bonnie says. "Mostly in the fall, during deer season, though I think she spotted one recently. You're allowed to shoot groundhogs in summer but not on private property like this."

I nod, trying to piece it together. "When did you last see Hannah today?"

"When she came by the kitchen for coffee—like I told you. And then I saw her from the window going across the lawn."

"She . . . she might have walked down here right after."

And stumbled onto her attacker. Was it really a hunter then, one who thought nothing of assaulting and killing her?

But then, unbidden, other names force their way into my brain, no matter how hard I try to keep them out.

Nick. Who'd quarreled with Hannah last night.

Marcus. Who seems to have been livid with Hannah, though I don't know why. Perhaps because he couldn't have her for himself.

No, it can't be one of Gabe's brothers. It *can't* be.

Behind us, leaves rustle in the wind, startling me, but I turn to see there's no one there.

"Can you start again?" I ask Bonnie, desperate to be back at the house.

"Yeah, I'm okay now."

Linking arms, we cover the rest of the passageway and then scurry up and across the lawn. There's no one outside the house, but as soon as we enter through the side door, I hear voices coming from the living room. We follow the sound to find Ash, Marcus, and Gabe standing in a circle, hands in their pants pockets, clearly having a discussion of some kind.

"Where's Nick?" I ask, still nearly breathless.

"I'm not sure," Ash says. "Are you okay, Summer?"

I shake my head. "We just found Hannah's body down by the stream."

"*What?*" he exclaims.

"She's dead, I'm almost positive. Her head . . ."

Marcus's face goes white before my eyes, and Gabe steps toward me, grasping my arm.

"Good love of god," their father exclaims.

"We need to call 911," I say. "And someone needs to find Nick. To tell him."

"Tell me what?"

Nick steps into the room from the front hall, dressed in jeans and a lavender polo shirt.

I take the deepest breath I can. "Nick, I'm so sorry," I say. "Hannah's—Hannah's dead. And, god, it looks like someone's murdered her. With some kind of blow to the head."

His face wrinkles, but in confusion instead of horror.

"What in the world are you talking about?" Nick says.

"Bonnie and I—" Before I can say another word, I hear footsteps in the hall, and a second later, Hannah enters the room.

All five foot eight of her. She's dressed in jeans and a short-sleeved yellow turtleneck, her hair and makeup freshly done.

As Bonnie lets out a scream of shock, I feel the blood rush from my brain. It's like I'm in one of those nightmares all actors have, in which you're about to go onstage and realize you've never even read the play you're performing in.

"I—We were down at the stream," I say. "We saw her . . . the body."

Hannah locks eyes with me. "Is this some kind of a sick joke?"

"Summer, what in the hell is going on?" Ash demands. Gabe is looking at me as if my hair's on fire. I gesture toward Bonnie to back me up.

"Just like she said, there's a body at the stream," Bonnie says, her voice tremulous. "A woman with dark hair—we thought it was you."

"*Keira*," Marcus exclaims, his voice strained with panic.

"It can't be her," I blurt out. "She was in the house when I left."

"*No*," Ash suddenly roars, and he tears out of the room into the main hall and from there into the foyer. We follow him, watching as he flings open the front door, and charges down the steps of the house.

"Dad, what *is* it?" Gabe calls out, running down the driveway after him, with Nick, Marcus, and me sprinting behind.

"Where's Henry?" I shout to Gabe.

"In the kitchen. With Jake."

When we catch up with Ash, he's just beyond the circular part of the driveway, in the long section that connects the house to the road, and he's staring at a blue BMW. His hands are laced through his thick gray hair, fingers digging into his scalp. "Jesus Christ, it must be *Jillian*," he says.

That makes no sense, but . . . her car is definitely sitting here. An image muscles its way to the front of my mind: the dark matted hair; the long slim fingers with painted nails. Like Hannah's. Like Jillian's, too.

"Jillian was here?" I say tentatively.

"She was helping me," Ash says. His eyes bounce with agitation. "We've got to get down there."

"Are you sure she's dead?" Marcus asks, pulling me aside and keeping his voice low so his father can't hear.

"Yes, unfortunately. The back of her head's open, from a blow—or a shot maybe—and there were vultures around, like she'd been dead for a little while at least. It also looks like someone might have tried to sexually assault her."

Or, it occurs to me for the first time, wanted to make it *look* that way.

Grimacing, Marcus turns back to Ash. "Dad, you can't go down there. It's a crime scene."

"Marcus, you had one fucking year of law school," his father snaps. "That doesn't make you an expert."

"Dad, he's right," Gabe says. "We have to all stay put and call 911."

"I'll do it," I say. "Since I can describe what I saw."

We hurry together back toward the house, where Bonnie's waiting on the front stoop, clearly doing her best not to fall apart. And Hannah? Nowhere to be seen now.

"Have you got your phone?" I ask Gabe in a rush.

"No, it's in the cottage."

"Mine, too. I'll use the landline in the den."

He nods limply, as if he's still trying to absorb what's unfurling. Before we take off down the hall, he asks Bonnie to check on Henry.

"Sure thing," she says.

The landline's on one of the small antique side tables in the room. I grab the receiver but before calling, I turn to Gabe. "I'm just—"

"Just what?"

"Worried. What if I say something that backfires?"

He presses his finger across his lips and eyes me expectantly, as if waiting for me to elaborate.

"Gabe, she was *murdered*," I say. "And what if it wasn't by a stranger, but by someone in this house?"

He flinches. "Tell them what you found. And leave it at that."

Steeling myself, I tap 9–1–1. After giving my name, I describe the situation, my voice trembling as I speak. The dispatcher runs through some questions, calmly and efficiently, and at the end I assure her that, yes, we'll remain in the house and await the arrival of the police.

"Did they say how long it would be?" Gabe says once I disconnect. He's been standing next to me the whole time, his brow furrowed.

"No, only that the police are being dispatched immediately. . . . Gabe, what could Jillian have been doing down there?"

"God knows."

But maybe *I* know. Or I could posit a theory. What if Jillian and Ash really *were* having an affair, and she came to the house today to see him, pulling her car into the lower part of the driveway so it wouldn't be so obvious? What if the two of them had arranged to meet in secret by the stream?

And then what? Did they agree to leave separately so as not to be seen together, and then Jillian, the last to depart, was attacked by a stranger? Or, oh god, did *Ash* kill her? But what would his motive be? It couldn't have been that she was threatening to tell his wife. Could she have been making demands now that Claire was out of the picture?

I realize that I have to tell Gabe about what Marcus and I witnessed. "Gabe, there's something I need to—"

He raises a hand, palm forward. "I know what you're going to say. Marcus told me last night on the phone—about Dad and Jillian."

I feel a millisecond of relief, but his knowing changes nothing about the current situation.

"Should your dad be calling a lawyer?" I ask. "I'm not accusing anyone of anything, but shouldn't there be someone guiding us?"

Before he can respond, Marcus appears in the doorway.

"Did someone say lawyer?" he asks.

"Yeah," Gabe tells him. "That's a priority."

"Dad's tracking one down now, a guy who does criminal cases," he says, looking pained as he says the word *criminal*. "You called 911 already?"

"Summer did," Gabe tells him, "and the police are on their way. Does anyone know what Jillian was doing by the woods?"

"According to Dad, she was checking out the area for the burial. Apparently, she needed to provide some information to the people digging the damn hole."

I guess that makes sense, sort of. "But how would she even know her way down there?" I ask.

Marcus shrugs. "Your guess is as good as mine."

"Do you think Nick's aware if anything was going on between Dad and Jillian?" Gabe asks. "He was around them a lot more than we were."

"Nick's so goo-goo eyed about his own love life, I doubt he'd notice if Godzilla made landfall and came up the

Delaware. But it's worth asking him. And we're all on the same page about the hug, right?"

"Of course," Gabe says. "I won't breathe a word."

When I don't respond immediately, they turn to me.

"Agree, absolutely," I say, but my stomach twists. What if this means I have to deceive the police? I can lie and make anyone believe me, but I don't want to have to do that.

"And everything else?" Gabe asks, back to looking at Marcus. "The less said the better, right?"

Marcus nods, but before I can ask what they're referring to, Gabe wonders aloud where Blake and Wendy are.

"Doylestown—they left around one," Marcus says. "Wendy's doctor arranged for her to have a sonogram there for some reason. They shouldn't be much—"

He stops short as the distant wail of a police siren penetrates the quiet of the room.

"Okay, here we go," Marcus says. "Brace for impact."

How in the world are we supposed to brace for *this*? It feels like someone's taken my life in their hands and is shaking it hard like a snow globe, making pieces come undone.

We hurry into the living room, where Keira's sitting with the just-returned Blake and Wendy, all three looking stunned as Nick debriefs them. Ash must still be trying to connect with an attorney because we can hear him through the open door of the study talking on the phone, his voice low and his tone urgent.

"And you're sure it's Jillian," Blake says, glancing at the three of us who've just entered.

"It must be," Marcus says. "Dad tried her cell and there was no answer. And anyone else is accounted for."

The siren cuts off abruptly and we hear a vehicle heading up the gravel driveway and lurching to a stop.

"Okay," Blake says. "Since Dad is tied up, I'll speak to the police first. Summer, you should come with me, to describe what you found. Everyone else should remain in the house for now, I think."

"I want Gabe to be there, too," I say.

"Fine."

When Blake, Gabe, and I exit the house, we discover an ambulance, not the police. But as the ambulance doors spring open, an official-looking SUV charges up the driveway, and moments later, two male state troopers climb out, dressed in gray pants, gray shirts, and black ties, their faces wooden.

Blake does as promised, introducing us in somber tones and explaining that it was me, along with the housekeeper, who found the body near a wooded area on the property. "We believe," he adds, "that it's Jillian Herrera, my father's assistant."

"You're not certain, though?" the older trooper asks, the one with a mustache too thin for his face, locking eyes with me.

"No, because she's lying facedown," I explain. There's no reason to waste time describing my initial confusion and the farcical scene with Hannah in the living room.

"And when was the last time Ms. Herrera was seen alive?"

"This morning." It's Ash talking, out of the house now and coming up behind us to introduce himself to the police. "She assisted me with some paperwork in the study and left about ten o'clock. Her intention was to return to the city, but first she'd offered to check out an area by the woods. I didn't notice until a few minutes ago that her car was still here in the driveway." He chokes up on the last few words.

"Why did she need to go down there?" It's still the older trooper speaking.

"She was looking at the place we plan to bury my wife, who passed on Sunday," Ash tells them. "Ms. Herrera was helping with the arrangements."

His voice cracks once again, but I have no way of knowing if it's mainly from grief or distress or fear. Could my father-in-law actually be a murderer? I try to push away the thought.

"You weren't surprised when she didn't stop in before she left."

"There was no need to. We'd finished our work and we planned to speak again tomorrow morning."

The troopers nod, their faces still stony. They inquire who else is here on the property, and after Ash goes through the list, they ask me to direct them to the crime scene, along with the housekeeper, and the two paramedics.

"I should accompany you, too," Ash announces. "This is my property, and I can answer your questions."

"No, the rest of you need to remain in the house," the trooper tells him. "Detectives from the state police are on their way."

"I'll get the housekeeper," Gabe interjects, and I realize that he doesn't want the troopers going into the kitchen and collecting her in front of Henry. He darts off and returns with Bonnie less than a minute later. As she and I depart with the police, I glance behind me, trying to make eye contact with Gabe so that he can give me a reassuring look. But instead he's staring off into the distance.

As if reading each other's thoughts, Bonnie and I lead the troopers and paramedics around the building, avoiding the house, then along the side of the boxwood grove and gardens and down the wide expanse of lawn.

Though the air is damp, the rain continues to hold off. Bonnie's put on a zippered cardigan since I saw her earlier, but I'm still in only a long-sleeved T-shirt. I shiver, but it's less from the weather and more from my nerves.

Pretend you're in a play, I tell myself. *Own the stage, own the room, stay in control.*

On the way, the troopers ask us a few more questions: *Did you notice anyone else in the vicinity when you were down here or hear anything suspicious?* No, Bonnie and I say in unison. *Did either of you have any contact with Jillian Herrera earlier today?* Again, no. *Is there any other way to gain access to where we're going?* Bonnie mentions an old logging road that cuts through the woods and ends not far from the stream. I've never heard of it before, but I'm relieved to learn another detail supporting the idea of an outside perpetrator.

We've reached the first meadow by now and one of the troopers asks if we have much farther to go. I give an estimate of under ten minutes and describe the rest of the route ahead. As we hurry through the wildflowers, their colors dulled from the lack of sunshine, I try to picture Jillian coming through here earlier. Was it right after she left Ash in the study? She must have looked at the sky and grabbed a slicker. I wonder again if she and Ash hiked here together. And then . . .

Finally, when we reach the end of the second meadow, Bonnie freezes in her tracks, as if she can't bear the idea of witnessing the scene again.

"It's to the left and then a few hundred feet," I tell the troopers. "She's between the stream and an old bird blind."

Thankfully, they instruct us to remain where we are before they start heading to the spot, followed not far behind by the paramedics, lugging their equipment.

"Come on, get the hell outta here," one of the troopers shouts a few seconds later. Not to a person, I realize, but to the vultures. I feel bile in my throat again as I picture the birds pecking at the head wound. There are sounds of movement next, the troopers traipsing through the grass and then the murmur of instructions being given into a cell phone or radio.

"You doin' okay, hon?" Bonnie whispers.

"Um, yeah. You?"

"Hanging in there. I mean, what choice do we have?"

Within a few minutes, two more troopers, a male and a female, come tramping through the meadow behind us, and we point them in the right direction, though the man returns a minute later, announcing that he's going to escort me and Bonnie back to the house.

"Can you tell us if she's definitely dead?" I ask.

"Yes," he says grimly. "I'm sorry."

We start the return journey. Part of me can't wait to be in the house again, but then I remind myself that there's no comfort waiting for me there.

The trooper leaves us at the back door, reminding us not to go anywhere until we've been interviewed. Inside the kitchen we find Jake folding napkins on the island, silent and bug-eyed, clearly a little rattled, but also revved up, I suspect. This might be the biggest excitement he's had all summer.

Gabe and Henry are there, too, parked at the table. Henry's riveted by something on his iPad, and Gabe assures him that he'll be right back, then ushers me into the dining room, making sure the door swings closed behind us.

"Is it definitely her?" Gabe asks.

"They didn't let us near the spot this time, but who *else*? What's happening here?"

"You just missed the two detectives. They're out front now, waiting for one of the troopers to escort them to the scene. And apparently a forensics team is arriving any minute."

"I guess it'll be a while then before anyone interviews Bonnie and me."

"It turns out we *all* have to give statements, and not from the comfort of the living room. At the state police station, wherever that is."

My stomach roils. I have no reason to feel guilty and yet I sense land mines ahead.

"Did your dad find a lawyer yet?"

"Yep, they've been on the phone. And Amanda's coming. I called and asked her to pick up Henry today instead of tomorrow. I can't have him around when there are police all over the place and people in hazmat suits."

I nod, aware it's the right thing to do. And yet it seems like a warning that the things we care about most in life are in danger of being wrenched away from us.

"I'm going to take Hen over to the cottage now," Gabe adds. "All I've told him is that Dad's assistant has been badly injured, and he needs to go back to the city. I'll pack his bag and hang with him there for a while."

"But aren't we supposed to stay put?" I ask.

"We're not leaving the *property*, Summer."

"Okay, okay."

After he departs, I stand there, uncertain of what to do next, my eyes on the oiled, wide-plank pine floor. Will I ever feel at ease in this house again? Will I ever be able to sit by the stream again, savoring the memory of Gabe's proposal?

"Summer?"

I look up to see Keira a few feet from me, tucking a hair behind her ear.

"Hi."

"Can I talk to you for a second?" she asks.

"Uh, sure."

"Did you hear we all have to give statements . . . at the police station?"

"Yeah, Gabe just told me."

She glances to the left, lips pressed.

"I know, it's scary," I say when she doesn't go on. "But we'll get through it."

"What do you plan to do—you know, in regard to Jillian?" I guess Marcus filled her in.

"You mean, am I going to tell the police about seeing Ash embrace her? No."

"Not about that. About Jillian's thing with Marcus and Gabe this morning. You aren't going to say anything to the police about *that*, are you?"

22

For the next two hours all of us except for Gabe mill around the first floor of the house. At one point, Blake, Nick, and Marcus press me to share more details about the crime scene, and I do, hating myself for the way I study Nick's and Marcus's reactions. But nothing about their demeanor seems suspicious. When the chance arises, I sidle up to Wendy, who's sitting quietly at the end of a sofa, still dressed from her trip to the medical center and hugging her leather tote to her chest.

"Was the sonogram okay?" I whisper.

"Yes, thank god, everything's fine," she says, smiling wanly. "I'm just shell-shocked from all this."

Ash spends much of that time sequestered in the study, talking on the phone, except when one of the detectives asks him to step outside to identify the body before it's loaded into the ambulance. When he returns, he looks shaken.

For our trip to the state police station, we've been put into two groups, and I'm in the first, along with Blake, Marcus, Keira, and Bonnie. We say good-bye to Wendy—because of

her condition, the police took her statement in the den—
and Marcus quickly ushers Keira into their car. I jump into
Blake's black Mercedes, along with Bonnie, who insists I take
the front seat.

"Would you mind cranking up the AC?" I ask Blake.

"Of course. You feel okay?"

"Uh, not great, no."

"If you're at all faint, put your head between your knees,
okay? It really works."

I thank him, but actually, I wish I *could* faint. I wish I
could face-plant on the asphalt the second we arrive at the
station, be hauled off on a stretcher, and then medevacked
to a hospital in another state where, for some reason, they
decide I need to be placed in isolation for a week.

Because I need time to concentrate, to decide what the
hell I'm going to tell the police. Jillian's been murdered, but
I feel sure Claire was, too. I contemplate hinting at my suspicions in the interview and yet I know that if I do, I'll probably sound utterly ridiculous to the police, and it's possible I
might complicate things even more for the Keatons. But then
does that mean Hannah goes free?

The jumble of thoughts is causing a weird rushing sound
in my head, like wind in a tunnel. And making it worse: my
anxiety over the conversation I had with Keira in the dining
room earlier.

"What do you mean?" I'd exclaimed, taken aback by her
comment about Marcus, Gabe, and Jillian, which clearly im-
plied something had happened that I shouldn't bring up to
the detectives.

"Oh, it's nothing important," she'd said. "They had some words with her about work stuff. In the driveway. I'm not going to bring it up, though. Marcus said we shouldn't."

I tried to get more out of her, but she scurried off. At least now I understand why Marcus and Gabe shot each other a look in the den and decided that the less said, the better.

"We're almost there," Blake announces, shaking me from my thoughts.

"Did Wendy give you any idea about the questions they'll have?" I ask him.

"She didn't have a chance to tell me much but said it was mostly what she expected—how well did she know Jillian, had she spoken to her that day, did she see anyone suspicious on the property. My guess is that it'll be pretty much the same for all of us other than my father. None of us knew Jillian well besides him, so we have very little to contribute."

Not long after, he makes a sharp right turn off the road and pulls up in front of a fairly large, nondescript brick building. In the utilitarian lobby, we see we're the first of our party to arrive, and the officer at the desk tells Blake to take a seat on the bench, and then Bonnie and I are led away by a trooper into separate interview rooms. The one I'm in smells faintly of spray bleach cleanser, and there's a long mirror on the far wall—two-way, I assume.

A duo of female detectives is waiting at the smudged metal table, both in dark, lightweight blazers, and though they don't rise out of their seats, they introduce themselves politely—Detectives Russo and Callahan. Callahan's the one who came into the house at one point and designated what groups we'd be in, but it's Russo, the older of the two, who asks me to take a seat across from them and explains that our conversation will be taped.

In acting classes you're taught that one of the best ways to project confidence is to claim territory, and I try to do that as soon as I sit, positioning both hands on the table a few inches from my body. Part of my nervousness is due simply from being inside an interview room at a police station, but it's more than that, of course.

The salt-and-pepper-haired Detective Russo kicks things off, asking for basic details, like my name and relation to the family, then telling me to describe how I happened to come upon the crime scene today, while Callahan takes notes. Needless to say, I don't mention that one reason I'd gone in search of Bonnie was to ask if she'd noticed any signs of someone drying poisonous leaves in the carriage house kitchen. Instead, I explain that I'd seen a coyote on the property the night before and had headed to the stream to warn her—also true, of course. Russo's expression never changes, but Detective Callahan's face contracts slightly, perhaps in skepticism, as if I'm trying to convince her of some mythical story, like those involving a winged horse or a she-wolf.

"Did you or the housekeeper touch the body—or go near it?" Russo asks. It's clear she's going to do most of the talking.

"I didn't, and I assume Bonnie didn't before I got there. It was hard for us to even look. And it was pretty clear it was too late to help her."

"Did you see anyone else in the vicinity?"

"No, not a soul."

"And this was at about what time?"

"Uh, I didn't have my phone with me, so I can't be precise. But probably about fifteen or twenty minutes before I called 911 back at the house."

Russo makes a show out of opening a folder in front of her, then thumbs through a thin stack of papers, skimming the handwritten notes on one of the pages before finally returning her gaze to me.

"How well did you know Jillian Herrera?" She asks it easily enough, still polite.

"Not well. In the six years since I've been with my husband, I probably only met her six or seven times, usually at certain events the Keatons had at their apartment."

"Did you see or speak to her today?"

"No, I never saw her," I say. "I had no idea she was even on the property, and that's why at first I didn't realize it was her lying on the ground. Bonnie and I thought it was Hannah Kane who was dead. Nick's . . . fiancée. Because of the dark hair."

So much for my vow to myself to keep things simple. The two detectives exchange looks.

"When did you realize it wasn't Ms. Kane?"

"When we reached the house and saw Hannah. She hadn't been around earlier."

"And the last time you *did* see or speak to Ms. Herrera? When was that?"

"Well, I saw her yesterday at the memorial service for my mother-in-law—on the lawn—but I barely had any contact with her. I did speak to her, though, on, uh, Monday. We discussed a few details related to the service, since Jillian was helping with the arrangements."

"Did she share any concerns with you about her safety?"

The question catches me off guard. Do the police think someone was *after* Jillian, stalking her? No, that's not it. What the question suggests is that if Jillian was killed by someone in the household, she might have felt nervous during the days beforehand, nervous enough to even hint at it.

"No—and she seemed perfectly fine to me. By the way, I need to point out something important. Before she died this weekend, my mother-in-law told me that local hunters had been trespassing on the property. There's apparently a way to reach the woods the Keatons own—the ones near where Jillian was found—from an old logging road."

Russo drums her fingers on the table briefly.

"Did your mother-in-law elaborate on that?" she asks. "Had she made any formal complaints?"

"I'm not sure if she did, but Bonnie is aware of it, too. I'm sure Ash—Mr. Keaton—would know of specific examples."

"And you hadn't noticed anyone on the property who shouldn't be there?"

"No, but I haven't strayed very far from the house this week."

Russo taps her fingers again. Her cuticles are ragged, bitten or torn, but right now at least it seems nothing could faze her.

"Just a few more questions, Ms. Redding. How well did other family members seem to know Ms. Herrera?"

My pulse quickens. This is when I might have to skirt the truth. *You're in a* play, I tell myself for the second time today. *Own the room, stay in control.*

"Probably not much better than I did—though Nick

might have had more contact with her. Because he works with my father-in-law."

"And how about your husband? Gabe, is it?"

Why is she asking about him specifically? *Only because I'm married to him*, I tell myself. It's surely just a routine question.

"Yes, Gabe. Jillian started around the time we met, so he only knows her as well as I do. Though he may have bumped into her occasionally when he dropped by his dad's office."

What the hell would she make of the fact that he was talking to Jillian this morning—but doesn't want to admit it? To my relief, Russo redirects the conversation.

"And just to clarify," she says after a few beats, "what is the reason everyone is staying at the house this week?"

"It was supposed to be our annual summer get-together week. A vacation. Then my mother-in-law passed, so we're all still here, but of course it's not a holiday anymore."

Russo's perusing her notes again, and Callahan has stopped writing, her pen poised right above the page.

"That has to be tough at moments," Callahan offers. "So many adults in one house."

It's the first time she's opened her mouth other than to introduce herself, and though I'm pretty sure what she's trying to get at, I refuse to bite.

"You mean, like sharing a bathroom, stuff like that?" I say, offering the perplexed expression I've perfected in the mirror over time. "There are several buildings, so people have plenty of privacy."

"I meant being with so many different relatives for an extended period of time."

"We actually enjoy it. That's why we do it every year."

And then without warning, Russo thanks me for my time and warns me not to disclose details about the crime scene to anyone else. She shakes my hand briskly, and Callahan sees me out to the lobby, where two people are slouched on a bench, though neither is Bonnie or Blake. There's also no sign of anyone else from the family.

I park myself on an empty bench, and within a couple of minutes, Bonnie is escorted to the lobby and takes a seat next to me. Her face is drained of color, and her hair's practically matted to her head. Though we exchange weak smiles, we agree silently that it's best to keep our mouths shut for now. About ten minutes later, Blake appears. We greet him with wan smiles, but it isn't until the three of us are halfway across the parking lot that he asks, "Everybody okay?"

Bonnie tells him, "Yeah, as well as can be expected."

I don't respond, because frankly, I'm not sure what to say. The interview unnerved me. I'm worried that with the state police on a mission, someone in the family could become caught in the cross fire. Worried, too, that my father-in-law might be a murderer. And regretful that I couldn't find a way to subtly direct their attention to Claire's death.

On the drive home, there's next to no conversation. Blake, I'm sure, would like to debrief me, but knows it's best to stay mum in front of Bonnie. Though she's a loyal employee, the Keaton family needs to circle the wagons in a crisis of this magnitude.

Finally, we're rolling up the gravel driveway. The front door of the house turns out to be locked and we wait a minute until Gabe swings it open, looking weary. He's been waiting with Henry for our return, he tells us, and now he's going to follow his father, Nick, Hannah, and Jake to the station. Bonnie takes off for the kitchen, and Blake and I linger with Gabe in the foyer off the main hall.

"So?" Gabe says, flicking his gaze back and forth between us. His face is ashen. Or does it simply look that way in the dim light of the foyer?

"I wouldn't call them hostile or aggressive," Blake tells him, "but it's clear they won't be treating us with kid gloves because Dad's got a big house on Durham Road. And it's obvious they have him in their sights."

"As a *suspect*?" Gabe says.

"Of course. She was his younger, attractive female employee. They asked me if it was typical for her to come to the house, that sort of thing. What's the latest with the lawyer, anyway?"

"He's based in Princeton and is driving over to meet Dad at the station."

"Good. I did my best to stress that someone must have gotten onto our land and crossed paths with Jillian in some horrible twist of fate. Or that it's possible some pervert had been keeping an eye on the house for days and followed her down there."

"And I told them to talk to Ash about something both your mom and Bonnie told me," I interject. "That hunters have been coming onto the property lately."

"Okay, that's very important," Blake says. "We need to highlight it for the lawyer." He looks back at Gabe. "My best advice would be to keep your answers brief, and don't volunteer information unless they ask. . . . Look, if you'll excuse me, I want to check on Wendy."

Gabe tells him that she's in the den with her feet up. As Blake departs, Gabe puts a hand on my shoulder. It's the first time he's touched me in a couple of days, and it feels the slightest bit strange, like a small bird has lighted there.

"You okay?" he asks.

"Yeah, but it was pretty unsettling. They asked me if Jillian had expressed any concerns to me this week."

Even in the dull light, I see his brow furrow. "Had she?"

I shake my head.

"Did you get the same feeling Blake did, that they have their eye on Dad?"

"If you ask me, the police seem to have their eye on *everybody*. The main detective asked how well all of us in the family knew Jillian. Just so you're aware, I told them that you knew her about as well as I did, which was hardly at all."

"And that's a hundred percent accurate. You didn't say anything about the hug in the . . ."

"Of course not."

"Good. Look, I know this has been a brutal day for you, Summer—especially finding Jillian that way. I feel awful you had to go through all that."

"I can't get the image out of my mind," I say, choking up for the first time today. "No matter how hard I try."

"I'm so sorry, I want to talk more, but I have to go. Amanda should be here in ten or fifteen minutes. You going to be fine dealing with her on your own?"

"Yup." By now I have an advanced degree in Amanda-handling. "Is Henry in the kitchen?"

"No, playing chess against himself in the dining room. I already told him good-bye, that I'll see him soon and we'll make up the lost time later this summer."

"Where does he think you're going?"

"I explained we all have to talk to the police about Grandpa's assistant being injured, that I'm going to the station now but you're on your way back. . . . I better split. Lock the door behind me, okay?" He turns to go.

"Wait," I say. My heart's pounding as I reach out and touch the sleeve of his cotton sweater. When he turns back around, his expression has shifted from worried to alert, wary almost. "What were you and Marcus talking to Jillian about this morning?"

"Who told you that?" he asks quietly.

"Keira."

He shakes his head. "It was nothing. Marcus saw me headed for a run and he followed me to the driveway to finish a conversation we started last night. Jillian was out there, putting on a pair of walking shoes from her car. She must have just finished with Dad and was planning to go down to the stream. . . . If I'd had any idea—"

"Was she wearing one of the tan slickers?"

"From the house? Why do you ask?"

"Because she had it on when I found her."

"No, she must have grabbed it afterward."

"And what did you talk to her about?"

"About work, about Dad."

"Did you ask if she was sleeping with your father?"

"No, that's not what I meant. We want to get Dad engaged in our business again, and based on things he said at the meeting on Sunday, Jillian was erecting her own share of roadblocks—which she had no right to do. For god's sake, she was his *assistant*, not his business strategist. Sorry to speak ill of the dead."

"Keira said you were having *words*."

He shakes his head dismissively. "No, but it did get a little heated. I asked her to butt out of stuff that was above her pay grade. That's why we decided it would be stupid to mention it to the police. Why distract them with something like that?"

From somewhere deep inside of me, I pick up the faintest siren sound, like a tornado warning that's miles and miles away but still close enough to scare you.

"What?" Gabe asks.

"It's just . . . I don't know."

"*What?*" he asks again, this time with the hint of a scowl.

"The timing seems weird, that's all."

"You mean us having a contentious talk with Jillian this morning? Well, needless to say, we had no idea she'd end up murdered later."

"I meant why be talking to her at all this week, with so much happening? Was Jillian such a big threat to everything that the conversation couldn't wait?"

For a moment there is silence so pronounced it almost has a sound of its own.

"What exactly are you suggesting, Summer?"

"I'm not suggesting anything, Gabe. I'm only asking what the rush was."

But *am* I implying something?

"You used the word *threat*. It almost sounds like you think Marcus and I wanted Jillian out of the way."

"Of *course* not, Gabe."

"First it was Hannah you thought was a murderer. Now it's me. Next you'll be accusing me of poisoning my own mother."

"Gabe, that's ridiculous." My heart is drumming so hard now I can hear it in my ears.

I reach for his arm again, but he yanks it away. He turns on his heels and leaves the house, slamming the door hard behind him.

23

Desperately catching my breath, I peek into the hall to make sure no one's there and could have overheard us. To my relief, it's empty.

I'm in shock from the conversation I've just had with my husband. How did it go so awry? I hardly think Gabe is a murderer. Not for a second. But it troubles me that at a time like this he seems more worried about his business than anything else. Plus, he's held back a couple of things from me lately—how upset he was with his mother the day she died, the discussion with Jillian. Which makes me wonder if there's *other* stuff he hasn't told me.

My priority right now, though, is Henry. After locking the front door, I hurry to the dining room, where he's sitting at the table, his eyes trained on the chessboard. The dogs are lying sad-eyed on either side of his chair.

"*There* you are," Henry says, glancing up. "Where did you go for so long?"

"I was doing my interview with the police and then talking to Dad. Did you grab something to eat?" There are a few types of cheese and cold cuts and several loaves of bread on the sideboard, which Jake must have set out before he left for the station.

"Yeah, Dad made me a sandwich. But did you hear? It's only Wednesday and I have to go home already."

"I know, and I'm sorry, too, but we'll make up for it later. We still have weeks more of summer to enjoy."

"I just want everything to be the same," he says, leaning into me. "The way it was."

I wrap an arm around his shoulder. "I know, honey. It's so hard to have Gee gone. But what she'd want more than anything right now is for you not to feel down. And you and your mom will probably do something fun this weekend."

I've barely uttered the words *your mom* when I hear a rapid knock at the front door. Of course, it could be the police instead of Amanda. I ask Henry to wait and I hurry back to the foyer.

"Who is it?" I call through the thick wooden door.

"Me, Amanda," she says, a note of exasperation in her tone.

I open the door and beckon her inside. Though Gabe does most of the interacting with her, our paths cross every couple of weeks in the city, so I'm pretty comfortable in her presence. Needless to say, though, we've never been in this house at the same time.

Her expression is harried, but overall she looks as pulled together as usual, her strawberry-blond hair arranged in an attractive sloppy bun. She's dressed in jeans so white they could trigger snow blindness, hip white sneakers, and a long-sleeved turquoise shirt with the sleeves rolled to the elbows.

Gabe once told me that after reading in a magazine that some celebrity considered jeans and button-down shirts her uniform, Amanda adopted it for herself, both for weekends and in her job as an event planner.

"Wow," she says after stepping over the threshold. "This is weird. It's been, what, at least seven years since I was here last?"

Leave it to Amanda to make this about *her*.

"Yeah, I guess it *would* be pretty weird."

"So what happened?" she asks, dropping her voice. "I read online that this woman worked for the family business?"

My heart sinks. If there are already posts about the murder on news sites, who knows what kind of speculation is happening.

"You know, you should probably talk to Gabe. I can have him call you tomorrow."

"You can't tell me *anything*?"

"The police advised me not to talk to anyone about it, sorry."

She gives me a "suit yourself" shrug. "Poor Henry," she says, her expression concerned. "I can't believe he's in the middle of this."

"According to Gabe, Henry only knows someone was injured. Let me get him. Do you want to use the bathroom before you go? Or have something to eat?"

"You know, I could really use a cup of coffee before the ride back."

"I'd be glad to make you an espresso?"

"Sounds great."

Before I can decide whether to leave her cooling her heels

in the living room or bring her with me, Henry comes barreling down the hall and flings his arms around her waist. The thing about Amanda is that though she may be prickly with Gabe, difficult to coordinate plans with, and slightly officious, she's a good mom and Henry is crazy about her.

"Aren't I lucky," she says, "seeing you five whole days sooner than I thought I would. Where's all your stuff?"

"Dad put it upstairs so it wouldn't be in the way."

"Okay, run up and get it."

As he rushes toward the stairs, I tell Amanda that if she waits in the living room, I'll be back in a few with her espresso. When I open the kitchen door, I find Bonnie wiping a counter.

"Oh, Bonnie," I say, "you must be bushed."

"I'm okay, really," she insists.

"I have to deliver an espresso to Amanda and see Henry off, and then I'll be back, okay?"

When I return to the living room, white porcelain cup and saucer in hand, Amanda's perched on one of the mint-colored armchairs, scanning the room with her eyes.

"Thanks," she says when I hand her the cup. "I was sorry to hear about Claire, by the way. I expressed my sympathy to Gabe, of course, but I've picked up from Henry that you were close to her."

"Yes. I was very fond of her."

"You're lucky," she says, after taking a sip and licking a tiny bit of espresso foam from her pink-glossed upper lip. "His mother never took to me. Which meant it was no fun having to spend so much time with his parents."

I knew Claire resented Amanda for the way she blew up

the marriage, but I had no idea that there was any issue prior to that.

"What makes you think she didn't like you?" I ask, keeping my tone even.

"She never came right out and said it, of course. But she'd leave me out of conversations. Rarely made eye contact unless she had to. When it came to making plans with us, she'd only talk to Gabe about them. And the slights were so subtle, it was hard to convince Gabe it was going on."

This is all news to me. "Do you have any idea why she acted that way?"

"I was never sure, no. I think she felt I wasn't supportive enough of Gabe when he was launching the business—and that I didn't leave enough time for him because of my *own* work. And then . . . there was that little indiscretion of mine, and that was the nail in the coffin, of course."

I bite my tongue. Who could blame Claire for being upset about her son being cheated on? Any mother would have been.

Amanda sets her cup on a side table with a clunk. "You may not be aware of this," she adds, straightening her back, "but it was Claire who told Gabe I was having a fling."

The revelation stuns me. Gabe never breathed a word of it to me.

"How—"

"How did she find out? Believe it or not, I'm pretty sure she had me tailed by a private investigator."

This is getting more nuts by the minute. "She had you *followed*? That sounds like a fairly drastic step."

"Not for a puppet master like Claire. She liked being in

control, making sure everything ran the way she wanted it to. You know, it was only a fling, and if she hadn't busted me and told Gabe, maybe we could have gotten through that rough patch." Her expression turns wistful. "Don't get me wrong, I know you're much better for Gabe than I was, and I'm glad he found someone like you. But for Henry's sake, I wish we'd never split."

I need to end this conversation now. She's not only bashing Claire but she's also clearly rewriting history: Gabe told me he was willing to try to work things out, but that Amanda considered the so-called fling a symptom of a marriage that they'd both outgrown.

I rise, signaling I'm done, and right then Henry comes charging into the room, hoisting his duffel bag onto his shoulder. He and I hug good-bye as Amanda heads out to start the car, and I almost can't bear it when his arms finally drop. He's been such a trouper throughout this whole nightmare.

"You didn't sneak Bella into your duffel bag, did you?" I tease.

He shakes his head and laughs briefly before his face darkens. "Summer, are you and Dad going to be okay?"

"Of course, honey," I say, feeling another pang. "What makes you say that?"

"I don't want you to get sick or anything."

"We won't, I promise."

As they drive off a minute later, I watch from the stoop, then wander back to the living room and start pacing. I'm still feeling sick about my exchange with Gabe, but now I'm also troubled by Amanda's comment that Claire was a puppet master. *Was* she? Was I so caught up in the thrill of being accepted into this dazzling family that I never saw it? Is it possible that she hired an investigator to look into Hannah, too? Which reminds me: somehow in the middle of this nightmare, I'm going to have to figure out how to address my concerns about Claire's death.

"There you are."

I turn to see Blake in the entrance of the room, blazer-free now and cradling a snifter filled with an amber-colored liquid, brandy probably.

"Is Wendy doing okay?" I ask.

"She's stressed, needless to say, but since the sonogram was fine, I'm not overly worried on that front. By the way, I heard from Marcus a minute ago. He and Keira decided to stop off someplace for a drink. I'm sure they're desperate for a change of scenery."

"How were their interviews?"

"Similar to ours, from the sound of it." He polishes off his drink, tipping his head back as he does, then lifts the brandy snifter. "Can I pour you a splash of Courvoisier? I'll gladly join you in another round."

"Better not. I actually haven't had much of an appetite since your mom died."

He nods somberly. "Me, either, to tell you the truth."

"This must be so awful for you today," I tell him, an idea forming of how I might be able to lead him to my suspicions about Hannah indirectly. "You've barely had any time to mourn the loss of your mom."

"I know. I feel like I've had to park my grief in the overflow parking lot and will need to come back to it later."

"One of the things that makes your mom's death so

hard to deal with—at least for me—is the suddenness of
it. It seemed to come out of nowhere. But Gabe says you
mentioned she'd been on heart medication for a while. Some
kind of diuretic?"

"That's right. And also amlodipine. It's a calcium channel
blocker that relaxes blood vessels so that enough blood and
oxygen can reach the heart. But nothing's foolproof, unfortunately."

"I think an aunt of mine takes both of those," I lie. "And
she mentioned once that other things can interfere with their
effectiveness. Do you think that could have happened in
your mother's case?"

He raises a single eyebrow, in a way that reminds me of
Gabe. "I'm not following."

"Well, I remember my aunt told me you have to be careful with diuretics. That if she were to take something like,
uh, digitalis, with them, it could make her heart beat too
fast."

"But my mother didn't take digitalis," he says.

"Right, I was speaking generally. That something might
mix the wrong way with a medication."

"Did your aunt end up with a problem?"

Backing into the subject is getting me nowhere fast, but I
don't feel comfortable blurting out my true concerns.

"No, no, she didn't. . . . Um, I should head back to the
kitchen and send Bonnie home."

"And I should get back to Wendy. If you need us, we'll
be in the den, trying to distract ourselves with terrible television."

Bonnie, I discover, is now at the table, sorting through a

stack of index cards and looking beleaguered, the dogs at her feet. Her hair's tied back now with a fat blue rubber band, the kind used to bunch broccoli or asparagus in the supermarket.

"Oh, Bonnie," I say. "You can't still be working."

"I'm just taking a minute to think through the menu for tomorrow. Claire and I had planned a cookout for Thursday, but that now seems—"

She's been working much, much too hard. "Actually, I don't want you to even think about coming in tomorrow. You need a break from all this, Bonnie."

"Oh, no, I—"

"I'm not taking no for an answer. I'll confirm with Ash when I see him, but I know he would want you to have some time off. Gabe and I know our way around a kitchen, and Keira's a great cook. Everyone will pitch in."

"Gosh, if you're sure, Summer, I would love that. Twenty-four hours to clear my head and recharge would help a lot." She fingers the gold cross that's peeking out from the open collar of her blue jersey shirt. "I think I'm still in a state of shock, you know—from what we saw."

"Me, too." I pull out a chair at the table, and it's only when I drop into it that I realize how much my entire body aches from fatigue—not to mention stress and fear.

"Do you think she suffered?" Bonnie asks haltingly.

The horrible image surfaces in the front of my brain again. I'd assumed Jillian suffered, based on the vicious wound on the back of her head. *What caused it?* I ask myself. *The butt of a rifle? A rock?* It would have had to be something sharp, I decide.

"Maybe not," I lie. "It's possible she died instantly." Of

course, if someone had attempted to sexually assault her, and the jury's still out on that, she would have been beyond terrified for a few minutes beforehand.

"I hope so. As you know, I wasn't always a fan of Jillian's, but I can't stand thinking of her dying that way."

I straighten a bit, as something in me stirs. "Why weren't you a fan? Because she was trying to micromanage the luncheon yesterday?"

"Not only that. I hated the way she was always calling here on weekends, when Claire wanted Ash to take it easy. Like she needed to show everyone how important and involved she was with the business."

I don't press beyond that. It's an additional hint of a more-than-professional relationship between Jillian and Ash, but I don't want to plant any seeds with Bonnie. She could end up saying the wrong thing to the police, inadvertently casting more suspicion on Ash than there already is.

Bonnie scoops up the loose index cards into a pile and squares it off with a few taps on the table.

"And I know this is awful to say," she adds. "But I'm glad for Nick's sake it wasn't Hannah. I was so sure it was."

"Did I put that idea in your mind when we were down there?"

"No, that was my first reaction, too—before I even ran into you. Because of the hair. And the coat."

"The slicker?"

"Mm-hmm. When Hannah came to get coffee this morning, she had one of the slickers on, too. I guess she assumed it might rain, just like Jillian did."

My heart skips.

Hannah and Jillian were both wearing those tan-colored slickers. Which means that from the back, they looked even more alike this morning than I'd realized.

What if Bonnie and I weren't the only ones to have mistaken Jillian for Hannah? And it was really *Hannah* someone wanted dead?

24

A s my mind races, I trace a couple of circles on the buffed wooden table.

"Did you notice where Hannah went when she left the kitchen this morning?" I ask Bonnie.

She shakes her head. "She left through the back door and I saw her strolling across the lawn, but I'm not sure where she was headed. I guess for a walk."

"Do you remember what time it was?"

"Probably between nine thirty and ten. Maybe a little closer to ten."

I trace more circles, trying to piece a puzzle together in my mind.

"How many of those slickers are in the side corridor?" I ask. They've hung there for as long as I've been coming to the house, though I've borrowed one only once, to race back to the cottage in when it was pouring.

"Six, I think."

This morning with the promise of rain, both women must have thought the slicker would serve their needs.

"Are there enough in women's sizes for Hannah and Jillian to have worn separate ones?"

Bonnie cocks her head, thinking. "Yeah, there are a couple of small ones. Though maybe Hannah came back and hung hers up, and then Jillian ended up taking the same one."

Probably not, though. If Jillian was preparing to visit the burial site at around ten, she headed down there not long after Hannah left the house.

I know I need to let Bonnie go home, but I can't quite drop this. "Did you tell the police about the slickers? And how we thought it was Hannah who was dead?"

"Yup, I told them about our mistake. And I think I mentioned the slicker, too. I was so nervous talking to them that my voice shook. They probably think *I* did it."

I shake my head. "Of *course* not. And how about the rest of the interview?" I ask casually. "Did that go okay?"

"Yeah, I guess. They seemed a little, what's the word, impertinent? Asking about Claire and Ash and how their marriage was."

My stomach clenches. "How did you handle that?" I ask, still trying to keep it light.

"I told them things were fine. And they wanted to know who was in the house and when, that sort of thing. . . . Does that mean they think someone *here* is the killer?"

"Oh, no, not necessarily." I'm trying to reassure myself as much as her. "But they have to cover all their bases, of course. Why don't you go home now, Bonnie, and I'll clear the stuff in the dining room later?"

"Are you sure?"

"Absolutely."

"Thanks so much, hon."

"One last thing," I say as she rises. Because of the murder, I never had the chance to quiz Bonnie earlier as I'd intended. "You've been tidying the carriage house this week, right?"

"And the cottage, too. Is there something wrong?"

"Not at all. I was just wondering—and please don't tell anyone I asked this, because it's so silly—if you'd noticed if anyone had been using the oven there. To dry herbs—or flowers maybe?"

She wrinkles her brow. "Drying flowers? No, I can't imagine why they would."

It was a long shot. Surely Hannah would have covered her tracks.

"But I assume they've used the oven to do a little reheating," she adds. "It was warm to the touch one day when I was over there."

"Sunday?"

"Gosh, I don't remember, Summer."

"Okay, thanks. I know, dumb question. I'll explain another time."

I walk her out the back door to her red Honda in the upper part of the driveway and she jumps in and rolls down the window. "See you Friday," she calls out and slowly backs out of the driveway.

Will I see her Friday? I wouldn't be half surprised if she calls that morning to tell us that though she's cherished her years with the Keatons, this seems like the right moment to move on.

Bella and Ginger have been trailing behind us, and now they're eagerly thumping their tails, looking up at me expectantly. It's probably been hours since they've been let outside. I don't love being out here on my own, and besides, there's something I urgently need to do, but it would be mean to ignore them. I lead them back to the patio, and tell them, "Go pee—though make it quick."

They scamper off, and for a minute they sniff around in the grass right off the patio, but soon they're fanning outward, nosing around a row of shrubbery. Ginger takes care of business fast enough and ambles back to me; Bella, however, suddenly strays from the circle of light thrown from the house and fades into the darkness beyond the bushes.

"Bella, come back here," I demand. Though I can't see her, I can hear her snuffling coming from the far side of the shrubs.

"*Bella.*" I'm nearly screaming now, desperate to get all of us inside, and two seconds later, she bolts toward me. I lead the girls indoors and after leaving them on their beds, I move quickly through the house to the side corridor where the slickers hang. It's dark, but I can see the outline of the remaining slickers, bulging a little so they almost give the impression that there's a cluster of people huddled against the wall. I snap on the light, walk over to the pegs, and count five coats all together. The one Jillian was wearing makes six in total, so Bonnie's estimate was right. Hannah obviously put back the one she'd worn this morning.

If she actually was the intended victim, someone in the family obviously wanted her dead. I try to imagine how things might have unfolded. The killer could have seen Hannah from a window like Bonnie did, assumed she was on a walk, and decided to act. It would have taken a couple of minutes for the person to hatch a plan and possibly snatch something to use as a weapon. But even though the murderer would have lost sight of the woman believed to be Hannah, he—or she—would know to follow the trellis-covered path to the meadows. It's the walk everyone takes, and it would re- quire only a few minutes to catch up. And then there she was, standing by the stream and facing the other way. Had the killer realized his or her mistake as soon as Jillian collapsed from the blow? Or not until later?

With a jolt it occurs to me that the police might want to examine the slickers, and the corridor, too, so I shouldn't be hanging out here. I snap off the light and head back to the kitchen, where I brew a cup of caffeinated tea in an attempt to stay alert. With the dogs eyeing me curiously, I let out a moan and sink bone-tired into a chair at the table.

As I nurse my tea, two names power their way into my brain again, the same ones I considered while rushing back from the woods, thinking I'd just found Hannah's body.

Nick. Bonnie heard him and Hannah sparring last night. Somehow Nick might have obtained incriminating informa- tion about her, perhaps the same secret Claire had learned. Had it sent him into a murderous rage? It's hard to imagine my charming, affable brother-in-law capable of such brutal- ity. And yet . . . I've occasionally sensed that beneath his jovial facade, there's something darker—perhaps a fear of failure, a concern that despite his designation as the family's golden boy, he's no match for his brothers in smarts or savvy.

And then there's *Marcus.* I've watched how he studied

Hannah, stone-faced, over dinner. I saw the fury in his expression as they talked in the glade. There are two possible explanations for his anger. He knows something incriminating about Hannah and wants her out of his brother's life. Or, despite what he's sworn repeatedly to his wife, he's never got over Hannah, is *infuriated* by the idea of her sleeping with his brother, and even worse, planning to *marry* him.

And either one of them could have tried to make it appear as if a stranger attempted a sexual assault and then resorted to murder.

But there's another name to consider, isn't there? *Keira.* She's clearly felt bothered by Hannah's presence. Could jealousy have propelled her to try to murder a possible rival?

Stop, I command myself. I can't let these ideas occupy any more space in my brain tonight than they already have. Nick, Marcus, and Keira are members of my family, people I love. Besides, there's still the possibility that Jillian was murdered by a total stranger, that this has nothing to do with Hannah.

But even if *I'm* not entertaining thoughts of suspects in my family, the police are. They're gathering information and trying to determine if any of us had reason to want Jillian dead. And after interviewing me and Bonnie, and learning about our confusion—as well as the fact that two women were wearing identical coats—they're probably also wondering which of us might have wanted Hannah out of the way.

Once again, I wonder if I should have shared my suspicions about Claire's death with the detectives. There's still time to tell them, of course. And it would be better to do it before Claire's buried. Maybe there's a way for them to look into the situation without identifying me as the one who raised questions.

But no, too dangerous, I think. What if it intensified the scrutiny on the Keatons, making the detectives surmise that if there's one thing rotten in Denmark, there's bound to be more? And am I still sure that Claire was poisoned, anyway? What if I'm looking at everything upside down, and some other dark drama has been unfolding here in this place I've loved so much? And Hannah is totally innocent?

I reach for my mug but don't even have the energy to bring it to my lips. Instead, I lean forward, resting my forehead flat on the table. Within seconds, sleep ambushes me.

When I wake, it's with a start and a rush of dread. The bright light confuses me, and it takes me a moment to realize that I'm not in bed, I'm in the kitchen, and there's muffled noise coming from the front of the house—voices, feet shuffling, doors shutting. Ginger and Bella have already jumped from their beds and are scratching on the door to the dining room. I glance at the kitchen clock. It's 10:14.

"Just a second," I tell them. Still half asleep, I rise from my seat and swing open the dining room door.

Everyone's back now. Not only Gabe, Ash, Nick, and Hannah, but also Marcus and Keira, coming in right behind them and crowding the hall. There's a stranger there, too, a tall and dark-haired man who looks to be in his forties. My heart freezes. A *detective.* But when I see him speak to Ash, and they look friendly, I realize it must be the attorney from Princeton.

Wendy and Blake emerge into the hall from the direction of the den, their attention clearly roused by all the noise, too.

"Okay, everyone," Ash calls out. "Grab something to drink if you want, and then let's regroup in five minutes or less in the living room. Paul only has a few minutes to spare."

Gabe seems to be looking at everyone but me. When he finally swivels his head in my direction, he briefly meets my gaze and then his eyes dart away. I feel sick with worry, not only about how his interview with the detectives went but also our ugly exchange in the foyer.

While he follows his father and the lawyer into the living room, everyone else swarms into the dining room, migrating toward the sideboard and somberly pouring themselves drinks and/or fixing a small plate of food. Blake indulges in another brandy.

I pour two glasses of sparkling water, noting that Nick's not far from me, as is Hannah. I don't favor her with so much as a glance, but I see the outline of her body out of the corner of my eye. Her confident, picture-perfect posture is missing in action tonight. She's probably thinking that this is *sooo* not what she signed up for. Or perhaps she's concerned that with police nosing into everyone's backgrounds, they might unearth unsavory details about hers.

As we all congregate as instructed in the living room, I hand one of the water glasses to Gabe, who accepts it with a dull "thank you," and take a seat next to him on the couch.

"The handoff went fine with Amanda, by the way," I tell him.

"Yeah," he says coldly. "I spoke to her."

Ash, who's been huddled at the card table with the attorney, rises to address us. His face is haggard, and he's uncharacteristically disheveled, the sleeves of his wrinkled shirt rolled up to his elbows, but there's a determination about him now, like someone who's gotten past the shock of a shipwreck and has resolved to build a raft from the pieces left behind.

"I know everyone's exhausted and eager to be in bed," he says, "but I feel it's essential for us to hear from Paul Mizel, the attorney who will be guiding us through this hell."

"Good evening, everyone," Paul says. "Thank you for your time."

He's debonair looking and even at this hour well turned out in a crisp white shirt, tailored blazer, and tan slacks. But there's a hint of the street fighter in his flinty brown eyes, I'm relieved to see.

"I know this isn't an easy time," he says, "and I'm going to do everything possible to help you through it. I've already had the chance to check in with Nick, and I'll debrief soon with each of you individually about your interview with the state police. But since it's late, and we need everyone to be fresh over the next days, why don't I give you a brief overview now, and touch base with you tomorrow. Sound good?"

We all nod without enthusiasm.

"Unfortunately, tomorrow's going to be another tough day," he continues. "The police will be back, searching the property. We've given them permission to do so, but not, let me stress, to enter the house or any of the outbuildings. I suggest doing your best to avoid contact with them, and under no circumstances should you answer any questions. If any of them asks you a question, you can just politely say they should speak to me first. That goes for any requests from the media as well. Frankly, I'm surprised they're not here yet, but they'll turn up soon enough. Do you have any questions?"

"I have one," Marcus says. "What about going back to the city at some point? Are we allowed to leave?"

Mizel cocks his head a little to one side. "They aren't actually requiring that you remain here, but I'd advise staying put for as long as feasible," he says. "For starters, we want to present a united front. And since the police will surely have additional questions as the investigation proceeds, you might end up having to rush back here if you leave now."

Marcus nods, and I see Keira bite her lip. There are no other questions, so Ash announces he wants to let Paul get on the road, and the lawyer departs with a promise to speak to us early tomorrow.

"A couple more things," Ash says after we have the room to ourselves. "For starters, I'm postponing the burial for a few days. This isn't the time for it. Also, we do have four extra bedrooms in the house, besides the one Marcus and Keira are using, so if any of you would feel more comfortable sleeping here, you're more than welcome. It seems impossible to believe that the sick monster who killed Jillian will show up on the property again, but there are no guarantees."

So that's the official Keaton stance on the matter: that a psychopathic, probably random killer is to blame for Jillian's death.

Looking grim as gravestones, the family members rise and disperse. Gabe nearly dashes out of the room, but I catch up with him in the hall.

"Do you want to stay here, in the house?" I ask quietly.

"No, we'll be okay in the cottage," he says, his tone still aloof. "There are decent locks on the doors."

I take a moment to tell Ash that I've given Bonnie the next

day off and then, after shoving leftover food from the sidebar into the fridge, I start with Gabe down the path to the cottage, neither of us saying a word. Though the sky is overcast, the rain never came, I realize. As soon as we're inside the cottage, with the door locked and the lights on, I turn to Gabe.

"Honey, you have to believe me," I say. "I wasn't accusing you of anything earlier. I'd never think you could hurt Jillian. That's absurd."

"Maybe not Jillian. But you acted like I was dancing on my mother's grave."

"That's not what I meant. It's just that the timing of everything caught me off guard. And though this isn't an excuse, I've felt in the dark about a lot of things lately. I had no idea you'd been having issues with Jillian. No idea you spoke to her."

"Well, how about you witnessing that scene between Jillian and my father and not informing *me*?"

"That was because Marcus wanted to be the one to tell you. . . . Please, Gabe, we need each other now more than ever. We can't let there be a rift between us."

He sighs deeply. "Okay. Okay."

This seems like the best I can hope for tonight.

"How did your interview go?" I ask gently.

"Ugh, it was exactly like Blake warned me. They clearly think one of us did it. But my brain's too fried to talk about it now."

"Okay. I'm going to pour myself a glass of wine to help me sleep. Do you want one?"

"No. All I want is to be in bed."

As he mounts the stairs, I open one of the Spanish riojas

and settle at the kitchen table to unwind for a few minutes. I pick up my phone, which I've barely looked at today.

It turns out I haven't missed much. There's an email from my agent saying she's booked me for yet another voice-over job a week from Monday. I'm glad for the news, but it's hard to derive any thrill from it right now.

Taking another sip of wine, I move on to texts, and see that there's a new one from Billy Dean. I've been so caught up in today's horror show that I've completely forgotten about our conversation. He's not only done his homework but dropped a bombshell.

Hannah DID go to USC but was kicked out soph year. Don't know why yet, but apparently it was very fishy. Still working on it. U really owe me for this one, sweetheart.

It doesn't line up with what Wendy's guy dug up for her, but it makes total sense, given Claire's hint to me about Hannah's undergrad years. Is this what she discovered? Is it even relevant to anything? I'm so confused tonight, I don't even know how to evaluate this piece of information.

The rain finally starts, drumming on the cottage roof. I take one last sip of wine and struggle up from the chair. Passing through the sitting room, I check that the French doors are locked, too. To my relief, the latch is on.

Ash's words from earlier play again in my head—that a sick monster somehow found his way onto the property today and murdered Jillian. *If only*, I think. Because for all I know, the monster is right here in our midst.

25

The next morning, I head over to the main house just after seven. Gabe and I both woke early after a restless night—when he wasn't thrashing around in bed, I was. Though things still feel strained between us, we at least had coffee together and managed a few words of conversation. About the text he got from Henry, via Amanda's phone, saying he was sad to be gone. About the fact that it'll be warm today but with thunderstorms expected in the late afternoon or evening.

Nothing, however, about Jillian's murder or the investigation. I don't think either of us wanted to go there this morning.

I'd brought Gabe's keys to the house in case no one was up yet, but it turns out I don't need them. The kitchen door is unlocked, and once inside I'm greeted by the aroma of fresh coffee wafting from a mostly full carafe. Though the dogs aren't anywhere in sight, there's fresh food in their bowls.

I pour myself a cup of coffee and then kick operation modified continental breakfast into gear. I dig out muffins and bagels from the bread drawer and drop them in a basket, which I cart outside along with plates, cups, a loaf of bread, and a bowl of fresh berries. Other family members, I'm sure, will chip in and help as the day progresses. I wonder how Claire would feel if she knew anyone besides her or Bonnie was running the kitchen right now.

Claire. For the first time since last night, I revisit Amanda's bitter view of her, that she needed to control everything, particularly her children's lives and destinies. On the one hand, it doesn't seem like the Claire I knew, and yet it echoes recent comments from both Wendy and Ellen about her being extremely judgmental. And hadn't she dug up a damaging secret about Hannah, one that led her to say, *You do the right thing—or I will*?

Maybe I didn't know my mother-in-law as well as I thought I did. Was I in denial all this time about who she was and what she was capable of?

My attention is torn away as the door to the dining room opens and Nick saunters into the kitchen, dressed in khaki shorts and a wrinkled pink polo shirt, his hair rumpled.

"Morning," he says, stifling a yawn and letting the door swing closed behind him.

"Morning, Nick. Did you decide to sleep in the house last night?"

"Yeah. Staying in an isolated carriage house the day after a murder seemed too close to a *Scream* sequel for my liking."

"What about Blake and Wendy?" I ask. I'm eager to tell Wendy about Billy's text from last night.

"Yup, they're here, too. She seems pretty shaken. I think they'd love to get out of here, just like the rest of us, but we're

all sitting tight for now." His gaze briefly roams the countertops. "Any clue where Bonnie's stashing the muffins?"

"I put a basket of them out on the patio."

"Sweet, thanks, Summer."

"Before you leave, can I ask how your debrief with Paul
went? I want to know what to expect." What I want even
more is to observe Nick when he answers a question or two
about yesterday. I'm wondering if he's worried the police
might suspect him. And though I hate to admit it to myself,
I'm still wondering if he actually killed Jillian, thinking it
was Hannah.

"It was all right, I guess. He seems like a smart guy."

"I'm so sorry about yesterday, by the way. Telling you
Hannah was dead. That must have terrified you."

He shakes his head. "Yeah, I wouldn't want to repeat that
moment, but I can see now how you made the mistake."

"Bonnie thought it was Hannah, too," I say, studying his
face. "Because she'd seen her walking across the lawn earlier,
like she was going for a walk."

"Right, Hannah mentioned she might do that."

Nick's never been a good liar. I used to wonder how he
managed to succeed in real estate, but I guess people in that
game often hear what they want to hear. And because he's
a gregarious, expressive guy, it's always been easy for me to
notice his tells—either his body language won't match what
his face is saying, or he'll scratch the side of his nose.

Well, he's scratching his nose at the moment. Is he simply
feeling embarrassed that he and Hannah had been fighting
and he had no clue what she was up to?

He excuses himself to grab a muffin. As he slips out the

back door, I feel a pang of guilt, for sitting here in this room I've always felt so happy in while trying to get a bead on my brother-in-law, attempting to sense whether or not he's a murderer.

I sigh, then try to redirect my anxiety. I collect the remaining dishes from the dining room, wipe the sideboard with a wet sponge, and then check the living room. As I'm returning through the hall, carrying a couple of drinking glasses, I hear a faint sound from the side corridor and turn to investigate.

Hannah's standing in there, her hand in the pocket of one of the slickers.

"What are you doing?" I ask.

"What am I *doing*? Why does that matter to you?" Her haughtiness might have been subdued yesterday, but it's back full throttle now.

"It just does."

"Well, if you must know, I wore one of these coats yesterday and I left my earbuds in them."

She's obviously telling the truth because the next moment she extracts two wireless earbuds from the pocket and holds them up for me. "Satisfied?"

"Actually, no. You shouldn't be around here. Jillian was wearing one of the slickers yesterday and the police might need to examine this area later."

"How do you know that?" she asks.

"I watch cop shows. Police examine things."

"No, I mean how do you know what she was wearing?"

"Because I saw her body, remember?"

She hesitates briefly and then brushes past me, looking suddenly flustered. It's easy to see that a certain thought is starting to form in her head, the way it formed in mine.

When I return to the kitchen, I spot Wendy through the window, sitting alone at the table under the pergola and drinking what must be a cup of tea. Just the person I wanted to see. I step outside and wish her good morning.

"Hi," she says, her voice subdued. "Want to join me?"

"I'd love to." I slide into the chair across from hers. "How'd you sleep?"

"Staying upstairs beat being in the carriage house, but mainly I want to get out of here."

"I know, and hopefully it won't be much longer." I pitch forward in my chair a little, so she can hear me as I lower my voice to tell her about the text from Billy. I'm worried she's going to think I'm beating a dead horse, but her expression reads pensive, not annoyed.

"Okay, my bad," she says. "I told my guy to only find out if she'd actually attended USC, not whether she graduated. She must have done something pretty serious to get thrown out on her ass, right?"

"I know," I say, grateful to have her interest back. "What do you think it could be?"

"People get expelled from college for plagiarism, but do you write many term papers in a school for dramatic arts?" I shake my head. "Maybe she presented someone else's play or screenplay as her own. Or cheated in another way?"

"I wish we could find out."

"Let me go back to my guy and ask him to dig deeper."

"Thanks so much, Wendy." If only Gabe was this receptive to my concerns. "I know we have a lot going on here, but I don't want to let this go in case it's a serious issue."

I'm about to rise when I see Wendy's attention snagged by something behind me. I turn to see four state troopers tramping across the yard, obviously headed for the crime scene. Two of them nod in greeting. Wendy and I return the gesture and then immediately look away, not wanting to encourage any further interaction.

"What do you think they're looking for?" she whispers.

"Evidence, I guess. Footprints through the woods— though the rain last night must have washed those away. Even the murder weapon."

She pulls her lips into a gesture of distaste. "Do you think they've found it yet?"

I shrug. "I have no idea."

There wasn't anything lying by the body, at least that I noticed. And then I see Jillian in my mind all over again, the vultures tearing flesh from the wound with their beaks. I shake my head, trying to chase the image away.

"What?" Wendy asks.

"Nothing." I'm not really supposed to be discussing the crime scene. In fact, I probably shouldn't have mentioned the detail about the slicker to Hannah, I'm realizing now.

With the troopers now out of sight, I bid Wendy goodbye and return to the cottage and to Gabe. In an attempt to busy myself, I strip the sheets from Henry's bed, make cups of coffee that I don't end up drinking, and try to read the news online—which Gabe seems to be doing, too—but I feel so anxious it's impossible to focus.

Just after eleven Paul Mizel, the attorney, calls my cell, asking if I have a few minutes to talk. I relocate to the kitchen and ease the door closed. It's not that I have any secrets from Gabe about the events of the last twenty-four hours, but he seems to be doing his best to chill and I don't want to disturb him.

"So you're aware," Paul starts, "I'm acting—for the time being at least—as 'pool counsel.' This means I'm representing and guiding all of you. There might come a time when people need or want separate representation, but we'll cross that bridge when we get to it."

His words send a chill through me. I'm not a lawyer—and, ha, I've never even played one on TV—but it seems the only reason one of us would need to splinter from the pack isn't a good one.

"Understood," is all I say.

"Let's work our way backward, shall we?" he says in a polite but efficient way. "I'd like to hear all the questions you were asked last night."

I go through the interview in as much detail as I can recall, and when I finish up by telling him how the red-haired detective insinuated that family members must have been getting on each other's nerves, he says, "Good, that's exactly the kind of information I need to be aware of. Now tell me what you can about the crime scene."

I do my best to describe what I saw, including the wound.

"Could it have been a bullet wound?" he asks.

"Uh, I've been wondering about that. If she'd been shot with a hunter's rifle—and as you've probably heard, there've been hunters around—I think the wound would have been bigger and messier. To me, it looked like a puncture wound, made with something very sharp."

"Can you make a guess about the weapon?"

"Maybe a pointy rock. Or . . . a tool even. You know, like the claw part on a hammer—though why would anyone be carrying one around the woods with him?"

"That's helpful, thank you, Summer."

"Does that mean the police haven't found the weapon yet?"

"I don't know. That's not something they'd tell me or anyone else at this stage, because they don't want people being interviewed to tailor their stories to the evidence or lack thereof."

I nod even though he can't see me. "Makes sense."

"My guess, though, is that they haven't found it. They asked how much of that wooded area belongs to the Keatons, which means they're planning a wider search today. And they're eager to get into the house as soon as they can."

"Are you going to let them?"

"They don't have a warrant at this point, so for now, no. Listen, Summer, I hate to wrap this up, but I have a few more people to touch base with this morning."

"Sure," I say, and sign off.

I wasn't expecting his call to be all warm and fuzzy, but I'd been hoping for something reassuring, like the fact that the police already suspected a local hunter and were conducting a house-to-house search or had put out an APB or whatever they're called. But our conversation has only unsettled me more.

About sixty seconds after I hang up, I hear Gabe's phone

ring, followed by the sound of the French doors to the patio opening. He must be talking to Mizel now.

I hadn't planned to leave the cottage, but as Gabe's voice drones from the patio, I find myself drifting out the front door and along the flagstone path. The yard is empty, and I assume the troopers I saw earlier are off in the woods.

I keep moving, something tugging at me that I can't quite identify. After reaching the patio, I wander to the eastern end of the house, and eventually find myself in front of the potting shed.

I stop abruptly and stare at the raw wooden door. I don't dare voice the thought in my head, but I know exactly why I'm here.

Approaching the structure, I look both ways, then tentatively push open the door. The same scent of clay pots and potting soil greets me as it did when I stopped in the other day, and the space looks unchanged from then. The vases I didn't use are still sitting on the counter, empty. I exhale. There's nothing here to see.

Before I turn to leave, I scan the room for a moment, particularly the wall where garden tools hang from black, rustic-looking nails: several small hoes, two spades in leather cases, and a shiny handsaw. Longer tools, including a shovel and rake, are nestled in one of the corners. Since I'm not a gardener, it's impossible to notice if a standard tool is missing. But as I zoom in, I spot an empty nail. And the tool next to it—which I think Claire called a digger—hangs awkwardly, as if it was positioned to partly fill the gap from a missing tool. A missing tool that was used as a murder weapon.

Panic swells from my core outward, but I tell myself that

there's no way to be sure. And besides, I need to erase this stupid idea that someone in the family murdered Jillian. It just can't be so.

By the time I return to the cottage, Gabe is off the phone. When I ask him how the call went, all he says is, "Okay. I mean, who knows?"

We could almost be strangers. I'm tempted to tell him we need to sort out what's going on between us, but I'm afraid that if I press, it will only make things worse.

Through a long series of replies to our family text chain, it's decided that everyone will fend for themselves for lunch and that Keira and I will oversee dinner with help from Gabe if necessary. He and I eat our lunch in the kitchen, leftover slices of tart from yesterday, and afterward, while Gabe reads, I make an attempt to work on my play. But my brain is too consumed with worry to do anything creative.

Five o'clock finally rolls around, and Gabe and I text Keira to say we're heading over to the house to help with dinner. It's a relief to step outside of the cottage and have a change of scenery. Halfway along the path, I'm surprised to see Ash striding toward us, looking very much like a man on a mission.

"What's going on?" Gabe asks.

"Nothing to be alarmed about," his father says. He's in a fresh, perfectly pressed cotton shirt and seems less agitated than yesterday. "One of the partners in Mizel's firm is being called out of town unexpectedly and Paul wants us to talk to him before he leaves so that he can add additional insight. We'll meet at their Princeton offices. You, Blake, Marcus, Nick, and me."

"When?" Gabe asks.

"As soon as we can get there."

"*Tonight?* But—but that means all the women will be in the house alone."

"Yes, I know. But Princeton's an hour away, and Paul says the meeting shouldn't go longer than ninety minutes. That puts us back here right as it's getting dark. Are you comfortable with that, Summer?"

"Sure," I say, knowing I can hardly object.

There's a sudden whirlwind as the men prepare to leave: Gabe racing back to the cottage to change into long pants and Nick and Marcus dashing upstairs to grab their phones. Minutes later they're climbing into two cars, Gabe and Blake in one, Ash, Nick, and Marcus in another. I watch from the wide stoop as they depart.

When I come into the kitchen a minute later, Keira's there, tapping her fingers on the butcher block of the island. She looks a bit agitated, like she's not any more pleased than I am about the way the evening's unfolded.

"I was thinking we could do a vegetable lasagna if you're all right with that," she says. "I checked and we have all the ingredients."

"Great idea."

"Why do you think they had to rush off that way?" she asks, sounding perturbed. "Could there have been some development?"

"From what I know, they just need to make sure the other law partner is in the loop. I mean, if there was any news, they'd tell us."

"You think so?"

"Jeez, Keira. Why wouldn't they?"

I didn't mean to snap, but her endless worry is making my own apprehension even worse.

"Why *wouldn't* they? Because people in this house keep secrets."

My stomach knots uncomfortably. "What secrets?"

"Ash and Jillian, for instance. Who knows what was going on there?"

"What else?"

She looks off, pressing her lips together.

"Nothing," she says finally.

"Keira, look, I know things are really tough. But we need to do our best to get through it. Why don't you tell me what you need me to do for dinner?"

Before she can, my phone rings from inside the pocket of my capris. Fishing it out, I see to my surprise that Amanda's name is on the screen, but when I answer, it's Henry who is on the other end.

"Hey, Hen," I say. "Everything okay?"

"I tried Dad, but he didn't pick up."

"Oh, you know, he's out for a drive with Grandpa now, and they're probably on that part of the road where the cell service is bad."

"Okay. Dad's not sick, is he?"

"No, no, he's fine." As I answer, I realize this isn't the first time Henry's sounded worried about us getting sick—and it seems like something might be going on in his little mind. I cross the kitchen, push open the swinging door, and step into the dining room. "Hen, why do you keep asking if we're sick? Does it have to do with Gee?"

I take his silence as a yes.

"Honey, Gee had a heart attack, which can happen to older people when their hearts aren't as strong. It's not something you have to worry about with Dad and me."

"But did getting sick make Gee's heart less strong?"

"What do you mean, Hen?"

"You know, getting sick, throwing up."

Unease ripples through me.

"Why do you think Gee was throwing up?"

"She told me she was. She told me that day."

26

I n my mind, I hear a sudden echo of the question Henry asked when I first told him that his grandmother was ill. *Is she throwing up?* he'd said. I should have asked what he meant.

"That's actually very helpful to know, honey," I say. "Where did you see Gee that day—in the kitchen?"

"Um, no. She was in the office."

"The office?"

"Grandpa's office. Where his desk is."

"Oh, right," I say, realizing he means the study. "What was Gee doing in there, do you know?"

"Sitting. And looking at a book."

"And she said she'd been sick?"

"She was holding a tissue on her mouth, and I asked her what the matter was, and she said she had an upset tummy. That's what she calls it when I throw up."

So Claire's stomach was definitely in distress that day. If only I'd paid better attention to Henry.

I sense him squirming on the other end of the line. "Am I in trouble?" he asks.

"No, no, you're not in trouble, Hen. I was just curious." I briefly comb through my memories, back to that afternoon. Henry must have gone to the house after I'd left for my run. And Henry, not me, was probably the last person to speak to Claire before she died. "I thought you'd been taking a nap with your dad that afternoon."

"I was, but I woke up and you were gone, and I wanted to find Ginger and Bella."

"Ah, got it. That makes perfect sense. Thanks so much for telling me. What . . . what did you guys end up doing today?"

"Nothing really. My mom said I shouldn't complain about not being at the house because it's going to rain a lot there anyway. If it thunders, can you hold Bella for me?"

As he knows, Bella's terrified of thunder. When it's far away, she worries and clamors to be in someone's arms. When it's close and boomingly loud, she goes into a full-blown panic and wedges herself into the tightest place she can find.

"Of course. And if you want, you can try your dad again in a little while. He'll be in a place where there's service soon."

I hate to rush him off the phone, but I have to follow up on what he told me. I hurry into the living room and pause on the threshold of the study. More than once over the past few days I've wondered what Claire was doing at this end of the living room and now I know. She'd been coming from the study, where she'd been sitting and reading a book. But what book? And why?

I step softly into the room and explore the floor-to-ceiling walnut bookshelves with my eyes. Though I've always thought of the study as Ash's domain, it was hardly off-limits to Claire. On a couple of winter afternoons over the years, I'd found her reading in one of the comfy armchairs, a fire crackling in the hearth nearby.

Based on what Henry said, as well as my own chronology of events, he must have come across Claire twenty or thirty minutes after she'd told me she planned to lie down. Maybe she stopped in the study to grab a book to take upstairs with her, but if she wasn't feeling well, why skim through it here first?

I didn't notice any book near her on the floor, which suggests that she'd put it away before she collapsed, rather than taking it with her, which seems odd, too.

I drift to the bookcases behind Ash's desk. Ordinarily I'd consider this area a kind of no-fly zone, but the normal rules don't apply anymore. Though the books aren't alphabetized, they appear to be clustered according to general topics: biographies, memoirs, history, a smattering of novels, art books, and on the lower shelves, several dozen oversize books on landscape design that must have been Claire's.

As my gaze approaches the floor, I see a volume jutting out more than the others, its glossy flap askew as if it's been jammed back in a hurry. I tilt my head to better read the spine and gasp in surprise. It's called *Plants That Kill*.

"Is everything okay with Henry?"

I spin around at the sound of Keira's voice and find her standing in the doorway, her expression puzzled.

"Yeah. He just wanted to say hi," I explain.

She continues to stare, clearly wondering what I'm doing standing behind Ash's desk.

"Oh, and he's missing a book," I fib. "I thought someone might have stuck it in one of the shelves here. You ready for me?"

"Not yet actually. Since they won't be back until close to nine, I think we should hold off on making the lasagna. Why don't we meet in the kitchen at around seven thirty? Wendy's going to help, too."

"Sure, fine."

I don't love the idea of being alone, but hanging in the house has no appeal either so I return to the cottage. My heart's hammering as things come together now more clearly in my mind. Just last night I was beginning to wonder if my suspicions were all a kind of mirage, the result of grief, and okay, maybe a smidgen of envy, colliding with an overactive imagination. But I wasn't wrong. Claire was definitely sick to her stomach the day she died. And very possibly looking through a book on toxic plants, wondering if that's where she'd find the reason for her gastrointestinal distress.

Hannah is as dangerous as I thought she was. Should I call the detectives who interviewed me yesterday? I shake off that idea. Maybe I should go to Ash with my discovery as soon as he returns. But he tends to be a conservative thinker, and it's highly possible he'll treat my theory with as much skepticism as Gabe did. I have to find *someone* to talk to, though, or I'm going to go out of my mind.

I try to distract myself by answering emails, and I also finally alert a few friends about Claire's death. At one point I text my mom, asking if she's around to talk. I haven't even filled her in on Jillian's death yet. But there's no response, and I finally remember it's Thursday and that means a trip to the movies for her and my father.

With nothing left to do, I simply continue to pace, gnawing at my cuticles.

At 7:25 sharp, I exit the cottage, locking the door behind me. Though the sun hasn't set yet, the sky is fairly dark thanks to the thick gray clouds crowding it. If there are any state police still down by the woods, they're probably packing up now. Far off to my left I see a faint flash of lightning. *That's all we need tonight*, I think—*a storm to knock out the power.*

Keira's already in the kitchen when I arrive, wearing a white apron over her jeans and jersey top and peeking into a pot of rapidly boiling water on the stove, and Wendy's at the island, drying lettuce leaves in a salad spinner. Keira's laid out peppers, squash, and zucchini for me on the table, along with a cutting board, so I slide onto a stool next to Wendy. As I dice the vegetables with a large kitchen knife, my mind keeps rushing to my call with Henry and the book about poisons, and what it all means, and I have to force myself to concentrate so I don't accidentally slice a finger off.

There's not much chitchat as we work, which is a relief. At one point, though, when Keira's busy dumping the lasagna noodles into the boiling water, Wendy leans toward me and whispers, "Nothing about Hannah yet, but my guy is on it."

I nod, relieved that at least Wendy's still taking me seriously.

When I'm done chopping, Keira collects the vegetables, transfers them to a waiting frying pan, and drains the lasagna noodles into a colander, moving around the kitchen like a seasoned professional. I'm not surprised to see her perform so well. Anytime that Gabe and I have eaten at her and Marcus's apartment, the meal's been delicious.

"Did you ever have Claire and Ash over for dinner?" I ask.

"No, never," Keira says.

"That's such a shame. Claire would have loved one of your meals."

"Oh, I don't know about that," Keira says. "It seemed like there was only room for one master chef in this family."

The bitterness in her tone catches me off guard, and I notice Wendy glance up, clearly surprised as well. Marcus told me that the Keatons intimidated Keira, but I wonder if Claire specifically made her uncomfortable. Is she another person who felt Claire was judging her, perhaps even trying to control her marriage?

The room goes quiet again, except for the sizzle of sautéing vegetables. Then, far off in the distance, I hear a rumble of thunder. And then another, this one longer and louder. Poor Bella bounds off her bed, skitters in my direction, and paws at my leg to be lifted. As I take her onto my lap, I check my watch. The guys won't be back for at least an hour still. I feel restless and uneasy, but I'm grateful at least that Hannah is keeping her distance.

And, then, as if I've mentally summoned her, the door from the dining room swings open and Hannah steps into the kitchen. Her face is shockingly red and blotchy. Maybe it's the result of a beauty regimen mishap, like some Umbrian clay, pore-purifying mask that backfired big-time, but I suspect what's really going on is that she's been mentally toying with the idea that whoever killed Jillian might have really been after her. And it's eating away at her from the inside out.

"I didn't realize you were making dinner tonight," she says. "Do you need me to do anything?"

"Oh, sorry, you must not have been on the text thread," Keira says from the counter, glancing over her shoulder as she layers the lasagna sheets into a pan with the vegetables. "We'll need a vinaigrette for the salad. Can you—?"

"I've got that covered," I interrupt, raising my eyes to meet Hannah's. "We don't need any more help."

Hannah goes momentarily rigid, then without saying a word, she turns and leaves, letting the door swing hard behind her.

"Care to share?" Keira asks. She's taken a few moments to slide the lasagna pan into the oven and now turns to face me.

"What do you mean?"

"Why you don't want Hannah in here?"

"I don't like her," I say. "More importantly, I don't trust her. And that means I don't want to be anywhere near her if I don't have to."

Keira's eyes narrow. "Did she do something to you?"

I shake my head and keep stroking Bella.

"Did she?" Keira urges.

And suddenly it's like a dam breaks inside of me. These two women are my sisters-in-law. They're not my best friends, and they might not have cared about Claire the way I did, but they would never have wanted her dead, let alone murdered. I have to tell them.

"Not to me," I say quietly. "But to someone else."

"Who?"

"Keira," Wendy interjects, "I'm glad Summer's finally looping you in. She's had some concerns about Hannah from the start, serious ones. It looks like she lied about her background, and she might also be a thief."

"Claire was concerned, too," I add. "She apparently dug into Hannah's past."

Keira pauses in front of the stove, a hand on each hip. "Does Nick know any of this?"

"I'm not sure," I say. "He's seemed upset with her lately, though I have no idea why."

Her expression clouds, and I wonder if Keira actually knows why Nick was agitated. Maybe it has to do with what she was discussing so animatedly with him in the side yard.

"The bottom line is that we need to get Hannah out of the picture," Wendy tells her. "If Nick marries her, it could be a disaster not only for him, but for all of us. But the trouble is, if we attempt an intervention with him, he'll probably dig in his heels."

"So what do you intend to do?" Keira asks.

"After we're past this current nightmare," Wendy says, "we're going to have to discreetly relay certain pieces of information and let him make up his mind."

After we're past this nightmare. And when will that be? Weeks from now? Months?

Hardly conscious of what I'm doing, I set Bella on the

floor and check the dining room to make certain Hannah's not lurking in there and listening in on us, then turn back to my sisters-in-law. "We can't afford to wait," I tell them. "We have to act *now*. Before someone else gets hurt."

"What do you mean, Summer?" Wendy asks. "What's going on?"

I take a deep breath. "Okay, you're going to think I'm insane, but bear with me. I'm pretty sure Hannah killed Claire."

Keira gasps and Wendy's lips part in surprise, then both women listen in stunned silence as I spill it all: the confrontation with Claire that Henry overheard, the missing foxgloves, the lost jug, the symptoms of digitalis poisoning that Claire presented on Sunday, the fact that Hannah knew the plant was poisonous, the foxglove blossom in my drawer, the newly planted foxgloves.

"I know the individual details don't seem like much," I continue, "but when you add them up, the result is impossible to ignore."

Neither of them says anything. Without warning, I feel myself choke up.

"*Please*," I nearly beg, "I need someone to believe me. We can't let Hannah get away with murder."

Wendy rises from the table and crosses to me, then touches my shoulder gently.

"It's not that we don't believe you, Summer, but it's a lot to take in." She turns toward Keira, who's still frozen in place by the stove. "What do you think, Keira?"

"I don't know," she replies. "I'm not a fan of Hannah's, but poisoning . . . It seems so nineteenth century."

"And that makes it all the more cunning," I say. "She was clearly counting on the fact that no one would even consider it."

"But does that mean there are two murderers around here?" Keira asks. "Hannah and the person who killed Jillian?"

"I . . . I guess so." It sounds unlikely to me, but if there's actually only *one* murderer at large, then what was Hannah's motive for killing Jillian?

More silence. Even the thunder has ceased. I catch Wendy and Keira shoot nervous side looks at each other.

"Look, Summer," Wendy says finally. "Why don't you let me discuss this with Blake? He's a doctor. He may have a sense of how feasible this could be—and also know what steps we can take to find out more."

I exhale in what feels like the first time in ten minutes. "That would be so helpful, Wendy," I tell her. Maybe I should have pushed my conversation with Blake further last night.

A marimba ringtone reverberates faintly from another room.

"That must be mine," Keira says. "I left it in the hall."

She hurries from the room, perhaps eager for a chance to escape from me and my lunatic theories.

"Don't worry," Wendy says. "Like I said, it's a lot to digest, but we have your back. Do you have any physical proof whatsoever? Something I can share with Blake?"

"Um, sort of," I say, and fill her in on what Henry told me earlier and about finding the book.

"Oh wow," Wendy says, a hand on her chest. "That's telling. And the book's there now?"

"Yup."

She nods. "Okay, I'll definitely talk to Bl—"

The door opens with a bang. We look over to see Keira, still holding her phone.

"You're not going to believe this," she says. "Ash started having trouble breathing on the way home, and they're in the ER with him."

"Oh, no," I exclaim. "Which hospital?"

"It's about halfway between here and Princeton. The doctor doesn't think it's serious. Just stress, maybe the start of a panic attack."

What if Hannah's done something to *Ash* as well?

"Is Blake with them?" Wendy asks urgently.

"No, he's already on his way back in his own car. He apparently left the meeting early because he wanted to check on you."

Wendy slips her hand into the pocket of her cotton sweater, yanks out her phone, and immediately taps the screen. "Blake, where *are* you?" she asks after the call's clearly gone to voice mail. "Call me. Please."

"Maybe he's in that dead zone," I venture.

I don't like this. I don't like it at all. Ash isn't well. Blake can't be reached. And we're alone in the house—with *Hannah*. Outside, dusk has morphed into darkness and once again I hear a far-off rumble of thunder. The houselights briefly flicker. I glance at the exterior kitchen door to confirm I turned the bolt after returning from the cottage.

Across the room, Keira removes her apron and tells us the lasagna has another thirty minutes to go, and she intends to wait in her bedroom and try to read. She departs without acknowledging the bomb I detonated a few minutes ago. Is she simply going to ignore it?

As soon as she's gone, I fish out my own phone and text Gabe.

Heard the news. Is there anything I can do? I could Uber there if you need me.

I can't help but feel a pang that he didn't reach out to me directly, just counted on Keira to spread the word. Meanwhile, Wendy is still urgently tapping away at her phone screen.

"Still no luck?" I ask.

"No, and it's worrying me. I think I'll try calling him from the landline in the den and see if the problem might be with the cell service here. What are you going to do?"

"I guess I'll wait here." My gaze drifts to Bella and Ginger, who are both staring at me intently. They're wigged-out by the thunder, but I also suspect they need a potty break. "And I guess I should take the dogs out."

"Good idea." As she steps toward the door, she turns back and smiles wanly at me. "I'll talk to Blake tonight, I promise."

"Thanks, Wendy, I appreciate that so much."

I'm pretty sure I can count on her to inform him. But will it be couched in the words *Summer's gone insane*? I have this terrible feeling that I might regret sharing my knowledge with my sisters-in-law, that nothing will result except a widening of the rift between Gabe and me.

Desperate for a task to slow my pulse, I whisk together olive oil and vinegar for the salad, then check my phone, hoping that Gabe's texted me back, but there's nothing. The only ones eager for contact with me appear to be Bella and Ginger, who are now waiting anxiously by the kitchen door.

I wish I could stall and take them out when everyone's back, but it wouldn't be fair.

I flick on the outdoor lights from the switch in the kitchen, unlock the door, and cautiously step outside, glancing up and down the patio. I'm not sure what I'm looking for. The coywolf? A sexual predator? All I know for sure is that it's dark out here, and there's an aggressive wind whipping through the tree leaves. I'm under the pergola so it takes a minute for me to realize that it's finally raining now.

"*Stay,*" I yell to the dogs, who by now are off the patio and sniffing around the lawn.

They take their damn sweet time, but I can hardly blame them. How much have they even been out today? As they press their noses into the wet grass, I stand near the doorway, my arms crossed over my chest, praying they'll make it quick.

"C'mon," I call nervously after a couple of minutes. Ginger raises her head with a cheerless expression that seems to ask, *Really?* but she lumbers toward me obediently, shakes off the rainwater, and trots into the house. Bella, however, refuses to budge. And then just like last night, she suddenly dissolves into the darkness.

"Bella," I shout. "Get over here."

A sudden streak of lightning splits the sky directly in front of me, briefly illuminating the night. Bella is now pretty far from the patio, I see, and exploring the underside of a bush. Leaving the back door open, I make a mad dash across the lawn, but as I'm about to swoop her up in my arms, there's a deafening clap of thunder and she takes off like a rocket toward the area north of the pool.

"Bella," I scream, unable to see her. "Don't be stupid."

I race back to the house, grab her leash from a hook in the kitchen, and nearly rip open the drawer where the flashlights are stored. After grabbing a torch and flicking it on, I tear back outside.

"Bella . . . Bella," I yell, approaching the end of the pool. The beam of my flashlight bobs as I go, making it hard to focus.

There's no sign of her. Torn between an urge to cry and another to strangle her, I pause long enough to train the light toward the small hill that descends to the tennis court. She might be cowering in the shrubbery there. . . . Nothing.

I start down the hill, being careful not to slip on the slick grass, the wind whipping my hair. Up until now, I'd been helped a little by the glow cast from the house, but I'm beyond it at this point. There's another huge bolt of lightning and then, almost simultaneously, the deafening sound of thunder rolling over the yard.

Finally, I hear her. A whimpering noise not far ahead. And a rustling, too.

"Bella, come here, girl," I call. "Bella, *please.*"

For a split second the wind ceases, and finally Bella inches into the beam of the flashlight.

"Good girl," I call out. I squat down and reach my arm out to her in a beckoning gesture.

Without warning, she flinches, her eyes trained on a spot behind me and to my right. There's a movement there, too, which I catch from the corner of my eye. And then a sudden whooshing sound in the dark.

A second later the top of my head explodes in pain.

27

Have I been struck by lightning? The pain's white-hot, like a wildfire's radiating from my skull through every inch of me. My legs give out and I pitch forward onto the wet ground, facedown. I try to grab a breath but manage only short, desperate gasps.

Help me, I think. *Someone, please.*

A dog barks in the darkness. Desperate yaps. *Bella.* I try to call to her, but nothing escapes my lips. I succeed in moving my hand and fumble for the flashlight but realize it's rolled to a spot I can't see. Something's in my left hand, though. I'm still holding the leash.

Other sounds now. The squeak of a shoe on grass, a swish of fabric. There's someone behind me.

And then I feel hands on my bare calves. They're pawing at the fabric of my capris. The person grabs hold with both hands and pulls. Fear shoots through my body, fighting for space with the pain.

I summon whatever energy I can find and heave my body

in a half turn to the right. And then the rest of the way. I'm facing upward now, woozy.

I sense the other person stumbling backward, maybe in surprise, and then, a few seconds later, rushing forward again. Feebly, I kick out with one leg, trying to halt the approach.

Even in the dark and rain, I finally see who it is. Because of the hair, the white-blond shock of it.

Wendy.

She's looming above me, her face twisted as she stares.

"Wendy," I say, more a moan than a word. "Wha——?"

I don't understand what's happening. And my head's pounding even harder now, the pain practically erasing all thought. Has she come looking for me? But there's a horrible sneer on her face.

"Help me," I manage. "Please."

She's gripping something—a hammer. But no, not a hammer, another kind of tool, whose head I can make out in outline. My heart lurches. That's what struck me, I realize. She raises it high now, ready to drive it down on my skull again. I force my left arm up and away from my body, and flick the leash like a whip at her. I barely make contact, but she yelps in surprise and staggers backward.

She comes at me again, the tool raised.

She's going to crush my skull.

I gasp for air and roll my body again, hurling myself into the shrub next to me. The blow misses my head but nails my shoulder, piercing skin through my shirt. I grunt in pain.

I force myself up onto my hands and knees, trying to fight my way through the shrub. Blood from my head wound runs into my eyes and my mouth, mixing with rain and tasting like metal. In the dense and prickly branches, I cover almost zero ground, and I let out a cry of despair, still trying to crawl. There seems to be no escape.

I see the light then. A flashlight beam, coming from behind and erratically slicing the darkness ahead of me. And a man calling out above the rain.

"Wendy, what the hell's going on?" I've never been so relieved to hear my husband.

"*Gabe*," I scream. As I twist around to see him, my head fills with swooshing sounds. "She . . . she's trying to kill me."

I sense him jerking back in surprise, halting in his steps. *Please, don't let her hurt him.*

"Get away from her, Wendy," Gabe shouts.

"You have no idea what's going on," Wendy screams.

"I said, get the fuck away from her."

He charges her, I can tell from the sound, and soon I hear their bodies dropping to the ground with a thud. Then scuffling, shoes slipping on soaking wet grass. I twist my head again, pushing against the pain, but can see only their outlines. I think Gabe's on top, but I can't be sure. I let out an anguished cry. "Gabe, are you okay?"

More scuffling. Gabe grunting, I think. Someone struggles to their feet. *Gabe.*

Then from behind us, the sound of heavy feet, booted maybe, tramping on the ground.

I wiggle a little, edging myself back out of the shrubbery, and raise my head, higher this time. There's rainwater and blood running in my eyes but I can see two beams of light penetrating the darkness.

"Freeze," two voices shout in unison.

"She was trying to kill my wife," Gabe calls out to them, jabbing an arm in my direction.

One of the beams of light ferrets me out, snagging me in the eyes and making me squint.

"Don't be ridiculous," Wendy protests from the ground. She struggles up and stands. Her clothes are sopping wet, and her hair's slicked back tight. "I was trying to *help* her."

"I said freeze," someone calls again. It's a trooper, I realize, from the outline of the hat, two of them actually. A man and a woman. "Every one of you."

"Please," I say, not moving a muscle. "I'm injured. She smashed me on the head with some kind of hammer."

"Are you bleeding?" the female voice asks.

"*Yes.*"

"You've got to help her," Gabe pleads.

"Officer Belker is going to call you an ambulance," the male trooper shouts to me. "And I'm going to put the other two of you in cuffs until we sort this out. Then we're going to wait for a second unit before we escort you back to the house."

As Gabe mutters his consent, I slowly lower my body facedown onto the wet grass. Could I be wrong about what's happened? *No.* I saw the weapon in Wendy's hand—and the rage on her face. A question fights its way through my wooziness. *Why?* Why would Wendy do this to me? My thoughts are like ragged puzzle pieces that refuse to align.

The hard snap of metal cuts through the darkness—handcuffs being secured—and there's a sudden burst of light in front of me, followed by a crack of thunder so loud I nearly levitate.

"We have to get my wife to the house," Gabe calls out. "Please. She's bleeding, and she shouldn't be out in this weather."

"I can walk," I say to the troopers, raising my head again. "But I need a little help."

A discussion ensues between the two troopers, too low for me to hear more than a few words: *risk . . . wait . . . statements.* Belker approaches and squats near me.

"You sure?" she asks.

"Yes, please."

By now the other three have started up the rise to the house. With Belker's assistance I manage to struggle to my feet and adjust my pants and then half stagger through the darkness, with her gripping my forearm. My head throbs like hell, but my thoughts finally start to fit together.

Wendy tried to kill me.

And . . . she tried to kill me with the same type of weapon used to kill Jillian. And dishevel my clothes.

But why? And why *Jillian*? Because she must be the one who murdered her. Only the killer would have known about the jeans around Jillian's ankles.

When we finally approach the house, I look ahead to the patio, where the male trooper stands under the pergola with a handcuffed Gabe and Wendy. Blake, Keira, and Hannah are clustered near the door. Bella's there, too, I notice, dripping wet and looking shamefaced.

"What in god's name is going on?" I hear Blake shout.

The trooper must order them to get inside because I watch the group quickly disperse into the house. He then calls out to Belker, advising her to take my statement in the kitchen. By the time she and I are inside, we have the room to ourselves.

"Are you okay to sit?" she asks. "That's a pretty ugly gash you've got."

"Yeah, but I don't want to lie down."

As I settle at the table, she wets paper towels and tells me to gently press them on the wound, which is on the crown of my head, a bit toward the front. It's only as I lift my arm to my head that I remember the blow to my shoulder, which is throbbing, too.

"I need to take your statement before the ambulance arrives," she says, withdrawing a pad and pen from her pocket. "Please tell me what happened tonight."

I explain about how I went after Bella and was frantically trying to coax her to me when Wendy came up from behind and bashed my head.

"Had there been an altercation between the two of you earlier?" she asks, locking eyes with me.

I picture my last few minutes with Wendy in the kitchen, talking about Hannah and the foxgloves. She seemed so sympathetic, so eager to help.

"Nothing. Not now or ever. And she killed someone else, I think." I touch a hand to my temple, trying to think. "Can you tell me . . . What's happening to my husband?" From far off, maybe in the living room, I can hear the sound of a raised voice, and I'm pretty sure it's Wendy's.

"Officer Palmer is waiting for a backup unit and then someone will take your husband's statement. Please try to stay calm for now."

As soon as the words are out of her mouth, the low wail

of an ambulance pierces the air, and I drop my face into my hands, relieved not to have to talk anymore. Soon I'm being lain on a gurney, and a paramedic stabilizes my neck with a surgical collar. There's no sign of Gabe, but as I'm loaded into the back of the ambulance, I can see Keira standing on the front stoop, watching.

The doors close with a double click, and a paramedic presses gauze against my head wound, assuring me that I'm going to be okay. I can feel how fast my heart is racing, so she probably thinks I'm fearing for my life, but it's not that. I'm worried about Gabe, worried that Wendy will somehow convince the police that it was a stranger who attacked me and not her.

As the ambulance zooms through the night, I can't help but imagine Claire, headed for the same hospital four days ago. And I think of my own mom, too, feeling the corners of my eyes well with tears. I need to call her tomorrow. Need to pull her into my life more.

Once we reach the ER, I'm evaluated quickly by a triage nurse and then examined by a warm, thirtysomething PA whose name tag says Amir Mohabbat and who orders a CAT scan of my head and cervical spine. I'm lucky to get both done quickly, and neither scan shows any serious damage. I'm praying Gabe will be waiting in the exam area when I return, but there's no sign of him. Though up until this moment, I've kept my emotions at bay, they surge now, a churning mix of fear, disgust, anger, and grief.

Once my tests are completed, Amir injects me with Novocain so he can irrigate the wound and suture it. He makes small talk with me about my career, asking with a wink if I think he could ever get work as an extra. I manage to grunt out a few five-word answers. Finally, just as he's finishing, the curtain parts, and I cry out with relief to see Gabe standing there, his clothes still a little soggy.

"Honey, please tell me you're okay," he says, his voice breaking.

I nod and glance at Amir.

"She's going to be fine," he says. "There's a nasty gash that I've just sewn up. Minor concussion. Nothing to stop her from doing Oscar-caliber work this year. She needs to keep the wound clean, take Tylenol for pain, and return if there's vomiting, blurred vision, or if the pain really intensifies."

I thank him for all his efforts.

"Can I take her home?" Gabe asks him.

"Let's give it another twenty minutes so we can observe her a little longer. Then she's free to go," he says and ducks out of the exam room.

"Does it hurt a lot?" Gabe asks.

"Only when I think."

"Ha. Good one. . . . God, I've been sick with worry about you."

"Gabe, if you hadn't come when you did, she would have bashed my head in."

"But it looked like you were managing to fight her off."

"Only briefly—with the dog leash. Ha, I've never been so grateful for that course I took on stage fighting and how to work with found objects. . . . What about *you*? They don't suspect you of anything, do they?"

"No, since my story matched yours. And Wendy seemed totally unhinged, screaming at the police and saying she was going to have their jobs. Poor Blake. The police arrested her and took her away."

I tap a hand against my forehead, as if it will help me pull my thoughts together. "Why did the troopers show up in the yard, do you know?"

"Keira called one of the detectives who'd given her his card. She noticed the back door open, realized you and Wendy were both gone, and worried that something might be wrong."

Finally, Keira's natural anxiety has been put to good use. "And the troopers came just like that?"

"Apparently, they were part of the search today and knew someone had already been murdered on the property."

"And how did you get home, anyway? I thought you were with your dad. Wait, how *is* your dad?"

"My father's fine. He had a panic attack. I guess this has all been too much for him. They wanted to keep him a while longer for observation, but Blake was worried about Wendy and felt he should get back earlier, so I left with him. To be honest, I hadn't been able to stop thinking about what you said—about Hannah possibly being a danger. The storm was so bad at one point, Blake ended up pulling off the road for a little while, and it was in an area with no cell service."

"I'm just so lucky you came when you did. Like I said, she would have killed me."

He shakes his head. "I know. But *why?*" he asks. "What possible reason could there be?"

"I wish I knew. I've been going over it again and again in my mind and I don't have a clue."

28

Gabe and I don't arrive home until close to one in the morning, but we're not surprised to see the house ablaze with lights. Marcus had texted Gabe to say that everyone would be waiting up for us in the living room. Everyone but Wendy, that is. According to Marcus, she's being held without bail.

I'm totally spent by now, and though the Tylenol has eased the pain a bit, my head feels like it's been wedged between two boulders. Still, I know I need to greet the family. They're desperate for answers.

Even from the hall I can see how distraught everyone is. As we enter the living room, Keira, Marcus, Nick, and Blake all jump up, begging to know how I'm doing, and form a loose circle around Gabe and me. Ash, looking pale and exhausted, remains seated, though, and Hannah hangs back, clearly shaken, her face even redder than before.

"Summer, what in god's name is going on?" Blake pleads. "I've been going out of my mind." His hair is standing on end, as if he's been raking his fingers through it for hours.

"Blake, I'm so sorry," I say, though I know that nothing I tell him will offer any consolation. "Wendy followed me out of the house and struck me as hard as she could. And she would have killed me if Gabe hadn't come along."

"But it wasn't her," he says. "She saw someone else strike you and she was coming to your rescue. She told me. We have to make the police understand that."

"Blake, I *saw* her with my own two eyes."

"But it was dark," Ash interjects from the armchair. "Can't you be mistaken?"

"I saw her, too," Gabe says. "As I came running down the rise, she had her arm raised, ready to hit again."

"But what earthly reason would she have to hurt you?" Blake says, his voice flushed with anguish.

"I have no idea, I really don't. But she clearly wanted me dead. She was using some kind of tool, like a hammer." As I say the last word, my mind fixes on a thought I had while lurching back to the house with the trooper. "And I think she killed Jillian, too."

The room fills with gasps. I see Gabe's mouth drop open in shock.

"No, no." Blake throws up his arms. "That's even crazier. My wife is not a murderer. And she barely *knew* Jillian."

"Yes, *why*?" Ash demands. "Why would she have any reason to kill Jillian? This isn't making any sense at all."

I shake my head, which only makes the throbbing worse. "I don't know. But she was going to try to make my death look like a failed sexual assault, too. So we'd all think the predator had come back."

The room goes utterly silent, and I rack my brain for answers once again, but come up empty.

"I think I know why." To my shock I realize it's Hannah speaking. She's still standing outside the circle, and as if choreographed, we all pivot to face her.

"*What?*" Nick says.

Hannah bites her lip hard, then takes a deep breath. "Because Wendy thought it was *me* down there by the stream. I was wearing the same coat as Jillian that day."

So maybe it's true, that the wrong woman was killed. But that doesn't explain why Wendy would have wanted *Hannah* dead.

"My god," Blake shouts, now angry as well as befuddled. "This is starting to sound like theater of the absurd. What could her motive possibly have been?"

Another bite of her lip. It's not for effect, I realize. She's totally rattled.

"Because . . . because of something I overheard," she says. "I'd gone outdoors Saturday night to sneak a cigarette by the side of the house, the side near the carriage house, and I heard Claire and Wendy talking on the patio." She looks at Blake. "Uh, I hate to be the bearer of bad news, but Wendy's been having an affair with some guy she met in Palm Beach and Claire knew because she saw them together there a few months ago. After you told everyone about the baby that night, I guess she decided to corner Wendy. She said that if she didn't come clean with you, she would. She'd make sure there was a DNA test because she thought the baby might not be yours."

Blake lets out a wail that could shatter the windows, and Gabe and Marcus rush to him. I stay where I am, pleading with my brain to work faster. It was a confrontation between Claire and Wendy that Henry overheard. Not Claire and Hannah. And it was Wendy who was threatened by the knowledge that Claire possessed, not Hannah.

Nick steps closer to Hannah, his eyes narrowed.

"How did Wendy know you'd overheard?" he says.

"I . . . I told her."

"*Why?*"

"I was just trying, you know, to help her—because I felt so sorry for her. I said I'd keep it to myself, and she promised to have my back when no one else could be bothered. I had no idea she'd try to kill me, for god's sake."

She's clearly floundering, out of her depth on this one.

"Jesus, Hannah," Nick says. "Wendy betrayed my brother. You didn't think *I* should know?"

"I didn't want to interfere. It didn't seem like any of my business."

"None of your business?" Nick yells, his face reddening. "Aren't I your damn business?"

Her expression morphs from flustered to wounded, and she turns on her heels and flees the room.

I take off, too, pursuing her down the wide front hall and then along the corridor that runs past the den. When I catch up to her, she's almost at the side door leading from the house, and she stops abruptly, clearly realizing she has to either venture out into the darkness or talk to me.

"What the hell do you want?" she demands angrily.

"Tell me what you know about foxgloves."

She purses her pillowy lips, bare now of her usual lipstick and gloss. I can see her sense of superiority surging back. "*Seriously?* You're asking me about flowers at a time like this?"

"Yes, *now*. If you know what's good for you."

"Okay, *okay*. I know they're poisonous. Claire told me when she gave me a tour."

"But you pretended you didn't know that when I spoke to you in the carriage house."

"I was just messing with you. You've been a total bitch to me from day one, and you know it."

"Did you pick foxgloves from the garden by the cottage on the morning Claire died?"

"*What?* No."

"Prove it."

"I wasn't out flower picking. Ask Nick. Or ask *Marcus*. He had me meet him outside that morning so I could hear how furious he was about me marrying his brother, and then when I was done listening to him spew, I played tennis with Nick and hung by the pool."

Then who . . . ?

My god. I've had it all wrong. It was Wendy who was threatened by Claire. And it must have been Wendy who picked the foxgloves and made the tea. Wendy who poisoned Claire.

If I'm remembering right, Blake went for a drive that morning, so Wendy had the carriage house kitchen to herself. That would have allowed her time to cut the flowers, dry the leaves in the oven there, and make the tea without being seen. And she would have had the house kitchen to herself, as well, in order to make the substitution. She was the one who told me Bonnie wouldn't be in until late.

And the *book*. The one on poisons. Wendy had been standing near that shelf when I'd run into her in the study.

But one thing doesn't add up. Why would she place a foxglove in my drawer? Why would she try to provoke me when she had no reason to believe I was onto her? And then it hits me.

"*You* put the foxglove in my drawer, didn't you?" I say to Hannah.

She lifts a shoulder, as if in agreement, and I swear to god, she stifles a grin. "If you don't mind, I need to get to my room and pack my bag," she says. "This family is nutso. Someone tried to *murder* me, and no one gives a shit."

"*Why*, Hannah? Why did you leave the foxglove?"

"Okay, I was messing with you again. You snuck into my room, for god's sake. Was I just supposed to let that go?"

I press my hands to my head, as my thoughts come together like the pins in a lock lining up.

"If you didn't pick the flowers near the cottage, where did you find them?" I ask.

"This is ridiculous. Why are we still talking about it?"

"Tell me."

"If you *must* know, from behind the carriage house. I happened to notice some of them there one day."

"Did you ever see Wendy picking any from that spot?"

"Wendy? You think her first plan was to *poison* me?"

"Not you, no. I need to know. Did you ever see her with any? In the kitchen of the carriage house, maybe?"

"No. I—"

"*What?*"

"I didn't see her, but she saw me with the ones I picked."

I jerk back in surprise. "Did she say anything?"

"No. But she looked at me kind of weird. And I told her not to worry, that I didn't have anything wicked in mind."

That's why Wendy wanted Hannah dead. Not because of the conversation she'd overheard. She probably trusted Hannah to keep her lips zipped about it because Hannah *needed* her. But she'd misunderstood Hannah's comment about the foxgloves. She must have taken it as a taunt, that Hannah had somehow figured out she was a murderer.

And when she thought she saw Hannah walking alone yesterday morning, she set out after her.

29

The second we pull into the driveway of the house on Durham Road, it's as if a switch has been flicked to make my heart start beating faster. I'm not sure exactly why. This isn't the first time I've been back since July. Gabe and I have driven out here a few times, though we haven't brought Henry yet.

Maybe it's due to the sudden, unexpected downpour. The raindrops pelting against the roof of the car, summoning me right back to that horrible night last summer.

"You positive you don't mind staying in the cottage?" Gabe asks. "The heating system isn't state of the art."

"No, I'll be fine. I packed flannel PJs."

What I don't tell him is that I'll feel safer and more at ease in the cottage. The big, rambling quality of the main house, which I always found so appealing, so *enchanting*, now makes me jumpy. When I'm in one of those rooms these days, I'm always looking over my shoulder, thinking I've heard unexplainable footsteps or a door opening somewhere it shouldn't.

After quickly unloading the car, Gabe and I do a mad dash along the path to the cottage, our duffel bags bouncing against our legs as we run. Ash told us he'd be lying down after lunch so we'll see him closer to dinnertime.

Someone, perhaps Bonnie, has clearly turned on the heat in anticipation of our arrival, and we find that the cottage is actually fairly toasty. Clean and tidy, too. While Gabe carries our bags upstairs, I switch on lamps on the ground floor, fill the teakettle with water, and open the fireplace flue.

By the time Gabe returns, a few flames are already licking up the sides of the logs I've lit. I finish making tea, and we both drop onto the sofa with our mugs. There's a pleasant November-y scent to the room, coming from both the wood-smoke and the bowl of fresh pine cones that's been placed on the coffee table. Watching the fire with Gabe has a calming effect on me, slowing my pulse.

And yet . . . I can't imagine ever feeling truly at ease out here again, even in the cottage.

It's not that I have any reason to be scared. Wendy's in jail and awaiting trial, and she can't lay a hand on us. From all accounts, the police have a solid case against her for Jillian's murder. Paul Mizel—who needless to say is no longer representing her—heard through back channels that the police searched the dumpsters behind the medical center where Wendy had her sonogram and ended up finding the murder weapon in one of them. A mini pickax. Online, it's described as a tool that helps gardeners break up hardened surface soil, but it's capable of puncturing someone's skull. Wendy must have grabbed it in a hurry from the potting shed when she spotted who she thought was Hannah making her way across the lawn. Then, the next night, she returned to the shed for the tool she used on me, which I've since learned was some kind of small hoe, sharp enough to do serious damage. If she'd managed to strike me several times in the head, she definitely could have killed me.

They also apparently found traces of Jillian's blood and DNA in Wendy's big designer tote, the one I saw her clutching in the living room the day of the murder. Obviously, she won't be seeing how much she can get for it through TheRealReal.com.

Proving that she killed Claire is going to be tougher. The police did test Claire's body for digitalis and the results showed that toxic amounts of it were present in her system. But unless Wendy confesses—and so far she's denied everything—we'll never know for certain if she was responsible. We may have to take consolation from the fact that she'll surely spend decades in prison for Jillian's murder.

Even now, with the benefit of hindsight, I'm still staggered by what Wendy was capable of. After it became clear that it was her, not Hannah, who killed Claire, I didn't understand why she felt so desperate to keep her affair under wraps. If she was so unhappy with Blake, why not simply leave him?

But what we learned later from Blake—who from a DNA test proved he *wasn't* the father of the baby—is that the man Wendy was cheating with is a twenty-nine-year-old associate of one of her clients, and he makes about fifty grand a year. Though Wendy would have done well enough in a divorce settlement, she obviously knew things would pale for her going forward. She wouldn't be able to count on Blake's income, and a prenup limited her from receiving any money the senior Keatons would leave upon their deaths.

And perhaps most significantly, the investment money Ash had offered her was being paid out over years, and any future funding for her prized gallery would clearly evaporate when the marriage did.

"Wendy liked me well enough to stay in the marriage and raise someone else's kid with me," a shattered Blake told Gabe. "But what she actually loved was her gallery and her lifestyle. That's what she couldn't stand losing."

So it was greed that drove Wendy every step of the way. And I guess panic, too. The morning after her confrontation with Claire, she'd clearly gone to the study—where I stumbled on her—to hunt down the book on poisonous plants, a title she'd probably noticed in the past. She would have already known from the garden tours *she'd* been given by Claire that foxgloves are dangerous. And she'd learned previously from Blake that Claire took a diuretic, which would make ingesting digitalis even more dangerous. By that afternoon, Claire was dead—silenced before she could breathe a word to Blake. It's possible Wendy even snuck into the house that afternoon and found Claire unconscious on the floor, and it was she, not Claire, who put the book back.

And then suddenly Hannah was a threat as well, though as I surmised before, Wendy must have assessed it as a manageable one. I can imagine the conversation between the two of them, Hannah telling Wendy that she needed more of a support system in the family and that if she agreed to be her advocate, Hannah would keep her mouth shut about what she'd overheard. That, I realized, must have been the reason Wendy went from describing Hannah as an interloper to acting sympathetic to her role as a newcomer. I have no idea if the background check was a complete fabrication, but either way, she probably lied about the results.

Everything changed, though, when she misread Hannah's sly remark to her about foxgloves, and she decided that Nick's fiancée had to be eliminated.

The decision to make the scene look like an attempted rape gone wrong must have been a frantic, spur-of-the-moment thing—an art aficionado trying to dictate our perception of events.

How freaked she must have been when she realized she'd killed the wrong person, and that Hannah was still in the picture, a real danger, she assumed. And then there was me, blurting out my theory in the kitchen, having discovered the book on poisons. She knew it might be only a matter of time before I recalled seeing her by the bookcase, remembered that she had her iPad by the pool even though she'd claimed it wasn't working, and started finding my way to the truth.

Looking back, I wonder if she actually experienced any cramping or fears of miscarrying, or if she made that up to cover for her mounting alarm. And of course, the trip for the sonogram gave her a way to dispose of the weapon she used on Jillian.

If she's convicted, it's not likely she'll ever see much of her child. For a time we wondered if Blake would agree to a role, but he says he can't bring himself to do so. Fortunately, the biological father is eager to raise the child with the help of his parents.

Those are the things I know, or feel pretty sure about. But there are other questions I still don't have answers for.

What was really going on with Marcus and Hannah? Late in the summer, Keira admitted to me that she'd suspected Hannah and Marcus were meeting privately during that awful weekend, and she'd not only confronted Marcus about it but had also shared her fears with Nick—the conversation I'd witnessed in the yard. I doubt Hannah harbored any feelings toward Marcus; rather, I think she liked the power derived from having two brothers in her thrall. Though things looked strained for a while between Marcus and Keira, they appear much better now.

I also don't know if Ash was having an affair with Jillian. He's sworn to his sons that he wasn't, but I suspect that he was at least moving in that direction. Nick admitted to Gabe that he had started to feel uncomfortable watching some of his father's interactions with Jillian at work, and that it might have been one of the reasons Ash was encouraging him to take on a new project, one that would keep him out of the main office.

Claire must have suspected, too. Perhaps she even was considering hiring a private investigator to confirm or disavow her fears. When she'd changed her will, she was protecting some of her assets but she also might have been sending Ash a warning that she didn't trust him.

And I still don't know what Claire discovered about Hannah. Gossip hound that he is, Billy Dean eventually learned that she'd indeed been booted from USC for some type of cheating. Maybe that's what Claire dug up, but I have no way of knowing.

By and large, I've pretty much stopped torturing myself at night with questions I'll never have the answers to. All families have secrets and I have to accept that.

At least Hannah's out of the picture. She'd sucked it up and spent that last night in the carriage house alone, then Ubered back to the city the next morning. Nick told us he was relieved, that he'd already begun to second-guess his decision to marry her. For one he'd found her behavior regarding the memorial service phony, and he hated that she'd insisted on speaking. Added to that were the suspicions Keira shared with him.

"You want more tea?" Gabe asks me, rising from the cottage sofa.

"Sure, why not."

Things have been good with us over the past months. We had a few rough conversations following Wendy's arrest, during which I told him how hurt I was by him not taking me seriously and he shared how upset he was that I thought he was being insensitive about his mother's death. But gradually, we moved on. We spent the rest of the summer lying low—working, reading, sampling interesting wines at home, avoiding the occasional calls from reporters, and orchestrating several staycations in the city with Henry.

Gabe returns and tops off our mugs and sets the teapot on the coffee table. As he settles back on the couch, a tear slides down his cheek, which is still windburned from the run he took first thing this morning along the Hudson River.

"Gabe, what is it?"

"Wow," he says, brushing it away with the sleeve of his sweater. "I didn't see that coming. I guess I'm feeling kind of emotional. I know it's important to come out and see my dad, especially since we won't be doing Thanksgiving at the house this year, but it's not getting any easier to be here."

"Oh, honey, I know. It must be so tough for you."

We haven't even considered bringing Henry to Bucks County the few times we've come. Master eavesdropper that he is, Henry's picked up some of the gritty, gory details about Jillian's murder, and in the end of course we had to tell him about Aunt Wendy going to prison. We've actually taken him to *my* family home a couple of times, and my parents have relished his presence.

"At least this might be the last time."

I raise my eyebrows.

"Nick called me earlier today and told me he overheard Dad saying he's probably going to put the property on the market."

"Jeez. But it certainly doesn't surprise me."

"He's apparently thinking of buying a place out on Long Island. Near the water."

"It's for the best, right? I know being in the house is hard for you. For me, too."

"Even being in *here* creeps me out."

"The cottage?" I say, surprised. "Why?"

"I haven't had the guts to tell you yet, but maybe now is as good a time as any. The day my mother died, when my father, Marcus, and I met, I found out it was her who was mainly against Dad investing more in our business."

It's what Nick had told me about back in July. And it's what I'd always hoped Gabe would share with me.

"She felt Nick deserved a turn?"

"Partly, but she also told Dad she thought Marcus and I needed to stand on our own feet for a while. I was so upset with her. That attitude was fine, but Dad had *asked* to be involved and we'd counted on it. I can still remember walking up the path to the cottage after the meeting, and then standing in this room, feeling livid. I took a hike to burn off my anger, but it didn't help very much. And then a couple of hours later, she was dead."

"Gabe, first, you had a right to be angry," I say. "It was unfair of your mom to do that after your dad made you a promise. And everyone gets upset with their parents at times. That's normal. The bottom line is that your mother knew you loved her."

"She was just so much more controlling than I ever acknowledged. Like trying to guarantee we were the family she wanted us to be. My dad told me earlier today that he's been going through some of my mother's digital files and figured out that she hired a private investigator after she spotted Wendy with that guy in Palm Beach. She had a whole freaking dossier on her."

That must have been what she did with Amanda, too, I think, but don't mention it.

"Maybe because your mom always seemed so perfect, it was easy to think of her that way. But all of us are human."

"Yeah, but a *dossier*. It sounds like the workings of a spymaster."

"But she was also protecting *Blake*. And that controlling

part of her had a flip side you loved. She created beautiful homes for you to grow up in. Perfect vacations. Wonderful times together."

"You're right. I can't lose sight of that."

I push forward and twist my body so that I'm facing Gabe.

"I have a confession to make, too. You've said more than once that you wished you'd heeded my concerns about Hannah. I wanted you to listen so badly and I hated that you thought I was being irrational, but some of what I was saying *was* irrational. I realize that now."

"In what way? I mean, you guessed someone had murdered my mother, and you were right."

"I know, but I refused to ever consider whether anyone else might have made the tea. It's taken me time to admit this to myself, but I actually *was* obsessed with Hannah. She was starring in a Netflix pilot, and it ate at me. And once I had my suspicions about the foxgloves, I let everything point me to her as the murderer."

"In the end the truth came out. . . . And I have to say, you've seemed so much more excited professionally these last couple of months."

When the fall hit, Gabe was patient about how much time I had to spend in rehearsals. The theater festival was two weeks ago, and it went better than I could have hoped. Though no Broadway producers are lighting up my phone—ha, yet!—a few new doors have opened for me professionally, and I'm pretty sure the experience helped tame my envy. . . . Okay, and I admit, so did the fact that when I checked IMDb, I saw that Hannah's pilot hadn't been green-lit after all.

"I *am* excited. I started another play, and I like it so far."

"That's great, honey. The other one was so sharp, and people loved it. And you in it."

I dig my phone from my pocket and check the time. "We should probably start thinking about walking over to the house. You going to be okay there?"

"Yeah, I'm sure one last time won't kill me."

"If your father does buy a new weekend place, it will mean a fresh start for everyone, Gabe. A chance to be happy again without so many painful reminders everywhere."

"You think so?"

"I do. I mean, everyone's pretty battered right now, but things will keep getting better, month by month."

Of course, nothing will ever be like it used to be, and I'm going to have to adjust to that. I'd be lying if I didn't admit that a little part of what made Gabe so appealing to me was the world he sprang from and inhabited—his charismatic, affluent, magical-seeming family. They had me at, *Summer, so nice to meet you; please come in and make yourself at home.*

But I can handle the change, I really can, I think. Despite the havoc Wendy wreaked, the Keatons are still the Keatons and I care deeply about them. Most important, I love my husband and I love Henry, and I see now that little by little we've been building our *own* special world. And hopefully, in the next year or so, our world will be a tiny bit bigger.

ACKNOWLEDGMENTS

Thanks to the wonderful experts on a variety of subjects who took time out of their busy lives to help me with my research for *The Fiancée*: Barbara Butcher, consultant for forensic and medicolegal investigations; Paul Paganelli, MD; Luci (the "poison lady") Hansson Zahray; Susan Brune; Joyce Hanshaw, retired captain from the Hunterdon County Prosecutor's Office; Will Valenza, Glens Falls police department, retired; Marsha Mercant; Grace Cushman; Steve Murphy; Jim White; Robert Lazaro. One of the fun parts of being an author is making things up, but there are some areas in which I want to be as accurate as possible and it helps incredibly to have smart people guide me.

Thank you, too, to everyone at Harper Perennial for another year of wonderful collaboration. That includes my extraordinary editor Emily Griffin, who has been a total dream to work with, as well as Amy Baker, VP/Associate Publisher; Theresa Dooley, publicity manager; Lisa Erickson, director of marketing; Robin Bilardello, art director (I adore this cover!), and Stacey Fischkelta, production editorial manager.

In addition, let me to thank my *own* fantastic team: Laura Cocivera, website editor; Imani Seymour, social media manager; and Bill Cunningham, tech support.

Thank you as well, to my wonderful husband, Brad Holbrook, and kids, Hunter Holbrook and Hayley Holbrook, for being my champions day in and day out.

Last but not least, I want to say the most heartfelt thanks to my fantastic readers, who stay in touch via Facebook, Twitter, Instagram, and katewhite.com, who review my books on Goodreads, Bookbub, barnesandnoble.com, and Amazon.com, and who share a little bit about their lives with me. I love hearing from you, and of course, couldn't do it without you!!

ABOUT THE AUTHOR

Kate White, former editor-in-chief of *Cosmopolitan* magazine, is the *New York Times* bestselling author of the stand-alone psychological thrillers *Have You Seen Me?*, *The Secrets You Keep*, *The Wrong Man*, *Eyes on You*, *The Sixes*, and *Hush*, as well as eight Bailey Weggins mysteries, including, most recently, *Such a Perfect Wife*, which was nominated for an International Thriller Writers Award. White is also the author of several popular career books for women, including *I Shouldn't Be Telling You This: How to Ask for the Money, Snag the Promotion, and Create the Career You Deserve*, and editor of the *The Mystery Writers of America Cookbook*. Visit katewhite.com for more information.

More Spellbinding Suspense from

KATE WHITE

"It's impossible to outwit White."
–*ENTERTAINMENT WEEKLY*

HARPER